The Weaving of Wells
Book Four in the Osric's Wand Series

_By_
Jack D. Albrecht Jr.
_&_
Ashley Delay

Copyright © 2016 Jack D. Albrecht Jr. & Ashley Delay
CoWrite, LLC.

ISBN-13: 978-1533315991

ISBN-10: 153331599X

Dedications

From Ashley:

For May with love—it often takes an adventure to discover who you are. I'm grateful to be a part of yours, and I hope you enjoy every step of the journey.

I wish you blessings and joy each day, I wish you to see the beauty and wonder in yourself that I see in you, and I wish you victory in every battle.

From Jack:

To my Jellybean—our little family has grown over the last year. At one time it was just me and my perfect little girl. Now, what once was two is four. You have another brother, and I have what you have always wished for me: a wonderful, loving wife.

You continue to grow and become more independent with every passing day. Your life will change in so many ways in these upcoming years, and I can't wait to see what life has in store for you.

Acknowledgments

The superb editing for *The Weaving of Wells* was done by Scott Alexander Jones: www.scottalexanderjones.com.

Our fantastic covers have all been created by Rodrigo Adolfo: www.radolfo.co.nr.

The World of Archana

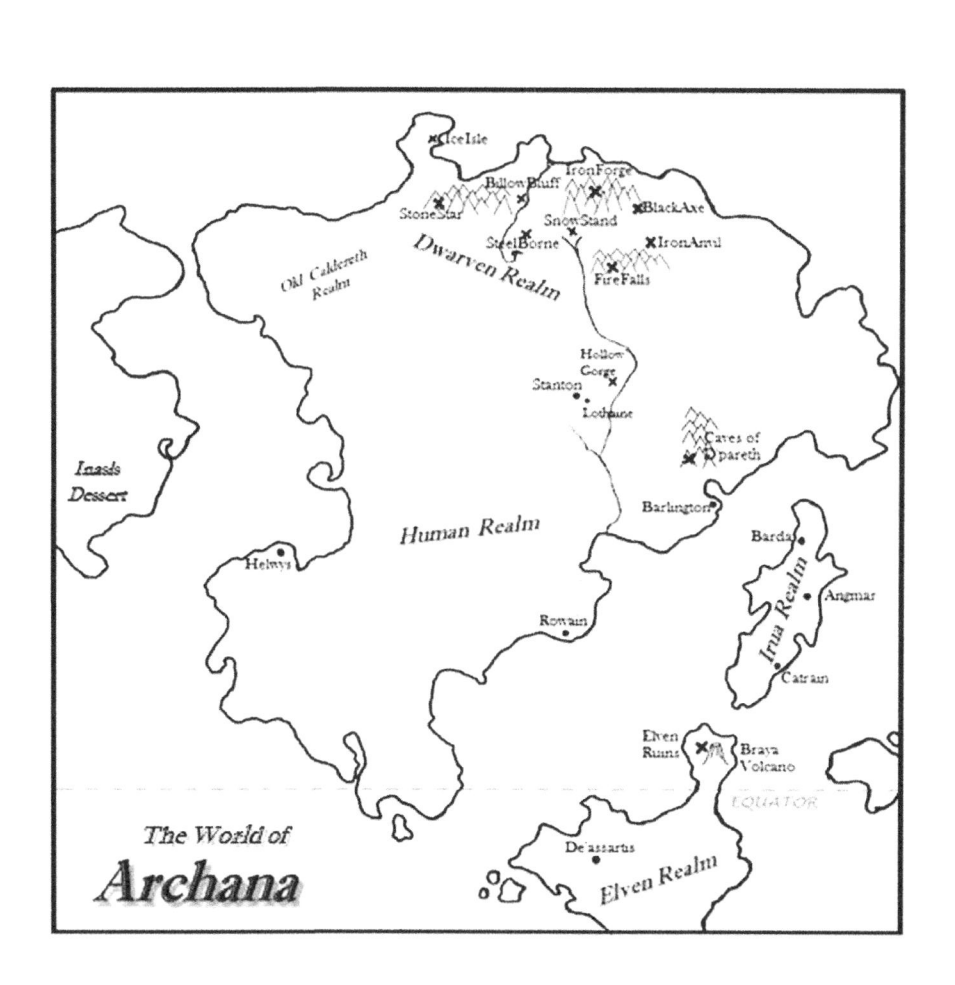

The Weaving of Wells

Chapter 1
Revelations

"Shiny!" Pebble clapped his paws and looked up at Osric expectantly.

"Here you are, sir." Osric looked up and saw a young man offering Legati to him. "We wanted to see her in your hands again, sir." A small group had gathered around his friends, a hopeful cast to their faces.

Osric took the sword and laid it down across his lap and smiled. In a wave of clarity, every truth washed over him as he looked up into the expectant gazes of his closest friends. He thought of the agonizing hours they had all spent trying to decipher the prophecy that had clung to them through all of their adventures. The answer to it all had been so simple, yet the timing of their attempts to answer the questions had to have been off by the slimmest of margins. He couldn't imagine how it had escaped their notice for so long.

Osric thought back to the power lock with Gus's wand, as he lay pinned under the collapsed ceiling. Pebble had seen it then, but Osric had never thought to look. The words of the prophecy danced through his head.

The wand that is not a wand... He thought about the hours he and Kenneth had spent mulling over those words while sparring to keep up their strength and skills on their journeys. *It will be wielded in practice by two...* How many times had they passed his wand around, each seeking something the others had missed, and each of them failing to find anything new in the simple stick and woven strands? *It will be known by one but not known...* Osric looked down at Pebble's big, brown, innocent eyes and laughed until he thought he would pass out. The prairie dog pup was growing quickly, but he still resembled the ball of brown fluff that had always seen what no one else had. Pebble was bigger than Gus now, but Osric knew he was still the playful pup he had grown to love.

"Pebble," Osric said with a sly expression as he recovered his breath.

"Yeppers?" Pebble asked.

1

Osric's Wand

"I think we all need to play a little game right now, don't you?" A wide smile grew on Osric's face. Gus looked over at them with a scowl. "Hey, Gus. I see something you don't." Osric stood up, sword in hand, and stepped forward. He was tall and lean, towering over the grumpy old prairie dog. Osric swept his sandy hair back from his forehead and looked down at Gus with confidence in his emerald green eyes.

"I don't know why you would assume anyone would understand what you are saying," Gus, Archana's most famous Wand-Maker, hesitated in his reply. "But your body language suggests we should."

Osric recognized the look on his face. It was a look he had worn himself on many occasions; the prairie dog's pupils dilated and his nostrils flared slightly. His senses were responding to the Portentist gift indicating that something important had occurred, but Gus still didn't understand the gift's pull.

Osric looked into the eyes of those who had gathered around them. A crowd was growing around where they stood on the grass outside the Aranthian barracks. He could see the anticipation on their faces—they didn't know what was going to happen, and indeed didn't know if anything would, but collectively their minds were locked in anticipation of some unknown portent. Osric knew that there would be a great deal of satisfaction for each of them in what was about to be revealed.

Bridgett took in a startled gasp of air as Osric locked eyes with her. He could see her focus change from the hidden realm of wandcraft as she met his gaze with a smile. Her russet hair fell softly along her jawline and tumbled down her back, and the silver flecks that Osric could see in her blue eyes brought back the memory of the first time he had met her. She was wearing the same earthtone dress, but the sun had darkened her skin and worry had left subtle creases around her eyes. She was even more beautiful now than she had been then.

"Give me a moment. There is something I need to do before we continue this conversation." Revitalized by recent events, Osric adjusted his grip on Legati's hilt and moved as if he had not been injured and asleep for over a month. He fastened his scabbard to his waist and sheathed the sword.

Those gathered began to whisper silently as the few moments grew uncomfortable for the bystanders. They weren't discomforted by the time it took him to prepare to sheath the sword, but by the intense lock that existed between Bridgett's and Osric's eyes, as well as the playful way Osric smiled while he moved.

"A day with many magical revelations shouldn't start without experiencing magic of a different sort." Osric stepped forward after the deep *thwonk* rose from the mouth of his scabbard as the sword slid into place. Grasping Bridgett's hand, he spoke softly but with great intensity. "Thank you for saving me. I have missed you."

Moving slowly, he planted a tender kiss on Bridgett's forehead. Osric caressed her right cheek softly with his fingers while lifting her face to his. He kissed her with all of the passion that had been pent up inside from months of anxiety for her safety and from the distance between them. She melted into his embrace, blushing as he finally released her and she noticed all of the eyes watching them.

"Boy, I am sure you both needed that, but couldn't it wait until after you explain why this Portentist gift is chiming like a bell tower?" Gus pleaded.

Machai grunted in a low laugh. A wide smile peeked through the dwarf's thick mustache, and his wide shoulders shook with his laughter.

"No, Gus, you've got to give them that. Both of them have been through a lot in the last few months," Macgowan spoke in their defense. His deep voice carried command in spite of the gentle way he spoke the words. Even so, nobody would defy orders issued from the hulk of a man that stood there, lips trembling in silent memory of the loss of his beloved wife.

"Don't just make an allowance for it. I think that kiss deserves applause!" Kenneth raised a cheerful shout, which was echoed by the bystanders. His tightly tied braid of long, black hair swept from side to side as he led the crowd in cheers. Though Jane's cooking had enlarged his waist in recent months, his arms were as heavily muscled as ever.

"Although I appreciate the thought you all have given to my love life, some things demand more prompt attention than world-changing magics do." Osric returned Kenneth's smile and bowed a jester's bow.

"Excuse me?" Bridgett looked indignant at the exchange.

Osric's Wand

Both Osric and Kenneth looked sufficiently chastised, turning their eyes downward to the ground in shame, but Bridgett wasn't through with them.

"If you insist it couldn't wait, you insist on applause, and you think a nod toward the crowd is warranted"—she turned toward Osric with mischief in her eyes—"then I'm afraid I must insist on a more impressive kiss."

Osric looked up with pleading eyes while searching for a way to extricate himself from the situation he had found himself in. He noticed a distinct upward turn to her lips, and a playful glint to her eyes before her words registered. Shortly thereafter, the laughter began to trickle toward his ears—first from his left, then his right. He couldn't resist the temptation to grant her wish, and so he did, taking her into his arms in a low dip that hushed the crowd.

When they stood again, Kenneth's chest was shaking in silent laughter. Bridgett turned her attention toward him, squinting in mock annoyance.

"Now is a good time for that applause you were talking about."

He answered with genuine praise in his vocalization, and he quickly had all but Gus joining in the joviality.

"And now would be a good time for your bow."

Osric bent in acquiescence before Bridgett stepped to his side and curtsied.

Cowbells sounded in the distance and caught the attention of each expectant ear, interrupting the playful display. Everyone glanced around, looking for the source of the sound. The old Vigile barracks stood as a backdrop to the lush, green grounds where most of the Aranthian training took place, but even those who typically joined in scholarly talks out on the early morning lawn were gathered close to hear the chatter. The sound grew steadily louder, and moments later a herd of cattle pierced the veil that encapsulated the Aranthian grounds and came around the corner of the barracks.

With a smile, Osric shouted. "David!"

The face of James's young assistant, with close-cropped hair and a wide, insecure expression present as always, peered out the window of the kitchen. "Yes, sir?"

"There's your cowbell!" Osric pointed toward the southern barrier, and David disappeared to the sound of pots clattering to the ground.

The Weaving of Wells

"Can we get back to more pressing matters, or should I be forced to endure more waiting while you attempt to conceive a child while we all watch?" Gus folded his arms and sat down impatiently.

"You're right, Gus." Osric looked from one face to the next, considering how best to proceed. The cattle lowed in the distance as all eyes were trained on him. Dozens of the men gathered couldn't appreciate the significance of the timing of the revelation, but those who had accompanied him on the first tentative venture outside of his home would.

The first prophecy he had been given on the dragon platform had told them all that a battle would still need to be fought once they had discovered what he now knew. It was almost comical how simple it all became when the truth found light.

"Gus, what does it take to initiate a power lock?" A smile creased Osric's face.

"What, am I a student of my own trade, now?" Gus deepened his tortured scowl.

"Ha!" Osric laughed and ruffled the hair on top of Gus's head. "If it weren't for that attitude, and my lack of understanding of this blasted Wand-Maker gift, we may have figured this out a long time ago. Don't look at me that way. You will see in just a few moments that I am right."

"I'll look at you any way I damned well please. Now, are you going to get to it, or am I going to have to spell your mouth shut until I figure it out on my own?"

"We both shared fault in the lack of discovery, so I'll try to share this with you as quick as possible. How did Pebble describe his finding me in the rubble?"

"He found you in a hollow, basically without a scratch on you. You were understandably a bit ragged looking, but you weren't injured seriously. Why do you ask?" Even through his greying fur and scars, Gus looked annoyed at the teaching tone in Osric's voice. His voice reinforced the emotion for those who couldn't see him.

"What state were my clothes in at the time, Pebble?"

The young pup smiled to be included in such a momentous day. "You were dusty and your shirt had ridden up on you." His playful understanding brought a smile and a nod from Osric.

Osric's Wand

"And remind me again about the times you examined me in an attempt to discover the truth behind what was going on?" Osric turned his attention back to Gus.

"I examined you on many occasions," he replied.

"Yes, but tell me when. Where were we when you examined me?"

"I examined you twice in the Caves of D'pareth, then again just before we left Braya after freeing the dragons from their cages, on multiple occasions within the barracks over the last few months, and at the Grove of the Unicorns. Oh, and I examined you on the first night after we left Stanton when you noticed the power growth for the first time due to the Anduro Amulet that Bridgett wears."

"No, you didn't examine me on that day!" Osric was unable to contain his excitement as he knelt in front of Gus. "And if you had, at least the mystery of my wand would have been solved."

"But now your wand is destroyed, so I don't see why we are having this conversation." Gus began to look uncertain, sensing that the end of the conversation was at hand.

"Has it been destroyed? The wand you created was an incredible wand, but was it the wand of the prophecy? Think, Gus."

"I've examined you on multiple occasions, so don't try to tell me that you are the wand; that's just plain silly."

"You're going to kick yourself when you see, Gus," Bridgett chimed in.

"Well, I'll be an enchantress's puppet," Kenneth exclaimed.

"We's gots a magic wand. They's gots to figures it out. Riddles and rhymes, till we runs outa time," Pebble sang playfully.

"Pebble, the one who looks when he's not supposed to. Come here Pebble!" Osric could barely contain himself for another moment, but Kenneth and Bridgett had both realized and looked for themselves at different points in the verbal byplay he was sharing with Gus. *How much longer until Gus looks with all the hints I have given him?* Osric wondered as he rubbed Pebble's belly, to the young pup's delight.

"The trouble, Gus, is that you were always looking at me or at the wand you created. There was always another wand. I'll ask you again: What does it take to initiate a power lock?"

"You grasp a wand and light the tip. Then the cycle is locked in until it is over, or death, or the wand breaks." Gus narrowed his eyes even further.

The Weaving of Wells

"Are you sure?" Osric smiled, toying with Gus. He hadn't had many opportunities to show that he knew more than the famous Wand-Maker, and to Gus's disdain, Osric was enjoying the moments he had left.

"Of course I'm sure. Now, where are you going with this, boy?"

"Kenneth, can you help me with a little experiment?"

"I don't know. I have heard the stories of that power lock, and Jane may never forgive me if I say yes to something so personal." He threw his hands up in mock protest.

"The only thing I'll hold against you is remaining a *child* when I want my hunter to be a brave man," Jane answered, stepping through the crowd and pushing him forward.

"All right." Kenneth stepped forward sheepishly in mock rebuke.

"Okay, you have just been trapped under a collapsing palace, and you find yourself waking up lying face up on a cold stone floor."

Kenneth dropped to the ground, playing the role he was given.

"You find yourself wandless, dusty, dirty, and with your shirt riding halfway up your body," Osric bellowed in his most impressive theater voice. *I can't believe I spent so many sleepless nights examining the wrong wand!* Osric thought.

"This had better be the end of the show or I'm going to ask for my money back," Gus spoke in flat tones with a hopeless expression on his face.

"Wait, if he's supposed to be me, let's complete the costume!" Osric unfastened his sheath and helped Kenneth fasten it to his right hip as he lay on the ground. "When you least expect it, something bites you. You try to draw your sword, but there isn't room under all the rubble." Kenneth complied with the stage directions, struggling with the sword, his face a grimace of dramatic fear. "Then," Osric continued narrating, "a handsome prairie dog pup scurries through an opening and brings you a new Gus wand."

With a quick motion, Osric took Gus's wand away and handed it to Pebble, who dutifully carried out his role in the reenactment.

"Oh, look! I've been given a Gus wand! It's a bit small for a human, don't you think?" Kenneth gazed teasingly at Gus. The crowd was growing as the conversation continued, and it seemed as though the entire Aranthian population was joining in the laughter with two of their most beloved acting out the scene in such a childish display. Gus was not amused.

"We'll forgo pointing out that this is a different wand than the one I was given, Kenneth. Soon everyone will see that it didn't matter anyway. Now, where were we?"

"You were given a Gus wand." Gus narrowed his eyes.

"Yes, that's right. Then Pebble reminds you that you have forgotten one important step in the ownership of a new wand by saying…" Osric pointed at Pebble.

"Yous gotsta lit the tip!"

Kenneth initiated the spell to light the tip of the wand

Gus's eyes went wide in surprise as both of his ears and his tail twitched uncontrollably. Osric leaned into his ear and whispered the last few lines as two distinct white lights began to emanate from the location where Kenneth lay. One light came from the Gus wand, and the other from Legati, connected to the spell by its contact with his bare torso.

"Let's get an accurate count of how many breaths the lock lasts this time. One… Two… Three… Four… Five… Six… Seven… Eight… Nine… Ten…"

* * *

"One hundred and fifty-four!" Gus shouted with a great deal of excitement as Kenneth attempted to sit upright. "I never thought that was possible! And the light that shot out from it could have easily blasted a hole in a solid wall like it did in the collapsed palace. Somebody hand me the sword, quick!"

Osric helped Kenneth to his feet and began to unstrap the hilt from his side.

"I haven't even looked at it myself yet. It just occurred to me when I was given the sword. It was a power lock from two wands, and one of them was the wand of the prophecy. I knew it, I just knew it." Osric smiled and laid the sword he had carried since his father had died in front of Gus.

"How is it possible that you never knew your father's sword was also a wand?" There was an almost playful tone to Gus's voice. "You've been carrying that for half your life."

The Weaving of Wells

"I think the unicorn that rescued me from the rubble is behind it becoming a wand. If my father had known this was a wand then he may have sold it during some of the lean years to buy us food."

"Ah, well let's see if your suspicions are correct. I've always wanted to get some answers to my questions about the unicorns. I knew it wasn't the wand I gave you!" Gus smiled up at him.

"I've always wanted to see what you two are talking about as it was happening." Kenneth stepped forward, followed shortly by Bridgett and then Pebble.

"There's more than enough room," Osric replied as he looked down and activated the Wand-Maker gift. What he saw was altogether as new as it was familiar.

Unlike the wands that Gus made, it was made of what looked like circular rings that decreased in size as they tapered away from the hilt of the sword. There were none of the typical linkings of strands to form a structure. Instead, the strange rings shared a common shaft that ran through the very center of the wand, and each of the individual rings was a distinctly different color. The structure was remarkably similar to another wand that Osric had looked at not too long ago, except that in this wand there were dozens of individual rings.

"Pebble, why does this wand look so much like one of your wands?" Gus inquired, but it was Kenneth who answered.

"He's the one that knows, but I think he is a bit too young to understand the significance of what he knows."

"Known, but not known." Gus smiled.

"All things are new to the young." Osric spoke with appreciation.

"Some of the hints he would give us in that blasted game I taught him are starting to make sense now." A genuine joy radiated from Gus as he looked at Osric with an uncharacteristically youthful smile.

"Yes, I believe you are right." Osric nodded in agreement. Then he leaned in close and whispered in Gus's ear, "And I think I'd like to know how he came up with his wand design too. Why don't you ask him?"

Gus stood right where he was and cocked his head to the right, asking, "Pebble, where did you get your inspiration for your wands?" A singular tremor shook his right ear.

"Osric's wand, silly." Pebble smiled.

Osric's Wand

"Well, I have to admit I was hoping for a bit more, but since he's known all along, I guess it makes sense." Gus shrugged, looking up exasperated.

"I thought there'd be more too." Osric returned the expression.

"I couldn't have done it without the unicorns helping me, though. I didn't have Osric's wand to look at always. Plus, it was tough trying to figure out how to do it the same way as his. It's still not perfect, 'cause those strands are hard to get at from below. They had to tell me how to do it five times before I got one right. Then it was easy, but I still can't make 'em quite like Osric's!" Pebble bounced around in excitement.

Osric and Gus both stood there, slack jawed and silent, waiting for more. Had Pebble really stated that unicorns had taught him how to make the wand? As far as the brightest minds on Archana were concerned, unicorns could not speak. Not only did he indicate that they had instructed him in wandcraft, but that they had done it five times.

"Who told you how to do it five times?" Kenneth was the one to break the silence.

"The unicorns," Pebble responded with the exaggerated impatience of a child. "You might hear me better over by them." He motioned for Kenneth to move next to Osric and Gus.

"I think he's picking up some of your mannerisms." Kenneth directed his statement toward Gus.

"I'm sorry?" Gus leaned in with his right ear.

"I said I think he's picking up some of your mannerisms."

"Not you, I'm talking to the boy." Gus scowled, yet a smirk remained on his face. It was as if he just couldn't manage to say it with a straight face. "You said the unicorns told you how to make these wands?"

Both of his ears twitched madly and his thin frame held in a tremendous amount of energy that looked ready to explode. Gus's entire body leaned toward Pebble in anticipation of the next few words.

"Yes!" He sighed. "The unicorns taught me how to make the wands. Goodness! You need to pay better attention, Pa. I already said it twice."

The Weaving of Wells

"You are correct," Gus spoke slowly as he chose his next words. "Now, how exactly did you get the unicorns to speak?"

"I never said they spoke. Their mouths can't make words, silly. They talk to the insides, like the dragons talk to each other, except for dragons can talk to us too." Pebble pointed to his ears. "But you have to be polite or unicorns won't say nothin'—not a peep. I told you that when we was at the Grove of the Unicorn." He said the last in exasperated annoyance.

"I don't remember you telling me any of that." Gus shook his head, more for the lack of attention he had paid his son than from disbelief.

"You tried to see their wands and they hid them from you. Then I told you to ask 'em first like you always told me." Pebble shrugged.

"I have most certainly told you to ask before you look into anyone with your gift, but you rarely listened," Gus said.

"Well the unicorns are so pretty that I looked *at* them first, before I looked *in* them." Pebble shrugged again matter-of-factly. "I said, 'Hello, you are pretty,' and she said 'thanks.' We talked for a bit before I asked to see her magics. Since I was so polite she said I could. But I never looked at anyone without asking since. Well, no one but all us here. I wanted to play games and you all said you would, so it was fair to look at you."

"I could see how you might think that." Gus bowed respectfully towards his son. Then he smirked a joyous smirk.

Not since his promotion to Contege, shortly before the attack on the palace, had Osric felt such satisfaction. By his guess, it had been far longer for the ex–world's greatest Wand-Maker—it was undeniable that Pebble had surpassed his father as the best. Gus beamed with tremendous excitement as he gazed as his pup. All of the onlookers attempted to hold in their sniggers, and a few unsuccessful mouths let loose an uproar at Gus's frivolous approach to his son.

Gus leapt at his son with gaiety. Both prairie dogs erupted with laughter as they tumbled about. Despite his youth, Pebble had nearly doubled in size since they had departed on their adventure almost a year earlier. Gus's thin frame kept disappearing beneath the chubby ball of laughter.

The cackles continued for some time as a visible load lifted from the small group of friends. Bridgett smiled as a happy tear slid down her cheek. Then her expression grew concerned and she leaned to whisper in Osric's ear.

"When you can tear yourself away, I need to catch you up on some dragon happenings. I'll be with Eublin. Don't hurry, but join me in the library when you can. You've carried such a considerable weight for so long, this time will do much to revive you." She motioned to the delighted gathering. Then she kissed him softly on the cheek and walked away.

Chapter 2
Mourning Epiphany

Kal groaned as he walked into the Wand-Maker's room for another day's work. Willam hadn't yet arrived, and Gus was never on time. But Kal liked to arrive early and take advantage of their new contraption. Peering into the hidden realm that could, until recently, only be seen by those with the Wand-Maker's gift, was thrilling. It was true that they hadn't created a tool that would allow him to manipulate the strands, but that was only a matter of time, by his reckoning.

He had to avoid Eublin to get to his station ahead of the rest. The gnome had been standing in the hallway on a pedestal for added height and visibility, trying to get everyone to sign some petition to change the way the hunt worked. The one thing Kal knew was to not get trapped in the hall with Eublin when he was on his pedestal.

He had detoured around that hallway and ventured by the kitchen to see if they had begun serving for the day. They hadn't set out any food yet, so he was left to let the internal rumblings continue for some time. While passing by the entrance to the barracks, he saw something that almost made him sacrifice an early arrival; a crowd seemed to be growing in the field, and laughter resonated from the area. For a moment he thought he heard Gus chittering playfully, and that's when he decided that he must be hearing things incorrectly, so he continued his hungry, weary walk to his small space within the Aranthian base.

The thought that he was a part of something as revolutionary as the Aranthians filled him with pride. This was his area; that was a hard fact to get used to. He still had to listen to the lectures of another master of the craft, but this time his own failings were due to something he couldn't control. He had the mind for wand-making, but not the gift. His stomach rumbled again just as he got to his station in the wand-making room. Kal grabbed his wand and focused on his attempt to summon a connection with the communication spell.

"David, are you there?" With so many people gathered around the grounds and Eublin on his mission to right the injustice of the hunt,

Osric's Wand

Kal didn't want to risk another trip out to get food or he might lose what chance he had to learn more about the Wand-Maker's gift.

"Hey, we're behind getting breakfast out, so make it quick or James will kill me!" David was thin and tall in the triangular display that appeared above the wand. Sweat poured out from under his blond hair, still visible in the transparent image.

"I didn't mean to bother you. I was just wondering if you might be able to bring a few plates to our office when you start serving? I tried to stop by earlier, but you weren't serving yet. You know how the passageways can get some mornings." Kal could hear several voices chattering and pans clattering about as the kitchen staff prepared the morning meal.

David's image turned toward Kal's right as he spoke. "James, could you spare me for a delivery when we serve? The Wand-Makers don't want to chance the halls this morning," he shouted.

"Ha!" James's voice bellowed in the background. "Gus is probably going to be a busy bee after this morning's epiphany. Besides, all the work you did to help us get ready for our cattle—you deserve an easy morning!"

The door cracked open and Willam stepped through, looking tired and casting a glance in Kal's direction. He raised a weary hand up in greeting. Then, seeing who was on the other end of the wand conversation, his eyes went wide.

David turned to face forward with a cocky smile. "How many plates should I bring?"

Kal looked at his stick-gathering partner, who nodded enthusiastically, then sat down across the table from him.

"That's two so far. Better make it three just to be safe. If you happen to see Gus in the mess, just bring us two."

"Okay, I'd better run. We're just waiting for the biscuits to brown, which should be anytime. Do I need to bring rulha as well, or juice?"

"Juice," Willam whispered with a quick motion of his head.

"One juice, one rulha, if you don't mind. Gus can get what he wants whenever he decides to get here." Kal smiled. Then something that had been said caught his attention. "Did I hear correct? Did the cattle finally arrive?"

The Weaving of Wells

"Yes, just a bit earlier. Osric called for me from the training grounds and told me they were here. We're going to be eating well for the foreseeable future."

"Osric's awake?" Kal now realized what had caused all of the commotion outside, and he grimmaced as he regretted missing the excitement in his hurry to get to his station. "Do you know if he plans to stop by our area today?"

"No idea. I didn't even know he was awake until I heard him shout my name from outside the window."

"Thanks. We can't wait for the food to get here, and thanks for the news." Kal ended the link and sheathed his wand. Taking a look around, he saw piles of wand material on every surface. "We need to clean this place up quick!"

"I'll move the sticks over here under the desk if you want to get the broom and sweep up all of the strippings and bark that are lying about?" Willam grabbed as much of the small scraps of wood as he could hold and started organizing them under the table.

"Sounds good, but let's get this done as quick as we can. I would like to try and show Osric that we are good for more than just gathering sticks. You think he can get Gus to make better use of us?" Kal moved to the back of the room, fetching the broom.

"I don't think we could fit another stick in this room if we tried. Gus is bound to let us learn something one of these days."

The door to the room opened and laughter burst inside. Kal quickly pushed a pile of debris against the wall and leaned the broom against the counter as Willam dropped his armload under the table. He looked nervous, and several sticks tumbled across the floor from his ill-timed toss. He kicked at the sticks closest to him, trying to make them find a less obvious place to rest.

"I still can't believe how different you seem." Osric's head came into view, and he was smiling while looking down.

"Shh! Don't spoil the surprise!" Gus bounded in, with Pebble, Jane, Kenneth, and Macgowan in tow.

Kal and Willam looked between each other at the sight of Gus hiding an obvious smile behind a fictitious frown. There was something strange in the way they all walked, as if weightless and unencumbered. It was simply baffling to witness.

"Why are you still here? Shouldn't you be gathering more sticks by now?" Gus nearly cracked a full-fledged smile.

Kal looked at Willam with hopeless desperation. He hadn't even been able to use the strand-sight device, and the worst part of it all was that his breakfast hadn't yet arrived and they would have to spend the day gathering sticks in the hot sun, outside of their safe enclosure. They wouldn't have time to get back and find something to eat until lunch, and David would be furious that they had made him bring food to an empty room. They wouldn't be able to get him to bring them their morning meal again anytime soon.

"We've got piles of them sitting around here. Why can't we take the day off and learn something for a change?" Kal berated himself in his mind. He had spoken too timidly. He sounded weak and reminded himself too much of a beggar.

"Yeah, Gus. Give the guys a day off and teach them something, why don't you?" Kenneth glared at the Wand-Maker sardonically.

"They've been putting up with you for months, so I'm sure they deserve more than a day off," Jane echoed.

Kal was starting to grow nervous with the way they were acting. Were they all drunk this early in the morning?

"Not so. I've been a perfectly hospitable instructor. Tell them I've been perfectly hospitable." The aged prairie dog looked back and forth between Kal and Willam, giving away no hint of his motivation.

"He's been perfectly hospitable." Kal's voice was less than convincing, eliciting a couple of loud chuckles, a guffaw, and two snorts from the gathered recruits.

"This is too much fun." Osric held his stomach as if he had spent too much time laughing. "But I have been indisposed for too long. I think I am going to excuse myself and see to the rounds that I have missed over the last month. Besides, Bridgett said she needed to speak to me about a possible threat. I think now would be a good time for me to see what that was about."

At last there was something familiar—Osric never stayed in one place for too long. Kal still didn't know what to make of the rest of the confusion. Once Osric had made his escape and everyone's attention returned, Gus regained his scowl.

"I don't think that you've convinced me. I need you to convince me that you felt I was cordial and attentive to your needs."

The Weaving of Wells

"Oh come on, Gus," Kenneth protested while Macgowan and Jane shifted uncomfortably.

"You two need more patience. At my age some things take time." Something that resembled a smile was on Gus's face. Kal was beginning to sense that a joke was happening at his expense, and he didn't find it amusing.

"Look, you have been, quite probably, one of the worst instructors Archana has ever seen. You are impatient, closed-minded, guarded with instruction, and you have a horrible habit of insulting everyone who could kill you without a second thought. You walk about this place as if you are the only authority on anything magical, and you inspire a great deal of nothing special from everyone." He shook with the nerves that it took to speak his mind.

Kal waited, anxiously anticipating what he knew was coming to him.

"You think I've been too harsh?"

Kal sent daggers at Gus with his eyes. He didn't like being belittled, and even less in front of a crowd.

"You have been the worst kind of intolerable," Kal answered.

"The worst kind, you think?"

"I don't have to think. There is no doubt that you are the worst kind of instructor. That's why the three men and one woman in this room are watching with such keen interest. They know you to be a vicious little tyrant." The words felt great! Kal took a deep breath of satisfaction, disregarding the uncertainty on display from the onlookers.

Gus took a long, slow breath and looked down, as if he were hearing what was being said for the first time and was actually listening.

He took a deep breath and replied, "I may have been less than I should have been." There was an unnerving amount of honesty in Gus's voice.

"May have? The executioner could answer with that amount of honesty, but not you." Kal held his breath, unsure of the brazenness in his words.

To his dismay, Gus took a short intake of air and looked at the dark-skinned hunter to his left.

Osric's Wand

"I think I've been correct in my statements about this poor lad, don't you?"

"He may prove to be fairly bright," Macgowan answered before Kenneth could.

Kenneth laughed with delight. "Took the words right out of my mouth," he replied.

"Fine. We've established that my skills as a teacher have left something to be desired. Will you accept my apology or will there be a trial later?"

"Ha!" Kal was certain now that this must be a joke. Surely Gus had not just offered him an apology.

"Look, kid," Gus shouted.

"Easy, Gus. You just started making progress," Kenneth replied with his hands raised.

"He has been horrible to us," Willam said softly, trying to support his friend.

"And you have learned a lot as a result!" Gus raised his chest in reply.

"Like how to be rude, or how to shout at those who don't have your gift? Maybe you'd like me to teach others to show up to work late? What part do you want emulated, because you haven't offered anything of value that I haven't mentioned!" Suddenly he felt his body lift off of the ground with his Levitation gift taking over. He leaned over the top of the table, looking down at Gus. His gift hadn't moved him in such a way since he was a child, but he had been holding in his temper for a long time.

"The man's got a point, Gus. You are rather difficult to work with at times," Kenneth said, supporting Kal's statement.

Gus sat there with a dumbfounded look on his face, blinking while sorting through the verbal onslaught. To Kal's surprise, Gus didn't retaliate, but took several deep breaths and smiled.

"I suppose I deserve every word of that, but things are going to change around here, and the first thing is this." Gus motioned for Kenneth to come forward. "What did you say I should name this contraption, Kal?"

Kal watched Kenneth grab Osric's sword off of the table near the door, half expecting him to leave the room to bring it back to the legendary wizard, but he didn't. Instead, the sword was brought around the table and he placed the base of the blade under the viewing tube of the strand-sight device.

"Strandiscope!" Willam nodded nervously.

"No, it's a strand-sight device." Kal felt the familiar tickle of curiosity bubbling to the surface. If Gus wasn't going to take the bait in an argument then something big had happened or was about to.

"That's it." Gus tapped his nose with a claw. "I hereby dub this a strand-sight device. Now, which one of you wants to take a look and tell me what you see?"

Before Kal could get his feet back on the ground beneath him, Willam had taken his position in front of the eyepiece, smiling apologetically in Kal's direction.

"We have a volunteer. The goal here is to show this to as many people as we can. I have to admit that I'm not quite certain how it works. It's become obvious to me that minds which haven't been subjected to a lifetime of hard, false truths can lend insight into magical mysteries that I tend to look past." Gus looked up at a room full of questioning eyes.

A moment of uncomfortable silence began to settle through the room. Kenneth's, Macgowan's, and Jane's eyes kept darting between Gus and Kal as if they were waiting for another outburst from one of them. Kal still felt that he was being subjected to some cruel joke, but Gus was the only one in the room who he could see attempting something of that nature. Macgowan was the strong silent type, not much of a prankster. Jane was too proud and too busy to bother with playing jokes on recruits, and Kenneth's humor was usually used to defuse tense situations rather than create them.

"Look." Gus had evidently sensed the distrust. "It appears to me that you two aren't in the mood for my attempts at being cute. Nor does it seem that you are in the mood for my attempt to apologize for being a bad teacher. So, dammit, let's try honesty and see how far that gets us." Gus nodded sharply, his voice rising in both pitch and volume as he addressed the room. "I'm excited, and I do need your thoughts on what is sitting on that device. So, if you'll kindly pick your jaws up off the floor, wipe the drool from your chin, and look through that blasted contraption!"

In no time, Willam had his eyes pressed down on the opening in the strand-sight device. Gus climbed up a chair and pulled himself up on top of the table where the strand-sight device sat, watching the examination with keen interest.

"Man." Kenneth shook his head as he watched Gus climb the table. "And he may never be nice again. I wish I'd known to say goodbye to the nice Gus. But we'll place a nice grave marker for him later tonight."

"Whoa!" Willam hadn't heard any of the sarcasm, but he began sliding the sword from hilt to tip and then back again below the glass. "What happened to this?" He looked up enthusiastically, backing away to let Kal take a look.

"A unicorn turned it into a wand right before the palace collapsed last year," Gus replied with a smile.

"Unicorns?" Kal inquired as he watched Willam step away from the device.

"Yes," Gus replied, motioning toward Pebble, who had made himself busy exploring the room's many sticks, unaware of the conversation happening behind him. "My brilliant son even had the help of the unicorns to make his wands. It seems the world has just been rude to the unicorns all these years, or they would have spoken to us all along, right?"

Pebble was still unaware of the conversation.

"No matter. That's what you heard, right?" Gus addressed those who arrived with him.

"That's my best guess, from what we heard. Though it seems an awfully large grudge to hold," Jane replied as Macgowan and Kenneth both nodded in agreement.

"It's a wand made of a mix of amulets and charms, right?" Kal looked at Gus for an answer.

"What?" The prairie dog looked shocked.

"Well, isn't it? I noticed the same charm at the tip of it that's in the necklace Bridgett wears." He was unsure of himself, but that was how he would have felt even if nobody else was in the room.

"When did you have the opportunity to examine that amulet?" Gus squinted his small brown eyes.

"Well, you sent us to watch over her the night she got back after being injured in the battle. I heard the stories that everyone told about your first adventures together, and I wanted to see what it looked like. I sorta snuck it out for a few minutes while Willam was asleep."

The Weaving of Wells

"You what?" The accusing expression on Gus's face told Kal that he had said too much.

"Willam was there in case she woke up, and I had it back before either of them woke, so I don't see what the big deal is. But that's it. Look, it's the exact same color on the third ring, right here." He pointed at a spot near the tip.

Gus stepped forward and looked down at Legati.

"You may just be right, boy. I'm impressed. Each ring behind the first seems to contain a different gift, but there are genuine life strands weaving their way through the entire wand. I've never seen a wand with life strands."

"Well, this is no ordinary wand. I've never seen anything like it. The charms seem to be working together, feeding off of each other, as if they are alive," Kal said, gazing at the sword in awe.

"Don't be daft, boy. Charms aren't alive, they're just spells trapped in objects." Gus pouted briefly as he noticed the scolding expressions on Kenneth and Jane's faces in response to his harsh words. "Although, I admit that if these are charms, they are not like any charm I have ever seen. Perhaps there is more to it than just a chain of normal charms trapped in a sword."

"If this thing isn't alive, then why does it have its own life strand?" Willam asked, causing Gus to fall silent with his mouth open as he stared at the amazing wand lying under the eyepiece of the device.

"There is much about it we still don't know. But, we will study it together and learn. Kal, how are these rings like charms? What do you see?"

Kal glanced over at Gus briefly, surprised at the patient, teacherly tone of the small, furry tyrant he was used to working for.

"Well, the first one seems to be leaching the levitation gift from my blood as we speak. It's like a charm, always active."

"Remind me to tell Largrid I was wrong. That device is amazing; I didn't even notice that with my gift." Gus turned his attention to Kal's hand, which now rested between the scope and the sword.

Tendrils that almost escaped Gus's gaze waved through the air as if blown by a breeze. Yet, when they contacted Kal they would fill with the pale yellow color that filled the hundreds of deposits throughout his body. Kal's gift would then be channeled through the life strands,

21

Osric's Wand

where they slowly began to build a new ring at the hilt end of the wand.

"Even now it grows more powerful. It finally makes sense. It's grafting your gift into the wand's makeup as we speak."

"So that thing is growing more powerful all the time?" Willam stepped forward with a look of sheer envy.

"It sure looks like it," Gus answered. "And, for safety's sake we should probably have Kal here teach Osric how to use the levitation gift before it surprises him in battle by asserting itself as a fully matured gift. The Invisibility gift was probably a bit easier to manage the first time, I'm sure."

Then he watched as the same tendrils, this time from the third ring of the wand, reached out to both Willam and Kal. Each time they journeyed to the two men and back, the tendrils carried a small sample of the magics within subsequent rings and deposited them within the bodies of the two men. Gus was astonished to see that along with partially formed gifts appearing in their bodies, there were also somewhat tenuous life strands twining around and adding to the life strands of both Kal and Willam. Gus was actually watching their power grow right before his eyes—no longer would the old saying "One gift, one measure of magic" hold true for these young men.

The wand was literally initiating the growth of new gifts on those around it. He wondered if the amulet-like segment in the wand was as choosy about whom to implant gifts in as Bridgett's amulet was about whom to endow with greater power fed directly to their gifts. Gus focused on the way the tendrils moved, hoping he could see the intent of the magic in the pattern of its movement—did it shy away from some, or did it favor some more than others?

"I just want to hold it." Willam grasped at the hilt greedily and pulled it out from under the strand-sight device.

"Just wait, boy," Gus said impatiently as he looked up.

The sword twisted slightly as it was pulled, causing it to draw the recently honed blade on the flat of Kal's hand.

"Ah!" Kal cried out. He turned a frustrated expression toward his friend as Willam tripped over his own feet and hit his head on the floor, lying limp where he landed. "Patience! You cut me, you prat!"

Gus blinked in shock, shaking his head. "He's dead."

The Weaving of Wells

"No he's not, he just took a tumble." Kal stood and pushed his fallen friend's legs with his feet. "Get up, Will. This isn't funny."

"I saw it happen when he cut you."

"Get up!" Kal dropped to his knees, shaking the limp body. He screamed at the others in the room, "Somebody help him!"

"We never even had a chance to save him," Gus spoke in a sorrowful tone. "Blood causes an immediate transfer of every gift within the sword. I was still using my gift as it happened. I saw it. Willam's life strand just snapped as his body was flooded with the new gifts and the power that came with them."

"No, that doesn't make any sense," Kal cried. "Osric has fought with this blade for months. He's cut guys in half with it, and it didn't kill him! Will can't be dead."

"I'm sorry Kal, but he is dead. Osric only acquired one gift at a time. He already had all the others whenever he used the sword, and each one made him stronger. The influx of every gift at once was just too much for him to survive. I'm so sorry." Gus gazed down at the still body of the young man. After a moment, he cleared his throat and spoke with calm authority. "Handle that thing very, very carefully. One drop of fresh blood and whoever is holding the sword could have the same fate. Kenneth, I think you're safe. You've been using Legati since the beginning and slowly acquiring gifts along the way." Gus began to shake, attempting to blink away the afterimage of Willam's death, as the others saw to getting Kal and the sword to safety. Pebble peeked out from behind a table with wide, watery eyes.

* * *

"Something has to change. The hunt had its place, I'm sure, but that was long ago." Eublin paced the room, tracing a finger on his chin.

"I'm just not sure what you want us to do about it. You've shown us that there are a large number of sentient minds who would love to live outside the hunt, but Osric has only known about this for a short time. He can't change the world overnight," Bridgett reasoned. She had found Eublin standing on his pedestal in the hall and nearly had to drag him away to the library to speak with him. Still, the subject had not changed from his preaching in the corridors.

"Yes, but he could do something."

"I'm sure he would if there was some direction for him to take, but you are talking about a massive social reform. The hunt has existed in its present form since its inception. If you have any ideas on how he might change something that spans all of Archana, I am sure he would listen."

"That's just it; it doesn't span all of Archana." Eublin's eyes grew wide in protest and he ducked out of sight behind a shelf filled with books. "But that's what they want us to believe. Thankfully some of these books were written by some well-traveled individuals." His voice was dull as he gruffed about, bending or climbing to retrieve a tome from the stacks. "Aha!" The note rose distinctly as his pale feet padded the floor, sounding his return. He rounded the shelf with a thick leatherbound book covered in dust. Eublin held a thin finger up to hold off questions until he could make his point. He rifled through the pages, searching for something, and his excitement grew when he found what he was looking for. He read the words aloud.

"Though the hunt became an important part of several realms, and with the humans especially, neither the elves, whose diet consists mainly of fruits and vegetables, or the irua, who feed upon nonintelligent burrowing creatures, have ever adopted the practice of honoring a sentient being for allowing itself to be eaten by another."

With a furrowed brow, Bridgett remembered the time she had spent in both locations. It hadn't occurred to her that she had been so far from the familiar world she had known. True, it had been obvious that their cultures were different, but she had a hard time believing that none of them observed any form of the hunt. Had she really gone that whole time without eating any meat?

"Don't you see? The hunt is what it is on this continent only. It was more than likely a result of having so many intelligent species living in one place. You wouldn't want to have a war because a lioness brought home a human, prairie dog, or squirrel for dinner. Something had to happen so that peace could be maintained with the multitudes."

"But there is more than one sentient species in both the elven and the Irua Realm. The nieko live in the Elven Realm, and the weasels live alongside the irua." Bridgett was thinking out loud, trying to sort through the information.

The Weaving of Wells

"Yes, but the elves don't eat meat, and I am sure the nieko share in the dietary habits of the elves. As for the irua and weasel world, there are dozens of tunneling, non-sentient species that live in their tunnels—the weasels have basically the same diet. The hunt only exists on this continent, and there are too many other possible sources of food that could be exploited. Cattle was domesticated into herds and raised for food because they lack the sentience of so many other species. There are many other herd animals, and the herds can be increased until hunting is simply not necessary. Even here, we are almost to the point that we can tend to enough livestock that the hunt will no longer be needed at all. For it to continue in its current form is simply ludicrous!" Eublin pleaded.

"Okay, while you make some good points, there must be a reason why the hunt has thrived for so long in its current form. Would you prefer that we just kill whatever creatures we want to eat without honoring them for their sacrifices? And, even if it is ludicrous, it won't be easy to overcome the normalcy of it. Do you have any ideas that could help us to change the widespread assumption that this tradition is normal and right?" Bridgett agreed with some of what Eublin was saying, but she couldn't imagine anything that could help bring an end to the hunt.

"I don't know. Red armbands were an idea that our group came up with, but then we realized that hunters approaching from different angles might not be able to see them. If we put the bands on every limb, they would be cumbersome. Nobody wants to feel like they are in danger if they forget to wear a piece of clothing, and what if the bands were to get damaged, lost, or fall off?"

"Sounds like that idea fell flat fast. I do agree with you, Eublin. I would prefer we didn't kill others at all, but I don't have a solution." She traced the table with her eyes, searching for ideas.

"Ideas are in abundance at every one of our meetings. The most popular idea has the Aranthian crafters designing a shield charm that wards off arrow and sword strikes. I don't have to tell you how impractical that idea is." Eublin's large brow furrowed in frustration.

"Yes. If a shield generated by a wand can't survive long under aggressive attacks, how could a shield generated by a charm hope to endure the attack?" Bridgett agreed.

Osric's Wand

"Yes." Eublin frowned, taking a deep breath and then sighing. "Lots of ideas, but nothing of substance. I only hope that all the minds we have gathered in this place can imagine a way for as much change to the hunt as they have for magic."

"I wish they could, but I just don't see how we can change that much of our world. We're just too small to have that much influence."

Osric took several timid steps through the door to the library. "I was listening to your conversation. I agree that no one should be forced to endure the hunt if they wish to lead a different life, but I'm just not sure if the Aranthians can force that change."

"Can we at least pour some of our energy into social reform, rather than revolutionizing magical knowledge? Surely you can see the former as equal in value to the latter?" The gnome's thin arms crossed his chest as he glared up at Osric.

"Eublin, I don't mean to—"

"Bridgett ready?" The irua boy, Trevar, peered up with a smile, interrupting Osric's reply.

Bridgett stood up and smiled at the boy and turned to Eublin.

"I'm afraid I need to continue instructing Trevar in Common. You two have a lot to discuss, it seems."

"Wait," Osric protested. "Don't you have news about the dragons that I need? And who is this young boy?"

"I do, but Trevar is the one responsible for bringing me into the Well of Strands, and if we ever hope to stop Dredek we will need to be able to communicate with him. I've been working hard to teach him how to speak Common while you were in bed, and he is making good progress, so we can't neglect his teaching now. Meet me on the elemental level when you are done here and we'll see if we've made enough progress to allow for a short diversion to catch you up." She kissed him lightly on the cheek, smiling apologetically as she left.

Osric watched with a longing stare as Bridgett left; then her words registered and he looked at Eublin with no small amount of worry in his eyes. "Did she say to meet her on the elemental level?"

"Yes, I do believe she did. Why do you ask?"

"We put them on that floor to isolate the danger to the rest of the barracks; that's no place to teach a child Common." Osric stood up to run after Bridgett, but Eublin stepped in the way with hands raised to calm his nerves.

The Weaving of Wells

"They have agreed to limit their experiments to ones that do not risk explosion, implosion, or mutilation until her lesson is concluded. Those elemental wizards are out gathering materials, so she can use the room for a while to test the boy. We worked it all out ages ago while you were still recovering."

The words settled in and the sense of urgency he had felt began to subside as he took a step back and sat down. Having Bridgett back was an almost overwhelming pleasure, but he didn't want to drown her with his overprotective nature; that would be a mistake. Eublin's next words echoed his thoughts precisely.

"She's a smart one. You don't need to worry about her so much. She wouldn't endanger the boy, so she made sure they would shut down any dangerous experiments before they arrived. In these parts, she is a force to be reckoned with. Ask anyone and they'll tell you the same."

Osric nodded, picturing Bridgett defending him after he had fallen in battle by thrusting a small knife into Dredek. "You're right. She's tougher than most would give her credit for." He smiled. "Why is she teaching the boy to speak Common, though? Aren't there a ton of irua here who could teach him much faster since they speak his native tongue?"

"Of course there are, but she needed something to take her mind off of you until we knew you were going to be all right. She was so worried about you that she was physically ill. Her bond with the boy was one of the few things that could keep her from wasting away at your bedside. And it seems that the child will not speak with others as he does with her, since she has whatever it is she needed for him to reveal the Well of Strands to her. He's a strange little boy, that one."

Osric nodded, wishing he hadn't worried her at all. He was glad to see she was smiling again.

"Now, do you have a few moments to spare?" Eublin asked. "I have some things I need to go over with you. I'm not expecting too much from you, but I would at least like to have your ear for a time."

"Sure. What's pressing on your mind these days, Eublin?" He knew what to expect, but the gnome deserved as much of his time as anyone else would get.

"Thank you. I'd like to show you a couple books that will challenge the way you feel about the hunt." Eublin pushed his spectacles up with a long, thin finger and walked around the table to two open books.

Chapter 3
Lesson and Learning

Bridgett sat on the floor with her legs crossed and fed a few more sticks to the small fire. Trevar sat next to her, his brow wrinkled in concentration. Bridgett smiled but resisted correcting the boy. His expression clearly told her that Trevar knew he had made a mistake. The story was one of her favorites from childhood, a silly tale about a bear who tries to catch a fish in a river but instead finds an enchanted boot. She had first told the story to Trevar in his native irua language with the aid of a translator. When she learned he was rather adept at fire-tellings, she thought this would be the perfect way to evaluate his mastery of Common.

The beginning of the story had gone well, though the images had faded from the flames a few times while Trevar struggled to remember the proper words. As he had neared the end of the tale, he said "foot" instead of "boot," and the depiction in the fire of a bear with a severed foot in its mouth had generated a look of surprise and confusion on the young irua's face. Bridgett managed not to laugh, and thus she was sitting quietly as Trevar tried to remember the correct Common word for boot.

"I cannot remember it." The disappointment he was feeling washed over her, wiping the smile from her lips, and she leaned close to him.

"Boot," she whispered. Trevar sighed and focused on the meager flames.

"The bear closed his mouth and raised his head from river. He is surprised to see it is not fish he caught. It is boot!" The boy smiled as the image reformed, a large boot hanging from the animal's jaws. Bridgett clapped her hands in delight and smiled down at the child.

"Very nice, Trevar. You are learning quickly." Bridgett tapped her wand on the rim of the firepit and the flames died out. "That is enough for today. I would like to speak with you for a while."

"Do we need Segan?" The boy sprung to his feet, ready to run and get the irua guard who often served as his translator.

"Not today. I believe you have learned the language well enough, and I would like this conversation to just be between us," Bridgett

Osric's Wand

said, patting the floor next to her. Trevar sat back down and looked up at her with wide eyes. "I want to thank you for saving my life in Angmar. If not for you, I would have died standing on that small ledge. I can never repay you for your decision to trust me."

"You tried to only help, not to hurt." Trevar grinned at her.

"I did want to help, and I could not have done so without you helping me. I am very grateful." She smiled back at him. "When those big creatures broke into the city, and the fighting started, you saved me again. You took me down the tunnels to the Well of Strands." Trevar nodded enthusiastically. "Why did you take me there?"

"So we could be safe, not die."

"Yes, but we could have hidden in the storage room. Why did you take me through the wall and show me the secret room where the well is?" Ever since they had left the irua city, she had been wondering why the boy had decided to lead her there. "You were part of the group selected to protect the Well of Strands, weren't you? I was an outsider."

"I do not know *outsider*. It is safer where no one can come. You can come because you are like me."

"What do you mean? Because I have the Trust ability?" Bridgett knew the sand-colored robes marked the individuals responsible for the well, and she could not believe that the irua who had nearly plunged a ceremonial blade into her chest was a Trust.

"No." Trevar scrunched up his face as he tried to summon the correct words in the unfamiliar language. "You have the strand the well needs."

"I don't understand, Trevar. What do you mean?"

"I don't know other words for you." He frowned into his lap and Bridgett felt his anxiety acutely. He feared he was disappointing her.

"That's all right. We can talk about it more another time." Bridgett brushed her hands together to clean off any ash from the fire and pushed herself to her feet. Trevar sprung up next to her and eagerly waited to hear what they would be doing next. "Let's clean up and see if we can find Osric, shall we? I thought he would be here by now."

Trevar nodded and collected the small stack of sticks from the floor next to the firepit. He carried them over to a large bin near the door. Bridgett picked up the two cups of water that they had been drinking from and washed them in a small sink along the back wall. She glanced at all of the odd items arranged on shelves nearby as she worked, wondering what each object could possibly be used for. The bags and containers of various rocks and soils and the vials of water seemed reasonable in a room used to study the elemental magics, but the strange statues, gems, and other unidentifiable substances left her wondering.

As she replaced the cups in a small cupboard above the sink, Osric entered the room. Bridgett didn't need to see him to know he was there; his unique combination of guilt, pride, and adoration created a signature effect on her Empath ability that left no doubt as to who was standing behind her. She turned and was greeted by his warm smile and a quick embrace. Yet, she could tell something was bothering him.

"Trevar did a splendid job today. His grasp of Common is improving rapidly." Bridgett indicated the young irua with a proud smile.

"So, you're the one who helped Bridgett through the irua tunnels?" Osric smiled, kneeling down to greet the boy.

"Yes. You are High-Wizard?" Trevar gazed up at Osric with a mixture of awe and surprise.

"I suppose I am. I owe you a great debt for taking care of Bridgett in my absence." He placed a hand on the boy's shoulder and then drew him into a grateful hug.

"Bridgett is good. She must be safe. You have my welcome." Trevar hugged him back awkwardly, and Osric nodded in agreement.

"Run along and get some lunch. You must be hungry after that wonderful fire-telling," Bridgett said. Trevar nodded and left the room with a beaming smile. She took Osric's hand and led him to a small table in a corner of the room. "He really is improving quickly. However, I still have few of the answers I think he can provide. Perhaps I am asking the wrong questions."

"You've done a great job teaching him Common in such a short time. I'm sure things will get easier in the near future when he can grasp the subtleties of the language. But after my long and unproductive chat with Eublin, I am eager for a diversion. So, I am here to learn what you can tell me about the dragons. What is happening with our winged friends?"

"Our friends are still loyal and willing to aid us in our travels as needed. It is the dragons we cannot call our friends which concern us. I know little of the motivations of these creatures, but I have learned something of their history."

"I wasn't aware there were dragons that we couldn't call friends. Go on." Osric leaned in to hear her words.

"It seems that not all of the dragons on Archana are as herd oriented as those we have met. While most of them look to the dragon elders for leadership and knowledge, some of the dragons have sought solo lives apart from the others." Bridgett held Osric's hand tighter. "While the captivity of the elders forced so many dragons into slavery for the other races, these independent dragons felt no obligation to obey anyone. They broke from the rest of the species and isolated themselves in distant regions. I do not know what has inspired the destruction, but it is those dragons which have set fire to sacred trees and fishing towns along the coasts."

"In the Human Realm?" Osric inquired.

"The Human Realm, Irua Realm, Elven Realm, and for all we know in many other places as well. The attacks have been sporadic and fairly well contained, but there must be at least four of these dragons based on the locations of the damage. The dragons I have spoken with say they have had no contact with the offenders for dozens of years, and they are confident that the telepathic link has not provided the other dragons with knowledge of the traveling spell. They know these dragons have no allegiance to the dragon elders, and so they will not risk putting the entire species at risk by letting that knowledge out."

"It would be dangerous to assume they don't have knowledge of the traveling spell, so I won't assume that. But the others don't have contact with the offenders? How is that possible? I thought they all communicated telepathically."

"I thought the same thing. We don't know for sure, but several possible theories have been raised. It could be that the link is still active and the dragons responsible for the attacks are very much aware of the spell. Although if that is the case, there could be as few as two of them. It is also possible that distance from the herd and so many years of silence has weakened or severed the link in these creatures. It has been proposed that these dragons have gone feral, losing any ability to communicate intelligently with the other dragons. It seems most likely to me that they have chosen to reject the link in order to protect their independence from the other dragons."

"Which would grant them the ability to tap into it at any time and learn about the traveling spell. When did these attacks begin?"

"The first attack was sometime before I traveled to the Irua Realm. We thought the first was on the elven forest, but there was an earlier attack along the west coast of the Human Realm." Bridgett shook her head in frustration. "As for the traveling spell, that is even more unclear. The dragons have a knack for collecting massive amounts of gold. If the rogue dragons have done the same, they may have found a way to permanently sever the telepathic link in order to keep their hoards hidden from the others. Although, we have to assume they could potentially know the spell."

"Has there been any declaration on their part? Do we know anything that could give us some hint as to their motives?" Osric's brow furrowed.

"We have had no communication with the rogue dragons at all. If they told anyone of their reasons, they didn't allow them to live to share the message." Bridgett shrugged. "Osric we have to find a way to stop them. I promised the elves that we would aid them when the attack occurred. I mean to keep that promise."

He nodded. "Maybe we need to pay the elves a visit and see if there is any news—after we sort things out here, of course?"

Bridgett's eyes were haunted. "If you could have heard that tree sing, you wouldn't wait."

"I will send some men to learn what may be done." Osric squeezed her hand, relieved to see her smile at his offer.

"Thank you." She stared at the table as she thought about what she had seen in the Elven Realm. The fear that had permeated the air when the elves realized the Mother was under attack had frozen her in shared empathic terror. "Osric—"

"I need you here. Please, don't leave when I have just gotten you back."

Bridgett smiled sadly but nodded. She would allow his men to go, but she would insist on speaking with them first.

* * *

Osric's Wand

Pebble held two stilts out in front of himself. He was impressed by the likeness to the performers' sets he had seen as the entertainers prepared and practiced for the anniversary meal. His stilts were, of course, shorter than those used by the humans walking through the streets, but he had gotten a good look at them before their pant legs had been lowered over the wooden supports.

He had to modify it a bit to accommodate his prairie dog legs, but the design was still very similar to that of the tall figures walking about as they juggled flaming torches, knives, or colorful bags of sand. He loved the long strides that the stilts provided the entertainers so much that he wanted to try it for himself.

Surprisingly, he had found that he already possessed all of the materials needed to duplicate the stilts. He had already been crafting wands from much larger chunks of wood, so he had more than enough of the material on hand in his wand shop. The act of carving the walking sticks with his wand had proven to be a fun challenge. It was more difficult than making wands, but still enjoyable.

He propped the leg extensions up against the front of a nearby chair. Then with a quick vocalization of the traveling spell, he found himself looking back at them from atop the chair. He sat, sliding toward them, careful not to knock them over. He slid his back paws in from the side—one brace above the paw, one behind his leg—and slipped his claws into a few holes of the footrest. The last step was to secure his legs with a few thin leather straps. He looked up at the closed window where the afternoon light still made its way through the border, gathering his courage.

Pebble slid off of the chair, bracing himself with his front paws as he tested his balance. He pushed off and took two tentative steps while growing accustomed to the new stride and height. Thrilled with the experience, Pebble surveyed the room. He giggled when he looked at the countertop—he could nearly reach it if he could keep himself atop the stilts for a few more steps.

The door to the wand shop opened and the bright sun blinded him just as his next step landed. As instinct brought his paw up to shield his eyes from the light, Pebble's right leg shifted slightly. The stilt slid out from underneath his paw, causing him to tumble down onto the

The Weaving of Wells

dusty floor and slide a few paces before coming to a rest next to a pile of carved sticks.

A young voice giggled from across the room and Pebble sat up, untying the straps so he could address the rude interruption.

"I am sorry to cause you a fall." The voice was amused and apologetic, though somewhat rough in diction and enunciation—but it was young. Pebble knew it immediately.

"Trevar!" Pebble smiled in greeting, forgetting the reprimand he had been working up to. "I saw 'em in the market. I built 'em, and I was gettin' the hang of it till you startled me."

"Oh." Trevar scrunched his face, searching for the words. "It looks fun?" There was clearly more to his question.

"Very good." Pebble nodded in appreciation of Trevar's quick mastery of Common. "That was correct. And yes, it was fun. I'd let ya try but these are too weak to support an irua."

"Yes, it is too small, but I bring fun for us, and food." Trevar brandished a small sack in his right hand and held a plate piled high with cheese, rolls, smoked sausage, and apple slices.

"Yum, lunch looks delicious, but my pa says I'm too young to play bones." Pebble looked around the room nervously.

"What is bones?"

"It is a game of bets and trickery." Pebble shrugged.

"Oh, this is no bones." Trevar shook his head.

"What is it, then?"

"It is…" Trevar hesitated. "It is magic puzzle of stone." He moved to the table, set down the plate, and overturned the blue bag. Seven small stones tumbled out.

"How does it work?" Pebble climbed up atop the wooden slab as Trevar sat down. "I like rocks. I was named after small rocks." They both nibbled on apples.

"These rocks do not do right," Trevar said.

"What do you mean?"

"You see." Trevar picked up three of the stones and tossed them in the air in an attempt to juggle. One rock hovered in the air in front of his head, one stuck to his hand, and the third diverted mid-toss and landed in front of Pebble's left leg.

"How did they do that?" Pebble was stunned and intrigued.

Osric's Wand

"I not know, but I see men juggle them, toss to others, and throw through hoops. They say was mind tricks only mastered by the clever," Trevar said, eyeing the rocks suspiciously. Pebble giggled and picked up one of the small stones.

"Mind puzzles!" Pebble tossed the rock into the air and they both laughed as it came to a quick, soft rest on his forehead and stuck. When it fell back to the table, he began looking at the strands within. "They're charmed! I just don't know how they work." Pebble placed a claw on one stone and pushed it. To his surprise, the pebble sat in the same spot but three others scooted away from him on the table.

"Why don't irua children learn to speak Common?" Pebble continued to manipulate the stones, trying to understand what was behind their odd behavior.

"They teach Common to most, but not to well guardians. I did not do learning with other children. I do learning with other guardians. We do very secret duty, so we do not speak Common until we pass tests of duty." Trevar was also playing with the stones and trying to determine how they worked, but nothing they did elicited an appropriate response from the rocks. All of their manipulations caused an unexpected response, often from stones other than those they were trying to affect.

"It's got randomy stuffs in it!" Pebble exclaimed. As he set a stone down on the table, another rose the same distance into the air as the one Pebble held was being lowered. He lifted the stone again slightly, and the one hovering above the table began to slowly rotate.

"What is 'randomy stuffs'?" Trevar looked over at the plump prairie dog.

"I meant to say that the charm inside randomizes which magic it pulls from Archana." He chose his words with great thought. "You shouldn't learn words from me. I still mess it up 'cause I'm young and rush my talking when I get excited."

Trevar weighed the words with a bit more thought than was required. "Big ones like your talk," he said with a serious expression.

"They think I'm cute." Pebble smiled big.

"This cute is true. I wish we had you at my home." Trevar ruffled the hair atop Pebble's head. "Our you is"—he concentrated—"not soft coat, smell bad, with sharp teeth. They bigger than you. They no speak too."

The Weaving of Wells

"They say only animals that use magic with intent can speak." Pebble nodded in understanding.

"What is intent?" Trevar asked questions like this a lot, but he was more comfortable getting the answers from Pebble. It didn't feel like a lesson when they were playing together.

"Intent?" Pebble paused and looked up absent-mindedly. "It means to do things you want to, not just 'cause you got scared or mad." He scrunched up his furry nose and added, "Or somethin' like that."

"Maybe it would be fun to set these like…" Trevar stood up and scooped the stones into their sack. Then something occurred to him and he changed his direction "Why is putting in sack so easy?" He paused.

"Dump them and do it again." Pebble stood up on the tabletop with skeptical eyes.

Trevar upended the bag and the stones fell out again. They scattered effortlessly and naturally, as if guided by nothing but chance and the smoothed edges against the table's surface. Pebble held one claw up in the air to tell Trevar to wait a moment as Pebble studied the spells on the stones. After a quick nudge of a rock sent two of the others hovering off of the surface, Pebble indicated that Trevar should collect them again. Once again, the rocks slid easily back into their bag.

"Super clever!" Pebble motioned for Trevar to give him the bag of stones.

"You see how the trick is?"

"I think so." Pebble took the bag and dumped it out. "But I need a hat."

He took the bag and turned around with a mischievous smile. When he spun back, the bag sat atop his head, tied by the strap under his chin. He smiled and bowed while Trevar laughed.

"You look like juggler man."

"I'm not a good juggler, but I like tossing rocks in the lake." Pebble picked up a few stones and skipped them lightly across the long part of the table. They slipped harmlessly, bounced off of the wall at the end, and scattered naturally based on the direction of the throw. "And I like to play catch."

Trevar flinched as Pebble tossed another rock toward him. Surprisingly, the rock arrived on target and would have been caught if it weren't for the fact that Trevar hadn't expected it to do so. He giggled with glee that the puzzle had been solved so quickly, and then attempted to toss the stone back—it diverted left and another slid off of the table, adhering itself to the blade of the axe by the wood pile in the corner.

"You got it!"

"Yup." Pebble smiled. "Touching the bag takes away the random. Here, you try it." He took the bag off of his head and brought it to the edge of the table, handing it to Trevar.

"I have idea. This is what I was to do, before." Trevar smiled, taking the bag and gathering all but one of the stones in his hand. He dispersed the stones throughout the room, placing them in odd locations: on bookshelves, under bowls, propping a book up, or buried under a pile of sticks. Finally he stood before Pebble and dropped the bag. He grinned down at Pebble. "Catch!"

Trevar turned around and threw the stone down sharply. Like before, the rock stuck to his hand and one that sat below the book shot across the room abruptly and collided with the one in his hand. Then they clattered to the floor in different directions.

"Neat!" Pebble jumped down from the table and scampered over to another of the stones. He attempted to pick it up and it stayed where it was, but across the room one of the stones began to slide in a circular motion at the bottom of a pot. It spun more rapidly when Pebble pulled harder at the stone held firmly against the floor.

Trevar picked up another as Pebble began to push his. The irua boy stumbled backwards, being shoved by the tiny stone in his hand. He pushed back and the rock Pebble held tight in his paw pulled him across the room.

They laughed and played with the stones well into the day.

Chapter 4
Prophecy's Demands

Serha held her skirt in one hand and the heavy book in the other as she rushed through the halls of the barracks. Eublin had given her access to all of his books, and several recruits had volunteered to help her sort through the vast stores of knowledge. She hadn't even known what she was looking for, but when she touched the book she was carrying, she had seen a vision that both terrified her and gave her hope. She needed to find the gnome and see if he knew anything about the book before she spoke to everyone else.

Serha found Eublin in the garden calling out to anyone who passed by about rejecting the murderous idea of the hunt. She hurried over to him and caught his attention.

"Eublin, I must speak with you immediately." The gnome responded to the urgency in her tone and followed her into a small office nearby. They both took seats, and she placed the book on a small table in front of the gnome.

"Do you know anything about this?" Serha's breath was short from her near run.

"Oh, let's see what you have found." Eublin lifted the big book and adjusted the small spectacles on his bulbous nose. "Yes, yes. I believe this one came from an old elven city. Were you able to read it?"

"No, but it triggered a vision that I do not fully understand. I wanted to know more about the book before I attempt to determine the significance of the vision."

"I see. To be honest, I cannot read this book either. I once had an elven acquaintance who was able to translate most of it, but he would not record the translation. He said it was a book of ritual. Much of what it contains is what he called 'The Story of the Stone Path.' It is one of the books I have the least knowledge of in my collection, I'm afraid. I've asked the few elves that are in residence here, but they all said it is an old dialect that they are not familiar with."

"That is unfortunate."

"May I ask what it is you saw in your vision?"

Osric's Wand

"At first I thought it was the Well of Strands, but after thinking about it, I am quite certain that that is not the case. I think we should speak with Aridis immediately." Serha's hands were shaking as she thought more about what her vision might mean.

"I happen to know where Aridis can be found. Osric has awoken and is likely having lunch with Bridgett, so we should also speak with him. Let us go, my lady." The gnome was not much taller than Serha's belt when they both stood up and headed toward the door.

"He is awake? That's wonderful!"

Serha carried the book with her, although she was sure that it would not do them much good since no one could read it. They found Aridis quickly, and he welcomed them into his chambers readily. Eublin caught a recruit in the hall and asked him to go find Osric. As soon as they were all gathered and Aridis and Serha had expressed their joy at seeing Osric alive and well—and awake—Serha described what she had seen.

"It began with a sea journey, by ship, but the crew could not see or hear me. The land where the ship docked was lush and green, and I followed an old stone road, half buried in moss and underbrush, deep into a forest. I walked uphill for most of the day, and at the peak I realized I was on an island. There was water on all sides, and the mountain I had climbed was at the very center of the landmass. The only structure I saw was a tower at the peak of the mountain. It sat in a small lake nestled in a crater, and it almost felt as if no other lands existed but the one small island. There was no door to the tower. When I approached the tower by way of a rickety bridge, a glowing entrance appeared and I was able to go inside by crawling through. Inside was a stone basin in the floor, about three strides in width and half that in depth." Serha spoke calmly but her voice conveyed her excitement and awe as she remembered how invigorating it had felt to stand near that circle of stone. "When I peered into the basin, a dark shadow crept across the floor and I felt as if I were suffocating. The closer it came to me the harder it was to breathe.

"Just before I would have fallen unconscious, a strong wind blew through the tower and knocked a book to the floor. As the pages of the book fluttered in the wind, the shadow retreated from me and went into the bowl on the floor. Once inside, the darkness seemed unable to exit the circular area, but it grew much darker as it pooled in such a small space. The book looked similar to this one, but it had distinctively different markings on the front.

"I knelt and looked closely at the shadow. Up very close, it looked like a massive army in marching formations. When I touched the book, it was obvious that my hand was not of my own body, but rather I was seeing everything through someone else's eyes. When my hand made contact with the page, a bright light washed across the floor and the army of shadows dissolved." Serha fell silent as she completed her tale, and she looked up to find genuine fascination and concern in the eyes of her companions.

"I agree with you that you did not see the Well of Strands." Eublin pushed his spectacles up his nose and scratched his head as he spoke. "From what Bridgett has described, it doesn't fit with what we know. However, we have been researching other areas of concentrated power. Smaller, less powerful regions. If we can identify enough of the elements of your vision, perhaps we can pinpoint the location of the well you saw."

"The area you described does not sound like one of the locations we have identified from the journals and maps in Eublin's collection. Tell me again what you saw before you entered the structure." Aridis stared at the book's well-worn binding as he listened to Serha speak.

"Lush greenery along an overgrown stone road leading to the highest point at the center of the island. The tower sat at the center of a small lake in a crater on the top of the mountain."

"It sounds like one of the islands off the west coast of the Elven Realm. That might explain why it was an elven book that triggered the vision." Aridis tugged on his beard and then looked up at Osric. "What do you think?"

"I think we have a trip to pack for. If the vision is correct—and we have every reason to believe it is, after all that has happened—we need to find the other wells before Dredek does."

"What do you think it means?" Serha looked at the other three people in the room with a serious expression, asking for their interpretation even as she formed her own.

"I would say it means our only chance of defeating Dredek's army is in using the Well of Strands against him, but the smaller wells may be our key to understanding how to accomplish that." Osric was already making a mental list of who he would need with him on the search for the well Serha had seen.

"Perhaps it can tell us more than that. It is interesting that it looked like an army, but I believe the darkness and the book are more important messages," Aridis said, watching him carefully and surprised that Osric seemed so healthy after his battle with Dredek in Angmar that had left the Aranthian leader unconscious for over a month. "Serha, do your visions usually seem so cryptic? Is this an actual event or more of a symbolic representation, in your opinion?"

"I have visions of both types, actually. Usually it is quite easy for me to tell the difference, but this vision was not so transparent. I believe it may be a combination of both. It would help if I knew whose eyes I was watching the event through, but even without that knowledge I can make some assumptions." She folded her hands in her lap and thought back to the vision carefully. "I feel that the man—at least, I am fairly sure it was a human male—was on the ship and traveled the road to the tower. The doorway I am less sure about. The glowing light could be symbolic for the enlightenment or knowledge of the entrance's location. Or perhaps the knowledge of how to gain entrance without a door, I do not really know. The well and the book exist, of that I am certain, though I cannot assume the book is still in the tower. As far as the shadow goes, I won't even attempt to determine its nature. It is as if the darkness hides itself from me even in my vision and my memory of it."

"You speak of the vision as an event that occurred in the past. Do you have a way of knowing this to be true?" Eublin asked, leaning forward in his seat excitedly. "Is it possible that this event has not yet taken place?"

"To be honest, I do not know. If I speak in past tense, it is likely only because the vision showed me something that I am now remembering as something I experienced. It is possible that I am seeing something as it will be, but that would make it even less possible to determine which elements are actual and which are symbolic." Serha stared down at her folded hands. "I am not sounding much like the master of my craft that I am supposed to be, am I?"

"Nonsense." Aridis did not hesitate to assuage her self-doubt. "We are all encountering magic and events that have no precedent in our knowledge or experience. You are doing better than any other Seer could under the circumstances. Doubting your ability to aid our world in its time of need will only keep you from doing so. Speak nothing of the sort again." Although his words were directed at the old woman, Aridis was holding Osric's gaze as he spoke.

"Wise words." Eublin clapped loudly once and hopped down from his chair. "If it is a trip we must be embarking on, we should certainly be preparing. I will gather all of my research on the wells and join you shortly." The others rose from their seats and went their separate ways with quiet determination.

* * *

The group met up again at mid'day in greater numbers. While Eublin and Aridis gathered their research and Serha prepared for the unexpected journey, Osric was briefed by Gus on the day's gruesome yet enlightening discovery about his acquired powers. He couldn't believe that Willam was dead, and he felt that it was his fault. He should have taken the sword with him. He should have realized the potential danger that was involved with the unusual power of the wand. Gus had described what had happened, in an uncharacteristically shaky voice, and Osric couldn't even imagine what it must have been like to see what had occurred. Gus's Wand-Maker's vision had been engaged as Willam cut Kal with the sword. The poor kid had been inundated with all of the fully formed gifts that Osric currently possessed, and it seemed the power influx of so many gifts was too much for the body to handle. The surge of power had been too much for Willam's life strand to handle, and it snapped right before Gus's eyes.

Though Osric grieved for the boy, his mind was overwhelmed by the implications of what Gus had seen. They had spent months trying to figure out how Osric was gaining so many new powers. It was obvious now that they had come from the sword, but there was more to it than that. Most of his gifts had developed gradually, although some had seemed to appear instantly or at least very rapidly between the occasions that Gus had examined him. If contact with blood had caused the gifts to transfer to him fully formed, then that would explain why he had gained the paun's ability of invisibility and the gift that allowed him to see the spoken spells in the book that had previously looked blank. Thinking about the vial, Osric still wondered how he had attained the ability to read the book. The only solution that came from all his thoughts was that the vial had to have contained blood, dried by the years, and the sword had been exposed to the blood when he had gone into the water to retrieve the vial. He wasn't positive, but it made sense. Then there were the various other gifts he had acquired after fighting with the sword; he had so many and the thought filled him with regret, gaining power with each life he took.

The others gifts must have been more gradual because they were gained by proximity to the sword rather than by blood contacting the blade. Kenneth's use of his sword during practice would explain how he had gained the gifts as well, though he wasn't sure how to explain Gus and Bridgett gaining the abilities as well. Perhaps being near the sword was enough to develop the abilities over time—Gus confirmed the theory as the story had progressed.

Osric secured his sword belt on his waist with trembling hands. The elation he had felt earlier in the day when he realized that his sword was actually the wand that had tormented him through the riddle of prophecy had given way to a heavy weight on his heart. Legati had been more than a sword to him all along, but understanding how his new gifts had been acquired did little to ease the demanding questions of why. There must be a reason why the unicorn had saved him that day as the palace collapsed, why he wasn't killed along with most of the other Ratification Ceremony attendees. If it was the sword, or the wand, that had given him all of his abilities, then why was he the one with the burden of gaining them? Could he ever use his abilities without feeling the guilt of taking the lives of so many whom he had gained them from? Although he had acquired several of his gifts over time from the people around him without any harm coming to them, far more of his abilities had developed after the battles at Braya and Angmar, and after the fight with the Kallegian in Stanton. So many of his gifts were a bloody reminder of the fighting he had been forced to participate in since he was thrust into the battle for peace on Archana, and he wasn't sure he would be able to use Legati again without feeling the weight of that guilt.

Osric's heart was pounding as all of the questions raced through his mind. He could still hear the echo of Aridis's words to Serha about self-doubt preventing their success, but he couldn't shake his own doubts. He wasn't sure he would be able to do what it would take to wage a war, never mind win one. He tried to think about what had to be done to locate the wells and learn what they could from them, but it took all of his strength to turn and address the gathered group who looked to him for leadership. What right did he have to speak to them, to try to motivate them, to lead them?

The weight of his sword against his leg felt both familiar and eerie, yet he couldn't imagine being without it. It may be a burden to carry, but it was his burden. He would find a way to shoulder it—he couldn't bear the thought of letting his people down after they had come so far with him. Osric straightened himself and tried to calm his thoughts—guilt was never an honest emotion. He looked out over the small crowd at his companions, his friends, and he set his mind on the next goal. They would take it one step at a time, just as they had all along, and eventually they would find the answers they so desperately needed. First, they had an island to find.

* * *

The greenery was just as lush and bright as it had been in her vision. The small bay where the boat had anchored was just as blue. Aside from her sight being distinctly her own, rather than viewing the beautiful island through the eyes of a stranger, Serha could be back in her vision. But she wasn't; she was on an unfamiliar coast far from home with a great many people depending on her. Serha had specifically described the location from her vision to a dragon, who then transported them all to the shore by spoken spell. Dragons, thanks to the Endurism ability, were one of the few creatures on Archana who could tolerate the vast use of magic needed to travel so far with the spell, but they weren't entirely sure they could make the image of the location specific enough to accomplish traveling there at all. The shape of the shoreline and the landscape near the water was unique enough that the dragon had felt confident it was an island she had seen before, and luckily they had all arrived safely. Now that they knew the island of her vision was real, Serha knew that it was her responsibility to lead them to the tower.

Serha's entire life had been devoted to receiving and understanding her visions and delivering prophecies. She had never had any doubt about her competency with her gift, but she honestly thought that finding Osric was going to be the last thing she did in her life. The vision she had received as a young girl, the one that had shown her finding the High-Wizard, was her first and still one of her most vivid visions as a Seer. At the time, she had been overwhelmed by the feeling that it had depicted the last days of her life, and she had waited for the moment to come with grim acceptance. She had always known that she would find Osric, but she had first needed to accept that it would be one of the last things she did before she died. Now she had seen that vision come to pass, yet she was continuing on to new lands with new purpose. For the first time in her life, she felt her gift had failed her. What she had experienced, what she had felt when she had her first vision as a child, had been wrong, and now her hands were shaking as she stared up at the dense forest before her. What if there was no tower at the top of the mountain? No well, no book? What if she was wrong about all of it?

"Any idea where that road was at?" Osric's voice broke into her thoughts.

Serha scanned the edge of the jungle, looking for something familiar. It didn't take her long to find the old, weathered, and cracked stones that had once been a road. Serha moved toward the old path with a stride more confident than she felt. She tried to push down her fears of failure by focusing on the many aspects of the island that were in fact the same as her vision. As she crossed beneath the first of the trees, a small bush dappled with bright blue blossoms peeked out beside the moss-encrusted tree trunk on her right. She smelled the heady sweetness that wafted toward her from the small flowers as her skirt brushed the leaves of the bush.

Two tiny birds hovered just above the blue petals, sipping nectar from the sweet flowers. Her father had called them flitterflies when she was a child, and she had chased them through the forest near her home on summer mornings, following brief flashes of bright feathers as they darted between blossoms. Serha's pace quickened as she followed the broken road, which was littered with leaves and overgrown with tree roots, toward the top of the mountain.

The sun climbed with them, marking the passing of the day as they swatted at insects and wiped sweat from their necks. The party traveled by spell when they could see far enough up the path for it to be worth the expenditure of magic, but much of the trek had to be taken on foot. The foliage was dense, and the path was vague and easy to lose beneath the trees. Tree sprites chittered in the branches overhead, and Serha could often catch sight of one of the small, furry creatures leaping from limb to limb above them.

Just as the muscles in her legs were protesting louder than her determination to reach the top could drown out, Serha saw a break in the trees up ahead and a swath of blue sky hugging the outline of a stone tower. Her breath caught in her throat, and she nearly jogged out from under the forest canopy. A carpet of soft grass cushioned her footfalls, and she crested the hill to find the tower at the center of a small lake in a crater. The bridge was just where she had said it would be. The rest of the party followed her up the hill, and she turned to see wide smiles and quiet nods of approval cast her way.

Bridgett knelt down in front of Trevar. His eyes were wide as he looked up at the tower.

"Are you ready? Do you think you can get us in?" Bridgett smiled at him warmly, and he returned the smile readily. He pulled his hand from his pocket and showed her the small stone rod. She nodded encouragingly and walked with him to the tower.

Trevar used the stone he was holding to draw an arc of symbols on the wall. Bridgett watched expectantly for the symbols to begin glowing, just as she had seen at the Well of Strands in Angmar, but nothing happened. Trevar looked confused as he held his hand in the air after drawing the final symbol.

"What's wrong?" Bridgett asked. The irua boy looked distraught, shaking his head in distress. "Have you ever seen any well besides the one you took me to?" Again he shook his head no.

"The symbols is not working. Wrong symbols?" His distress and confusion seemed to be regressing his recent grasp of the Common language.

"I'm not sure. I don't know what the symbols mean. Do you?" Trevar nodded at first, but he didn't say anything. Then, he scrunched up his face a little and shook his head, staring down at the ground.

"Oh, it's going to be all right. We will figure something out." Bridgett squeezed his shoulder and walked back over to the rest of the group.

Osric's Wand

"Bridgett, what's wrong?" Osric's voice blatantly conveyed concern, but he couldn't help but smile when he looked at her.

"He wasn't able to open the door. He thinks that the symbols he knows might not work for all of the wells."

"Blazing strands! I didn't really have a backup plan for getting in." Osric ran his hands through his hair.

"I have an idea, but you're not going to like it." Gus was perched on Serha's shoulder.

Osric looked over at him and grimaced. "Well, like it or not, I'm willing to hear it."

"Serha can get in," Gus said slowly, "with the traveling spell."

"Absolutely not." Osric glared over at him. "Have you forgotten what can happen when someone uses the spell without being able to see the destination? It's too risky."

"Do you have a better idea?" Gus puffed out his little chest and glared back. Osric's shoulders sagged.

"No, but you're right. I don't like it." Osric looked at Serha. "It isn't a decision I can make, though. Do you understand how the spell works?" Serha nodded. "This is more dangerous than any other time we have ever used the traveling spell. Not only can you not see the location you are trying to travel to, but the only way you have ever seen it is in a vision. There is no way to know what is inside the tower now. It is entirely possible that attempting this will kill you."

"Osric, we can't let her do that. We don't know what will happen to her," Bridgett objected vehemently.

"Actually, my dear, you cannot stop me." Serha squared her shoulders and looked at Osric. "Tell me what I should do to succeed."

"Serha, did you hear anything I just said? I'm really not sure it is possible. You could die."

"So, I just have to have a clear image of where I want to go, and then I speak the spell and I go there, right?"

"In a most simplistic manner, yes, that's how it works, but there have been incidents where people have died because they appeared in an altered environment," Eublin said, quietly but adamantly. "For example, focusing on a clearing with a small tree near a childhood home can lead to appearing with a large branch through one's torso due to the growth of the tree over the years. We can only assume that

The Weaving of Wells

your vision was either from the past or the future, thus it is possible that the interior of the tower is not as it was when you saw it."

"I understand the risk. But if there is no other way to get into the tower, then I am willing to try. We must learn what we can about the wells. It may be the only way to save the irua race and any others Dredek may seek to destroy."

Osric eyed her with a mix of admiration and fear. He was torn between needing to understand Dredek's purpose in seizing the Well of Strands and needing to protect Serha from potential harm. He didn't want anyone else to die.

"Serha, can you show me the vision? Is that possible? If I could see what you saw, then I could travel into the tower and you would not have to take on the risk yourself." She smiled warmly at Osric's obvious concern for her, but she shook her head.

"If the vision were meant for you, then perhaps I could, but that is not the case. This vision came to me for a reason, High-Wizard, and the danger is no greater for me than for you. However, you must go on to win this war. I am just an old woman."

"Wise and modest. You speak too little of yourself, old woman." Aridis's eyes were shining with moisture as Serha prepared to speak the spell.

"Serha, there is another danger we have not discussed." Osric's voice strained with anxiety. "The spell around the barracks prevents anyone from entering uninvited. I have felt the pain that trying to breach this protection causes, and you would not survive it. Only my added abilities allowed me to live through it. We have no idea what type of magic protects this tower. There are spells woven into this stone that I have never seen before. If they are as effective as the ones around the barracks, you won't get through alive. I can't let you do this."

"Osric, I understand the risks involved. There is no other way." Serha took a deep breath and pictured the tower as she had seen it in her vision. Every detail that she could recall was clear in her mind, and she focused carefully on a space in the center of the floor far from any object in the room. "Eo ire itum."

* * *

Osric's Wand

Serha felt a sensation of falling forward, but after a brief moment the feeling passed. As she looked around, she felt lightheaded and her vision seemed foggy. The walls of the tower around her were hazy, and she felt as if her feet were stuck in thick mud. With great difficulty, Serha crouched down and looked at a book lying open on the floor. It was the same one from her vision. Several symbols were written along the spine of the book, but the pages were faded, and her vision was so blurry that she could not read any of the writing. Serha picked up the book. She clutched it close to her chest and tried to walk toward the round opening in the floor. She couldn't move her legs.

Confused and disoriented, Serha struggled against the invisible force that kept her from moving. She felt drawn toward the well, as if she needed desperately to reach it, but she couldn't break free. The darkness she had seen in her vision bubbled up from inside the round opening in the stone floor. It slowly moved toward her, like a thick smoke. She had the disturbing feeling that it was watching her, laughing at her, and just before she would have been enveloped in the gruesome shadow, Serha recited the traveling spell and her vision went black.

* * *

Serha awoke to the sensation of a cool cloth on her forehead and a warm blanket spread over her. Her limbs felt heavy and stiff, and her eyes ached terribly. Aridis squeezed her hand and spoke softly as she opened her eyes.

"You gave us quite a scare. Do you remember anything?"

When she could see him clearly, Serha blinked and sighed with relief.

"That is not an experience I will forget anytime soon. Where is the book?"

The old man's brow furrowed as he stared at her eager expression.

"What book do you mean?"

"The one from the tower of course. I brought it back with me," Serha said. She shifted up into a sitting position and realized she was on soft grass near the crater and the lake. The tower stood silhouetted against the bright blue sky just across the water.

The Weaving of Wells

"Serha, you never went anywhere." Aridis watched her with concern. "You recited the spell and immediately collapsed on the ground outside the tower. You have been unconscious for half the day."

"What? That isn't possible. I traveled into the tower, but I couldn't move. I picked up the book, and I traveled back out just before the darkness reached me. It was terrifying."

"I have been by your side every moment since you collapsed. Could it be another vision?"

"Aridis, I have been receiving visions for over one hundred years. I can always tell when I am seeing a vision, and this was different. This was real." Serha had an overwhelming urge to either get up and move or to vomit. She opted for the former and struggled to her feet. Every bit of her body protested, but once she was up and walking she started to feel better. Osric caught her eye from a short distance away, and he hurried over with Bridgett, Gus, Eublin, and the irua boy.

"Serha, are you all right? How are you feeling?" Osric's concern for her was clear in his voice and in his urgent approach.

"I think so. I still feel a bit sore and quite confused. Aridis says I collapsed when I spoke the spell."

"That's right. We were so worried, but we didn't know what was happening." Bridgett embraced the woman warmly. "Thank Archana you are back with us."

"Actually, that's what I am confused about. As far as I know, I traveled into the tower and retrieved the book from my vision, but it seems I never left at all. If this was just a vision, it is different than any I have ever had. And I have no explanation at all for why I collapsed."

"I would wager it has something to do with your proximity to Osric and Bridgett, or rather the magical devices they possess, along with whatever protection spells are built into this tower." Gus scampered closer and Bridgett lifted him to her shoulder. "That sword and amulet can have an unusual effect on one's power, and we are only beginning to understand how and why. Attempting to get inside may have triggered any number of rejection spells, causing you to collapse. Your amplified ability may have taken over when you fell unconscious, and that could explain why you felt it wasn't a vision at all."

Osric's Wand

"Gus, that actually makes a lot of sense. If that's true, then Serha is probably very lucky that the traveling spell didn't work. If she had managed to get inside, the protection spells may have done a great deal more damage than just causing her to black out for a while." Osric stood and stared out at the tower, shaking his head. "Serha, I am very glad you are not injured, but I have no idea what to do now."

"We aren't going to learn anything from here. We either go back home and give up, or we knock the tower down." Gus glared at the impenetrable tower.

"I don't think either of those is the best option. Serha, you said you held the book in your vision. Can you describe it?" Eublin asked.

"There was something wrong with my vision, er, my eyesight. Everything looked very blurry, but I could see that there were seven symbols on the spine of the book. I couldn't read anything inside, though." Before Serha could describe the book any further, Trevar jumped up from where he was sitting on the grass nearby. He hurried over with a hopeful look on his face.

"Seven symbols? Can you show it?" Trevar asked.

"Well, I am not sure I can draw them correctly, but I will try." Serha used a stick and scratched what resembled the symbols she had seen as best as she could. The irua boy watched on, and he grew more excited with each symbol she drew. When she was done, he took the stick and drew a slightly different symbol under three of those she had drawn.

"It look like this?" he asked anxiously. Serha looked carefully at the images that both of them had drawn.

"These two which you drew are better than mine. But this last one isn't right. I got the best look at the last symbol, and I am sure I drew it correctly." The last symbol looked like an inverted cone with a coil wound around it. The image the boy had drawn looked more like a triangle inside of a coil or a spring. The symbols were somewhat similar, but the differences were distinct. Serha erased the first two symbols of hers that Trevar had corrected. "These are the symbols on the book. I am sure of it."

The irua boy's face broke out in a wide grin, and he ran toward the narrow bridge that led out to the tower. Bridgett and the others ran after him, calling for him to wait. When they reached him, he had already started drawing the symbols on the wall of the tower with his

The Weaving of Wells

stone rod. The seventh symbol was one he had never drawn before, and his movement was slower and more careful to get it right. By the time he completed the last one, the symbols were beginning to glow brightly and Bridgett let out a squeal of excitement while everyone else stared in awe.

The symbols grew brighter and brighter until everyone had to shield their eyes. When the glow faded, the group looked back at the tower wall and found a small, arched opening. They all moved toward the small doorway, and the boy's expression of glee suddenly turned to one of fear.

"No," Trevar called out, holding out his arm and blocking their way. "I must protect it." Tears filled his eyes.

"What? We have to go inside, Trevar." Osric spoke softly, but his voice was strained.

"Only Bridgett." The determined set of his small frame showed that he would not let anyone else pass.

"Look, we need to learn as much as we can about this well. If we can't go inside, how are we going to learn anything? You have the Trust ability, so you know you can trust me, right?" Osric knelt down and spoke to the child with forced cheerfulness.

"You can be trusted, but you cannot learn. You do not have the connection. Only Bridgett." The boy stood his ground and glared at Osric.

"Osric, I don't fully understand it yet, but the irua who oversee the Well of Strands are very select—and very secretive. I am still trying to get him to explain why he took me there." Bridgett took Osric's hand and squeezed it. "If I am the one who can enter, then let me enter and see what I can learn. I will keep working to make Trevar see that you must be allowed inside the wells."

Osric shook his head adamantly. "But I have to—"

"I believe what she was trying to say is that we know there are at least a dozen other locations like this. If they are also walled in, then we may need the child to access them all if we are going to learn more about the wells than just what this one may hold. She understands the danger, and she has the ability to travel out of any situation she may find herself in with a few words. It's not like there is anyone waiting inside to hurt her, unless you think someone else may have one of those stone sticks and a Seer to show them the necessary symbols."

Osric's Wand

Gus stood at Osric's feet, successfully keeping himself from shouting but still as sarcastic as ever.

"You're right." Osric's shoulders drooped and the frustration dissipated from his expression. He pulled Bridgett into his arms and kissed her quickly. "Be careful. We can't just assume that Trevar knows as much about this well as he does the well in his homeland, obviously. If you see anything that makes you nervous, come back out. And keep your wand at the ready."

"Always. I'll tell you everything I see when I get back."

"Look closely." Gus's tone implied that he meant she should look with more than just her eyes. She smiled down at him and then followed Trevar through the opening.

The interior of the tower looked much like the stone chamber that housed the Well of Strands in Angmar. There was nothing to break the surface of the walls as far up as Bridgett could see in the light of her wand—no doors, no windows, not even cracks or seams in the stone.

Trevar touched his wand to the wall, but nothing happened. Bridgett expected the intricate whorls of light to spread out in a glowing display along the stone, but it seemed that Trevar was unable to affect this well as he could the one in Angmar. With the only light radiating from the tips of their wands, Bridgett gazed around at the inside of the tower.

The circular bowl in the center of the round room was much smaller than the one in Angmar but equally proportioned. With her Wand-Maker's vision firmly engaged, she moved closer to dispel the shadows and peered into the concave space. Her breath fluttered from her chest at the beauty of the strands—the source of all life and magic on Archana—and she gazed deeply into the intertwining pattern for several moments. The strands, like thin ribbons of light, radiated outward from the bowl and pierced everything in the room. The colors penetrated the stone, leaving it brighter as though it held a charge of energy. Bridgett remembered the way her entire body felt lighter and more energized when she had stood barefoot on the stone of the Well of Strands.

It was still quite disorienting to see the world in two ways at once. The tips of their wands dimly lit the room, and she could see the shadows that danced away from her toward the edges of the circular, stone room. Yet, with her focus on the strands, the room seemed as

The Weaving of Wells

brightly lit as a lake in full sunlight. It took a great deal of effort to navigate the room and to observe the objects it contained while still using her new ability to view the magical strands that permeated everything in sight.

With great concentration, Bridgett forced her attention away from the well and around the rest of the small space. There was a small table and chair, a bookshelf containing a few texts stacked haphazardly and a variety of jars and boxes, and a large wooden chest spread out around the well. Based on the heavily woven strands that encircled the lid of the chest, Bridgett saw that it must be spelled in addition to the large lock that adorned the latch. She still did not fully understand what she was seeing when she looked at the strands, but the pattern seemed too regular not to be an intentionally orchestrated spell.

Serha had described the book from her vision in detail, but in the stack on the shelf, Bridgett did not see any texts with seven symbols on the spine. Luckily, she also didn't see any evidence of the dark fog or liquid that Serha had warned her about. The stone basin in the floor held nothing but strands of magic from Archana. Bridgett gathered up the books in one arm and turned to scan the room before leaving. Trevar was crouching on the floor near the desk with his back to her. Bridgett walked around the well and came up behind him.

He was staring down at an open book on the floor. He looked up when Bridgett approached him, and she was assaulted by the strength of his emotions. Her Empath ability threatened to overwhelm her as tears flooded her eyes.

"Trevar, what is it?" Her voice was weak and choked with his feelings.

"It is everything. It is how to get in. It is the one we need." Speaking with her seemed to calm him down, and as his influence on her gift waned she was able to identify his emotion. What she thought must be sadness or terror, to have such an effect on her, was nothing of the sort. The intensity of the emotion must have been due to the recent, agonizing lack of it for both of them—it was hope.

Chapter 5
Patterns on Parchment

Osric entered the Tipsy Tree with a heavy heart. He took a seat at the bar and nodded to Leisha. She had a steaming mug of rulha in front of him before he had scanned the room and its meager collection of scattered patrons. He smiled his thanks and sipped the beverage slowly. Within moments Kenneth had taken the stool next to him.

"What is it with cryptic languages and unreadable books that we can't seem to avoid?" Osric's frustration was tempered by his friendly sarcasm.

"You're just such a mysterious guy, Os. Of course one mystery after another falls in your lap."

"Right. I knew it was my fault." His half-hearted laughter showed he was only partially joking.

"So what is it this time?"

"That book we picked up from the island well is exactly what we need, and we aren't any closer to being able to use it. Trevar is sure it's the key to the well locations and access, but he can't actually read it. No one in this city seems to have any idea what language most of it is written in, never mind being able to translate it," Osric said. Kenneth whistled softly into his mug of mead and shook his head.

"Just our luck. How can the kid be sure it's the right book if he can't read it?"

"Something about the symbols. He was taught the book exists, but he had never seen it before. He insists no other book would have those symbols on it. He seems sure, so I see no reason to doubt it until we can get it translated. If he's right, it could mean the only way we can defeat Dredek without sacrificing every innocent life that pledges to our cause."

"So what are we going to do?" Kenneth finished off his drink and shook his head when Leisha offered a refill. "How are we going to find someone to read it?"

"I've got Aridis and Eublin working on that. I am more concerned about being ready to pursue the wells when the locations are discovered. I need you to make sure the men are ready. I also want to do some specific recruiting."

"What do you have in mind?" Kenneth turned his full attention on his friend.

"Up until now, we have been taking in any trustworthy body who wants to help. If we are going to successfully use the wells, we are going to need specific gifts and skill sets. I wish I knew more about how they work, but Bridgett has been able to get a bit more information from Trevar since we found the book." Osric looked around as the bar began to fill up with regulars seeking an evening meal. "Let's head back to the barracks and I will fill you in."

Kenneth nodded and rose from his stool. "I need to stop by the Vigil assignment post at the palace. There are a few men I will need to speak with later when we are done, and I don't want them out on patrol when I call for them."

"Just meet me in the south dining hall when you're done." Osric left a few coins on the bar and headed back to the barracks.

* * *

"Sprites seem attracted to the magic in this place." James smiled and leaned back in his chair. "They take care of tending the fields as if they were created to sculpt perfectly tailored grounds. There are more of them every day, and whether that is from mating or whether more just gather in our enclosure, I don't know. And their tending has caused remarkable improvements in our yields from the garden. Orson's contribution to the gardens aside, I think the sprites have done more to improve our crops than anything we could have done."

"So do you think it's the barrier that is bringing the sprites, or the magics we are experimenting with inside?" Osric squinted, unsure of the direction the conversation was taking.

"I am hopelessly lost when it comes to things of that nature. Food is my specialty." James chuckled.

"I think it is both the barrier and the experiments." David, the young lad who helped run the kitchen, spoke nervously from where he stood fidgeting behind James's chair.

"So, what's the problem with them helping us keep the grounds tended?" Osric asked. James had asked Osric to stop by the kitchen

Osric's Wand

because they needed his help with something, but as the conversation progressed, Osric was having a harder time grasping the problem. "Are they causing trouble for our new herds?"

James's belly moved in silent laughter. "Absolutely not. The herd is doing great. We've set aside several mates for the bull so we can start raising our own cattle, and the sprites have started tending to them as well. They seem to have a sense that tells them to keep the cattle grounds a bit taller than the rest, which leaves the cattle with more than enough to eat."

"But there aren't enough." David's voice barely reached Osric's ear.

"What's that?" He leaned in to elicit more volume.

"There's not enough cattle, especially for the size of the group now." David dragged his boot on the floor, staring at the marks it left on the dusty stone. It wasn't a lack of passion, Osric sensed, but merely a byproduct of timidity that caused him to behave the way he was. The lad was demonstrating a great deal of courage in just speaking with the riot of emotion that was inside his head. "Four hundred and forty-three live within our walls, at last count. And we're still growing, so it's probably closer to five hundred by now."

"How many head are in our herd?"

"Twenty-five," the young kitchen attendant answered with a bit more authority.

"And how many animals does it take to feed us?" Osric turned his attention to James, who looked thoroughly bored with the conversation.

"Although I do appreciate his rationing state of mind, which is the primary reason I chose to bring him in, I believe he is incorrect in these matters." James sighed and sat up in his chair before continuing.

"We consume roughly a head a day, but that is not an entirely accurate statement. As we speak, some of that meat is still being made into meals, like the sausage that is curing or the dried meat for our travelers. But one a day will remain a fair constant until our stockpiles have been built up, for at least the next few months."

With so few head to work with, Osric could see why the boy's nerves were worn thin. The herd that had promised them a great start to self-sufficiency would be eliminated before the month's end, and James was speaking of months at the current rate of consumption.

The Weaving of Wells

"However," James continued, "we have our hunters who can add other food to our stock, and many of those recruits have only recently completed the training they began when joining our cause. With the new recruits adding to the already skilled hunters, things don't look so bad. And I still have my arrangements with hunters and gatherers outside of the Aranthian habitat. Many of them are excited about my latest venture into opening a dining hall, and they look forward to having another way to make a few coins for a day's hunt. With the prices we have set, I'll make sure they are paid well for their efforts too. If my figures are correct, the hall could supply a great deal of meats that the Aranthians need just from hunters eager to earn a better wage for their efforts."

Osric knew he was referring to the old Vigil barracks that existed outside of the protection spell. Through some extraordinary magic that he didn't entirely understand, he was able to pull their current habitat out of that world and anchor it in a place of its own that only the trustworthy could access.

"Just when were you going to tell me about your plans to open a dining hall? We need you here." Osric was beginning to feel concerned.

"Come now, Osric. At nearly five hundred men in this safe haven, I have too many hands working for me to man just one kitchen. It's come to a point where I have to expand or I'll lose people from sheer boredom. We already cure all of our own meat, from bacon to"—his eyes searched the ceiling in vain—"to whatever you can think of. Now I have the opportunity to do something I have long dreamt of. And in doing that, I will be able to give sustainability, real sustainability, to a group that has not only captured my heart but my imagination."

James had locked eyes with Osric, and there was a fire in the fat chef's words.

"I'm just not sure if we have the coin in the coffers to start another project at this time." Osric's head swayed back and forth as he tried to gently break the worst part of the news to a man who deserved a chance at achieving his dreams. No small part of Osric's mind yearned to have his chance at the slow and measured life he had always desired too. It broke his heart to have to say no. In spite of his own misgivings, James's chest began to rumble with laughter.

Osric's Wand

"The purchase is already made. Eublin is using the twin of the space we use here for the library, and I purchased a bit more than the old kitchen from the Ryhain for my project. Do you think I ate my way through every bit of money I earned with a cart that cost me seven day's maintenance a year?" As blood filled his face, his cheeks turned red. "I've supplied half the honey in Stanton for over a decade with my beehives. I have twenty casks of mead I've made, and my cart did very well. I… I've knocked down walls, decorated, and built a stage. I've even got three floors of seating for the music that will be there: the main floor, and two balconies. Pebble has been selling wands out of the old blacksmith shop for a few days, and crowds are growing. I've named it the Meat and Meadery, and I open in three days. It'll be the best place to eat in this town, and I'll be two hundred strides from Pebble, the shop of the best Wand-Maker on Archana! People will travel for miles just to see that adorable little guy. I know because my first five days of business are completely booked—all three seatings!

"This is something I want to do, not only for myself, but for the Aranthian organization. Halls like mine survive off of hunters, and with the volume I'll be serving nobody will miss one elk or deer, or seven. Not to mention the fact that the entire operation will be run by our men, our Aranthians." James ended his speech with a flourished smile and head waggle.

"He hasn't even told you that there is another thirty-five head on its way from one of our new recruit's own farms, has he?" Kenneth approached from behind Osric. "You probably didn't even tell David about them, did you?"

"Well, ah…" James suddenly stumbled over his words. "He's got to learn to trust his elders. I know more about what is in store than anyone in my kitchen. I can't be expected to explain everything to them or they won't appreciate the magic that is me." His thick cheeks turned a distinct color of red.

"So, more cattle are on the way?" Osric clarified.

"Thirty-five should arrive by mid week. One of the newly trusted sold his farm to join our cause. He kept thirty-five head as part of the selling agreement, and they are en route from Dragsden." James glared at Kenneth for spoiling the mystery. "And we still have our

The Weaving of Wells

hunters out getting a couple different animals each week. We are in no danger of going hungry in the near future."

"So, what exactly did you want to ask me? I am a bit lost as to what this was all about. Didn't you say you needed help with something?" Osric felt a bit uncertain. If they had spent all this time just to give him the news that James was opening a dining hall, what could the favor be?

"Well, I told you already. I need your permission to man the second kitchen with our people—the Aranthians." James looked at Osric, befuddled.

"Oh." Osric sat up as several excited voices entered the room.

"Osric, we have got things to discuss." Aridis smiled as he led Bridgett, Eublin, Serha, and Gus into the room.

"Of course. Come in." He turned to James and David with a smile. "You have my permission to use the men you need. Will that help?"

"Fantastic." James stood up and turned to David, patting him on the shoulder. "Now, let's leave these people to discuss more important issues. We'll send out some food and drinks for you all to enjoy as you talk."

"Thank you, James." Osric shook his hand and turned to focus on the new matters.

"Still up to filling me in?" Kenneth asked.

"Sure." Osric turned to Aridis and said, "I was about to get Kenneth up to speed on the situation with the book, but it sounds like you have something new. What is it?"

"We were hoping to hear that you had come up with a plan for reading the book. Did you find anything in the spoken spell book?" Bridgett asked. Osric shook his head, but before he could respond, Kenneth interrupted.

"Wait, I feel very left out right now. What do we know about this thing?"

"Nothing useful," Gus spoke up in his grumpiest voice. "We think it will save the day, but we can't learn anything from it. No surprises there, so this is probably just another waste of our time."

"Gus," Bridgett scolded, "that isn't quite accurate. We know that the book contains the locations to the wells, as well as the symbols necessary for Trevar to get us in."

"You mean to get *you* in," Gus interrupted.

"And we think the language is a code of some sort, not an actual language that none of us have ever seen before. Between Aridis, Eublin, and Serha, if it were in a known language we would have identified it by now, even if we couldn't read it," Bridgett continued, ignoring Gus's sarcastic remark. "Trevar recognizes some of the symbols, but he can't read enough of it to translate the book for us. He thinks he has identified the portion of the text that lists the locations of the wells, but we can't make sense of it. There are maps, but none of the markings seem to correlate directly with the location of the well we visited, and if the text explains it, we just don't know enough yet to tie them together. Unfortunately, Trevar has no knowledge of where the symbols he uses to enter the well came from. He was never taught the history of the marks. He was only taught how to perform them properly to gain access."

"So then, whoever created the wells probably created the symbolic language as well. Do we know who that was?" Kenneth asked.

"Not exactly, but I am hoping we will soon find out." Aridis rested his gnarled hands on the long wooden table they were gathered around.

"How are we going to do that?" Osric asked.

"I have sent for someone who may be able to tell us. I am not sure, however, when he will arrive."

"But you are sure he is coming?" Osric wished that Aridis would be more forthcoming with information, rather than dropping cryptic hints and phrases so often.

"I am confident that he will be located and persuaded to aid us, yes."

"Great," Gus spoke up. "So we don't even know where he is, never mind if he is going to agree to come here, or if he can be trusted to help us if he does. You are a wealth of confidence for our cause, old man."

"Enough." Osric slammed his hand on the table. "Let's stop focusing on what we don't know for a moment and try to decide what we can do with what we do know. Gus, it would be immensely helpful if you could forgo the sarcasm and put your brilliance to work on solving some of these problems." Osric ran a hand through his sandy hair in frustration, his stern expression showing no remorse for his reprimand. Gus crossed his arms at his chest and grumbled under his breath as Osric continued in a calmer tone. "Assuming this man arrives to help, and he can tell us who created the wells, that still doesn't help us read the text. We need to find someone who is good at deciphering symbols. Perhaps Trevar knows more than he is aware of regarding the meaning of the symbols. That would be a start at least."

"There may still be something in the book of spoken spells that can help with that," Eublin said excitedly. "I have stopped looking for an obvious spell, and now I am going through the whole thing again seeking a combination of spells that might work together to help us decode the symbols."

"I like that idea, Eublin. Gus, can you help him with that?" Osric's tone made the question sound more like a command than an inquiry. "Aridis, see what you can find out about this man you have sent for. If you can't give us any more information now, perhaps you can learn something new you would be willing to share. Kenneth, ask some of the Vigils and see if you can find someone with experience in symbols and codes. The more experience in multiple languages, the better. It seems likely that there was a starting point to this language from something familiar. If we can find that starting seed, perhaps we can discover some of the meanings from there. Isn't there anyone here among the Angmar refugees who is part of Trevar's sect? Maybe they would be willing to teach Bridgett how to enter the wells, since Trevar says she has whatever is necessary to be trusted in the wells."

"I'll see who I can find, right away," Kenneth said, nodding with determination as the room cleared out and everyone rushed away to seek answers.

"Bridgett," Osric sighed, leaning back as the weight of his concerns pressed heavily upon him. She stood behind him and rested her hands on his hunched shoulders, easing some of his tension with deft fingers. "I will join you for dinner, and we can discuss our next move. Have you eaten anything today?"

"Honestly, I don't think I have," Bridgett said. She looked down at his creased brow with concern, touched by his consideration for something so simple when he had so much on his mind. The food James had promised arrived just as everyone else left, and Osric and Bridgett enjoyed their meal in the quiet comfort of each other's company.

Chapter 6
The Hermit

Stargon crouched against the rocks, clinging to the side of the mountain securely with his claws. The dragon had been flying over the hills and valleys surrounding the mountain pass for days, and he was beginning to curse Aridis for sending him to do the impossible. Everything else that the old wizard had requested of him the last few times they spoke at Lost Lake, Stargon had accomplished. Now, much time had passed and he had yet to complete his last task. Stargon had never failed Aridis before, and he understood the necessity of his task, but he wasn't sure he would be able to succeed this time.

The land still felt unfamiliar as Stargon gazed down from his perch and scanned the path below. Aridis had asked for the dragons' help in locating many places, but Stargon wasn't sure he would ever find this one. Perhaps Aridis had been wrong about what to look for, or maybe a rockslide had occurred and the path was no longer where it should be.

Stargon pushed off the side of the mountain, spreading his wings to catch the air current, and let out a cry of frustration. He would fly one final pass over the area, and if he could not locate the exact place Aridis had described, he would have to admit failure and return to Lost Lake. He had seen several streams with similar characteristics, and he had seen a few of the rare flowering bushes, but he could not find the two together.

Stargon flew just under the dense clouds, following the narrow valleys below. His keen eyes searched for signs of the strange flowers as he swiftly viewed the twisting and turning streams that cut through the rocky terrain. He turned in a wide, slow circle, and just before he would have given up and traveled back to his homeland, a small flame caught his eye. The light was more of a flicker than a fire, but it was enough to draw the dragon's attention and send him gliding down toward a rocky outcropping. Night was coming on fast and daylight was fading behind the peaks. Stargon landed on a wide ledge of stone and pierced the twilight with his gaze.

<u>The Weaving of Wells</u>

The small flame was coming from the center of a large, red flower. The leaves of the plant were broad and dark, slowly curling away from three flowers near the center of the low-growing bush. Each flower's five petals were pale yellow at the base, gradually warming and darkening to a vivid red and deepening to black at the tips as they curved toward the small flame in the center of the flower. Other than a few scraggly trees and hardy grasses fighting for purchase in the rocks, the glowing bush was the only flora in sight.

The bush sat protected by several large rocks in the center of a narrow stream of water rushing along the curve of a valley. It was just as Aridis had said it would be, and Stargon sighed in relief. He was still far from accomplishing his actual task, but finding the final location in his journey was a good start. He needed to be at the area at sunrise, although Aridis was unable to give him much more information than that. Stargon curled up on the warm slab of stone and waited to see what the morning would bring.

Stargon woke hungry long before dawn. He found a meal easily enough in one of the large scavenger birds that circle high over the remains of unfortunate desert inhabitants who wander too far from home. Stargon returned to his rocky perch and intently watched the curve of the stream around the flaming flowers. As morning arrived, the sun crept across the rocks and brightened the sky to a brilliant blue. Soon, he was surprised to see a man slip from between two large boulders and approach the water's edge. The man knelt, filling a skin from the stream and then quickly splashing his face and arms with the crystal-clear water. Stargon stood up and spread his wings wide to attract the man's attention. The dragon's shadow stretched out over the mountainside in the morning sunlight, and the man stood up slowly, shielding his eyes from the sun as he gazed up at Stargon.

The man scanned the ridge, looking for a rider. He approached the dragon slowly with his fists clenched. Stargon watched him carefully, trying to determine if he really was the legend Aridis had sent him to find. He was tall and heavily muscled, with a long blond beard braided down one side. Stargon found it hard to believe he was as old as Aridis claimed, but he had the markings on his skin as described. The massive dragon folded his wings against his sides and waited calmly as the man climbed up to him.

Osric's Wand

"You're a long way from a dragon platform." The man's voice was gruff, as if he rarely used it.

"You are Pendres?"

"What are you doing here? What do you want?"

"I was sent to find you. There is a wizard in the Human Realm who needs your help. War is threatening every realm."

"I can't help anyone. Leave me alone." The man glared up at Stargon, and the morning light caught the deep red pigments of the ink along his temple.

"It seems you can do a great deal to help. I need you to return with me." The dragon's tone was quiet but insistent.

"How did you find me?"

"I was given directions. However, it was no easy task. Why are you hiding?" Stargon eyed the man warily.

"Who says I am hiding?"

"Your remote location and self-imposed exile speaks for itself. When was the last time you visited the Human Realm?"

"A lifetime ago. What do you want?" The man's eyes still scoured the surroundings for an unseen rider as he bit off his terse questions.

"I was sent here to find you because prophecy ties you to the end of this war."

"I can't help you. I'm not a soldier anymore."

"I do not know what role you are to play," Stargon spoke carefully but with little patience, "but prophecy has cast you in it, with or without your cooperation."

"I'm done with war, and with prophecy, so you should just be on your way." Pendres glared up at the dragon.

"I was sent a very long way to find you, and if the High-Wizard's success rests on your shoulders, you will be returning with me. You can come willingly, come along unwillingly, or I can just eat you now." Stargon growled through curled lips.

"If only it were that easy, I would drape myself across your teeth. I would experience all of the pain but fail to gain the welcome release of death; otherwise I would encourage you to eat me." The man had a strange expression of longing and disgust on his face. "Now, tell me more about this High-Wizard."

"He is powerful, but humble. He freed my kin from the cages on Mount Braya, and he defeated the Kallegian to defend his home and his people. Even the unicorns are in awe of him." Stargon hadn't thought about what he would need to explain to this strange hermit, as it had been a long time since he had come across a human who hadn't heard the stories of Osric and the feats that made the High-Wizard a household name. The only signs Pendres showed that he was impressed with what he heard was a slight tightening of his jaw and a narrowing of his eyes. Stargon continued, "Nearly every walker that I respect in the slightest rallies around him, aiding him in his mission, but they are outnumbered and lacking the experience and skill of the enemy. Still, Osric is more powerful than any other, and he will win. Somehow, you are going to contribute to his victory. It has been foreseen."

Pendres slipped the straps of a small pack from his shoulder and then rifled through the bag. He pulled out a fruit that resembled an apple with white skin, and he took a bite as he listened to Stargon speak, juice dribbling into his thick beard.

"And the war? What is worth the bloodshed and destruction of war?" Pendres asked.

"The turgent of the Human Realm has launched an attack against the irua in their home city. The turgent has taken Angmar."

"Angmar?" Pendres sounded shocked and he viewed the dragon suspiciously. "The Well of Strands?"

"They are hoping you can help them understand the well, among other things."

"I fought that war once already. I never want to be there again." Pendres shook his head and turned to walk away from the great creature.

"The man who sent me here to find you believes he knows why you are still alive. He said to give you a message if you declined the request to aid him. He said that he knows how to end time for you." Stargon called out the message from Aridis clearly, although he was quite sure his mission would fail. Pendres turned back slowly, expressions of anger and pain flashing across his face.

"Who sent you here?" Pendres's voice took on a vicious edge.

"An Obcasior. I would be glad to take you to him and introduce you."

"Yes, you will take me to him, but I wouldn't bother with the introductions."

"If you attempt to harm him, I will eat you after all." Stargon narrowed his swirling eyes with suspicion. "Slowly, and more than once if necessary."

"I won't harm him unless he gives me reason, but I have some questions for him. I never intended to be sought out again." Pendres used the lowest bone of Stargon's wing as a step and launched himself onto the dragon's back. "Where exactly are we going?"

"A city called Stanton. Have you ever been there?"

Pendres said nothing in return.

"Don't you need to gather some things? Humans always travel with so much stuff." Stargon swiveled his neck to allow him to see his passenger. Pendres adjusted the straps of his pack and glared back at the dragon's swirling eye.

"I have everything I need."

* * *

Stargon landed on the Stanton platform the next day with a travel-weary passenger on his back. He had waited until Pendres had fallen asleep late at night as they flew to travel most of the way back to Stanton by spoken spell. Although he had to spend much of the morning dodging questions about how they had made the journey so quickly, Aridis had made it clear how urgent it was to return swiftly. Pendres had finally let it drop and resumed his brooding silence. Aridis was waiting on the platform when they arrived.

"Pendres, thank you for coming. I realize my summons was likely unwelcome."

"Your friend here, and your cryptic message, left me little choice." The man swung himself down from Stargon's back and approached the dragon's head. "I have had no need for coins in a long time. I have nothing to offer but my gratitude. I do not hold you responsible for my presence here, but I do thank you for delivering me here safely."

Stargon's lips curled away from his massive teeth in a fearsome smile. "Your gratitude is sufficient, so long as you remember what I have said."

"I remember." Pendres nodded at Stargon. His expression showed no fear of the dragon eating him, but it was obvious he held a great respect for the creature. He turned toward the old man who had sent for him, studying the appearance of the Obcasior in one long look. His crooked frame, draped in tattered cloth and leaning heavily on a tall staff, seemed unimposing. His grey beard hung nearly to his waist, strangely contrasting his bald head. However, his eyes glinted with ancient knowledge and a quick wit, and Pendres silently vowed not to underestimate the man. "So why am I here?"

"That tale is long and complicated, and you have traveled far. Let us go and speak somewhere more comfortable." Aridis led him away from the dragon platform toward the market district of Stanton. Aridis needed to know more about the man than he could learn from his gift or from old stories before he would present him to a Trust. He wasn't even sure the man would pass the test and be invited into the Aranthian sanctuary. Pendres followed him silently, observing his surroundings in the new city and contemplating his own thoughts.

The market was bustling with people shopping and gossiping, trading and haggling, or just enjoying the autumn sun and a mug of mead. Aridis smiled and waved to many, and exchanged brief pleasantries with a few, before slipping into a small inn just beyond the market. He greeted the woman behind the bar warmly and she waved him through with promises of warm food and rulha to follow. Aridis led Pendres to a small room in the back of the bar with a rough table and chairs. There were no windows in the room, and the only decoration was a small dingy tapestry depicting a drogma hunt hanging above a plain ewer and basin on a shelf in one corner. Sconces on the walls containing small, cool flames provided light. Pendres noted that there must be a Fire Elementalist on the premises, or else one made the rounds each day to light the sconces in the local establishments. The men took seats at the table and Aridis broke the silence immediately.

"I wouldn't have sent for you if there were not a great need for your aid."

"You got me here, but that doesn't mean I will aid you." Pendres eyed Aridis grimly. "Who are you?"

"I am an old man tangled up in the paths of prophecy and the ugliness of war. I suppose one could say the same about you."

"How did you know where to find me? How did you even know to look for me?"

"The *how* is far less interesting than the *why*. It was a combination of obscure books and my Obcasior gift." Aridis spoke casually, pausing to respond to a soft knock at the door. A girl brought in two mugs of warm rulha, bowls of thick vegetable stew, and a plate of cheese and fruit. He paid generously and sent the girl away with a smile. "Are you familiar with it?"

"I have known a few over the years. Though certainly none who could use the pathways to find someone like me. Is your gift varied, or just that powerful?"

"I have had a long life to learn its particularities, though that probably sounds silly to you. I have only known one other Obcasior, and his gift worked the same as mine, if not quite as efficiently," Aridis said. Pendres nodded, but he did not comment on the reference to his age. They sat in silence for a while, eyeing each other and eating the simple but flavorful fare of the tavern.

"And these books you speak of—they mention me?"

"Not exactly." Aridis spoke slowly, enjoying his meal. "Prophecy speaks of you."

"I have no interest in prophecy," Pendres said.

"That does not keep it from being interested in you."

"So why me? What do you know?"

"Ah, not as much as I would like. I know you were a soldier in the war when the Well of Strands was created. I know you are still alive, and there are many stories and myths which attempt to explain why, though I doubt any are accurate."

"If that were all you knew, you would not have brought me here." Pendres finished his meal and sat sipping his mug of rulha.

"In times such as these, that would be enough. However, it is true that there is more to it than that. I know little about you because there is no way for me to know if what I have read is accurate. Yet, I have reason to believe that my suspicions are correct, even if I cannot say it is knowledge."

"So what is it that you suspect?" Pendres eyed Aridis suspiciously, growing tired of the word games.

"I suspect that a spell was cast upon you during the war, though why and by whom eludes me. If I am correct as to which spell was used, then I suspect I know how to break it." Aridis steepled his

The Weaving of Wells

fingers before him and leaned in, his voice growing softer even as it gained intensity.

"Go on." Pendres leaned forward in his chair, his interest obviously piqued for the first time since the conversation had begun.

"I have found references to a spell sold by a Seer in the time of your war, in the proper region, that likely would have been available to those who knew you before you left to fight. If cast properly, with sufficient power and motivation, it would guarantee the survival of the subject until the end of the war. It would ensure that you could return from the fighting. Was there someone who would have had the desire and ability to cast such a spell?" Aridis's voice held compassion as well as curiosity. Pendres's eyes narrowed as pain flashed hotly across his features. The expression confirmed Aridis's suspicions, and he did not pressure the man for a response. "I do not fully understand why it is so, but I believe the spell is still working. It seems most likely to me, based on my research, that the spell should have ended when the war ended. The only reasonable conclusion is that the war did not end."

"That doesn't make any sense." Pendres shook his head as he spoke, attempting to understand what Aridis was saying. "The war ended. The well did what it was supposed to do." Pendres spoke with conviction, although Aridis could sense a nagging doubt, and the reference to the well's purpose caused Aridis's eyes to widen slightly with hope.

"Do you know what it was the well did? Why it is worth a war that could last hundreds of years?" Aridis asked. Pendres did not acknowledge the question, although he now knew what Aridis wanted from him.

"Even if the war hadn't ended after the well was built, the caldereth were wiped out over three centuries ago. I was there for that war too. Or did your prophecy fail to mention that? Surely if it wasn't over before, it would have ended when the last caldereth died. Not only is the war over, it has been long forgotten along with an entire race of people. What on Archana are you talking about?"

"I believe that the wars you were fighting in then, both of them actually, are the same war that we are fighting now. The paths of history, as well as those of prophecy, indicate that events played out in the proper order and direction so as to keep the war active over all of that time. I realize it doesn't seem to make sense, but I think my companions and I can explain. I would like to present you to a Trust." Aridis watched him closely.

"I am finding it increasingly difficult to trust you, so I think I will pass." Pendres glared coldly at him.

"You have been given little reason to trust me, but if I am correct, you have nothing to lose. Well, nothing but an eternity of uncertainty. Or perhaps you may prefer to watch the world burn down around you until the inevitable end of the war arrives and you are finally released from the spell." Aridis glared back at him. "But wouldn't you prefer to help determine which side wins?" Pendres said nothing in return.

Aridis rose from his seat and leaned forward until his beard nearly brushed Pendres's knees.

"The man who should win is looking forward to meeting you. What shall I tell him of you?" Aridis asked. Pendres sat for several moments in silence with a contemplative look.

"I wish to consider what you have said for a while before I meet anyone else who may call you friend. Does your demand for my presence afford me a night's sleep in this inn?"

Aridis nodded slowly and a small smile touched his lips.

"Your room has been prepared, and any meals you need are already credited. I will send someone to greet you in the morning and receive your decision."

Pendres nodded silently and Aridis left the room.

Chapter 7
Future's Walk

Serha walked up to a door she had never approached so early in the morning. It was time, she knew it. Before she could raise her hand to knock, Aridis opened the door and greeted her with a wounded smile while wiping at his wet cheeks. She didn't want the day to be any more difficult than it already was, so she spoke with as much strength in her voice as she could muster.

"I feel like taking a nice walk before the day gets too hot, and I could use some company. Would you please escort a feeble old lady for a trip outside?"

Aridis nearly broke, but her glare forced him to remain resolute. His lower lip trembled as he smiled.

"I would walk with you another hundred days." His voice trembled.

"You are a sweet old man. Come." Serha held her thin, strong arm out and took Aridis's hand in hers.

They passed through the hallways in the barracks in silence. Not a soul moved in the halls, save for Eublin, who was already too engrossed in his books to be aware of his surroundings and took no notice of the two. It was an almost bitter silence, but Serha welcomed it.

Her life had been devoted to delivering words of prophecy in faraway lands. Her gift had brought her before the highest seats in all of the lands, and to the lowliest child hidden within the trash behind buildings while looking for warmth.

She had delivered words of doom and salutations of joy. Once, she had been tasked to deliver ominous news of the coming extinction of an entire race, and she had spoke of births that accompanied new gifts. Words had been her partner through it all; even in the long, lonely walks between destinations, her words had been with her. Words of joy, words of praise, words of training, words of rejoicing, words of love and of death—always she had carried words. It was fitting, in her mind, that this day should be met with the absence of words. It was as if her words were in mourning, and they too longed to feel the loving caress of the wind offering its soothing touch in remembrance of the long, fruitful life she was leaving behind. But unlike man, who mourned by wailing, words offered only silence in condolence.

The cool breeze came from the east as the two aged friends departed the invisible shelter at the barracks. She faced west, heading into the trees and wishing for a few blooming flowers to greet them, but even the traveler's companion hid its purple bloom in the early dawn.

While they walked, she could feel words attempting to gain an audience in the way her companion shifted his gate. She could sense his tentative attempts at communication in the way the air would catch in quick intakes followed by a long slow release. She felt for him, knowing what they both knew, but she savored a few more moments of silence while the smells of the forest lingered in the humid air.

"When did you realize how close this day was?" Serha's words were soft, but the breaking of the silence was sharp as she finally bid Aridis to speak.

"This morning I awoke early and even the wind whispered of my coming pain. I dreamt all night of this day, and there was no denying that it was no dream," he answered.

"I'm sorry." She smiled. "I began this path with the first vision I was given as a child. All pathways led here, for me."

"Are you sure there is no other way?" His voice pleaded with her.

"Our world is on the verge of a great awakening. If we do survive, everything will change—it already began with magic. Today an event takes place that will bring about many different paths in the way Archanans live their lives."

"But if this day happens as the stones tell it, nobody will remember you." His argument was feeble, and his voice portrayed his knowledge of the fact.

"I know you will remember me; that's enough for an old woman like me. I must admit that I always hoped for an end like the one that the Seer who brought Osric his first prophecy enjoyed, and I would have loved to be buried below the funeral rune. Serha Aranthian sounds nice, don't you think?" For the first time, her own lips quivered—the time was close.

"You can still have that day. Come back with me and spend your last days with an old man who has been waiting for you his whole life." His pleading took on a desperate quality.

"What a lovely thought." She sighed.

"Damn the hands of time that steer us toward an end we cannot see. Our lives are meant to direct the path of every life that follows, but what of happiness?" Aridis protested vehemently.

"It is a selfish mind that insists on survival as long as it does not have to endure the sting of unhappiness."

"I would settle for death today, if I may have some small measure of a peaceful walk with a mind such as yours."

"Then a small measure you shall have, my dear friend." She could see the hunger for a different resolution in his eyes. Sure, the bright and vibrant color of youth had departed from them a long time ago, but the shimmer of moisture still lent its aid, tempting Serha's heart to alter her path.

"How is it that two disparate gifts such as ours can share so much in common that our meeting rekindles feelings of long-lost friendship, in spite of the fact that we had never laid eyes on one another?" She smiled a sad but genuine smile.

"Magic is a difficult thing to understand," was his only reply.

"And you will have another age to ponder all of the meaning it may hold, and you will guide many minds long after I am gone." She looked over at him with kind, brave eyes.

"It will be a lonely existence without you."

"Aridis, you and I both knew how this day would end when you opened your door to greet me. Could we just enjoy what is left of this walk in one another's company? Or do you want to continue to sulk right up until the end?" There was nothing accusing in her tone—no malice, no impatience or frustration in her voice. The words were a query of sorts, and the inflections carried nothing more. She just wanted to know how he wished to proceed.

He faced her with regret in his eyes, and he shook with the desire to share a different path. He searched her eyes for an answer that he couldn't find. Reluctantly he sighed, tucked his chin to his chest, and closed his eyes while he gathered the courage to proceed.

"You want to enjoy this trip as if it were any other day?" he asked in all sincerity.

"If I had but one wish, that would be it." Serha smiled and nodded as a tear fell from her eye.

Osric's Wand

"Then it would be my pleasure to give you what you ask for." Aridis put his right arm around her shoulders and kissed the tear off of her left cheek. "Can I ask you which flowers are your favorite?"

"Traveler's companions have always been my favorite."

Aridis bent his creaking knees and plucked one of the purple blossoms from between the long blades of grass along the path. He tucked the flower behind her ear and wrapped an arm around her subtly trembling shoulders. She leaned into his embrace and resumed their stroll.

As they walked along the path, he held her, the only thing left for him to bring comfort in these last few moments or hours. Both of them knew there was no way to inspire the changes Archana would need without it, but it was no easier to take each step knowing what was to come. Serha shook slightly as Aridis leaned in to give her a kiss on the cheek.

* * *

"Quickly, place him on the table and get me some water. Put half of it in the pot over the fire, and the other half needs to be chilled—we don't know what's wrong yet and I want to be ready," Bridgett shouted as the group of Hunters brought Aridis's unconscious body into the room.

Osric looked on with worry-filled eyes, staying a safe distance out of the way. Nearly everyone who knew Aridis had been informed that they had found him in the woods, bloodied and unable to speak, and were on their way to lend whatever aid they could.

In moments, Bridgett had cut the robes off of the old man and was wiping every wound clean with a warm cloth to better assess the damage. She worked fast and steady, with practiced patience, while speaking to herself in hushed tones.

Kenneth joined Osric, mouthing questions about what had happened. Osric shrugged and shook his head, but stood in silence watching Bridgett work. Eublin, Gus, Pebble, Macgowan, and Jane joined in the silent vigil.

Aridis was breathing at least, and none of the wounds seemed to be life-threatening to Osric.

The Weaving of Wells

"He's got a nasty bump and bruises on his head, and a few scratches, as if he fell down or was hit over the head by someone. I think he'll be fine when he wakes up." She wrapped his head in a cool cloth and turned to face the group.

Just as she turned with sad eyes, Aridis whimpered, letting out a long slow whine. His eyes opened slowly, and then came the weeping. His face contorted in agony as his cries rang out.

"No, no, no." His voice was soft and pleading. The old man's chest rose and fell with the ferocity of his cries, while his hands moved to cover his eyes.

"Aridis, don't get up. You took a nasty blow to the head. You shouldn't be out walking in an unfamiliar forest without some company." Bridgett moved to his side and placed a comforting hand on his shoulder. Her attempts at consoling the elderly man had no effect. "It's okay. Everything will be fine after you get some rest."

"Serha's dead!" The words burst out from his mouth between sobs.

"What?" Osric stepped up to the bed. "Was she with you?"

Aridis nodded shakily. "She was hunted." He rolled onto his side.

"I'm sorry, my friend. We all know how much she meant to you." Osric attempted to comfort the frail old man, but his own grief and anxiety prevented his efforts from being effective. Osric had come to care for the Seer, admiring her both for her talents and her compassion toward his people. She had savored life, and the thought of it being taken from her was somehow wrong. Though she had lived a long and full life, she was still vibrant and almost playful in her seriousness. It simply wasn't fair that she had lost so much time that she could have spent with friends and loved ones—time she could have spent giving to the world what only she could give.

Osric's grief was heavy, if more subdued, than Aridis's, but he was also struck by the anxiety of never understanding the visions Serha had seen surrounding the books and the wells around Archana. There was still so much they needed to learn, to see, and now Serha was gone and so was her gift.

"She told me she wished to be buried beneath the stone at our borders." Aridis still wept, but his words were growing more clear as he expressed her final wishes.

Osric spared a moment to look towards Eublin, whose eyes burned with passion as well as sorrow. There was a life's worth of intensity buried in the expression, but he held his tongue. Osric nodded out of respect to the gnome for keeping his call for social reform to himself, for the time being. Still, Osric knew that there would be a reckoning to come. No small part of him wished to join in the call, but how could they change a world of culture with the strength of one man's cries?

He needed time to figure out how to deal with his new powers—to learn how to incorporate a constant stream of new abilities in a way that was good for something more than boasting of the power within. He needed time to figure out the whole truth behind his wand—what new magics his wand could introduce to him. He needed time to repair the separation that he and Bridgett had endured—their relationship deserved the time that faulty prophecy had taken from them. He needed time for Machai to get the dwarves to join their side—they couldn't hope to gain access to the Well of Strands without their help. He needed time to learn what was behind the dragon attacks—for as far back as known stories were told, dragons had always been friends to walkers. And now, it seemed, he needed time to figure out how he was going to help Eublin change the hunt—maybe the most daunting task of them all.

The hunt was a tradition that claimed to keep all of the species of Archana at peace. Meat was something that was highly sought after, and if it weren't for the hunt, wars might have broken out based on the fact that families needed meals in order to survive. Populations of cities and animal colonies would have grown so large that there would not have been enough farmland to sustain them. Then wars would have been fought over the shortage of land to cultivate crops for the masses. It was the hunt that kept all of Archana from erupting into war at any given moment.

These were the ideas behind the tradition that Osric had grown up hearing, internalizing, and repeating. He truly did believe that the hunt kept the world fed while also keeping Archana peaceful. He had never thought to question the ideas, but then again, he had never thought he would be leading an army into war. These days he had to question everything he had ever known, and that included the hunt. Could the gracious acceptance of a loved one serving as someone else's meal truly keep the world at peace and keep the populations in check?

No, it would take decades for problems like that to arise, and Eublin was very convincing with his arguments that those were

The Weaving of Wells

problems that could be solved in the intervening time. Osric was starting to see that there was wisdom in the gnome's words. It was time for the hunt to change or to evolve into something that wasn't quite as open to interpretation as the hunt had been for so long. It was time to provide a way for some to have an existence outside of the hunt, but what would a world like that look like? How would they implement such a drastic change? What could he do?

Yes, he needed time...

Unfortunately, time was one of the many things they had too little of. Soon Dredek would be ready to achieve his final goal, to revive the caldereth. Who knew what would happen if the caldereth controlled the Well of Strands? He felt as if he knew too little about the race to know what Dredek would do once he had brought his people back from the dead. They had learned a great deal about the way the caldereth taught their people, and about their language, the way they lived, mated, and farmed. The instructional lessons recorded on the stones had given them a picture of a culture that strove to advance their understanding of magic, educate and train their youth, and maintain healthy, happy communities in the frigid environment they favored, but there was still so much they didn't know.

To be fair, while studying the stones had been a priority, it took a long time to filter through all of the material to find something useful. Dozens of stones were still waiting to be viewed because they still had not figured out how to duplicate the viewing device. Only one stone could be activated at a time, and there were many other things that needed to be accomplished by the small population of the Aranthian compound.

They had no idea how the caldereth had known so much about the Well of Strands, or why they had believed that moving their entire population to the well's site was necessary. They had not learned much about the magic that the caldereth knew, as the lessons were largely focused on what young members of the society needed to learn first. They didn't know exactly why Dredek had lived for so long, although it was clear that the normal caldereth lifespan was significantly longer than a human's. They certainly hadn't learned how Dredek was capable of taking another's ability and fusing it into himself. Most of all, nothing on the stones could tell them the lengths to which Dredek's mourning would drive him. The emotional turmoil

Osric's Wand

that he had sensed from Dredek in their fight caused Osric to doubt that this was the fight that all of the prophecies had been warning him about, but it was obvious that Dredek was willing to kill as many people as it would take to bring back his people. If he would go to such lengths to revive his race, what might he do once they were alive and he felt the need to protect them or provide them all with the wealth and the power he had grown accustomed to himself?

Time was not something they could waste, and now Serha was lost to them, which left a hollow feeling in Osric's gut. He surveyed the shocked faces in the room. Bridgett kept her face low to hide her tears as she tended to Aridis. Gus had a blank, worried stare on his face as he looked across the room.

Eublin had made himself useful by fetching several pots of water to warm over the fire, but he carried himself with sunken shoulders. Kenneth helped Bridgett tend to the wounds on Aridis that still needed attention.

Through Aridis's wailing, the binding of wounds, silent mourning, and several bodies moving in and out of the room, wisps of smoke swirled in the corner of the room. A thickly muscled man with a braid down one side of his beard sat in a chair, hidden from view by his lack of movement. He puffed quietly on the end of a wooden pipe and kept to himself while the room bristled with sullen life. He wore a look of long-felt sorrow that teemed with ancient turmoil.

Chapter 8
Buried in Sand

A shaky hand moved slowly down the cold stone wall. Dredek braced himself internally as the raking tremor gripped his body. His only comfort came in the form of a thick woolen cloak he pulled tightly around himself. The tremors were expected, but still they tested his strength and forced him to curl tightly on the floor in the corner of the small, dark room.

"It will pass." The whispered voice of his personal physician, Jalyn, was as soothing as his expression. "But you must give yourself more time before attempting to merge another gift. You didn't wait long enough since the last, and it very nearly cost you your life."

"The opportunity presented itself and I had to have this gift—it will aid in more ways than you could know." Dredek forced his body to relax and unclenched his fists while stretching out on the floor.

Jalyn had been loyal for reasons Dredek could never glean in all of the years he had known him. It was comforting to him to not understand the purpose behind the loyalty after such a long life of searching for truths.

Decades had passed while he searched for a way to revive the bones he had kept hidden. He had searched through libraries, citadels, barracks, bookstores, and all manner of hidden locations in palaces across Archana. Knowledge had been a lifetime pursuit, while carefully disguising his caldereth heritage. But all of his hiding was near an end... even if he was forced to endure a few months of discomfort. He was happy to keep the reasoning for Jalyn's devotion a secret, if it made him feel better.

But this time the tremors were more persistent than they had ever been in the past. Osric had been the worthiest opponent he had been up against to date. The sword of his was truly spectacular. The way he used it to gain the powers of those he faced was remarkable. He was a powerful man, but he lacked the experience with the gifts that Dredek had so carefully mastered over the years. It had to have been the density of the strands bound to the life strand within the inexperienced boy that caused him so much pain in taking the gift and its associated power. For most, the rending of a gift from one's life strand would be enough to sever it and end the life, but Dredek was sure Osric had survived—a worthy opponent indeed.

"But still, master, you need to rest if you hope to regain your strength." Jalyn spoke in soothing tones that caused Dredek's body to relax. Voice was a gift that never interested Dredek, but he did enjoy being in the company of one with it.

"I intend to rest just as soon as I can verify that everything is going as planned. We've been here far too long to not have found a trace of the well's location. And these men who keep interfering with our efforts must be stopped."

"Yes, master, we have those with the sight seeking areas with high concentrations of strands hoping to find a pathway, but there are so many places like that in these tunnels that we keep running into rooms that lead nowhere. And our troops continue to search for the few irua holdouts that must be left, but they are far too good at evading us. We had a few robed irua that we thought could lead us to the well, but we found our guards unconscious when we went to interrogate them. The guards spoke of two Aranthians rescuing the hostages, shortly before they were executed for failing you."

"We do not have as large an army as I would like. Let's keep the executions to a minimum for a time." It wasn't as easy to speak as he had expected. It hadn't taken as long to recover from rending Osric's strands as it had on the other occasions he had stolen a gift, but the finer control of his body was taking a great deal longer with every gift he appropriated.

"As you wish, master. How would you like to go about finding the ones who can lead us into the well?" Jalyn bowed.

"I've told you to have those with the sight look closely at the life strand. The ones we are looking for have two strands, but it is nearly impossible to see the difference. The second strand carries no power and coils itself around the life strand. It's nearly invisible. Only those who know about it would know to look as close as is needed. Make sure our men take the time to look closely at the prisoners. We may already have what we are looking for. They won't all be in robes. That coiled strand is the key to unlock the door, and once unlocked our plans will be hard to stop."

The Weaving of Wells

Jalyn placed a calm hand on Dredek's shoulder and looked him in the eyes. "You really must rest. You've not given yourself the time you need to recover. We will find these men, but if you are to achieve your goals then we need you strong. The new gift is speeding your recovery, but the rest of your senses haven't adjusted. You must give them the time they need."

"Jalyn, you have been very attentive since the battle, and indeed you have been for years, but I assure you I know what is best for me. Have you found a large shallow basin for me yet?" Dredek glared at his assistant, not wanting him to continue forcing the issue with his gift.

"I have been given news that one was found several levels from our current location and is being brought to us forthwith. If we were more familiar with these tunnels, I am sure it would have arrived by now. Can I ask what you need with it?"

Dredek closed his eye as the world began to spin, uncontrolled, and he steadied himself against the stone wall to his back. "It will help me to heal, but the how of it is for me to know." He took several deep breaths. "And what of the other supplies we need? Have we located any more?"

"We have located several food stores selling mostly grains and roots. They are nothing special, but more than enough to sustain our army while we are here."

"Yes, of course." Dredek motioned with his hand for Jalyn to continue.

"Several levels have something resembling farms, and they have a most peculiar way of lighting the crops. Once we understand how the devices work, we will be a lot closer to being able to sustain a large population. Water was the easiest to locate. There are several springs and wells located throughout each level."

"Of course, these are the simple tasks I gave you. Have you found any of the items that I asked you to find?" Dredek looked at his companion with disdain. There was no doubt that Jalyn knew exactly what was being asked.

"Well, uh. We have located kadmel root and wolf's essence, but we are finding it difficult to locate any petrified deadman's stalk. I'm not sure where else we could look." Jalyn produced a small sack from his satchel and sat it on the bedside table.

Dredek bent over and grasped the small pouch he had brought with him into the room and tossed it shakily up to Jalyn. "I found this within an hour of entering these tunnels. It shouldn't be hard to locate some that has been petrified when it is so easily found in the city."

"I know it may seem…"

"Enough!" Dredek had had enough of the conversation. "You will find me what I need or I will find someone who can. Look in every apothecary shop and home in these tunnels if you have to. I need that stalk."

"Of course. It will be done." Jalyn nodded as a man entered the room holding a bowl. "Just in time. Set that on the table next to Dredek and leave us."

A tall human male in standard military dress carried the basin to the table and set it down. After a nod of respect in Dredek's direction, he turned and walked out of the room. Jalyn filled the wide, shallow bowl with water and stood patiently waiting.

"Now, if you would kindly leave me to my business and make sure that nobody disturbs me." Dredek dismissed Jalyn with a stern expression and a wave of the hand.

Jalyn looked hurt by the easy manner with which he was sent away but bowed his head as he backed out of the room.

Dredek took a vial from his belt and emptied it into the water, mixing it with his finger. Then he sat waiting as ripples met the edges of stone and washed back over the bowl growing smaller with each pass. Soon, the distortion caused by the waves faded and he was left with still, calm water, darkened only by the contents of the vial.

Once all motion had ceased, the water changed to a vivid silver color that reflected nothing. Dredek smiled as he leaned over the bowl—the earth and stone surrounding him didn't bother him nearly as much as it had when he activated the one gift that had been with him through all of the years and peered at the strands within himself. This mirror of sorts was not his creation, but a gift created for him by the woman who held his every hope for the future—a woman whose bones lay buried in a chest he had kept safe since her death.

The Portentist gift stood distinctly separate from the gifts that he had become familiar with. Shimmering in a bright purple color at the top of his neck, the orb sat vibrating in a disturbingly unsecure fashion. He slipped his wand out from the band that held it to his upper arm and turned it on himself.

It was delicate work, linking the gift into a more centralized location. It would never fit him like a gift that had grown over time, but these steps were the next best thing, and with every small measure of stabilization, the world became clearer and more defined. It was an act he had performed many times, and he had grown much more proficient at stabilizing the abilities in his own body over the decades.

He continued to work, slowly linking the gift into a more stable setting—he felt more alive with every passing second. When he had completed as much of the work as he had the strength for, he leaned back against the wall and shook with the effort it had taken. The short times spent stabilizing his new gift would go a long way toward helping him recover, though he still needed some time alone before he would feel like himself again. There were times he would have to be around others, but he had to minimize the number of times when his soldiers would see him in his compromised state. Summoning all of the strength he had left to keep from weeping, he let himself slip into calm and silent rest.

Chapter 9
Another Below

The spell's effects dwindled as Machai steadied himself, leaning against a frost-covered cliffside and counting his companions as they appeared. The traveling spell was worse on some than others, and he stood patiently as the small group of dwarves gathered their wits and the disorientation faded.

They had chosen a familiar location a quarter day's climb from the entrance to FireFalls, and Machai relished the sting of the cold air against his skin. His men grunted and grinned as they gazed around at the frigid landscape they had always called home. After the scorching heat of the irua desert, and the intensity of the fighting, the northern mountains provided a peaceful reprieve. Machai gathered the group together and spoke in hushed tones.

"Ye be the best companions I could be fighting alongside, but even ye willn't be enough to be overpowering Dredek's army. We need to be getting inside and convincing the clan to join us." The dwarves nodded silently as Machai continued. "But ye be sent out with a wagon of swords, and ye be coming back with me. It willn't be easy to be swaying Thenar to the cause."

"It be that cur Aron's fault that we be empty-handed for the weapons. Thenar willn't be blaming ye for that debt," Lynth said.

"Ye be young, Lynth, which be not a flaw." Machai shook his head in disbelief at the younger dwarf's words. "But ye be naïve if ye be thinking that Thenar willn't be blaming us all for such a failure. Ye be sent out with a shipment of weapons, but ye be not returning with the gold he be promised. He willn't be caring that Aron be breaching fair-trade agreements by ambushing us on the road, and he willn't be caring that Aron be threatening me or taking Osric hostage. He will only be blaming me, and Kablis as the shipment overseer, for allowing Aron's men to be loading the gold back into the wagons and taking it with the weapons back to Rowain. For Thenar, we may as well be the ones who be stealing the weapons—or stealing the gold, for that matter. Ye shouldn't be expecting a warm welcome home."

The Weaving of Wells

"It be that bad? What can we be doing?" Lynth asked, staring at the snow scattered across the toes of his boots.

"Ye just be keeping yer head about ye, and we'll be watching out for ye." Machai attempted a reassuring tone, but he was worried that they hadn't all considered just how angry Thenar was going to be. He turned his attention to Kablis, knowing that at least one of his companions understood what a mess they were walking into. "The first thing we must be doing is getting inside without drawing the attention of the guards. Kablis, ye know as well as I, since we be training most of 'em, that it willn't be simple."

"What be yer plan?" Kablis asked.

"We need to be getting inside without being seen. Me plan be to be avoiding the guards entirely."

"Can we be traveling in by spell?" Kablis didn't sound confident in the suggestion, but it seemed like the simplest choice.

"Nay," Machai said. "Ye be knowing as well as I that there be too many protection spells on this mountain to be risking triggering one. I cannot be knowing if the protection spells be enough to keep us from traveling directly inside. I be willing to risk some of us getting caught, but I willn't be risking any of us getting dead."

"Can we be coming down the shaft of the lift?" one of the others asked softly, and Machai didn't look around to see who it was.

"We be risking the same spells whether it be traveling through stone or through the shaft. That opening at the top of the mountain be as protected as any entrance or the walls themselves be. We be having no choice but to be opening the doors." Kablis answered the next obvious suggestion without waiting for Machai to reply.

"We locate 'em before they be locating us, and we be using the traveling spell to stay between 'em and out of sight. It'll be best if we all be arriving undetected, but it be harder to travel as a pack. We be splitting up. The more that be getting in unseen, the better our argument'll be. If ye be seen, be making it take a while to catch ye, but don't be using the spell. It'll be giving the rest time to be getting inside. Ready?" Machai glanced around at each of them, acknowledging the silent nods and looks of determination. He wasn't sure just how cool the welcome would be when they arrived, but he intended to show Thenar that the new revelations in magic would prevent their stronghold from being as safe as it had once been. If they could get to the doors undetected by using the traveling spell, so could Dredek's men or any other enemy with evil intentions. The FireFalls clan wouldn't be secure unless they were willing to aid Osric in winning the war and restoring order to Archana. When he was sure they were all ready, he gave the signal to split up and take positions to locate any clan sentries.

Machai and the dwarves with him knew the surrounding mountains at least as well as anyone stationed in the area. Between their skill and experience with the terrain, and the traveling spell, they moved rapidly toward the entrance in silence.

This approach would be different than the last time he visited his home; he needed to be unseen by any patrols that may be on the mountainside. Last time, he had landed on dragonback and didn't care who saw their approach. This time, he needed his kin to recognize the threat that new magic could present to their home or all hope of gaining support could die before it had a chance. He wasn't showing up under the best of circumstances either.

The dwarves who were with them had been charged with delivering weapons, and he had a hand in stopping the delivery. Though Dredek still gained the weapons, it was because of Machai's allegiance to the Aranthians that the dwarves received no payment. Coupled with the fact that the ones charged with the delivery were now a part of the organization that was responsible for their lack of payment, he knew they would have to have a very good reason for asking more from FireFalls.

Quickly, Machai surveyed the surroundings knowing that one of them would have to make their way to the door while taking advantage of the surroundings to stay concealed. One of them would have to place a palm on the door to open it for the others. He knew that others on the mountainside would be watching for intruders, and though a group of dwarves would not be frowned upon, or even stopped when approaching, they needed the element of surprise to lend credence to their argument. They had to be careful.

Halfway up the slope, two guards leaned up against a tree smoking pipes and eating cheese. Machai heard them before he saw them. The sun stood high in the sky, which did not help them find cover. Luckily there were more than enough large rocks and trees to block their approach until one of them could see the door and travel to it. He ducked behind a tall bush, shielding him from view of the two visible guards, and surveyed his surroundings.

He noticed a location that could easily hide someone from view, but he didn't see anyone from his current position. Machai looked around for a spot that would give him a better view without putting him out in the open. Off to his left he spotted a tree that provided a perfect view behind the obstructing rock. So he spoke under his breath, imagining himself at that location. Machai appeared behind the tree, though a small broken branch was piercing the muscle at the back of his arm. He held his breath to avoid making a sound and pulled the offending object out, grimacing as it tore at his flesh. He knew the risks of the spell, but even the most experienced could make mistakes. Bending the branch out of his way, he flattened himself up against the tree and peered slowly from behind to see the concealed guard signaling to another man, and he was pointing in Machai's direction. His heart raced at the thought of being the one caught in their group.

He sat, silently waiting for someone to find him, not wanting to give away anyone else's location. If he were to be found, he would have to make a run for it so as to not give away the knowledge of the spoken spell. He would still be able to make an argument for troops, but it would be less convincing than walking in without being seen. He could hear footsteps from the other side of the tree, and a voice rang out.

"Ye there, halt or we'll be cutting ye down!"

He tensed, preparing to make a run for it, but one from his group burst out from behind a bush and began to run back in the direction they had started from. Two more of his men panicked and joined in the flight for safety, drawing two hidden guards into the chase. Machai couldn't be sure, but he thought one of the dwarves fleeing across the snow was Lynth.

Machai breathed a sigh of relief that his location had not been discovered, glanced back at his wound with annoyance, and then looked into the distance for his next cover. Luckily, the hidden scout location was now empty, which meant that four fewer eyes were now surveying the mountainside for intruders. He wished his three men luck in their retreat, hoping they would make it a long distance before being caught, but how many would end up joining in the retreat was unclear from his hidden location. He couldn't risk making an accurate count, as it would compromise his location.

He had come nearly half the distance with one use of the spell, but he still couldn't see the door. The crevice leading to the door would provide a great deal of cover while the door was opened, but by his estimate it would take two more uses of the spell before he could safely arrive at the entrance to their mountain home.

Appearing behind the furthest tree that he could clearly see behind, Machai was happy to find that no hidden obstacles had pierced his body. Making sure he was concealed from view, he peered through the snow-covered landscape one more time, searching for hidden eyes. He made out three guards at heightened alert, standing ready with wands out, scouting the path he had already passed. He smiled as the long, dark crevice leading to their home was now visible, and he thought he could see one of his men walking inside. Luckily, from their current vantage point, the alerted guards wouldn't be able to make out anything near the opening, and one spell would have him inside.

Appearing just inside, Machai quickly stepped into the shadows, turning around to make sure he hadn't been spotted. There was no sound to indicate he had been seen, so he quickly started down the dark corridor, feeling his way through rather than lighting his wand. He could smell the familiar scents of home in the stone beside him, and at least two of them had made it as far as this.

A few moments later, he could see the familiar glow of a hand on the door, indicating it was being opened. A burst of warm air breezed by him, smelling of metal and oil. They had made it. Machai grunted in appreciation as he greeted three of his companions inside the door.

"Ye be slow as always, Machai. I be surprised ye be making it at all."

"Aye, Kablis. Ye be quick, but ye flushed out the guards that be chasing the tails of three of yer men." Laughter fled from Kablis's face at Machai's words, and he stared down at the smooth stone passage rather than meeting the eyes of the disappointed dwarf. Machai softened his tone as he said, "They be making an honorable sacrifice. It be true that we needn't all make it unseen, and yer boys led them away to be clearing the path for the rest."

The Weaving of Wells

As Machai finished, two more crept silently up behind them. Their faces showed both the success of their arrival as well as defeat. The first broke the silence.

"We be the last. Ye saw the three be running back, leading the guards away." He directed his words to Machai. "We be near ye, but well concealed. Not long after, we be seeing three more caught in an avalanche spell. They be snared by the guards before they could be getting their feet under 'em and running away. The guards willn't be too far behind."

"Aye. Be we confronting Thenar now?" Kablis asked.

"No, let us be making our way to yer chambers first," Machai said.

Kablis nodded and the six dwarves moved quietly but swiftly along the corridor as the door closed behind them. They stopped at the chasm in the floor only long enough for Machai to place his hand against a well-worn space on the wall and use his wand to summon the stone lift that would take them to another floor and hopefully to safety from the approaching guards. They needed to seek out some friends, and he only hoped that they would find those who would help them before anyone else found them first.

Machai stood on the lift with his five successful companions, dreading the inevitable confrontation with Thenar. He hoped to put off the encounter for a while—not because he feared the result, but because he wanted to feel out the clan and determine how much support and resistance they had for Osric and the Aranthians. The platform's descent halted several levels down into the mountain, but not as far as he had taken Thamas when they had arrived at FireFalls the last time.

Machai and his companions stepped off of the lift in silence, heading down the smooth stone passageway that led to the private quarters of many of the strongest warriors in the clan. Each wore a solemn expression as they considered whether they would be welcomed home with open arms or with raised weapons. Any of the dwarves they were striding toward would have the power to raise an alarm and have them all imprisoned before they could speak to anyone about their mission. It was a risk they would have to take.

They passed several arched doorways carved in the stone and continued on until the passageway opened up onto a large common room. Only three people were in the room at that time of day, as most

Osric's Wand

others would be engaged in various training, work, or the mid'day meal. Machai almost sighed with relief when he saw who was present, but the tension did not entirely leave the group.

Two women sat at a table near the center of the room playing a game of bones, and they didn't notice the arrival of the six men. The young dwarf in the corner of the room did notice, and he came running immediately when he saw them enter.

"Papa!" The boy rushed up to Kablis with an excited grin. The grizzled old dwarf smiled from ear to ear as he embraced his son.

"Ye be taking care of yer mother like I be ordering?"

"Aye. Ye be gone so long, though. She be growing grumpier by the day." The young boy was still beardless but beginning to fill out in the shoulders, and Kablis roared with laughter at the angry face his son donned doing an impression of his mother. The noise of the reunion drew the attention of the two dwarven women, who approached with warm smiles. Machai was familiar with them both.

"Aye, it be nice to be welcomed home with smiles from ye lovelies. Can we be hoping we be not as hated as we be fearing?" Machai draped an arm across each of their shoulders as he greeted them.

"Nay, ye be not hated. But ye do be drawing down the wrath of Thenar more with each passing sun." The women were well past working age, and their skin was greying and cracked like weathered stone. They still giggled like girls at Machai's flattery, but their eyes shone with the wisdom of their years and the words held a clear warning for the long-absent group. Machai nodded silently in acceptance and sent the women back to their leisurely game of strategy and chance with a grateful smile.

Kablis knelt down and spoke softly to his son.

"We need to be speaking with some of the men, Dandren. Do ye be knowing who be angry and who be loyal to yer papa?"

"Aye. I be listening just as ye be teaching me. Krind and Morgo be worried and missing ye most. Threed be grumbling much about yer being gone. Krind be thumping 'im twice already for calling ye a betrayer."

"Ye be doing well, son. Can ye be going to fetch Krind and Morgo? But ye cannot be letting anyone know we be here." Urgency and import were heavy in Kablis's tone.

The Weaving of Wells

"Aye, papa, easy." Dandren grinned up at his father's companions with confidence.

"Good. Be bringing 'em to our chambers quickly." Kablis sighed and smiled as he watched his boy run off to the lift.

"Yer lad's grown a deal since we be leaving home."

"Aye." Kablis watched until Dandren was out of sight, and then the men hurried to his chambers to await the arrival of potential allies.

Although the wait was not terribly long, it was filled with tense silence, and the room was shadowed with the men's dread. They were confident that they still had friends there, and they knew some would support them in attempting to recruit a force to aid Osric. Yet, they were also aware of the potential backlash for even asking, nevermind the rumors that may have been spread about the reason they were gone so long after losing the largest and most valuable shipment ever sent out from the stone walls of FireFalls. A failure like that, without the swift return and an explanation from the offenders, would likely be seen as dishonorable at best, treasonous at worst. Dwarves crafted and used weapons; they weren't defeated by them.

They heard Dandren approaching, an ungainly skipping down the stone halls, before they saw anyone turn in through the archway that led to Kablis's rooms. Machai realized he was holding his breath when he sighed with relief at the sight of the two dwarves Kablis had sent for. They were smiling at the youthful excitement of their guide, and they rushed forward to embrace Kablis and several of the others as soon as they saw them. Machai had never been close to the two men, but he knew of their reputation for honor and loyalty. If they still supported Kablis, in light of what they may have heard about him, then there was still hope for their mission.

"It be good to be seeing ye. We knew ye'd be back, and ye'd be telling yer side of the tale." Krind slapped Kablis on the shoulder as he spoke.

"It be quite a tale at that. We be needing some help first, lads, before we be sitting around and yapping."

"Ye be naming it, we be providing the aid," Morgo assured him before turning with a grin. "Machai, ye lil devil. Ye be stirring up a hornet's nest with yer last argument with Thenar. What be yer aim this time?"

Osric's Wand

"We be needing a force to be marching to war." His words raised the eyebrows of both men. "But first, let's be sitting down and telling ye what be stirring outside our little hive. Archana be a mess, men."

Chapter 10
Alliances

Morgo and Krind sat in quiet conversation with each other while Kablis and Machai told the whole story over again. When the two friends of Kablis had heard everything the men had been through—first in Rowain when the shipment of weapons was lost to Aron and his men, then in Stanton when the Turgent's men had attacked the city, and again in the Irua Realm when Dredek had stormed the tunnels and then severely injured Osric—Morgo and Krind had readily agreed to do anything they could to aid Machai and Kablis in recruiting a force. It was clear that there was more going on in the world, particularly with the discovery of new magic, than the dwarven stronghold was prepared to withstand. It was only a matter of time before someone or something took an interest in the Dwarven Realm as well. The two had rapidly gathered a few of their closest friends they were sure they could count on to support them as well. Even if they weren't as willing to march off to war as Morgo and Krind were, these dwarves would surely stand against an enemy that dared to steal a massive shipment of enchanted dwarven swords for an army.

When Kablis and Machai finished telling the newcomers their story, the men sat back in thought with varying expressions of anger, disbelief, determination, and conviction on their faces. Phel sat on Machai's right, tugging on his red beard as he considered the situation. He was one of the dwarves who had crafted the weapons sent to Rowain, and he took the loss of the swords and axes personally. Gerbim was next to Phel, a smaller dwarf than most and also quicker to anger. He had the sight of Wand-Makers, but the dwarves used the ability to enchant their finely crafted weapons. He hated the idea that his skills had put such deadly weapons into the hands of a madman. Pavyn, the last of the new allies, worked with Machai training young dwarves in combat. His Hunter ability was the keenest Machai had seen until he had fought alongside Kenneth and Osric.

"I be fighting beside ye most of our lives, Machai. I be fighting beside ye always. Ye have me aid in yer mission." Pavyn spoke up first. "But I cannot be knowing if ye can sway Thenar, and I be far from his good graces these days. Ye willn't be winning any arguments with 'im by raising me name."

Machai nodded his appreciation and sat silently, waiting to hear where the other two stood.

"I be thinking ye all be crazy. Even if he be armed with me best weapon, no caldereth imposter can be getting through the FireFalls protections. I'd be happy to be thrusting me finest blade in his chest if he be trying." Before Kablis could interrupt with an objection, Phel said, "But if he be seeking to be putting me blades in the hands of animated corpses, I be traveling with ye to the furthest reaches of Archana to be thrusting me blade into 'im there. There be no excuse to be corrupting the good magic of Archana that way."

"Aye," Gerbim added. "He be evil, and evil ever be finding a way to be spreading its tendrils afar. Ye be having me support as well, boys."

Machai and Kablis smiled and released tense breaths. They were overwhelmingly relieved to find that they had support from so many talented dwarves. However, having the pledged aid of friends was only a fraction of what they had come home for. They needed to raise a significant force to join the Aranthians, and they couldn't do that by convincing two or three dwarves at a time. Machai stood and squared his shoulders, looking around him at the other ten men in the room. He wouldn't be appealing to Thenar alone, but he wanted to be sure he took the right men with him for the job.

Although Thenar would hold Kablis primarily responsible for the lost shipment, the seasoned dwarf had been one of the clan leader's most trusted men. That's why he was given the responsibility of heading up the delivery of weapons in the first place. Even if Kablis's presence angered Thenar, Machai needed to show that he had the support of such a widely respected dwarf, and Kablis had been there with him at the battles. If Pavyn was already on Thenar's bad side, he should stay behind. Batrel, Lers, Ieal, and Tagel had been with Kablis on the delivery, and they were the only four of Kablis's men who had made it through the battles and into FireFalls without being detected. Morgo and Krind would be valuable allies in the discussion, as both commanded a great deal of respect with the clan. Morgo ran the forges where all weapons and armor were made, and Krind was the kiln

The Weaving of Wells

master. They both oversaw many men, and their opinions would go far in persuading men to aid the Aranthians. However, Thenar would not look favorably upon the two abandoning their posts to discuss taking so many able fighters far from the walls of the clan stronghold. It would probably be best if they returned to work and used the time to get a feel for the minds of their workers on the matter. Just before Machai could announce his thoughts on the matter, a familiar but unwelcome face appeared in the doorway.

"Well, what be this? Do ye be having a reunion celebration while yer companions be rotting in the dungeons?" Threed's gravelly voice was full of contempt. "Or do ye be recruiting for yer next plot of treason?"

"Ye be out of line, Threed. Yer words be earning ye a thrashing. These dwarves be more loyal to the clan than ye be to anything but yerself," Krind snarled. "I willn't be hearing no more of yer accusations."

"Ye willn't be having to be listening to me, betrayer. Did ye not be thinking that when we be catching Kablis's men as they be running with tucked tails that we'd be coming for ye? Thenar be waiting for ye all," Threed spat back.

Machai could see the confused faces of many armed guards hovering in the passageway behind Threed. Rather than allow the turn of events to lower the conviction of his allies, Machai strode forward and slapped Threed on the shoulder.

"That be fantastic. We be needing to be speaking with Thenar about a few matters. It be good to be seeing ye again." Machai smiled widely at the dwarves behind Threed, and the tension in their postures seemed to lessen. He turned back toward his companions in the room. "Be ye ready, boys? Thenar be expecting a report, and we be making a few requests, aye?"

"Aye." The response was hesitant from some and adamant from others, but all ten dwarves rose up together and joined Machai at the door. Machai stared Threed squarely in the eye.

"Will ye be escorting us, then?"

Threed glared at Machai's implication that he was there to lead the willing party, rather than his own view of having captured nearly a dozen rebels. He turned and marched up the stone corridor without a word. Machai, Kablis, and the others fell into step behind him, saying hello to familiar faces and laughing with the guards as they always had. Even if Thenar wanted them under guard, there was no reason to let the guards think that was necessary. Machai and Pavyn had trained many of the men who were sent to apprehend them, and many had served under Kablis or alongside his men. Machai needed to keep them thinking of him and his companions as friends and clan brothers, rather than letting them be swayed by the rumors of betrayal and treason spread by the likes of Threed.

Thenar was waiting in the Grand Hall, a cavernous but richly adorned meeting hall carved into the stone of the mountain several levels below where the group had been. The ride on the lift sounded as lighthearted and casual as ever, much to the disgust of Threed, as the men jostled and joked with each other. Machai's confidence had taken all of the bite out of the dwarf, and he made no attempt to chastise the men, for fear of losing even more authority. He was one of Thenar's favored aides, a bit on the thin side with an unusually neat beard, and he had a small, jingling pouch always lashed to his belt. Threed stood at the entrance to the hall in a victorious pose as the guards led Machai and the others in with more serious expressions than they had worn on the journey from Kablis's quarters.

Thenar struck an imposing figure on the raised dais at the front of the room. His long, gray beard complemented the silver chainmail that draped his torso. A heavy cape trailed from his shoulders, runes of power embroidered onto the thick fabric in threads of gold along the hem. His hands were still hard from the calluses of daily weapon training, and his aged and wrinkled skin was thickened and greyed, resembling stone more than flesh. His sharp eyes took in every detail of Machai's confident show and the hesitant dread of most of his party. Though he had tolerated Machai's arguments the last time they had spoken, Thenar showed no indication that he would allow the same level of insubordination in such a public display as this would be. Machai prepared himself for the oncoming tirade.

Thenar eyed the party silently from his position on the raised platform. As the quiet dragged on, the group grew more uncomfortable and less confident in their convictions. Ieal and Tagel fidgeted slightly, but the others stood still, defiant against the silence. Finally, Thenar spoke with age and authority resonating in his gravelly voice.

The Weaving of Wells

"Ye be defying me orders. Ye be sacrificing me men. Ye be engaging in acts of war that I be not declaring. Ye be compromising the security of our home." He spoke slowly, accentuating each phrase with an angry but controlled snarl. "Ye be treasonous wretches, and ye be earning the name of Betrayer. What say ye"—his eyes pierced like daggers into each of the men in turn before resting on one—"Kablis?"

"Ye be correct that I be defying ye, Thenar." Kablis stood straight-backed with his head up, meeting the eye of his clan leader directly, but his voice was calm and respectful. "But ye be wrong that I be treasonous. Me actions be in the interest of the clan, and ye be too quick to be naming me Betrayer. Though ye be not declaring the war, it be only a matter of time before the war be declared on ye."

"Who be ye to be deciding the interest of the clan? Ye, who be losing the largest shipment of weapons we ever be sending through our gate? Ye, who be listening to the sniveling of a soft-hearted sap rather than the iron word of yer clan leader? Ye, who be letting half yer men turn tail and run on an approach to yer own door?"

"Where be me men, Thenar? Threed be saying they be in the dungeons. That be no place for loyal members of yer clan." Kablis's tone remained calm, but those near him on the floor could see anger rising in his eyes.

"They be me men, Kablis, not yers!" Thenar's voice climbed to a roar. "Ye should not be worrying about them." The implied threat hung heavy in the air between them.

"Aye, Thenar, they be yer men. Every one of them be loyal to ye and to the clan. As be every dwarf here on the floor before ye. We only be wanting to defeat evil before it be at our door."

"Ye be speaking of war and of evil as if it be a concern of mine. I be caring little for the petty fighting between humans. The squabbling between those men be nothing to me but gold in me coffers and bread in yer belly. I be fearing no human!" Thenar slammed a fist into his palm for emphasis.

"Aye, but Dredek be no human." Machai spoke for the first time since entering the room. Thenar's gaze snapped toward him, fury in his expression at the interruption. Machai continued in a calm, pleading tone, "Thenar, we be needing to be speaking of matters beyond the cost of yer shipment and the blow to yer pride. This man be using magic that we never be hearing of or be seeing before, and it be a terrifying thing that he be seeking. Please, let us be putting aside this conflict and be discussing the necessity of war."

"Ye be crossing me one time too many, Machai. Be silent, or be paying the price."

"Thenar, I be willing to be taking any punishment ye be doling out for me failure to return when ye be ordering it, but Machai be correct. We need to be assembling a force to be aiding the Aranthians in their cause. Defeating Dredek be more important than me own desire to be gaining yer forgiveness," Kablis said, his hands open before him in supplication.

"These doors be standing fast against many forces, and they shall be standing fast against any that be coming against them again. I willn't be sending me men out to be dying just to be saving the lives of a few humans. Ye be cowards to be doubting the ability of our stronghold so easily." Thenar's anger was evident in his volume and tone. Machai could no longer restrain himself from yelling back.

"Ye be mocking Kablis for half of his men being caught by men we be training to be catching them, but ye should be more concerned about the six of us that be making it inside using magic unknown to our clan. If *we* be using it to be breaching our defenses, what will ye be doing when an enemy be doing the same?"

"Ye be gaining access to FireFalls with yer palm, just as ye always have. Do not be trying to scare me with yer tales of new magic."

"Thenar, ye must be listening! Six of us be arriving at the door to FireFalls without being seen by our guards. Ye only be knowing we be here because the other six be Kablis's men, and we be having no reason to be hiding from ye. One dwarf, near death, be all one needs to be getting through the door once he be reaching it. Ye be a fool if ye willn't be seeing that. And an enemy may be using men he be considering disposable. What be keeping 'em from using the magic to be gaining direct access, the risks be damned?"

"Guards! Be getting this insolent fool out of me sight," Thenar yelled. The guards on the floor rushed to do his bidding, though none showed any delight in the task. Threed stood back in the doorway with a victorious sneer as Machai was led off at swordpoint.

Kablis and the others watched in shock with varying expressions of disgust and worry on their faces as Machai was led off from the chamber. They were used to Thenar's heavy hand when it came to

*** The Weaving of Wells ***

protecting the clan and maintaining order and rule, but they found it hard to believe he would go so far as to put their clansmen in the dungeons like criminals when they were only trying to prevent war. Kablis's expression quickly turned from disbelief to anger and then to acceptance. He stared up at his clan leader on the dais. Never before had he felt so little respect for the old dwarf. Suddenly the chainmail looked duller, and the heavily embroidered cape looked gaudy and pompous. Kablis no longer trusted that this bitter old man had the best interest of the clan in mind, and he couldn't stand by as he made such important decisions out of spite and anger.

"Thenar," Kablis called out clearly, his voice echoing off the chamber walls, "I regret to be defying ye once again, but ye be too blinded by yer rage to be deciding this point for the future of the clan. I be declaring a gathering. Will ye be bound by the ancient law and uphold the rites of our ancestors?"

"Aye, Kablis," Thenar hissed down at him. "Ye shall be having yer gathering, and ye shall be bound by its oaths. I be giving ye three days. With all yer new magic, that should be sufficient, should it not?" Thenar turned his back on the group and exited from the back of the dais as Machai was marched off to the dungeons.

Kablis sighed in frustration, hoping he had not just severed a lifelong friendship with his clan leader. He wasn't even sure they could accomplish a gathering, never mind win them over, but he would need Machai to pull it off.

* * *

Kablis sat at a large table, along with those who had accompanied him to the hall for the confrontation with Thenar, as well as the six of his men who had been captured on their attempt to enter FireFalls. Thenar had released them from the dungeons after granting Kablis his request to hold a gathering, but Machai still remained in a cell deep within the mountain.

"If we be wanting to have the gathering, we be needing Machai and more time. Do any of ye be having any ideas?" Kablis's concern was apparent in his creased forehead and constant fidgeting, but none of the dwarves seemed to know how to solve the problems Kablis raised. He glanced around the table at them, hoping someone would be able

Osric's Wand

to think of a way to get Machai released. "Aye, we be facing a mountain of trouble, boys."

"I be having an idea," Morgo said. Everyone turned to him expectantly and waited for him to share his thoughts. "Let us be going to the other clans. Perhaps there be a more reasonable dwarf to be hearing our plea than Thenar." A few of the men laughed softly, but Kablis nodded thoughtfully.

"Ye may be onto something. We cannot be seeking an army from other clans against Thenar's wishes, but we will need to be traveling to other clans to be raising a gathering. It may be that we can be recruiting a bit as we go." Kablis turned to Gerbim. "It willn't be solving our problems, but it may be helping at least. Gerbim, can ye be finding old Agrik? We need to be planning how to be finding our gathering members."

"Aye, he should be easy to find." Gerbim rose from the table and left the room. The others sat in silence, pondering the difficulty of their task. Gerbim returned surprisingly quickly followed by a dwarf in patchwork leather clothes. Agrik was an ancient-looking dwarf, with skin more wrinkled and gray than Thenar's. He shuffled in behind Gerbim and took a seat at the table across from Kablis.

"Ye be summoning me for a purpose, but ye should be knowing I do not like being disturbed."

"Aye, Agrik, I be knowing. Ye be the wisest dwarf I be knowing, and we be needing yer aid." Kablis spoke with great respect in his tone. "We be intending to be raising a gathering, and I be needing yer expertise with the codes."

"Aye." Agrik's voice was slow and gravelly, as though his long life had worn away any sense of urgency. "Ye be needing me expertise indeed."

"Can ye be telling us what ye be knowing of the process? We cannot be failing in our attempt, and ye be knowing more than any dwarf in this clan about the gathering." Kablis's words were heartfelt, even in their flattery.

"Aye. If ye be sure a gathering be necessary, I can be telling ye what ye be needing. It willn't be an easy task, though."

"Aye, I be assuring ye, it be necessary. And we be prepared to be doing what be needed," Kablis said.

The Weaving of Wells

"The gathering be an ancient tradition." Agrik settled more comfortably into his seat, and his speech became more animated as he continued. "In the Dwarven Realm, before FireFalls or any other clan be existing, there be only one clan of dwarves. There be no clan leaders then." Everyone listened intently to the old dwarf's words, though all had heard the tale at the feet of their elders as children. "When the clan be needing a decision, and the minds be unsettled among the wisest of dwarves, a gathering be called. It be consisting of the nine eldest dwarves in the clan, and they be the ones who be deciding the fate of the matter.

"When the great freeze be coming over the mountains of the north, and the air be so chilled that it be death to be breathing it in, the clan be calling the last gathering of the unified age. The eldest nine be meeting in the depths of the old mountain home, eyeing the flames of the fire that be keeping their blood from freezing, and they be arguing for seven days. The more they be arguing, the more the ice be building up outside, until every entrance be sealed in by the coldest ice any dwarf ever be feeling. The clan be trapped inside, and the gathering be a failure." Kablis summoned a mug of mead from a nearby tray and placed it before Agrik. He returned to his seat without a word of interruption. The old dwarf nodded gratefully and took a long draught before continuing his story. "They be finding no means of agreement on how to be saving the clan. The fighting be getting worse, and they be nearly coming to true blows. Soon the clan be breaking into factions. Some men be siding with one elder, and others be siding with others, until the clan be fractured into nine rivaling groups.

"The ice be so thick that no one could be going out hunting, and soon there be too little food for the masses. Great famine be devastating the dwarves, and nearly a third be dying before the ice be starting to thaw. By the time the sunlight be piercing through and granting the dwarves access to the outside world, the one clan be too far severed to be reconciling. The nine elders be leaving the old mountain, and nine clans be forming with them. Before the clans, with their new leaders, could be getting off the slopes of the old home, a Seer be stopping them on the frozen path. She be crying out a prophecy, and her words be echoing off the snowy cliffs.

"*Sundered stream of ancient ties, when nine seeds sever strength of one. Fear divided, anger torn, defeated by the ice and stone. If gather ye beyond the gate, beware the breaking of the line. The dwarven fall be imminent, if ye fail to gather each of nine.*

"To this day, no dwarf be willing to be risking the fall of the realm. If ye be wanting a gathering, ye need to be gathering the descendants of the nine."

"Aye Agrik, ye be telling the story of the nine clans better than any dwarf I ever be hearing." Kablis refilled the old man's mug as he spoke. "But that willn't be helping me to be finding the descendants. Can ye be telling me how to be knowing who they be?"

"Aye. Ye be needing a Chronicleer." Agrik sipped his second mug of mead slowly.

"A what now?" Lers asked, leaning forward in his seat.

"A Chronicleer." Agrik grinned slyly in Lers's direction. "Ye willn't be knowing one, lad." Agrik turned his attention back to Kablis. "There be no Chronicleers here in FireFalls, but ye should be asking Machai where one be."

Before Kablis could object that Machai was currently imprisoned in the dungeons, Agrik tipped his old bones from his chair and shuffled out of the room. Kablis stared after him with his jaw slack and frustration resurfacing. After a moment, he threw his hands up in the air and grumbled.

"If we can be sneaking into the mountain, we might as well be sneaking down to the bottom of it."

Chapter 11
The Descendants

Kablis pressed his back against the wall and waited for the two guards to round the corner ahead of him. He had managed to reach the lowest level of the mountain without incident, but he couldn't use the traveling spell to locate Machai because he had no idea which cell they were holding him in. Once he found the correct cell, he would have to find a way to speak with him without drawing the attention of the dungeon guards. He had passed nearly a dozen cells, all of which were empty. It was rare for the dwarves to have any prisoners, as few outsiders knew where the clan was, and everyone in the mountain worked toward the interest of the clan rather than against it.

Kablis moved slowly and deliberately, trailing behind the guards in silence at a far enough distance to remain unnoticed but close enough not to risk another guard coming up behind him. Just before he rounded the corner, Kablis heard Machai call out, "Can ye be bringing me a book at least?" One of the guards grunted and mumbled something, eliciting a loud laugh from the other guard. Their footsteps continued down the corridor, and Kablis eased his head around the corner. A small torch was burning outside one door in a long line of cells. Kablis assumed it was the only occupied chamber, and he waited until the guards were a good distance away before approaching it. The cell doors stood recessed into the wall far enough that Kablis could stand against the bars without being visible from down the passage. He hoped no one else would be coming along before he finished speaking to Machai.

"Ye be catching up on yer reading?" Kablis kept his voice low, but Machai glanced over at him through the bars with a smile.

"Aye, if ye mean me reading the passage of time in the cracks of these stone walls. What be yer plan for the gathering?" Machai wasted no time in seeking information about the progress toward recruiting the troops they had come for.

"We be needing a Chronicleer. Old Agrik be saying to be asking ye where one be."

Osric's Wand

"Aye." Machai nodded in thought. "I be knowing one, but I cannot be telling ye where he be. We must be speaking with Osric."

"That be difficult with ye in there. Do ye know where they be keeping yer wand and axe?"

"Aye." Machai grinned. "I be keeping 'em in me chambers."

"What?" Kablis didn't understand how that could be.

"I be knowing that Thenar would likely be overreacting. I be making sure I had me lucky charm on me." Machai pulled a small stone from a pouch on his belt, and it glowed slightly in his cupped palm. "It be keeping the spells on the cell from blocking me magic. I be using the traveling spell to be retrieving me things as soon as they be leaving me here alone. It be making no sense to be caught outside of me cell, since then Thenar would be having proof of me treason, so I be sitting here since. Ye be taking longer than I be hoping."

Kablis shook his head in disbelief and grinned. "Well, let us be grabbing yer gear and be going. We be having a few trips to be making." Both dwarves whispered the spell and then appeared standing in Machai's chambers. Machai gathered his weapons, his wand, and his traveling pack, and the two hurried down the corridor to Kablis's rooms to meet up with the others.

Machai drew his wand and established the link to contact Osric as Kablis explained the events in the dungeon to the others. A diaphanous image of Osric appeared in a display of light above the tip of Machai's wand, and the walls of the Aranthian barracks could be seen in the background behind him.

"How are things going there, Machai? Have you had any trouble convincing the dwarves to join with us?" Osric's optimism was apparent in his tone, though the dark circles under his eyes and the wrinkles in his brow showed how hard the past year had been on him.

"Aye, there be trouble anywhere I be going, but I willn't be letting ye down. We need to be speaking with Ero. Can ye be telling me how to be finding him?"

"Ero? What do you need with the eagles?" Osric asked, both surprised and concerned by the unexpected request.

"We be needing a Chronicleer, and I be hoping that Ero will be wanting to help ye again."

"I don't think the eagles will be willing to aid us in battle, but Ero may help us if it is his gift you are in need of. You will find him in the

The Weaving of Wells

Caves of D'pareth, near the eastern coast. I am sure if you can get close to the nesting grounds, Ero will find you." Osric held his hand up for them to wait. "I've got a better idea. I'll summon a dragon for you and have it take you to the eagles—we don't want you to attempt traveling that far if you've never been there."

"Aye, we cannot be traveling that far anyway. We be getting tired from the extensive use of magic here."

"What have you been doing?" Osric asked.

"It be a long story, but I can be telling ye about it when I be returning with the troops I be promising ye."

"I look forward to hearing about it. I will have Greyback to you soon. Be careful, Machai." Osric severed the link between wands and the image from Stanton disappeared. Machai turned to the others and nodded, a somber greeting after his time in the dungeon cell.

"Kablis and I be taking a short trip. I need ye to be learning what ye can about who be willing to aid us and who be determined to thwart us. When we be returning, ye must be ready to be leaving yer home if ye be with us. I cannot be telling when ye may be returning." Machai needed each dwarf to understand the stakes of joining the Aranthians by fighting with him. Thenar was unlikely to view their actions as anything other than treason, regardless of what the gathering may determine as lawful. Each man nodded without hesitation, and Machai hurried out the door with Kablis to the entrance of his mountain home. They moved swiftly and silently, avoiding others in the halls in hopes that Machai's absence would go unnoticed long enough for their allies to scatter and avoid being accused of breaking him out.

The dragon platform was located down the trail, not too far from the great doors that separated their clan from the rest of Archana. By the time Machai and Kablis arrived, Greyback was waiting patiently on the large stone platform.

"Aye, ye be as lovely as ever. Have ye fared well since we be seeing ye last?" Machai greeted the familiar dragon warmly, rubbing his small fist on her scaled snout.

"I have been doing well, and you are as fierce as ever." Greyback nuzzled the hand affectionately. "Are you sure you wish to go to see the eagles? My first visit there didn't go very well."

Osric's Wand

"Aye," Machai responded. "But this time ye will have me and me blade on yer back. If any wee eagles be seeking to attack ye, I will be having eagle stew for me supper."

Greyback grinned in a fierce display of sharp teeth, and she lowered her wing to allow the dwarves to climb onto her back. Kablis checked the gear on her back, making sure the harnesses were well secured for their flight, and they lashed their packs behind the small seats before tightening the harnesses over their shoulders and letting Greyback know they were ready.

The dragon launched herself off of the stone slab with her powerful hind legs and propelled them into the air with her wide wings. Greyback carried them swiftly into the sky, and soon the mountain faded into a hazy, snow-covered hill far below them. As she leveled out their flight, Greyback recited the traveling spell.

"Eo ire itum." The sensation of falling was even more disorienting in mid flight than on the ground, and Machai gripped the straps of his harness tightly and squeezed his eyes closed. When he opened them, it was a very different range of mountains that spread across the land beneath them.

The snow-covered peaks had been replaced with jagged, mossy cliffs, and the roar of the ocean reached them even at the great height where Greyback hovered.

"You see that valley there, off to our right? That's where I landed with a wounded wing. I would take you to one of the ledges, but I fear the eagles might think we are attacking."

As Machai eyed the many dark crevices and crags along the cliffside, he noted two large shadows dancing across the rocks. With some effort, he was able to spot the giant eagles that were casting the shadows as they flew around the peaks of their home.

"Surely, they be seeing us from that vantage point. Can ye be taking us down to the ground?"

"Of course." Greyback navigated around the lower rocks and flew out away from the mountains toward the grasslands. As soon as she had gotten away from the dangerous rocks, she landed gracefully in the open, where the eagles would be sure to find them.

Machai and Kablis had only dismounted and glanced around the area when the shadow of an eagle passed over them. They looked up just as one of the giant birds was landing nearby.

The Weaving of Wells

"We honor you, sister of the air. Do you bring us friends or foes upon your back?" The eagle's voice was softer and higher than Machai expected for his size, but he hadn't had the opportunity to speak with many eagles. Greyback responded with equal respect in her tone.

"May the winds bring you wonder. The dwarves are allies and friends of the High-Wizard. They come to seek aid from Ero, and they mean the eagles no harm." The dragon spread her wings wide to the sun as she spoke, and the eagle nodded before taking flight. Machai watched the bird glide gracefully on the currents of air, as if they were lifting him intentionally to his home. Soon, Ero landed silently next to Greyback, greeting her warmly as though they were old friends.

Machai had not spent much time with the bird, but he had gotten to know him briefly at the battles for Braya, where they aided in freeing the dragons, and Stanton when the Kalegian had attacked. He knew the eagle to be honorable and greatly knowledgeable, as well as being a friend to Osric.

"Hello again, dwarf. What brings you to my cliffs so far from your mountain home?" Ero asked.

"Me kin and I be seeking to be aiding Osric by recruiting troops from me clan, but me clan leader be having other ideas. Me kinsman, Kablis, be calling a gathering to be overruling him, but we be needing the talents of a Chronicleer to be identifying the nine members of the gathering." Machai nodded toward Kablis as a brief introduction and continued quickly. They had very little time to accomplish their goals, as Thenar had only allotted them three days to raise the gathering. "Will ye be willing to be aiding us?"

"I doubt that it is troops that Osric will be needing to end this conflict, but I don't believe it would be harmful to have the dwarves working with the humans to bring peace to Archana. I will help you if I can. What exactly is it that you need?"

"We be needing the identity of the descendants of the nine dwarves at the last gathering of the first clan. According to prophecy, we cannot be holding a gathering unless we be maintaining the lines of those original participants. Those nine elders be establishing the nine clans of the Dwarven Realm, so it be likely the blood ties be staying within the clans." Machai explained as best he could, but he was not entirely clear on what Ero would need to do to provide them with the information that they needed.

"Tracing genealogy is not usually my specialty, but as the lines are tied to prophecy, I may make an exception. Tell me, what will come of your clan if your gathering succeeds? Is this war worth the risk?"

"I cannot be saying what will be happening if we be gaining the troops, but we be assuring that Dredek be keeping the advantage over the Aranthians if we be failing. I willn't be letting Osric down." Machai squared his shoulders and gritted his teeth as he finished his declaration with a determined growl.

"Well then, shall we see what we can learn about the family lines of the dwarven clans?" Ero settled himself down into his feathers, tucking his wings in tight at his sides and closing his eyes. "Tell me the names of your nine gathering members, and I will see if I can glean who among the living has their blood running through them the swiftest."

Kablis slowly spoke the names of the eldest nine members of the first clan, giving Ero time to utilize his Chronicleer ability and trace the heritage through the ages. Machai sat in wonder, as the giant eagle appeared to be merely sleeping. Yet, after a long, silent pause Ero would scratch at the ground and open one eye to gaze down at the product of his movement. When the process was complete, there were nine names and clans etched into the dirt at Ero's feet.

Machai recited the names, committing each one to memory. The success of his mission relied on the nine dwarves, spread through the cold mountains of his realm in their respective clans, and the sun had nearly set on the first of three days.

"Ero, ye be performing a valued service for me and me kin this day. If there ever be anything that I can be doing for ye in return, ye need only be asking. I be owing ye a great debt." Machai made a formal bow and held an open hand before him in a gesture of gratitude.

"This was a satisfying use of my ability if it will serve to unify the walkers and lead to peace in Archana." Ero slowly nodded in acknowledgement of the gesture. "It is enough that you would return my effort with your own if ever I have need. Now, I know you are in a hurry. Be on your way, my friend."

The Weaving of Wells

Machai smiled in thanks and the two dwarves ran quickly back to the waiting dragon and requested a swift return to FireFalls. Greyback roused herself from her relaxed position and allowed them to scramble up her wing to the seats on her back. She had barely cleared the tops of the cliffs when she spoke the spell and transported them back to the northern mountain range, landing on the dragon platform within a few moments of when they left the Caves of D'pareth. Machai and Kablis unlashed their packs and hopped down to the stone platform. After thanking Greyback profusely with grateful words and a generous offer of coin, Kablis asked her if she would request the aid of eight more dragons willing to travel around the Dwarven Realm. She assured him that she would have dragons waiting upon their return, but that she would not accept their coin. While the dragons often still accepted payments for transporting walkers, keeping their treasure hoards growing, none of the dragons would take coin for aiding the High-Wizard or any of the people who had helped free the elder dragons from Braya. Machai added his words of gratitude before Greyback flew off, and the dwarves traveled by spoken spell directly to the front gates of FireFalls.

Machai's jaw was stern with determination, but the light steps that he and Kablis took assured the others of their success in identifying the gathering members. They indulged in a moment of celebratory congratulations from the assembled dwarves, but then they quickly set to the task of organizing the retrieval of nine dwarves.

"I be seeking Festil, blood of Gring in IronForge. Morgo, ye be finding Rhemt, blood of Metzel in SnowStand. Krind, Hern, blood of Stasp in BillowBluff. Batrel, be going for Furtl, blood of Myx in SteelBorne. Lers, be seeking Jom, blood of Tunft in BlackAxe. Phel, ye be heading to IceIsle for Kant, blood of Behg. Gerbim be finding Legin, blood of Ware in StoneStar. Pavyn, will ye be seeking out Prex, blood of Gyln in IronAnvil?"

"Aye," eight unanimous voices cried out.

"Aye, and Kablis be seeking Irto, blood of Uvet," Machai said. "He be a close advisor to Thenar, but we be hoping he can be swayed." He dismissed the group of dwarves with an ancient phrase of parting: "Be swift as water, be sturdy as stone, be sharp as ye blade, and be ye soon home. The dragons be waiting, boys."

Chapter 12
Portent Hunt

It felt good to be walking for long periods again. Though his strength wasn't ready for a fight just yet, he was more than comfortable making excursions out into the tunnels to look for the things he needed. Dredek was finding the Portentist gift more than useful in that respect.

It had taken some getting used to, understanding the gift's pull, but soon Dredek found it easy to determine the direction the gift was indicating with every distinct pull. At times the gift was rather alarming, as there were many dangers in the world that could hold import if one was foolish enough to partake. Learning that each pull of danger held different levels of urgency was a humiliating lesson. Everyone knew the dragon's claw plant was dangerous when ingested, but his early experiments with the Portentist gift had him diving for cover when the door to a room containing the plant was opened. Luckily, he had been off searching rooms on his own when it had occurred.

He kept his daily searches as yet another step to help him to regain his strength, and it was working. He could feel the strength returning, and he had been able to spend a great deal more time stabilizing the Portentist gift. He thought back to the fight that he had had with Osric, wishing he had been able to retrieve the sword wand before he had to flee. All of his troubles would have solved themselves if he could have learned how to use the wand to gain powers as fast as Osric had.

Getting stabbed by the woman had been the turning point in securing the wand, and if she hadn't arrived after he had already bonded the Portentist gift, rendering him virtually useless in battle, then they would never have escaped. But it made no sense to dwell on things beyond his control. He had gained another gift, and if his calculations were correct he would have more than enough power to complete his goals.

He had to focus on current issues, and locating deadman's stalk was the most pressing issue on his mind. Luckily, one of the irua they were holding captive told them about several large apothecary shops

The Weaving of Wells

on some of the lower levels. He decided to leave the two furthest locations to the younger humans in his army. The Portentist gift had signified that the closer location held something that was important to him. He needed the time to figure out if it was merely deadman's stalk, or possibly something else.

The tunnels were dark, lit only by his wand, but it was more than adequate for his eyes. It was the perfect exercise to help him fine-tune his use of the Portentist gift. Turning right, Dredek was greeted by an expansive opening—the light from his wand only lit a small portion of the room. If it weren't for the ceiling of stone above him, he would have sworn he had just turned into a market street. The walls were lined with small globes that began to come to life as he passed, and light slowly filled the expanse as he moved deeper into the chamber.

After the lamps came to life, Dredek looked closely at his surroundings. Water flowed from a central fountain. A large statue of an irua male stood in the center with a weasel perched on his shoulder, and water cascaded above a hand held over a spire that rose from the center of the pool of water. The way the lights reflected in the square made it appear that the water flowed up and into the outstretched hand.

Light continued to grow in the distance, and abandoned shops stretched on as far as he could see down rows of buildings. Portent had brought him to the location, but it was difficult to sense a direction from its pull. Dredek paced the area surrounding the statue, allowing the gift to become more familiar.

He allowed himself to drift, and two blue doors grew closer as he let his instincts guide him. Light brown walls stood sentry to the side, and a sign over the door displayed a bowl of bubbling liquid. Dredek felt compelled to enter the building.

He opened the door. As the light of his wand fought off the darkness, he saw wooden bowls stacked on shelves and dried herbs tied together and left dangling from hooks. He followed a path that led him around the low countertop laden with candles, and he opened the first drawer nearest the back wall. Three petrified deadman's stalks rolled to the front of the drawer with a clatter. Dredek smiled as he pulled them free and stuffed them into a pouch at his waist. It was almost enough for what he needed, and he continued to explore the room.

Osric's Wand

Another drawer contained twine, swine bones, beeswax, ink, three quills, and a heavy coin box. At first, Dredek disregarded the contents to continue searching, but after a moment of thought he stowed the beeswax, ink, and quills in his pouch alongside the stalks.

He still felt the presence of something crucial to his plans, but what it was that kept pressing its urgency he could not tell. He turned over every bowl and opened every drawer, but not another stalk was found. He began to pace, walking to the back of the room and then to the front repeatedly.

His footsteps echoed throughout the small space, and after a time he could tell his location in the room by the tone of the footfall alone. Each knock of his boot filled him with rage as the source of the meaningful draw on his gift evaded him.

Thwonk, thwonk, thunk, thwonk, thwonk.

Dredek began to loathe whoever had built the shop. The walls and shelves appeared to be built of sturdy supplies, but he must have run short of materials when building the floor.

Thwonk, thwonk, thunk, thwonk, thwonk.

Each time he crossed the room he grew angrier, and imagining how he might kill the man was his only comfort.

Thwonk, thwonk, thunk, thwonk, thwonk.

He could rip the life strand directly from his body or pull it taut as a lute string, pulling more and watching as each anchor snapped one at a time while screams of pain rang out and echoed throughout the corridors. Until, days later, he would let the life strand and another new gift become a part of his own growing power.

Thwonk, thwonk, thunk, thwonk, thwonk.

Or, he could use his discovered ability to rend life strands merely to end the man's life, not taking the gift for himself. He wouldn't have to go through the long recovery process if he simply let Archana have its magic back. The man probably didn't have a very useful gift anyway, or he should be able to raise the funds to cover the supplies for a decent floor.

Thwonk, thwonk, thunk, thwonk, thwonk.
Thwonk, thwonk, thunk, thwonk...

Dredek stopped as the memory of Aeya, his mate, forced its way into his mind. He trembled with pain as his memory of her replayed, as it often did in moments of stress.

The Weaving of Wells

"Make sure to remind Gidaun to check my calculations, love. The boys and I should not be too long, but if you are leaving camp tonight, I want to make sure our records of the natural well are correct." She had been radiant in her lavender dress. He had heard others describe his race as clammy and pale, but as he remembered her face, that description did not fit. Her white skin was dewy and opalescent in the dim light of the room.

She had been in charge of collecting data on the many untapped minor wells they encountered on their trek to the Irua Realm. He, not being a Wand-Maker of any note, had been delegated the task of scouting the next day's route for his entire race. That was the last conversation they had had before he left on horseback in the dark to scout a route to the next well. Verifying her calculations had been her way of making sure he was heading in the correct direction, but he loved the way her long, thin arms moved about gathering books and bags.

He hadn't understood half of the things in her books, but over the hundreds of years of solitude since her death, he felt that he had gotten to know her better through studying her math and notes. She had been so careful, so meticulous in every detail. That was one of the many things he had adored, one of her many attributes that was so endearing. She had never let anything leave her desk until she was sure it was done right. It had been worked and reworked before any eyes other than her own had witnessed the contents.

He had kissed her softly on her shoulder, then bid Chehl and Tweggan goodnight. Watching the three of them walk off into the encampment was the last memory he had of his family alive. The human army had moved in and slaughtered every caldereth the next day. He returned three days later, after scouting, to discover the massacre, but if all went as planned, he would have another life to live with them. He would be able to tell them how much he had missed them.

A tear fell from his cheek and Dredek stepped back to watch it fall. The tear was his gift, his seed of love and of hope. Only he was the one to bear the sins of the last few decades to bring about the resurrection of his people. But that seed, that seed would grow.

Thunk, thunk.

Osric's Wand

His footsteps echoed again throughout the room, yet there was something more to it that he had missed as he had been throwing things around in the room.

Thunk, thunk.

Dredek stomped his feet hard in the center of the room and looked down. The footfalls in this spot had echoed, but not only in the room he now occupied. There was something else, and that something else was below.

He summoned the Wand-Maker sight and looked down, hoping to see some magical trigger that would release a mechanism to open a door, but he saw nothing. He then looked closely at the wooden panels, but nothing stood out. He decided he would have to take it one board at a time; he knew there had to be a pattern—something that would hint at a way to get to the opening below.

Before he could start, he noticed that a group of three of the wooden planks stood slightly higher than the others in front of the desk at the back of the room. He studied the oddity carefully, and as they extended away from the wall, a full stride passed before any nails secured them in place. The next two on either side of the three were shortened, but showed the same pattern. A triangular shape was laid out in rough, staggered boards, but only the edges had been secured with nails.

He pressed on the end of a short side panel. It took a bit of force before it gave way, flipping up as if on a hinge and revealing a metal handle. He wrapped his slender yet strong hands around the cold metal and pulled hard. The even, flat bottom of the triangle raised up to hinge on the point at the back of the room. A small stairway led beyond the back of the room and into a great darkness that slowly began to light itself with a soft white light.

With a weary eye, Dredek scanned the stairs. There were no magic traps, but there had been no magic in the door either. He stepped slowly back and then carefully went down the wide wooden staircase, watching carefully for some hidden trap. Portent surged that danger was approaching rapidly as his foot brushed the top of the third step. Dredek dove backward out of the stairwell and onto the floor of the shop. Three small thuds rose from the stairs in quick succession.

He rolled over, groaning from the former exertion, and sat up to rub his right knee where he had slammed it into the top step when he had

The Weaving of Wells

tumbled onto the wooden floorboards. He turned to look in the stairwell. Three large, barbed darts with green-feathered tails pierced the backs of three steps—a viscous black liquid dripped from the barbed shafts and hissed as it hit the wooden stairs.

A voice swore in the irua language from somewhere below and Dredek jumped to his feet, drawing his wand. Footfalls sounded as three irua burst from below, casting spells blindly in their attempt to escape the room. The poorly aimed spells were easy to avoid, so Dredek stepped aside as the blasts knocked over a bookshelf. With a simple flick of his wrist, he locked the door with his wand from across the room. Even with the natural speed of his race, he wouldn't be able to leap over the staircase and round the counter before they were able to unlock the door, but it would slow them down. And if he could manage to stun them, he had a chance of being able to capture them.

In a flash he moved out of the way of another blast—now they were taking the time to aim before casting. He pulled one of his daggers out from behind his back and threw it, knocking the wand out of the hand of the middle irua, a woman. The wand broke in half, taking one of the spell sources out of the equation. Dredek grinned a wicked smile as the other two turned with wide eyes to focus their attention on him.

The man at the door was thicker than most of the irua he had seen since capturing the city. He wore a thick woolen cloak, split at the neck, and his silver hair lent an ominous cast to his stern expression. Was this a family? They each had some characteristic of the older man at the door, and the younger man stepped in front of the wandless woman with fear and panic on his face.

Dredek dove behind the raised stair cover as both of the men cast spells at him. Quickly, he stood back up and darted out, stunning the younger male. The silver-haired man screamed in horror, launching himself across the room in a rage. After that, it was easy work to stun him and then the girl.

With the three unconscious, Dredek circled the desk and peered inside the eldest of the three. He had the gift of Brawn, but nothing that interested him. It wasn't a gift worth stealing, and he was in no condition to attempt another merger at this time. There would be no time to add another gift before reviving the caldereth; he needed to gather his strength for that feat alone.

<u>Osric's Wand</u>

The young boy's gift amplified his hearing, but he was wearing several useful charms that would ward away spells with more than a stun to them. He took them off of the boy. He had no use for them himself, but getting answers from someone was difficult if they were impervious to the torture.

When he got to the girl, he found a gift he was altogether familiar with. It wasn't his gift, but another exceedingly rare gift. Aeya had been an Auctus as well. An Auctus could manipulate the structure and growth patterns of a plant without injuring it. With a great deal of skill, one could cause a plant to grow at an astonishing rate, and then stop it when it reached the desired size.

Aeya had had a special way of wielding her gift. Their home had been full of plants that she had carefully cultured over her lifetime. Several had been manipulated and altered to become completely different plants.

He had been so caught off guard by the sight of the gift that he nearly missed the sight of the curled, fibrous, and nearly invisible strand that wrapped itself around the young woman's life strand. Dredek sat down, contemplating the discovery of the key into the Well of Strands and saddened by another forced remembrance of Aeya. Yet, in spite of his pain, he knew what he had to do. He knew, but he needed a few moments to gather his thoughts and his strength. The short battle had taken more out of him than he had expected.

I'll have to bind their hands and feet, he thought while they were unconscious, *and then I'll sit and rest. When I'm feeling better I should call Jalyn to bring a few guards. I should be able to greet them on my feet by then.*

Chapter 13
IronForge

Treethorn was as fast as Machai remembered, and though he feared the wind would tear him from her back at any moment, Machai found he was still quite fond of the petite green dragon. She was just as pleased to see him again, and her aerial antics turned his face a pale shade of green.

The sun had set, but Treethorn was familiar with the cold mountains. Since being released from her volcano prison, she had spent as much time as she could flying around the various realms of Archana. With the aid of the traveling spell, she had seen more of the world in a few months than any dwarf had seen in his lifetime. The gift of Endurism, the same ability that allowed dragons to use an immense amount of sustained magic to keep their bulky bodies in the sky, allowed them to use the spoken spell time and again without experiencing the fatigue felt by other creatures.

Treethorn had traveled as far by spell as was safe, but the IronForge clan's home was located deep in the most treacherous region of the northern mountains. She couldn't risk appearing too close to the jagged peaks or in the throes of an ice storm, so they would fly north for some time before reaching the dragon platform. Machai tried to calm the gnawing fear in his stomach that any of them might fail to find the gathering members—that he might fail. He tightened his leather hood against the cold wind and grasped the restraints tighter as Treethorn sped through the skies at top speeds.

She slowed considerably as they approached heavy, black clouds hanging in their path.

"You won't have time to go on foot, but this is going to be a very unpleasant last leg of our flight. I had hoped the weather would favor us, but that isn't the case."

Machai felt the first stinging bite of sleet against his face as she spoke, and he bent forward to expose as little skin to the elements as possible.

"Ye just be getting us to the platform, little dragon. If ye can still be flying, I can be riding it out." He gritted his teeth against the frozen air, and Treethorn increased her speed. She couldn't fly any faster, as the ice storm was quickly limiting her vision and her wings were accruing a heavy coat of ice, but if she went any slower they would be in the cold too long and die from exposure. Machai let go of the straps with one hand, moving his fingers rapidly to restore the circulation, and drew his wand. He struggled to focus on the spell and his ability, but in spite of the frigid air that whipped around him he managed. It took all of his strength to maintain the spell, but he was able to use his Fire Elementalist ability in combination with a shielding spell to create a bubble of warm air around them. Luckily Treethorn was so small or he may not have been able to keep the shield around her whole body.

The ice melted quickly from her wings, and her muscles relaxed enough to smooth her movements and steady his wand hand. The warmth eased his own tension as well, and the shield blocked much of the wind. Though the sustained spell tested his stamina to its boundaries, he was able to keep them from freezing. There was nothing he could do to improve the dragon's visibility, and his heart raced as rocky cliffs and icy peaks seemed to rush toward them with no warning. The lithe little dragon evaded them all, and they landed safely on the platform near IronForge as the moon was reaching its nightly apex.

Machai slipped from the dragon's back, barely keeping his feet beneath him on the icy platform. With what little strength he had left, he used his gift to light several fires on the stone slab around the dragon and his wand to erect a minor shield above her. The storm would continue to rage, but she would be relatively comfortable as she awaited his return. Machai sheathed his wand, too tired to ease his own discomfort from the cold and ice, and hunkered into his cloak as he made his way toward the entrance of IronForge.

While FireFalls's door had been secreted away in a crevice, surrounded by the beautiful mountains and valleys Machai called home, IronForge needed no such precautions to prevent visitors. It was nearly impossible to reach the fortress without flying in, and the frequent ice storms deterred anyone from wanting to. The narrow path that led away from the dragon platform was dangerous enough, but at least the stone and gravel provided some traction to the ice and snow. Just ahead of him, Machai could make out the last span of his journey

The Weaving of Wells

to the doors of IronForge: an iron bridge that spanned a great chasm, swaying in the icy wind.

Just before the bridge, a cave was carved into the mountainside. Machai ducked inside and warmed his hands above the small fire that was always burning there. He wasn't sure he could wait out the storm before crossing the bridge, for this far north the ice could be hurled from the stormclouds for days without letting up. He sat against the stone wall furthest from the cold wind blowing across the entrance and rested. He needed to regain enough of his strength to travel by spell to the solid stone beyond the bridge, as each step on the icy metal could send him sliding off of the edge and plummeting to his death.

Machai struggled to fend off his exhaustion with thoughts of how important his mission was. Usually, after expending so much magic, he would need a hearty meal and a full night's sleep to recover. He could afford no such luxury as sleep or sustenance. He sat motionless for longer than he felt he should, but he hoped it was enough. Rising from the stone floor, he warmed himself briefly close to the flames and stepped back out into the icy onslaught.

His footsteps were hesitant on the slippery stone as he approached the treacherous bridge. The wind blew sheets of ice toward him, whipping his cloak against his body and stinging his eyes. He was able to make out only the slight impression of the great iron doors that stood beyond the swaying bridge, and he waited for a lull in the storm to clear his vision. He needed a view clear enough to ensure that he would appear on solid ground across the chasm. Luckily the wind, seeming to hear his silent plea, calmed for a moment just before the moon dipped behind the steep mountain and stole the light he needed to see. Machai spoke the spell in the brief intermission, hoping the sense of falling was from his transportation and not the wind driving him down into the black abyss.

He appeared before the doors, assured himself that it was truly stone beneath his boots, and gazed up at the immense iron barricade that marked the entrance of the IronForge clan. The wind resumed its vicious attack, ice pelting his cloak and clinging in his beard. Machai wrapped the cloth strip that kept his hand shielded from the ice and wind tighter and gripped the large metal striker firmly. The hammer was embedded in the stone and hinged on a spring. He drew it back toward himself firmly, and when he released his grip the hammer reversed direction and struck the door solidly. The reverberations of the gong strike echoed throughout the chamber beyond the door, and he hoped a warm welcome awaited him.

He grew concerned that his summons would go unanswered as the night grew colder and darker. He considered using the striker again, but before he could pull the hammer back, a small square concealed by the pattern of the door slid aside to reveal a flickering light inside.

"Who be daring the mountain in an ice storm?"

"I be Machai of FireFalls, seeking admittance and an audience with Festil, blood of Gring, the mighty founder of IronForge."

"Ye be daft to be coming here in this weather. Be ye mad, or be ye desperate?"

"I be only a touch of both, me friend. A gathering be summoned, and I be seeking a member of the nine."

"Aye, ye be desperate then. Mean ye any harm to IronForge or its clan members?"

"Nay, no harm at all. I be here as a dwarven cousin, friend and ally to IronForge."

"Aye, ye be true." The small door slid closed and Machai heard a loud creaking just before the warmth and light of the mountain's interior spilled out to embrace him.

Machai stepped through the iron gateway into a well-lit tunnel. Large fires roared on either side of the door, though like the fire in the cave no wood fed the flames, and Machai welcomed the warmth that thawed his bones and left his cloak melting puddles on the stone floor. The Trust who had queried him through the small window waved a hand impatiently at him, and he hurried after the retreating figure.

The tunnel went deep into the mountain, making Machai feel at home in the almost familiar passageway. However, rather than encountering a gaping chasm at his feet, they passed through several crossways where small openings in the stone walls blew warm air across the tunnel.

"What be the winds?" Machai asked his guide.

"Spells of protection. If ye be passing before me, rather than after me, ye be catching on fire instead of feeling a warm breeze on yer cheeks."

The Weaving of Wells

Machai nodded silently, glaring at the dwarf's back for failing to tell him so before they started walking down the passage. At regularly spaced intervals, torches were set into iron brackets just above their heads. The light made the space seem larger than it was, but the thick smell of smoke made the stone walls seem imposing. Machai wondered why the area was not better ventilated. He looked around, taking notice of the various protections that were in place to protect the clan from intruders.

In addition to the winds, Machai noticed a portcullis as they passed beneath it. The grooves in the stone in which it would slide down to block the tunnel were nearly imperceptible. In several places, there were lines of small holes in the walls, with arrow tips glinting just inside. Machai wondered how they were triggered, as his guide didn't seem concerned about walking past them. Just beyond the last of the recessed arrows, they passed under another portcullis. Machai realized that a fairly formidable force could be caged between the two grates, and triggering the arrows would decimate the majority of those within. Though he was sure there were other ways of getting in and out of the mountain, Machai was impressed that the entrance was so well defended. An army may make it across the iron bridge and through the doors, but it was likely to be completely wiped out before anyone could reach the end of the main tunnel. After one last gush of hot air, Machai and his guide emerged from the passage into a large open chamber.

To his left and right, several smaller tunnels branched off, and directly across from him two staircases led to higher and lower levels in the mountain. The Trust turned to Machai and then indicated a stone bench against the wall near the opening of the tunnel they had just come from.

"Be taking a seat. I can be seeking Festil, but ye may need to be speaking with Gorin first."

Machai sat on the bench, trying to recall if Gorin was the name of the IronForge clan leader. As a boy, he had learned much of the history of the nine clans. He had known the names of all of the clan leaders then, and most of their children's names as well, but he had forgotten many of them over the years. His work in training young dwarves to wield weapon and wand had required little knowledge of politics and even less of diplomacy with the other clans.

<u>Osric's Wand</u>

Before he could recall for sure, two young ladies appeared from one of the tunnels to his right. Both had blue kerchiefs tied over their heads, covering brunette curls, and both wore white aprons. The first carried a tray on one hand and a mug in the other. The second placed a small table before him so her companion could unload her burdens. They turned without speaking to him, but they giggled as they retreated into the same tunnel again. Machai shook his head slowly, wishing they hadn't left so fast, but he was grateful for the meal. A dark bread, a soft white cheese, and a dried fruit that he didn't recognize were arranged neatly on the platter. The mug held cold water, and Machai had nearly finished it all when he heard the sound of jingling chainmail and heavy boots approaching.

The armored dwarf came up the staircase across the chamber. A short sword was scabbarded at his hip, but no helmet covered his blond hair and beard. A thick scar traced the length of his face, from his left temple to his jaw, and he scowled at Machai as if he were the one who had given it to him. He stopped in front of Machai, eyeing him suspiciously before speaking.

"Ye be seeking Festil for a gathering of nine?"

"Aye." Machai stood up, but his tone was polite.

"Ye willn't be speaking with him, unless ye be convincing me of yer mission."

"Ye be Gorin, the leader of IronForge?" Machai asked.

"Aye."

"Though I be short of time, and the ice be raging outside yer iron doors, I would be speaking with ye of the state of Archana. Then, ye will be seeing me need for Festil and the gathering of nine."

"Aye," Gorin said, seeming to come to some conclusion about Machai as he briefly assessed his words and manner. "Be following me to me chambers, and ye can be saying yer piece."

Machai followed him across the room, and they ascended the stairs to the next level up. They spoke little as they walked, and the stone walls with interspersed torches changed even less as they moved further into the mountain. Upon entering Gorin's rooms, however, Machai was struck by the lush decorations and the elaborate furnishings. The main corridors may be plain and unadorned, but the clan leader's chambers were a study in generations of spending gold on frivolous novelties and domestic comforts.

The Weaving of Wells

The front room was carpeted in thick rugs, and heavy, brightly colored tapestries covered every wall. An elegant chandelier was suspended in the air above a large round table. Eighteen chairs encircled the wooden table, and the finish was such a glossed stain that Machai could see his face reflected in its surface. Tables and shelves held jewel-encrusted statues, large gilt-framed paintings, old books and scrolls, and crystal trinkets. The richness and beauty of the room was overwhelmed by its clutter and opulence, and Gorin looked like a rough and unpolished rock amid the gold and gems. Through an open doorway in the far wall, Machai could see a massive four-poster bed draped in dark red curtains and skirted with layers of gold linen and lace. Several swords hung on the walls around the bed amid portraits of stern-faced dwarves in gleaming armor.

Machai could not help but shake his head, wondering if Gorin relished the luxury of his surroundings as much as those who had come before him. Surely it had taken many generations for the variety of items to be collected in one place, and Machai hoped that the current clan leader cared less for gold than the collection implied. Then, Machai wondered why Gorin had chosen his chambers, with such decadence, as the location for their discussion.

"Why do ye be calling a gathering? Surely the FireFalls clan be needing wiser dwarves to be making decisions than Thenar, but a gathering be a bit extreme," Gorin said loudly, refusing to hide his dislike of Machai's clan leader in tone or in volume. Machai bit back a sarcastic retort about the impossibility of finding wisdom in such surroundings.

"Thenar be seeking to be protecting the clan, but we be in need of dwarves who can be seeing the distant future as well as the near. There be a wizard in Angmar seeking to be raising his kin from the dead, and it be likely that he has found the power he be needing to succeed." Gorin's eyes went wide at Machai's words. "We be calling a gathering to seek the consent of the nine clans to be marching an army out to meet this madness."

"Aye, Thenar be content behind his stone mountain, huh?"

"Aye," Machai said. "We willn't be ignoring the threat of new magic in the world, but we cannot be recruiting enough men with Thenar threatening charges of treason."

125

Osric's Wand

"I believe we can be aiding each other, Machai, and ye may yet get yer army. I will send Festil with ye to the gathering if ye can be obtaining something for me in exchange. I be knowing that FireFalls recently be acquiring a large shipment of gems for imbuing. Ye be bringing me a number of these gems, and I will be giving ye what ye be wanting."

"IronForge be a clan of mercenaries now, Gorin?" Machai glared at the greed on display in the room as well as in the clan leader.

"Not mercenaries—merchants. We be good at seeing profits where others be seeing *problems*." Gorin's voice dropped low as he emphasized the last word, making Machai angrier at the intended threat.

"Nay. I willn't be paying ye a single coin." Machai stepped closer to Gorin. "When was the last time anyone be knocking on yer door in the middle of an ice storm?"

Gorin's brow furrowed and he took a step back, startled by the change of topic.

"It be happening rarely, if at all."

"How do ye be thinking I be making it here tonight?" Machai didn't wait for Gorin to respond. "I be traveling here from FireFalls in the time it be taking yer servants to polish one gaudy trinket in yer rooms. I be crossing the iron bridge without ever touching foot to it. And if I can be arriving at yer door with so few *problems*, ye can be sure that others will be able to as well."

"Are ye threatening me, Machai?" Gorin's hand rested lightly on the wand secured at his hip.

"No. I be offering ye a great reward for aiding the Dwarven Realm in a time of great necessity. Ye will be sending Festil back with me for the gathering, and as soon as the storm be lifting ye will be supplying three hundred men with weapons and armor and be marching them to the Iron Valley. All of yer men who be passing me scrutiny for battle will be taught new forms of magic and strategy to help defend yer home and yer people from the magic that could be used against ye by yer true enemies."

"How dare ye try to be persuading me to be handing the lives of me men over to ye on the threat of some distant and ambiguous magic. Ye should be spending time in me dungeons for yer insolence."

The Weaving of Wells

Machai recited the traveling spell so softly under his breath that Gorin could not have heard him over the angry rush of his own blood in his ears. He appeared directly behind Gorin, seated at the round table. Before the clan leader thought to look around for him, Machai spoke.

"Now ye be sounding like Thenar. He likely believes that I be in his dungeons right now, since that be the last place he be sending me."

Gorin spun around, his mouth hanging open and his hands clenched into fists.

"How can ye be doing such a thing? Ye don't even have a wand in yer hand."

"As I be saying, there be new magics spreading across Archana. Do ye be wanting yer men to be learning new magic, or to be open to attack by it for lack of the proper defense strategies?" Machai asked, resting his empty hands lightly on the smooth, polished table. Gorin stood silently for a moment, glaring at Machai and cracking his knuckles.

"Three hundred men, ye said?"

* * *

Treethorn landed on the dragon platform near FireFalls just as the sun was coming up over the mountains. The ice storm had subsided slightly during the night, and with Festil maintaining a shield and Machai warming the air around them with his gift, they were able to make it to calm skies, where the dragon could safely use the traveling spell. Machai slid down the dragon's wing and helped his shaky companion to the ground. Though it had been a while, and a great deal had happened since then, Machai could still remember how disorienting the spoken spell was the first time he experienced it. He understood why Festil was unsteady on his feet, but they had little time for him to gain his bearings. Machai thanked Treethorn for exposing herself to such harsh conditions on his behalf, and he offered to reward her with a generous amount of coins from his pouch. After all she had gone through for him, Machai would willingly part with the small fortune. However, she refused that payment with an indignant laugh and flew off to bask in the warm sunlight and to seek a hearty meal. Then, Machai hurried Festil through the halls of

Osric's Wand

FireFalls to Kablis's chambers, hoping they would find that most of the nine gathering members had arrived during the night. Only five new faces greeted him when they walked into the room.

"Where be the other three?" Machai asked as he sank into an overstuffed chair against one wall.

"There be no word yet from Phel, but IceIsle be a long way." Kablis took the seat next to Machai. "Gerbim be reaching me by wand. He be finding Legin in StoneStar, and they should be here anytime. Morgo went to SnowStand, but Rhemt be heading for Barlington on trade. Morgo be following the river looking for the boat he be on, but since me wand be silent it be likely he still be searching."

Machai eyed Festil and the other dwarves from the various clans, and he wondered what they would need to hear to be convinced that war was the correct choice for the Dwarven Realm. Festil was fairly young, but the stern gaze of the IronForge clan was firmly etched in his features, and he had shed the instability of his shock at traveling by spell. His blond beard was trimmed straight across at his chest, and he wore his long hair in a single braid down his back. Krind had welcomed Festil warmly when he followed Machai into the room, providing warm food and mead to the newcomer as he ushered him to the large table in the center of the room. The guests sat around the table, trading stories of their clans' recent happenings and discussing the various ideas they each had about what a gathering would entail. They knew why they were there, but none of them had ever been present at a gathering.

Machai slipped in and out of sleep while sitting in the chair, the exhaustion of having used so much magic catching up to him, as conversations and laughter drifted around him. Around mid'day, Gerbim arrived with Legin and with news of Phel, who had spent the entire night arguing with the clan leader of IceIsle. Kant was the leader's uncle, an old dwarf that had rarely left his clan's walls in recent years. However, his spine was still straight and stong and his hands still thickly calloused from weapons training. Phel had tried to make the leader of IceIsle see that Kant was needed to complete the gathering, but the protective younger dwarf refused to yield. Phel had contacted Gerbim, seeking advice on what he should do, when Kant walked up and slapped a wrinkled hand on his nephew's back. The old

The Weaving of Wells

dwarf had listened to the men argue all night, and when it seemed that Phel might give up, Kant had looked his nephew in the eye and said, "Ye be too kind and too foolish to be of me blood, and ye be too young to be dictating me life or me death. A gathering be the highest honor ye may ever receive as a descendant of Behg the Brutal. I be going now, with or without yer blessing. It be me right and me responsibility to be knocking some sense into these foolish young dwarves who be bent on a foreign war."

Phel and Kant arrived shortly after Gerbim, and the absence of Morgo and the last of the nine gathering members settled over the room like a fog. Machai roused himself from his sporadic slumber and sent a young dwarf who earned coin by running errands to get a tonic from the healers. He needed something that would restore alertness and ease the magical fatigue. It was an expensive remedy, but Machai would have no time for the sleep he needed until after the gathering was over.

When the small vial of foul-smelling liquid arrived, Machai drank it quickly with a grimace. He struggled to keep it down, but once his stomach had settled he began to feel a bit better. Soon, he was nearly back to his normal self, and he found Kablis in the next room.

"How can we be aiding Morgo to be finding Rhemt so we can be getting this gathering over with?" Machai asked. Kablis glanced up with a worried expression.

"I cannot be saying, though I wish I be knowing. Perhaps if we be sending more men? We be sure he be on a boat, but Morgo cannot be traveling any faster than the dragon can be flying. We be fearing that the spoken spell may be taking him past the boat and he could be missing it."

"What be the furthest south the boat could be stopping before Rhemt be heading east for Barlington?" Machai asked.

"There be a small port city on the coast, though I cannot be recalling its name. Rhemt be either gaining a ship to be sailing along the coast from there, or calling a dragon somewhere between the forks and the coast. It be impossible to be saying where he be disembarking if he be taking a dragon over land."

"Aye. Be calling us dragons. Ye be traveling to the coast and flying north, and I be starting at the forks and doing the same. Whoever be finding the boat first can be calling the others by dragon. We need to be finding it fast." Machai waited only long enough for a nod of confirmation from Kablis before turning and rushing into the outer room. "Krind, Kablis and I be heading out to aid Morgo in the search. I need ye to be bringing Agrik in to be preparing these men for their service in the gathering. I cannot be saying what he may be needing for preparations, but ye be getting him anything he be asking for, aye?"

"Aye." Krind placed the pitcher of water he had been pouring for their guests on the table, smiled reassuringly at the dwarves gathered around and waiting anxiously, and hurried from the room to find the old man who knew more of dwarven lore than any other alive. Machai followed closely on his heels, but he turned toward the stone lift rather than trailing Krind deeper into the mountain. He needed to reach the dragon platform quickly, as each moment of delay in finding the ninth member put the gathering at greater risk of failure.

When Machai reached the platform, Kablis had just arrived and was summoning the dragons. In one corner of the large slab of stone that served for a landing space was a small, narrow structure. The stone brick walls stood only a bit taller than Kablis, and the roof was made of thickly thatched straw treated with sap from the lentum trees that grew along the mountain springs throughout the region. The sticky substance kept the small building surprisingly immune to the elements, protecting the riding gear that was stored inside.

Just inside the door, mounted into the wall, was a pulsing green emerald spelled to link up with the dragons' telepathic abilities. Kablis placed his hand over the stone charm, worn smooth not by polishing but by the touch of dwarven hands over the generations. The warmth of his hand activated the spell, and once the pulsing became a steady glow, Kablis tapped the emerald twice with the tip of his wand, signaling that he needed two dragons to respond to the summons.

They waited only moments before the first of the mighty creatures appeared in the sky above them. The dragon's wide wings stirred up the snow around the platform as he beat them quickly and powerfully to slow his descent and land gracefully before the two dwarves. A second dragon was not far behind. Machai approached the first one, a massive grey-colored male he had never met before. He bowed low before it, and the dragon watched him silently with blue eyes the size of Machai's head.

The Weaving of Wells

"I be immensely grateful that ye be responding to me summons. I know the dragons be an honorable and free species, and ye be under no obligation to be carrying me aside from yer loyalty to the High-Wizard. I be loyal to him too."

"You know more than most, dwarf, yet you still summon us. Where is it you ask us to carry you?" The voice rumbled deeply from the great dragon's throat.

"I be needing to reach the forks of the river, south of Stanton. Me companion be needing to fly further, to where the river becomes the sea." Machai indicated Kablis with a nod. "We need to be finding a boat that be traveling downriver. We be asking ye to carry us out of great need, but we willn't make demands of ye. If ye be willing to aid us and the High-Wizard's cause, we would be extremely grateful for yer help. We cannot be paying ye what ye deserve for yer service, but we will be paying ye what we can."

The dragon did not respond immediately, and from the still posture of the second dragon, Machai assumed that the two were communicating through their telepathic link. Kablis stood near the smaller female, waiting for the decision.

"Keep your coins, dwarf. We will aid you out of gratitude for your role in our freedom." The surprised expression on Machai's face made the dragon rumble with laughter. "Do you think you are unknown among the dragons, Machai? I know who you are, and I would be honored to carry you wherever you wish to fly."

Humbled, Machai bowed again in gratitude. "Ye be doing me a great honor. May I be asking ye for yer name?"

"I am Cinereus, and this is Zephyr. Ready your gear, my small friends."

Machai and Kablis worked quickly, helping each other to secure the harnesses onto each of the dragon's backs. They lashed their gear behind the seats, and when they had strapped themselves in they called up to the dragons, announcing that they were ready to fly. Machai nodded over at Kablis, hoping one of them would be able to intercept the boat before they lost Rhemt on land, and Cinereus launched himself into the air with a powerful lunge from his hind legs. His wings beat against the cool air, lifting them high into the air above FireFalls. The sun was still a few fingers above the highest peak, but the end of the second day was coming swiftly. They needed to locate

Osric's Wand

Rhemt and return to the clan before night. Machai wanted time for all nine members to be fully prepared for the ceremony of the gathering, and he wanted to be able to rest before pleading his case before them.

"Once we clear these last few peaks I can utilize the traveling spell. You want to begin your search where the Dimon River meets the Diutinus River, near the village of Bridges?" Cinereus's deep rumble carried easily on the wind.

"Aye. That be a fine place to be starting. Be heading north with the Diutinus, and I be grateful if ye be helping me look for the boat. Yer eyes be much sharper than mine, especially from such a height." Machai held tightly to the straps of his riding harness, but the larger dragon's flight was much less unsettling than Treethorn's agility and speed.

"We will find it. If it is that important to you, and to the High-Wizard, I will make sure we find it," Cinereus said. They were soon soaring with the currents of air that swept along just beyond the mountain range, and Machai heard the dragon mutter softly, "Eo ire itum."

They appeared just above the point where the two rivers joined. All that was before them was land painted with the caress of the evening sun. Cinereus banked right slightly and then took a wide, slow turn to the left, looking back at the long, winding tail of the Diutinus River to the south, swollen from the addition of the Dimon's swift waters. As their direction changed, so did the view.

"Nothing, as far as I can see, to the south." Cinereus turned his head to the north as his massive body navigated the wind.

"Aye, north it be!" Machai shouted over the wind as he admired the landscape.

To the south it had been green, with small patches of white where snow had very little chance to last through the day's sun. To the west stood a small mountain chain, far in the distance, but still visible from the altitude gained on dragonback. Machai remembered the tales of how Osric's journey began in those mountains, and he was grateful that he had stumbled upon Osric's party in the Elven Realm—even if it meant he would be giving up his own home to aid the Aranthians in their cause.

Then their flight brought them fully in the direction the river was coming from, and much larger patches of white filled the landscape in

The Weaving of Wells

the northern direction. He couldn't make out the majestic peaks of his home, and the land looked almost flat from his vantage point strapped into a seat on dragonback.

They took the right fork of the two, which led all the way to the mountains he had known since he was a lad. The small village, Bridges, lay nestled in the fork of the rivers, protected from sporadic flooding by neat, winding walls. Two great bridges spanned the rivers and tied the village to the roads leading west from the Dimon and east from the Diutinus. From Machai's height, the quaint village was only a spattering of thatched rooftops, late-blooming flowers, and a few animals penned in by even fences. Machai drew his gaze from the little town and focused on the sparkling water rushing along on its course. The banks were far apart, and the dark-blue water showed its depth, providing an ideal waterway for small cargo ships to traverse the entire realm in only a few days.

They saw only two boats near the village, but they were far too small to be the trading vessel of a dwarven clan—likely only a wealthy family or a merchant enjoying the evening on the water.

"Can ye be taking us a bit lower, Cinereus?"

The dragon dropped closer to the water, where Machai could easily make out individual trees along the bank and large fish leaping from the current in the evening light. Cinereus increased his speed slightly, sure that they would be able to identify the ship from such a distance without having to sacrifice additional time. The village fell behind them quickly, and the quiet countryside spread out across Machai's vision on either side of the water. He spotted a family of lions lounging along the riverbank, and further on, numerous deer were drinking from the river or grazing in the fields nearby. Several small fishing boats were on the water as they traveled, but nothing like the one they were looking for.

Just as the sky began to blush in the west, Cinereus called back that he had spotted a ship. A moment later, Machai could see sails up ahead, and he dared to hope that the search would be over so soon. However, when they came up closer, the ship was clearly marked as a merchant vessel from one of the human cities near the coast.

The air was growing cooler as they flew north and night approached, and Machai pulled his fur-lined hood closer around his face to fend off the bite of the wind. Still, after the bitter cold and stinging ice of the storm he had flown through to get to IronForge, the cool air of this flight was nothing that could distract him from his mission.

The sun continued its journey beyond the horizon, and Machai struggled to distinguish the rocks and trees along the riverbank from the hulls and sails of small ships in the dark.

"Can ye be the eyes in the dark, Cinereus? I cannot be seeing a thing."

"Of course. There is another ship up ahead, and it looks large enough to be the one you are seeking. I will fly in closer so you can get a good look."

"Aye, I be thanking ye greatly. Let's be hoping it be the right boat and we can be ending this wild chase." Machai gazed up along the melodic water, but he could see nothing that looked like a sail. He hoped the dragon was right.

Cinereus flew on into the night, banking and swerving with the curve of the river. Far below him, the water moved smoothly along its course, sweeping steadily south toward the sea. The sound of the water was faint, merely a whisper beneath the rush of the wind. Machai had forgotten how far a dragon can see, and he leaned forward impatiently in his harness, eagerly waiting for his vision to identify the silhouette of sails against the starlight reflecting off of the water. His legs were beginning to grow stiff from his position on Cinereus's back when he finally spotted the ship.

The cog sat low in the water with the weight of its cargo, its large single sail billowing in the wind as dwarves moved about on the wooden deck. The ship looked to be in good repair, if still a few years out of dock. A large complement of men was carrying out various duties, but with several of them concealed behind the massive sail, Machai couldn't get an accurate count from his seat. The captain was a stout dwarf with a long, thick mustache, bald head, dark cloak and boots, and he was surrounded by men gesturing to the sky as the dragon flew by. Beyond that, Machai could make out little in the dark from his seat. Cinereus sank lower, approaching as near to the ship as he safely could. Machai looked for the identifying markings along the side of the hull, and he let out a sigh of relief when the moonlight revealed the dwarven runes.

The Weaving of Wells

"That be the one we be wanting, Cinereus. Ye be saving me skin tonight." Machai rested a grateful hand against the smooth scales of the dragon's shoulder. "Can ye be contacting the other dragons and letting Kablis and Morgo know the search be over?"

"Of course. Would you like me to land, or do you intend to board the ship from here?"

"Can ye be keeping us alongside so I can be hailing 'em?" Machai didn't want to waste any time.

"I can try, but I won't be able to get you close enough for you to gain the ship without the spell. I will keep it steady enough for you to unharness before traveling."

"Aye, that'll have to be doing then." Machai waited until the dragon was as close to the ship as possible. He could see the dwarves scrambling across the deck, lowering the sails, and loading a small cannon mounted on the starboard railing. He called out to the captain, "I be Machai of FireFalls Clan. I be seeking Rhemt, blood of Metzel, the mighty founder of SnowStand. Will ye be granting me permission to be coming on board?"

The crew of the boat moved methodically, quickly carrying out the captain's orders, and Machai was impressed that Cinereus seemed to be unfazed by the weapons aimed his way. He kept them steady in the air, using great, smooth beats of his wings to keep them aloft while slowly following the progress of the boat downstream. A gentle wind had picked up, but the words of the ship's captain still reached Machai clearly.

"Aye, if ye want to be leaping from yer dragon, ye can be doing so. Ye'll be welcome aboard as bait for me next fishing trip." The crew roared with laughter, but Machai took the captain at his word and spoke the traveling spell. He appeared standing in the center of the deck, and it took him a moment to feel stable on the gently swaying surface of the ship after being on Cinereus's back for so long. Machai's hands were empty and held palms open out at his sides. The shock of the crew would wear off quickly, and he didn't want them to perceive him as a threat. The ship captain approached Machai, one hand on the sword sheathed at his hip. "That be quite the trick. Since I be inviting ye onto me ship, ye better be telling me why ye shouldn't still be fish food."

"Rhemt be the last member of nine needed for a gathering. Ye cannot be feeding me to yer fish, or ye'll be finding yer ship enveloped in flames. I be meaning ye no harm, and I be hating to threaten a cousin clan, but I be at the end of me patience. Be turning over Rhemt, and be continuing on to trade or be sailing back to SnowStand. I do not really be caring which, but the gathering cannot be going on without him, so I willn't be leaving without him." Thin blue flames licked Machai's clenched fists as he spoke. He was so exhausted, he doubted that he could wash the entire ship in fire if he had to, but the captain didn't know that. The crew eyed Machai uneasily, keeping their distance from the unfamiliar dwarf with unusual abilities, but his threatening words brought their hands to their wands and weapons. The captain eyed him warily, sizing up Machai's power in the flames lapping the skin of his fingers and wrists.

Machai had gambled on the gifts present in the crew, hoping there was no one on board who could easily counter the threat of fire on a wooden ship. From the anger and hesitation in the captain's eyes, Machai decided he had won the wager. The captain caught the eye of a crewman behind Machai, and with one jerk of his head the man ran off toward the narrow steps that led to the small chamber beneath the deck that wasn't occupied by cargo. A moment later, he returned with a second dwarf. The newcomer was dressed in finer cloth and was older than anyone else on board, but he had the rugged boots and twinkling eyes of a young adventurer. He came readily to the scene with a look of curiosity.

"Ye be asking for me, Captain?"

"Aye, Rhemt. Ye be disembarking early. Gather yer things and be assigning the lead position on the trade."

Rhemt looked confused, and he glanced around at the situation more closely. His gaze took in the crew and their looks of disdain for Machai, the fire surrounding Machai's fists, and the stern set of the captain's jaw. He settled his eyes on Machai.

"Ye be stirring up trouble? What do ye be wanting with me?"

"As a descendant of Metzel, ye be the last member of a gathering of nine taking place tomorrow. Ye need to be returning with me to FireFalls." Machai kept the fatigue out of his voice by clinging to his frustration of the past two days traveling all across the continent to seek the members.

The Weaving of Wells

"A gathering ye say?" Rhemt glanced over at the captain and then back to Machai. "Ye can be extinguishing yer hands, lad. Ye willn't be needing to be creating fear and tension between our clans. A gathering be sounding fascinating." The elder dwarf grinned and walked back down the steps to retrieve his pack. Upon his return, Machai nodded respectfully to the captain, gripped Rhemt's arm tightly, and spoke the traveling spell under his breath. The two dwarves appeared on the bank of the river in time to hear the cries of surprise lift from the crew as the ship continued on down the river and into the night.

"Fascinating!" Rhemt exclaimed, seemingly unfazed by the unusual method of travel, and he followed Machai through the trees toward the open field where Cinereus was waiting.

Chapter 14
Morning

 Machai woke early with a pounding headache, the residual consequence of too much magic and too little sleep. They had arrived back in FireFalls late the night before, but the addition of the ninth member of the gathering had eased the urgency of his stress slightly. There was still a great deal to be done, and the success of his mission still hinged on the approval of the gathering to send an army out from the realm, but he had regained a glimmer of hope that he could still pull it off.

 Machai rode the stone lift up through the shaft of the mountain until the brisk morning air caressed his cheeks. The lift stopped, lying flush with the surrounding snow-blanketed stone, and Machai stood there and gazed out at the valley that gave his home its name as the sun brought a blush to the eastern sky. In the evening, the snow and ice turned to fire spilling down the mountain from the orange light of the setting sun, and the trees looked to be aflame. On mornings like this, however, the light brought bright white clarity to everything Machai could see. As the sun climbed into the sky behind the tall mountain peaks, the snow glistened like diamonds and the trees were haloed by shimmering light. The breathtaking view breathed new optimism into the weary dwarf, and Machai whispered a blessing to Archana and asked for resolution to the tension and conflict among his brethren. He wanted only to be able to fight for what was good and right in the world without his own kin and clan leader seeing him as a traitor. Osric was depending on him, but he hoped he would not be marching out from his home for the last time, an army at his back or not.

 Machai bid good morning to the sun as it washed the valleys below with cold light and then touched his wand to the lift. As he sank back down into the mountain, he closed his eyes for a moment and tried to etch the image of the sunlight and snow embracing his home into his memory. Come what may, he would be able to summon the sight at will and bask in something beautiful. The stone lift carried him deep into the mountain, past the levels containing the kitchens, the armory,

The Weaving of Wells

the private quarters, and the craftsman's labs. He stepped off of the platform as it came to rest at the tunnel to the Great Hall. There, the gathering would decide his success or failure.

When Machai entered the hall, Kablis, several of their supporters, and all nine of the gathering members were already present. They were seated in small groups, against the wall or along the dais, sharpening and polishing weapons or engaged in hushed conversations. Machai entered with his head high, walked purposefully through the large room, and stepped up onto the dais. His weapons and armor had been brought down ahead of him, and he sat down among them and began to check his blades over, focusing completely on the task at hand and trying not to contemplate the trial ahead.

Machai had been training and working with weaponry all of his life, and he had been in many battles, but never one couched in ritual or against his kin and clan cousins. The story of the gathering emphasized the debate, but the ceremony was far more complex and dangerous. Agrik had been with Machai and the nine members late into the night explaining how the gathering would work, how the tradition had evolved, and what they would be expected to do once they had committed to the ceremony. Though Kablis had challenged Thenar to the gathering, it was Machai's battle to fight. Thenar had smiled smugly when Threed had informed him that Machai, not Kablis, would be engaging in the contest of wit and arms against the clan leader.

The gathering was scheduled for mid'day, when the sun was at its apex, and the participants were growing anxious as the time approached. Shortly before the appointed time, Thenar arrived in the hall fully armored in gleaming mail and plate. He carried his highly polished helmet in one hand and a parchment scroll in the other. Threed followed behind bearing Thenar's weapons and a scowl as his eyes landed on Machai sitting upon the dais. However, Thenar looked calm and he greeted the members of the gathering with welcoming smiles and hearty handshakes.

Kablis joined Machai and helped him into his armor, securing the buckles of his chest plate while speaking reassuring and calming words to keep his nerves steady.

"It be a battle of words. The blows be a ritual only. Ye cannot be defeated if ye have no opponents. Be brave, and for blade's bounty be persuasive." Machai nodded silently, breathing slowly and running his arguments through his mind until the words became an echoing chant in his head. Thenar was arrogant and ignorant in his refusal to aid the Aranthians, and Machai was determined to convince the gathered—or defeat them.

Machai allowed the familiar space to calm him as he waited for the nine dwarves to don their armor and arm themselves. The cavernous room echoed with the sounds of low voices, jingling chainmail, and scraping metal. The height of the dais was minimal, but it was enough to provide Machai with an unobstructed view of the room. There were no furnishings other than a large brass bell near the door, but the walls were adorned with dusty tapestries depicting elaborate scenes of ancient battles and dwarven lore. Torches that were nested in iron brackets lined the walls, casting a warm glow throughout the room, and they burned without consuming fuel or emitting any smoke. The stone floor was worn smooth from the feet of generations of dwarves, and one of the stairs on the left side of the raised platform was cracked with one corner crumbling away. Machai thought it was appropriate, as he felt like he was a small piece of the clan being broken apart from the whole. Even if he won in the gathering, the harmony of the clan had been fractured by the need for a gathering in the first place. Machai's attention was drawn back to the impending debate as the nine gathering members made their way up the steps and onto the dais.

Thenar moved in closer to Machai with a smug expression on his face. The two stood nearly shoulder to shoulder, and the nine others formed a loose line behind them.

"Ye shall be wishing ye had stayed in the dungeons before I be done with ye." Thenar's words were a low growl, only loud enough for Machai to hear. Machai gripped his sword tightly, and his response was just as quiet.

"Do ye be surprised that I be slipping out of yer dungeon cell? It be a pitiful task compared to organizing a gathering in a mere three days, but we be managing that just fine as well. Here we be. Do ye still be underestimating me and the new magic that be sweeping across

The Weaving of Wells

Archana? Imagine what we could be doing if we were truly yer enemy, rather than yer kin."

Kablis set the bell to ringing, and a steady stream of spectators entered the chamber. The Great Hall was nearly filled, as most every member of the FireFalls clan had turned out to watch the gathering, when Agrik nodded toward Thenar to indicate that mid'day had arrived and he could begin speaking. Thenar unrolled the scroll he held and looked out at the crowd before reading. Once he was finished, Machai would give his speech. As the Summoner, or the one who called the gathering, Machai would speak first and Thenar would respond. Then the questioning would begin.

"FireFalls, today we be welcoming representatives of the nine clans to our mountain walls. A grievance be raised, and today we be settling it with the honor and tradition of a gathering. Ye be here to be witnessing a debate which be deciding the fate of many of ye and yer families. Our ancestors, when they be the one clan of all dwarves, be wisely seeking answers and agreements in the sacred rite of battle, and we be doing the same to be honoring their names."

As Thenar read off each name of the nine members, the dwarf raised his sword to loud cheers from the crowd. "Hern of BillowBluff, blood of Stasp! Jom of BlackAxe, blood of Tunft! Irto of FireFalls, blood of Uvet! Kant of IceIsle, blood of Behg! Prex of IronAnvil, blood of Gyln! Festil of IronForge, blood of Gring! Rhemt of SnowStand, blood of Metzel! Furtl of SteelBorne, blood of Myx! Legin of StoneStar, blood of Ware!"

Thenar waited for the roar of the crowd to settle down, and then he continued reading from the scroll. "Today's gathering will be determining if ye shall be forced to be marching to a war that be not yers. I and Machai be debating, and ye shall be seeing the verdict. There be no axes, no maces, no wands, and no magic allowed in the engagement. There be only swords and the strength of each dwarf." He turned to the gathering members. "Ye be understanding yer rules?"

"Aye." Nine voices echoed in response.

"Ye be prepared to be judging the debate based on what be best for the Dwarven Realm?"

"Aye." Again, all nine responded in unison.

"Ye be charged with the honorable execution of our realm's most sacred ritual. Ye be the voice and the judge of yer clan. Ye be the blood and the arm of yer ancestors. Ye be the final say in this debate." Thenar nodded at the men, and they formed a well-armored ring around Thenar and Machai as the crowd looked on silently. Machai eyed the nine men with resolve, confident that he could sway them though still nervous at how much depended on the next words he spoke. He widened his stance and felt the comfortable weight of the short sword in his right hand, and then he turned to face the nine dwarves he had helped to bring together in the hall and proceeded with his speech.

"Ye men be gathered here today, some at our request and others at our demand, but all to be participating in an honorable tradition of our dwarven heritage. Ye being here for the gathering be a mark of yer direct descending from our nine mighty clan founders. Ye all be having the blood of fierce warriors and strong dwarves in yer veins." Machai gripped his sword tighter and furrowed his brows. "Ye all be having the blood of foolish men in yer veins." All nine of the gathering members, as well as those watching, stood still, shocked and surprised at Machai's disrespectful words. He stood quietly for a moment, his eyes scanning the faces of the nine men who could very well determine who won the war, and he let the shock and confusion stir their emotions and thoughts. When it seemed inevitable that the discomfort would boil into anger and dissent, Machai raised his sword and his voice. "Ye be hearing the story of the last gathering as be I. So ye be knowing a gathering can be uniting a clan, or be severing it. We be knowing the clan leader be strong, and be brave, and be wise. We also be knowing the clan leader can be wrong."

Thenar scoffed and sneered at Machai, but he stood still on the dais and did not interrupt.

"Nine men be at that last gathering too. It be the responsibility of those nine to be determining who be right. The problem be that all nine be thinking he be right, and be thinking the other eight be wrong. Either all nine be wrong, or only one in nine clan leaders be right." Machai did not pause to allow the few sniggers that erupted to penetrate through the crowd. "Ye may be thinking that I be criticizing clan leaders because I be debating with mine. Ye be wrong. I be criticizing the clan leaders because they be destroying the unity of our people. They be so caught up in who be right and who be wrong that they be failing to see that they should be putting their differences

The Weaving of Wells

down with their swords. If those nine gathering members be not fighting, be not debating, then they could be saving the clan instead of sundering it. We could be one mighty clan, be united by our ancestors rather than be divided by them.

"Today ye be charged with judging a debate. Ye be the voice and sword arm of yer clan, and ye be the aye or nay that be sending a message about the Dwarven Realm to every other race on Archana. Ye be in a position to be saying ye be strong and brave and wise, or ye be wrong as those nine be wrong. Ye be able to be seeing the world as it be, splintered and scared, on the precipice of great evil and destruction, or ye be seeing yer clan, me clan, as those nine be seeing a need for new clans. Be hearing me tale, and be considering not what be the position of yer clan, but what be the future of yer clan, of the realm, of the world." Machai took a deep breath and gently laid his sword on the floor. He straightened, hands held out with his palms up. He gazed out at his kin filling the room. His eyes narrowed and he clenched his teeth, then he turned his back on the crowd and faced the line of nine squarely. "Many of ye be hearing I be a traitor. At least one of ye be thinking I be a manipulative lurg. There be little reason for ye to be thinking otherwise, but I be assuring ye, I be no traitor. There be a wee bit more truth to that second one.

"By now I be sure ye be hearing of Osric, the High-Wizard, and the role he be playing in much of the political turmoil in the Human Realm over the past year. I be meeting him first on me journey to Braya to be delivering a wagonload of weapons we be selling. There be much I willn't be telling ye about me time in Braya, but I can be telling ye that I be seeing two of the most incredible things I ever be seeing in my life up unto that day. One be the most disgusting display of cruelty and disregard for another creature, and the other be the most impressive feat of magic ever to be accomplished, and it be in the service of another creature. That second one be done by the High-Wizard. I be accompanying him on his travels as he be seeking the man who be sabotaging the peace treaty signing in Stanton. He be finding him, and it be the man who be usurping the human Turgency. This man, Dredek, be not human. He be of a race that we be thinking extinct, and he be a few hundred years old." Machai watched the eyes of the nine widen and their lips turn down with doubt. "That be not the most surprising thing about Dredek. He be using all that time to be gaining political and magical power, and to be perfecting the art of wielding unknown and dangerous magic. Recently, he be invading and conquering the irua city of Angmar. There, in the very near future, he be planning to be using obscenely powerful magic to be raising his kin from the dead." Several of those in the gathering gasped, and confused and shocked cries rose up from the crowd behind Machai. "If ye, me kin, be wiped from the face of Archana, I cannot be saying I be not seeking the same. I cannot be saying I be thinking Dredek foolish, nor that his desire to be seeing his loved ones again be evil. Yet, I can be saying that animating the dead be unnatural, and it be terrifying. There be no way to be knowing if it be possible to be bringing his people back whole. But, even if it be true that he can be raising the dead, I willn't be standing aside as he be making new dead in the process. Dredek be killing innocent people, regardless of species or race, and he be gaining more power by the day. He be killing those who be standing in his way, and that I be calling evil.

"I be a proud member of the FireFalls Clan, of the Dwarven Realm, but that cannot be keeping me from being a proud resident of Archana. I be spending me life training me kin to be fighting, but what be the purpose if we cannot be using our skill in battle to be battling the evil that be raising up against Archana? Just because there be no soldiers at our door, no evil wizard in our realm, that be no justification to be turning our backs on others who be scared, suffering, and in danger. It be true that Dredek may never be turning his gaze upon the Dwarven Realm. It be true that this be not a dwarven war. But if the wrong side be winning, it be only a matter of time before we be regretting any decision we be making that could be making it otherwise. If we be turning our heads to the danger that be growing in Angmar, we be sending a message to Dredek, to others like him that we be not knowing of yet, and to Archana the whole. If it be coming to be that we be under attack by the magic that Dredek be capable of, or worse if that be possible, no people will be aiding us in our time of need. We need to be uniting as a realm, as a world, to be doing anything we can to be bringing this war to a successful end.

"Ye may be thinking that the irua be deceptive and undeserving of our aid. We be trading little with the irua in the past, as they be not the honorable sort we be claiming to be. But if we be judging them based on the character they be showing in this war, we be wrong to be calling them the enemy. There be wicked men among the humans, as I be seeing for meself last year at Braya, but there be good men among them too—perhaps better men than we be if we be standing aside and letting the irua be massacred. The Aranthians be a small group of mighty men. They be many races, and they be led by one of the finest humans I ever be meeting. Osric be the first leader to be actively engaging in war on behalf of another race. It be true the Human Realm was attacked as well, but only because they be hosting the Ratification Ceremony for the peace treaty signing. Can ye men be sleeping soundly if ye refuse to act so honorably and so generously as Osric? Can ye be refusing to aid the irua in this time of undeserved brutality and slaughter, just because ye be not liking 'em? Is that who we be?" Machai paused for a moment to take in a few shaking heads and a few disapproving looks, attempting to measure the reactions of the nine men around him. He continued in the same measured and confident tone.

"I be returning to me home to be seeking aid from me kin. I be asking Thenar to be sending a force to be joining Osric's troops, the Aranthians. Thenar be refusing, and he be punishing me for what he be perceiving as betrayal. If he be truly believing that I be betraying me clan, I cannot be believing that we'd be standing here before ye. Thenar be granting the request to be having this gathering, but he be granting us only enough time to be arranging for yer arrival if I be speaking true in me claims about the evolution and discoveries in magic. And here we be. We be living in a time of great portent, when magic be far more complex and dangerous than we be realizing. Magic be a way of life, a part of our world that we be taking for granted, and if we be ignoring the men of Archana who be using incredible magic for great good, and for great destruction, we be scared, stupid, weak little men who be not deserving to be proud of our power and prowess in battle. Is that who we be? I be not believing that Thenar be thinking we be scared, or stupid, or weak. I be not thinking any of us be, especially the descendants of our nine clan founders. FireFalls be a mighty clan since it be established, because the men who be leading FireFalls be what a leader should be. Thenar be brave and intelligent and strong. He be acting in what he be believing to be the best interest of the clan. But Thenar still be wrong!

Osric's Wand

"I be needing yer help to be showing Archana that we be dwarves of great loyalty, honor, and pride. We be every bit as determined to be finding the person responsible for destroying the peace treaty signing, attacking an innocent realm, and dabbling in magic that be dark and dangerous. Soon, I be leaving, but I be hoping ye willn't be letting me go alone. I be needing men with me who be brave and selfless, men who be skilled in fighting with and against magic, dwarves who be desiring a peaceful world beyond the borders of our realm. I know there be men like I be describing here in FireFalls, and I be forced to be leaving these warriors behind if ye be siding with Thenar in this gathering. I be sure that men like I be describing be here before me, among ye nine, and it be up to ye now to choose if it be ye." Machai locked eyes with each of the nine gathering members for a moment, weighing the effect of his words on their emotions as best he could, and then he slowly bent and retrieved his sword from the floor near his feet.

Thenar stared at Machai, conflicting emotions causing his eyes to narrow and his lips to pull tight in something between a smile and a grimace. His clenched jaw made it clear that whatever mixed feelings he might have about Machai and his speech, anger was still the most prominent. He tore his gaze from Machai and held his hand up to the crowd in welcome. Many voices rose up in support of the clan leader, but most of those gathered stared on, silently waiting to hear how Thenar would respond to Machai's praise and accusations. Thenar turned to the nine men on the dais, avoiding looking back at Machai, and when he spoke his voice was clear and confident.

"Machai's words be full of passion, but they be lacking in something that be more important: reason. If we be running off to be fighting every battle that be breaking out between other races, we be ever marching to our deaths. I be the clan leader, and it be me job to be ensuring the safety and continuation of this mighty clan. FireFalls be not a clan of thugs and mercenaries. We be not a clan fueled by the anger of humans or the fear of foreign feuds. We be not a clan who be trembling at fancy magic spells or distant necromancy. And we be having no reason to be fearing that this Dredek feller be knocking at our door." Thenar paced back and forth within the ring of dwarves, projecting his voice to address the nine members of the gathering as well as those who were watching from the lower floor. "But, if he be

The Weaving of Wells

standing before the door of FireFalls, will we be trembling then? Will we be quaking before his rotting kin? Will we be hiding in our homes if he be casting wicked magic at our walls? Nay! If he be foolish enough to be threatening our home and our families, *then* me brothers, then we will be crushing his skull in our armored fists and be grinding his bones under our boot heels." A few of the onlookers cheered, but they were quickly silenced by the discouraging looks cast their way by Kablis and his companions.

Thenar continued, "How can we be honoring our ancestors, who be carving these halls from the cold stone of the mountain, if we be fleeing from our walls to be saving the skin of a human who be too weak to be winning without dwarven warriors? If Osric be so ineffective in his battles, who be we to say he shall be the victor of his war? Who be we to say he should be leading the heroes of our southern neighbor realm? Who be we to say he be the man we be wanting to follow into battle? Machai be speaking of loyalty to a foreign ruler who be falling in every battle he be fighting. Machai be speaking of an organization in its infancy, forged in a war we be playing no part in, but unproven in times of true hardship. There be no reason to be believing the Aranthians willn't be a mere memory in a few years' time, no reason to be thinking that Osric willn't be the catalyst of tragedy in the tale of humanity, no reason to be discussing marching to the lines of a war that be someone else's battle. It be me responsibility, as yer leader, to be knowing when to be sending aid and when to be refusing. I willn't be sending me men to slaughter, to be led into battle by a wailing child who be playing at war with a foreign warlord—one who be fully grown in his tactics and thirst for destruction. I willn't be sacrificing me men, yer brothers, to be risking the blood of dwarves for the pride of a human.

"Machai be right that ye be having the blood of fierce and strong warriors in ye, but he be daring to be calling yer ancestors—our first clan leaders—fools?! He be away from these mighty mountain halls for too long, and he be forgetting what it be meaning to be a dwarf. He be forgetting that the unforgiving stone and ice of these northern lands be demanding staunch loyalty and stern discipline or it be consuming ye and burying ye alive. He be forgetting that it be me duty first and foremost to be protecting the lives of me clan members.

"It be true that we clan leaders can be wrong, I willn't be denying it. Yet, it also be true that only clan leaders, and those that be closest to them"—he gestured with his sword to the nine gathering members—"can be understanding what it be taking to be leading a clan. Machai be a good fighter, and he be a good teacher, but he be naïve in the necessities of me responsibilities.

"He also be running a track record of blatantly disregarding clan welfare when it be coming to his decisions about this war. He be sent to Braya to be making a delivery, and it be taking much longer than anticipated to be returning with the clan's payment as he be getting himself tangled up with Osric and his rebellion. That money be needed to be feeding and providing for the clan families. He be belligerent upon returning, and he be leaving against me wishes when he be needed here to be training others to be defending our home. Ye may be tempted by his words of bravery, loyalty, and wisdom, but he be leaving his home to be intentionally sabotaging the largest shipment of weapons FireFalls ever be filling, and the clan be losing enough money to be providing for our people for an entire year, not to be mentioning the weapons. Machai be told to be returning home, and we could be working together to be forming a plan to be recovering from the loss, but again he be disregarding me authority. Machai be going off to war with the Aranthians and be leaving his clan to be suffering the losses of goods, coin, and his skills with no consideration for what his actions be doing to his people.

"Aye, I be calling Machai a traitor. When he finally be returning, he be recruiting the men he be dragging into his rebellion and he be turning them against the clan. His only defense be that the magic he be using to be sneaking into the mountain be dangerous in the wrong hands. After all he be doing to be betraying the clan, I be saying it be his hands that be wrong, and I cannot be tolerating such traitorous behavior. He even be escaping from the dungeons to be using what he be calling dangerous magic to be bringing ye men here today. Does this be the dwarf ye want determining the fate of me men? Of yer men?" Thenar stood on the dais, one hand raised and pointing at Machai and the other gripping his sword. He let his arm drop slowly, turning and gazing out at the crowd beyond, then spinning slowly to squarely face each of the gathering members.

The Weaving of Wells

"Be taking up yer swords, men, and be using yer wisdom and strength that be inherited from those mighty dwarves ye be descending from. Be embracing yer clan, and yer loyalty to the Dwarven Realm, and be asking what ye may. Be letting the gathering commence."

Thenar and Machai moved back to back as the nine armed and armored dwarves slowly tightened their circle around them. As the nine dwarves drew their weapons, Machai and Thenar raised their swords and prepared to meet the gathering members in ritualistic battle to defend their arguments and seek victory against the other. Neither of them had ever participated in a gathering, but the method of the sacred rite was well known from the stories they had all heard.

As the nine dwarves slowly circled around them, they brought their swords up to meet the blades of the two combatants. The clear clang of steel echoed throughout the chamber, one after another, as Thenar and Machai returned the strokes with controlled movements. Legin of StoneStar was the first to engage in the interrogation phase of the gathering, swinging his sword in quickly toward Thenar's left shoulder. The clan leader reacted swiftly, blocking the blow with his own blade, and Legin asked his question as the circle came to a stop in its revolution.

"If ye be denying Osric the reinforcements, will the Dwarven Realm be earning a formidable enemy?" Legin's strikes were slow and controlled, easy enough for Thenar to parry while he responded.

"There be no reason for Osric to be declaring the dwarves as his enemy. He be young and inexperienced, but I be not thinking he be stupid. Besides, he be leading a small rebellion. New magic or no, he be no threat to the Dwarven Realm." Thenar expended only enough energy to block Legin's half-hearted attack, knowing that he would need his strength and stamina to last through the ordeal. Legin only grunted and stepped to his left, initiating the rotation of the ring to resume around Thenar and Machai. Festil of IronForge, whom Machai had recruited through his brother the clan leader, engaged next.

"Machai, ye be demonstrating unfamiliar and impressive magic in me brother's chambers. Who else be having the skills ye be showing off to be manipulating me clan into compliance?" Festil thrust his sword toward Machai's armored shoulder, but Machai blocked the

Osric's Wand

stroke easily, sweeping Festil's blade down toward the floor. His only response to the open animosity in Festil's tone was a grim smile.

"Most of me allies in the Aranthians be using the same techniques I be demonstrating for yer brother, among many other more impressive feats, and we be learning the skill from Osric. It be hard to say what magic Dredek be knowing, but it be safe to say it be at least as terrifying as mine. Soon, the men who be aiding me in strengthening the ranks of the Aranthians and resisting the terror of Dredek's magic be knowing it too." Machai's words caused a spark of desire to flash in Festil's eyes as the IronForge dwarf weighed the truth in Machai's promise to teach the traveling spell to anyone who joined him. Though Machai was confident that Gorin would send the three hundred men as promised in order to gain the benefit of new magic, Machai still needed Festil's vote in the gathering to secure the win. He disliked the idea that Festil may join with him only out of greed for the knowledge Machai could provide of magic, but he would accept that over Festil siding with Thenar out of anger for Machai manipulating his brother into sending Festil to the gathering. Festil delivered a final sweeping strike at Machai as he shifted his weight and the circle resumed its rotation. Machai blocked the blow, following through with the movement and catching the sword of the next man in line and blocking that as well.

Rhemt of SnowStand, one of the eldest of the gathering members and the one Machai had chased down on the ship, asked his first question of Thenar. His sword strokes were reserved, as though he didn't want to distract Thenar from his answer with the ritual combat of the gathering.

"Thenar, if it be SnowStand that be under attack by this Dredek feller, would ye be refusing Machai his army then?"

Thenar's brow wrinkled fiercely and his eyes narrowed, the dwarf's question clearly causing a feeling of disgust in the clan leader.

"Of course I willn't be withholding me men from aiding a dwarven clan. That be not the same thing at all," Thenar said. Rhemt nodded slightly, but rather than moving on in the circle, he quickly reversed his grip and brought his sword down quickly toward Thenar's right hip. Surprised, Thenar stepped to his left and just managed to block the blade as Rhemt asked another question.

The Weaving of Wells

"And if it be FireFalls that be under attack, will ye be expecting the aid of others if ye be seeking it?"

"Aye, but I be not seeking aid from within the dusty tunnels of the Irua Realm. If trouble be coming to the Dwarven Realm, the dwarves be made of sharp enough steel to be handling it." Thenar swung his sword at the older dwarf, but Furtl stepped in from Rhemt's right and blocked Thenar's blade with his own. Furtl attacked with a quick flurry of strokes as he continued with Rhemt's line of questioning, keeping Thenar on the defensive in more ways than one.

"If the irua be thinking yer peril be genuine and unjust, and they be marshaling a force to be aiding ye, would ye be turning their army away when ye be in need?"

"Nay, but I willn't be trusting 'em either." Thenar kept his feet rooted to the wood of the floor as he blocked each blow. "If they be wanting to be dying, I be thanking 'em. But if they be marching an army into me realm, it be hard to be saying if they be ally or enemy."

On the other side of the circle, the sword and the questions of Hern from BillowBluff engaged Machai.

"How can ye be putting the welfare of the irua and yer pal Osric over the safety and unity of yer clan? Ye be willing to be sending dwarves to the death, but ye willn't be allowing Osric and the irua to be fighting what be their own war?" Hern asked.

"I be claiming no hierarchy of what anyone's life be worth. The lives of me kin and me clan be close to me heart, and I willn't ever be seeking to be causing them ill, but me desire for me kin to be safe cannot be causing me to be leaving the irua and the Aranthians to be dying a needless death. Me kin and me clan, and all yer clans too, be the most efficient and effective force at wielding a weapon I ever be seeing, and if there be dwarves fighting alongside the Aranthians and irua then far fewer of all three be dying. The Aranthians be far too few to be matching Dredek, as his men be having the advantage of superior numbers and superior weapons. It be our fault they be armed so well, I willn't have it be our fault that they be so much greater in numbers too."

Hern's fierce glare was little changed by Machai's response, but he halted his bladework and stepped to his left. However, the circle was breaking down as each member of the gathering began drawing his allegiance and focusing his questioning on either Machai or Thenar.

Osric's Wand

Fertl and Jom were hurling alternating questions at Thenar as he deftly defended against both of their swords, so Hern was stalled for the moment near Machai.

Irto stepped around Fertl, coming up on Machai's left side and further desynchronizing the circle. Irto, the member from FireFalls, struck a half-hearted blow at Machai's blade and picked up the questioning where Hern left off.

"Do ye be pledging yer sword to Osric because ye be losing love for yer clan and our leader? Or maybe ye just be hungry for the power these new magics be promising?" Irto spoke louder than he needed to, as if the accusation were actually meant for another's ears. Machai noted that Irto's next sword stroke was slow in coming, although he was only aware of the hesitation because he knew what Irto was capable of; Machai had had a hand in training him, after all.

"Nay. Me loyalty to me clan and to Thenar be no less solid than yers be. I be seeking to be aiding Osric only because it be the right thing to be doing. I be always true to me clan and me realm in me heart, but I also be a citizen of Archana. It be wrong to be turning a blind eye and a cold heart to the world that be around us, even if it be a distant land from our borders that be in peril. Me loyalty to Osric be forged in me observing his virtue and his commitment to be righting the wrongs that be perpetrated against our world, and it be tempered in me fighting alongside him and seeing his strength and humility when all odds be against him." Machai watched Irto closely as he spoke, and subtly embedded in the FireFalls dwarf's grimace was an approving smile. Irto continued aiming sword thrusts, which Machai easily blocked, while speaking loudly over the noise of the fighting.

"I be not hearing ye be denying that ye be seeking the power of new magic. Be that a confession of yer true intentions?"

"I willn't be denying these new magics be powerful, but ye be a fool if ye be believing that that be me motivation for fighting in this war. No spell be worth dying or killing for, though Dredek be likely to be disagreeing with me. Still, it be beneficial to me clan and me realm to be learning as much as we can be of magic. Magic be powerful because it be born of Archana, and it be no less wondrous when it be used for destruction as when it be used for protection. We who be seeking to be protecting Archana be in need of magic as powerful as those who be seeking to destroy her. The work that Osric and the

The Weaving of Wells

Aranthians be doing in the study of magic be of great import to this war, but it be of even greater import to the future of our world."

Irto nodded slightly and lowered his sword, stepping off to his left far enough to disengage from Machai but not so far as to be seen as confronting Thenar. The gathering members were tiring, breathing heavily and raising their swords a little slower. The questions came out between grunts and gritted teeth, and sweat rolled down their faces and onto the gleaming links of chainmail at their throats. Thenar bled from a gash on his cheek, and his movements were losing their gracefulness. Torchlight glinted off his armor and the sheen of his skin alike, and he bared his teeth in a snarl as he blocked the attacks from multiple directions. Machai fared better, as his battle had been less intense and his stamina had been improving over the past months, but he too bled from small wounds and felt the fatigue in his arms and shoulders from the weight of his armor and sword. The day was passing swiftly, and the crowd was growing louder as they reacted to skillful blows or seemingly insufficient responses.

As Prex from IronAnvil and Jom from BlackAxe hurled accusations at Thenar about his diminishing the honor of dwarves and being a coward for hiding within his vast stone mountain, Kant of IceIsle focused on Machai with his sword and his tongue, each equally sharp.

"Ye be entitled to be traipsing off to Stanton or the Irua Realm at yer will, but ye be in no position to be disregarding and disrespecting yer clan leader. Yer no coward, but ye be arrogant and naïve. The Dwarven Realm be the solid place it be for generation after generation because we be not tolerating a dwarf who be insubordinate and ineffective at executing orders. No matter yer passionate and persuasive words, ye belong in the dungeon for yer sabotage of the Rowain delivery. Ye may be convincing these others ye be innocent of the charge of treason, but ye never be convincing me ye be not a criminal against the realm and yer clan." Kant's bladework was skilled, and Machai channeled his anger, inspired by Kant's words, into his sword. He blocked the old IceIsle dwarf's attacks deftly, and before responding he stepped forward and swung his sword down hard toward Kant's shoulder. Kant blocked with his sword and the stroke landed low on his blade, the force and vibrations causing Kant's fingers to loosen and driving him backward. Machai stepped back into place and replied to the accusations while Kant kept his distance and caught his breath.

"I be meaning no disrespect, but the Dwarven Realm be scattered in nine clans because the mighty dwarves who be founding the clans be unable to be issuing effective orders. They be using this very ceremony to be sundering the realm, and it be the ability of this generation to be either uniting it or be repeating the mistakes of our ancestors. Ye be saying I be naïve, but it be naïve to be thinking this realm be solid. We be fractured and fighting, failing to be binding our strength and our honor in our actions, failing to be rising to the need for greatness in a world that be on the brink of atrocity, failing to be meeting our potential as the mighty warriors and leaders that our ancestors should be if they be putting their differences aside for the good of the clan. Our ancestors be great men, mighty and honorable in their own rights, but they be failing the realm when they be giving up on unity and abandoning each other because they could not be agreeing. We can be great men too, or we can be striving to be even greater than they be. We be valuing tradition, as our blades meeting here today be showing, but we need not be blinded by it. Let us be seeking to be the greatest Dwarven Realm that ever be. Let us be standing beside our clan leaders and be following them into battle for virtue and right, rather than standing against each other with blades raised and insults flying. Let us be bringing the clans together under one banner, bound by our blood and our burdens and our desire to be defending Archana from brutality and wickedness. Let us be marching out from our mountain fortresses and be showing the world that the Dwarven Realm be a realm to be celebrated and feared, a realm of justice delivered swiftly by honorable hearts and enchanted blades, not a realm of factions but a realm of heroes!" Machai thrust his sword skyward as he concluded, raising a thunderous cheer and applause from the gathered audience. The dwarves who had been fighting with Thenar had stopped to listen to his speech as well, and tears were shining in old Rhemt's eyes as he nodded in approval of Machai's words.

Fertl, Jom, Prex, and even Festil resumed the ritual with a new vigor, trading well-timed and coordinated attacks against Thenar. They no longer questioned him or accused him, but rather focused all of their energy into subduing him with their swords. Irto stood to one

The Weaving of Wells

side, eyeing Thenar's battle with interest, but he was not willing to raise his blade against his own clan leader.

Kant and Hern refused to be swayed by Machai's call for greatness and glory, and they came at Machai with fierce determination. Machai, invigorated by his own words, fought them off efficiently, pacing his strokes to fend off the fatigue of such a long engagement. Thenar did not fare so well, and it was only a matter of time before his four opponents overwhelmed him. Legin and Rhemt had joined Irto on the sidelines, supporting Machai by choosing not to oppose him. Thenar fought well, but he was heavily outnumbered, and the tradition of the gathering required that he avoid maiming or killing his opponents. The fighting was supposed to be a ritual, not a bloodbath. The dwarves who stood against Thenar were striking precisely, timing thrusts and strikes where the others left openings in the clan leader's defenses. And Thenar was tired. He trained now less than he did when he was young, as the responsibilities of leadership were demanding of his time and his energy. Even with perfectly controlled movements, his sword was growing heavier with each breath. As Thenar contemplated his impending loss, his focus was broken and he made his first significant mistake. Prex landed a well-timed blow to Thenar's chest plate, and he overcompensated to keep from falling backward. Had he been fresh in the fight, Thenar would have planted his rear foot and barely moved from the impact. As Jom moved in with the next blow, aiming at where Thenar's sword should have been, Thenar lunged forward and took the full strength of Jom's sword strike on the shoulder. Dwarves made some of the strongest armor on Archana, and also some of the best weapons. With the dense muscle of the BlackAxe dwarf behind it, the blow severely dented Thenar's shoulder cop. He cried out as much from shock as from pain, and he lowered his blade. With his teeth bared in a ferocious grimace, and his left arm hanging limp, Thenar called a halt to the gathering and conceded. He stood on the dais, surrounded by some of the most powerful and skilled dwarves in the realm, and declared Machai the victor of the gathering. Machai caught the eye of Kablis in the crowd and the two exchanged smiles of relief and resolve. They had won the day, but the work was only beginning to prepare for the battle ahead.

Chapter 15
Departure

Two days after the gathering had decided that Machai would get his troops, much had been accomplished to ready the dwarves for their departure. Nearly two hundred members of the FireFalls clan had volunteered to follow Machai and Kablis into war, and Machai had asserted that they would not force anyone to fight with them unwillingly, even if the gathering had given them the authority to do so. Thenar had no choice but to allow them to go, and the last thing Machai wanted was troops who resented his rebellion against their clan leader fighting by his side.

The necessary armor and weapons had been secured. Rations, tools, clothing, tents, blankets, and water skins had been collected. Maps of the Irua Realm and the regions they might travel through had been rolled and packed, and a variety of other tools and supplies were still being gathered. There were several people Machai needed to contact, but his morning had been filled with discussions with many of the gathering members to determine what contributions he could expect from the other clans. He had put off speaking with those members who had opposed him in the questioning, but inevitably he would have to face them and take an account of where their clan leaders stood. Machai hoped that the leaders would honor the gathering victory rather than being swayed by the prejudices of their clans' representatives.

Festil had left early for IronForge, and his tone and expression toward Machai had been more respectful after his victory than it had been since he had arrived in FireFalls. His congratulations sounded genuine, and Festil had the familiar gleam of greed in his eyes when he confirmed that he would be among the three hundred dwarves who would meet up with Machai. He ended their conversation with a reminder that Machai had promised they would all learn the "spell to sneak up on me brother and be scaring 'im outta 'is breeches."

Rhemt, the old sailor from SnowStand, had initiated a wand conversation with his clan leader while lying on a bed with ice wrapped in cloth packed around his limbs to ease the ache in his

The Weaving of Wells

muscles from the unusual exertion of the gathering. The leader of SnowStand had interrupted the old man as he sang Machai's praises for his valiant speech and commendable swordsmanship and promised to send one hundred fully equipped clan members immediately. Machai hadn't even had a chance to speak with him about the details before Rhemt started up again and the clan leader quickly ended the communication link.

Machai sat with Furtl and Jom when they established communication with their clans. SteelBorne was hesitant to commit any troops without speaking to Thenar, but Furtl was able to convince his clan leader that he would bring a letter from Thenar acknowledging the gathering result. BlackAxe was willing to send the manpower, but they had a shortage of gear due to a recent cave-in that had buried one of their three armories. Much of the contents were recovered, but it would take time to restore the damaged gear to a usable state. Between the two clans, Machai was promised another one hundred and fifty troops, but he would have to hope that Osric could provide the lacking armor and weapons.

The leader of IronAnvil, FireFalls' neighbor to the northeast, was curt but professional. He pledged fifty troops when he heard about Machai's victory. Prex tried to persuade him that no other clan was sending so few men, and that the gathering had convinced him that a full commitment to support Machai and the Aranthians was prudent, but he was unconvinced even by the idea of new magic and skills.

Machai spoke to the leader of StoneStar last, and he had been disappointed and concerned by what he had heard. There had been several reports of small villages along the west coast of the peninsula being razed by dragon fire. StoneStar was some ways inland, in the foothills of the Stonehorn Mountains, but they feared they would be overtaxed by the relief needs of nearby villagers, and they were leery of sending any of their men away. When Legin heard this, he had informed Machai that he would help assess the situation and if they could spare the men he would uphold the decision of the gathering and send them. However, Machai was leaving immediately, and he was not confident that anyone from StoneStar would be joining in the war effort in the Irua Realm.

IceIsle was on the peninsula, much closer to the region where the dragon had been reported to be actively attacking, and Machai was worried that Kant would not do the same as Legin in advocating for his cause. He decided to send Kant home to evaluate IceIsle's situation without seeking troops. He found the IceIsle dwarf easily enough and shared the news with him. Flushed with concern for his clan, Kant gathered his belongings quickly. Machai saw him off, wishing him and his clan well and asking that he call on FireFalls and the Aranthians if the clan was in need of aid against the dragon. Machai wasn't sure what aid they would be able to offer, with the resources of able fighters stretched so thin already, but he hoped to prevent the clans from severing their relationship further over the gathering and the war.

The only clan that Machai had not yet spoken to was BillowBluff, and Hern had made it clear in the gathering that he did not support Machai and his efforts to recruit troops. BillowBluff was located on the eastern edge of the Stonehorn Mountains, northwest of SteelBorne. Though these mountains were far more forgiving than the range surrounding IronForge, it was still rough terrain. The clan leader, Staspin, was as hard as the stone and as inhospitable as the cold wind that blew past his door. Still, Machai hoped he would be more understanding of the stakes of the war than Hern, and he intended to make it clear that he was not placing his loyalties to Osric above that of his clan.

Machai found Hern having a drink with Thenar in the clan leader's dining room. Maps were spread out all over the table in front of them, and both dwarves scowled as they looked down at the charts. Machai cleared his throat as he stepped into the room.

"Be ye here to be gloating?" Thenar's speech was slightly slurred.

"Nay." Machai held his hands open at his sides, a gesture of passivity. "I be hoping to be speaking with Hern."

With red eyes, Thenar stared at Machai for some time before waving him in and sliding back the chair next to him. Machai took the seat.

"Ye be a thorn in me boots, boy, but ye be putting on a commendable show and winning fair. I willn't be holding a grudge that ye be besting me in the gathering," Thenar said. Machai exhaled slowly, hoping briefly that they could reconcile their differences before he departed for Stanton. "Still, ye be defying me one time too many, and for that I willn't be forgiving ye. Hern here be speaking with Staspin, and in accordance with the gathering tradition, BillowBluff be sending one hundred and fifty men to be joining yer army. It be all they can be sparing."

"That be very generous. I be grateful to ye and yer clan." Machai directed his heartfelt words to Hern across the table. Hern only glared back in silence.

"Aye, ye be getting yer army. I be hoping ye be happy leading the men, knowing ye be never returning to yer home." Thenar polished off his drink and slammed his stein down on the wooden table.

"Thener, I…"

"Ye what, boy? Ye be sorry ye be defying me every chance ye be getting? Ye be whining that it be not fair to be taking yer home from ye? What?" His final word was a hoarse shout as Thenar rose from his seat and loomed so close to Machai that he could feel his clan leader's hot breath on his cheek. "Ye be fighting that battle to be getting yer way, but I be fighting to be keeping the trust and loyalty of me clan. Ye may be feeling victorious as ye march from these walls with two hundred of me men, but ye be the one who have to be telling them that marching behind ye means they be not welcome to return!"

"Ye would be banishing good men from FireFalls for fighting for those who be too few or too weak to be fighting for themselves? Be ye so shortsighted in yer anger at me that ye be punishing all who be fighting for what be right?" Machai kept his tone soft and respectful, but he could feel the flames of rage heating his blood and pulsing in his clenched fists.

"Nay, Machai. I be punishing all who be fighting for *ye*." Thenar's words were a low growl.

Machai stood up and Thenar backed away, although he never broke eye contact. As angry as he was, Machai was still terribly saddened by the finality of Thenar's words. Machai had succeeded in what he set out to do; he would be bringing Osric an army—and one twice as large as he had promised, at that—but Machai would be giving up his home to do so. It was a cost he had known was possible, but that didn't ease the weight he felt pressing on his chest, making each breath feel like he couldn't get enough air in his lungs. In the end, his sadness overwhelmed his anger, and Machai could not even form a response to Thenar's unspoken challenge of violence. He merely nodded in resignation, gave a shallow and stiff bow, and turned and walked out of the room.

By the next morning, everything was packed and ready for departure. Machai stood on a flat, elevated rock just outside the crevice that led into the mountain of his home. Gathered before him were almost two hundred of his kin—men he had grown up with, men he had always looked up to, and many men he had spent his life training for battle—all armed and ready to march away from their home. Thenar's words rang in Machai's head like a clanging bell announcing the death of a warrior. It took all of his strength to raise his voice and address the crowd.

"The mighty dwarven clan of FireFalls be a proud line, a line to be proud of. Ye men be gathered here today because ye be believing that FireFalls, and the rest of Archana, be worth fighting for. Ye be hearing me words and heeding them, that the High-Wizard be a worthy man to be leading ye into battle against the force of a wretched man. Osric be worthy of every word of praise I ever be speaking of him, and ye be good and brave men to be here with me today. If ye truly be believing in this war, in the High-Wizard, and in me, then I be asking ye to be raising yer blades and be following me off of this mountain." A forest of sharp steel was thrust into the sky amid a chorus of raucous shouts, but Machai raised his hand for silence. "But, before ye be following me, ye need to be knowing what it be costing ye, for no battle be free for the defeated, nor for the victor. Thenar be a good dwarf, a good leader of the FireFalls clan, and he be mighty furious that I be seeking an army for another man's war. I be believing he be wrong that this be another man's war, but he be sure he be doing what be right for the clan. Therefore, any man who be following me into battle be earning Thenar's wrath." Machai gazed out over the expectant faces gathered before him and took a deep breath. "If ye be leaving with me, ye willn't be welcomed back. Anyone who be joining me in this army be a welcome member of the Aranthians, an honorable and just group founded to defend those who be in need of it, but no longer will ye be a member of the FireFalls clan." A wave of silent shock spread throughout the crowd. They knew that Thenar would be angry about his defeat, and they didn't expect him to be happy that so many of his clan members had joined the recruited force, but no one had expected Thenar to go so far as to banish anyone who followed Machai.

Machai watched on, fearing that he may be leaving FireFalls alone after all, and he held his breath waiting for the first of his kin to walk back into the mountain. His eyes landed on Kablis, and he watched as his friend and greatest supporter slowly raised his arm and pointed his sword tip into the sky. Soon, others joined him, thrusting their blades upward and cheering loudly. A feeling of relief, camaraderie, and pride overwhelmed Machai as the beginning of his army chanted the name of their new clan.

"Aranthians! Aranthians! Aranthians!"

Not a single dwarf left the crowd to return to Thenar and FireFalls. Machai leapt down from his rock and walked away from the mountain, two hundred men marching behind him on the glistening snow toward the Iron Valley.

Chapter 16
Coiled Potential

Dredek had a few days to rest and recover by the time Jalyn had found the rest of the ingredients he needed. The last of the dead man's stalk had been discovered a short time before in a lower level of the city, but they had found an abundance of the other materials he needed in the room that their new captives had been hiding in. He spent the last two hours mixing everything he needed, and he was nearly ready to begin distilling the medicine that would speed his recovery.

True, his recovery had come faster than ever before, but it had been a more severe injury to himself than any rending of strands had caused. If he had any hope of reviving his kin before the humans or irua could mount a response to his conquering of Angmar, he would need his power soon. Though deadman's stalk was deadly in most cases, his people had learned a method of refining the petrified stalk that, in small doses, brought about the healing of both magic and body at an unprecedented rate.

He dropped the twelve stalks into the boiling cauldron, adding the wolf's essence, and then a handful of kadmel root. The last two would work together to nullify all poisonous properties of the deadman's stalk. He would have to add more of them at specific times during the process, but for the time being he would need to make himself busy while he waited for the boiling water to dissolve the stalks and turn a bright shade of purple, eventually simmering down to a viscous liquid and turning black. Waiting for the color changes to occur could take days, so getting his captives to cooperate was his next objective. Even so, he wished there was something he could do to speed up the process of distilling the medicine.

He left the room, knowing there was no reason for him to remain in the small chamber for the time it would take for the change to happen, and Jalyn would make sure one of the attendants would keep water fed into the pot. He needed to stretch his legs. The long time spent under the sand without seeing the sun was rather unnerving.

Leaving the tunnels for any reason was not possible. Too many of his men would see that as a weakness, so he had to stay inside for the

The Weaving of Wells

same reason he waited until he could stand after his last battle to call for the guards to haul the prisoners to their cell. The only option left to him was to walk the gardens and farms that were placed on every level of the city. The grow lamps and well-lit expanses they provided helped him to displace his desire for the surface's sunlight, and they were well ventilated so far under the sand.

He turned into the grain field and inhaled the odor, closing his eyes. The earthy, sweet smell of soil wafted up from the ground and caused memories of home to flood back into his mind. There were no snow-covered fields of arugula, spinach, cauliflower, and mustard trees, but earthy vegetables had similar smells, and something about the smell of the grain in this area brought him right back to his home. He sat down on the path surrounding the field, pulled out the book his mate had penned centuries ago, and lost himself in memories and calculations.

"Dredek, we've found a man in our ranks who can translate the irua language. We're ready to begin the interrogation at your leisure." Jalyn startled Dredek out of his thoughts.

"Next time could you announce your presence at the door? I nearly killed you." Dredek stood up, whipping the soil from his backside and making sure Jalyn saw his displeasure.

"I'm sorry." Jalyn bowed and backed a few steps away. "You wanted to be informed as soon as we were ready. I'll be sure to announce myself in the future."

"Take me to the prisoners." Dredek glared at his servant, but he stood up straight and motioned for Jalyn to lead the way.

They left the farm behind as the cold, dark halls of Angmar greeted him. They were a poor trade for the lush farm, but it did wonders for refocusing his thoughts. He already knew that the young woman had the strands needed to grant him access to the well, but whether she knew where it was, or how to enter it, he did not know. He was determined to find the answers to his questions, and when he was done distilling the deadman's stalk, he would be ready to bring life to the bones of his people.

Soldiers moved through the halls carrying baskets of food and treasures they had found in several small stashes throughout Angmar. They had yet to find a site that could be considered the city's coffers, and searching for gold, food, and a few small groups that had failed to escape the city consumed most of their time. Dredek made sure the army felt appreciated for the time being. He didn't need to have armed men and women attempting to take power at a time when he was in no condition to do anything other than flee, and the treasure they found was the reward for all of their efforts.

The halls didn't smell nearly as good as the gardens and farms, and each time they turned down a new path the smells changed. He could almost tell what task had been done on each stretch of the way to the holding chambers. One smelled of heat and metal, obviously a forge. Some rooms smelled of spices and alcohol, no doubt the meadery. Another room smelled of linen and lye, so it must be a laundry. But the halls smelled of damp clay and mildew, which lent to the constant headache Dredek had.

Jalyn opened a door to yet another dimly lit hall, but this one ended at a set of bars. All three of their new prisoners were inside the first cell, but the passageway split off to each side, where more cells were filled with captives taken at an earlier time.

"Where is our translator?" Dredek turned in a slow circle, unsatisfied with the promptness of his help.

"I was told that he was here. I'll check with the men outside the door and see." Jalyn stepped toward the door.

"No need, sir. Both of the gentlemen in the cell speak Common." The guard behind him spoke nervously. "Only the girl doesn't."

"We've been chatting with our captors since you put us in here." The eldest male looked up at Dredek with resignation.

"I wish someone would have informed me of this revelation. This news may have changed things." He shot a sharp look at Jalyn. "I think you can find the way out, don't you?"

Jalyn looked up with wide, terrified eyes. "I didn't know. Nobody gave me this information."

Dredek held his gazed steady. "You are well versed in excuses, Jalyn. But right now you should be gaining some experience in retreat, or this man's punishment will be yours." The guard dropped to the ground without a sound, blood pouring from his nose and mouth.

Quickly, the hall was vacated, leaving Dredek alone to get the answer he needed. He turned to the older man and spoke. "May I ask what your name is?"

The Weaving of Wells

"My name is Freyn. Please, let my children go. I will give you anything you want." He stood at the cell door. His words were pleading, but there was nothing but strength in his voice.

Dredek paced in front of the cell, meeting the man's eyes. "My name is Dredek. And what names were given to your children?" He motioned to the boy and girl at the back of the cell with his wand.

"Keth, my eldest son, and Visah, my only daughter." Freyn narrowed his brow and watched Dredek carefully.

"And how is it that two of you speak Common, but the last of you doesn't?" Dredek would much rather have been getting answers directly from the girl. He was suspicious of the fact that she couldn't speak Common. It seemed that most of the irua they had encountered could speak the widely utilized language quite well.

"Some families are called upon to give a child to serve with the Proferre. They are permitted to spend time with their families, but they spend most of their lives with the sect. Outsiders are not permitted to speak to them, so there is no need to teach them Common."

"They take your young away from you? Sounds like cruelty to take a child from her parents. Are there other examples of cruelty among the irua?"

"We were honored to be chosen. Very few are given the opportunity to serve. The Proferre is our highest calling. There is no cruelty involved in becoming a Guardian." There was great sincerity in Freyn's voice.

"And how does one access the Well of Strands?" Dredek leveled his wand at the young boy. "Just to make sure you give me the answers I need, in case you lie to me, or attempt to delay me."

The boy threw himself against the back of the cell, screaming out in pain, and then fell to the ground, shivering. His father and sister ran to his side, concern evident on their faces. The rise and fall of the boy's chest was their only comfort, but his fear-filled face and rapid breathing brought tension to the cell.

"Why?" The father's pleading tone was sorrowful. "Why would you do that? I'll give you anything you ask. Please, just leave my children out of this!"

"I need to make sure you realize how serious a situation you have found yourself in." Dredek didn't like this sort of activity, but it was the only way to make sure he got answers quickly. "It will hurt more next time."

"Please, don't hurt either of them. I will ask her." Freyn turned to his daughter, speaking quickly in the language native to the irua. "Nan wey, chulenek va ya glen?"

She looked hesitantly away from her father, and then to Keth, and back again before she answered. "Nan wey chulenek va ya e sas ah yey va garspa. Ta klet chulenek aya, solo."

"She says the well can only be accessed if you have what is needed. You can't access it on your own."

"Yes, I know about the extra strand. I need to know how to enter the well since I have already located someone with the strand." Dredek nodded at the girl, and then looked back at Freyn. He waved his wand in the direction of Keth, but he cast no spell. "Ask her."

"Nan wey, yey keb sas et leh trabis?" He looked at his daughter with stern, pleading eyes.

"Sas ness skib nan etch em nan flet es nan bate. Aya lep ncskin." Visah shrugged nervously.

"You have to write the runes on the wall and an opening will appear." Freyn spoke very clearly, but his speech was rushed—almost panicked. His gaze kept sweeping to his children and then back to Dredek. He stood between the wand and his son with his chest puffed out.

"And only one with what is needed can write the rune?" It was a cold voice that Dredek chose to elicit replies. He couldn't risk his prisoners guessing how much he dreaded having to hurt the child to get what he wanted.

"Nan sas ah yey va garspa ness skib nan etch?" Freyn asked Visah, unsure himself of how it worked as he had never trained with the sect that protected the well.

"Peg," Visah answered.

"Yes." Freyn turned back quickly to face Dredek.

"Good job, father. Now tell your daughter to take me to the well and open the door. Tell her to take me by the most direct route or I will kill her father and her brother." Dredek locked gazes with Visah and he donned a most serious expression, turning the wand toward Freyn. "You will tell me exactly what she says, or I will kill her and find myself another of the well guardians. Do you understand?"

"Yes, I understand." Freyn trembled almost imperceptibly and pointed at their captor as he spoke to his daughter. "Voy Dredek leh nan wey iz neskin aya." He locked a hateful gaze on Dredek. "Leh nan mair yestin o ta lep brusein es saftin crag sen."

"Sen klet, aya va shamin." Visah shook her head slowly, tears streaming down her scared face.

"She says it is forbidden." Freyn repeated her words for Dredek in Common between clenched teeth.

"Len ness!" Keth shouted at Visah, desperation in his voice.

"Aya va shamin!" she yelled back at him.

"Ta lep brusein se!" he shouted at his sister again.

"Enough!" Freyn shouted at his son. Both siblings shrank back and looked up at their father.

"What are they going on about?" Dredek stepped closer to the cell. "And remember to be honest." He flicked his wand as a reminder. Keth curled into a ball, closing his eyes in anticipation of pain.

"She says that giving you the information is forbidden. He says that she has to give you the information or you will kill him." Freyn held his hands up in surrender. "Please, wait! I can talk her into it!"

"I've already told you that I will not tolerate delay." He pointed his wand back at the boy. The girl screamed

"No!" The father moved in front of the wand. "Please, just give me a chance to reason with her. There is no need for this!" Both of the younger irua wept in opposite corners of the cell.

"I am running out of patience," Dredek said with his jaw clenched. The shouting was wearing at his nerves. "Make it quick!"

"Yes. I understand" Freyn backed away and knelt, ready to leap between Dredek's wand and his daughter and spoke in a soothing, yet pleading, voice. "Visah, len ness voy Dredek leh nan wey iz neskin aya. Brey, Es goya essen vat. Es saftin essen vat. Sen es vat. Brey!"

"I'm growing tired of this. I need to know what you're saying!" Sparks hit the wall at the back of the cell. Dredek wasn't proud of it, but his patience had nearly run out. He almost allowed himself to kill the boy, which made his hand shake perceptibly.

"I told her she must help you. I said that her family needs her to. Her brother needs her to, and I need her to." Tears were streaming down the father's face as he held his daughter's hands. "Visah, brey. Brey."

Osric's Wand

"What is *brey*?" Dredek lifted his chin.

"*Brey* means please." His large hands reached up and caressed his daughter's head as she buried her face in his chest. Her long strawberry-blonde hair hid her pale, tear-streaked face from view and Freyn's hand moved gently across it. He spoke in a whisper, over and over again, saying, "Brey Visah, brey."

The sight of the family huddled together for comfort in a time of danger was hard for Dredek to watch. Had his mate comforted his sons on their last day? Had Aeya spoken soft lies to dull their fear in the dark winter night? Did they see the army coming, or did they die asleep in their beds? Dredek didn't know, and now he was the one bringing the fear. But it must be done; there was no other way to bring them back. He shook himself out of his daze as Visah began to nod in agreement with her father's plea.

"Peg, es ness." She pulled away from Freyn's embrace. Her lips quivered when she looked to her captor. But there was something in her eyes, something primal that allowed her to gain some courage.

Dredek wasn't entirely sure what she had said, but he knew from the Portentist gift that she would show him the way. "Good." He nodded. "Now, I hope you can understand that I can't have you conscious when we open the door. I won't kill you, you have my word." He had already been forced to kill too many men to bring about his plans.

He slipped a small vial from his satchel and held it out for the father to take. "It will make you sleep, but no harm will come to you or your children. I swear it." His voice was softer than he had intended and Freyn looked at him, confused. "Give it to the boy, first, but no more than two drops—one, if you can manage it. He will fall asleep before he finishes swallowing it."

Freyn unstoppered the glass and smelled the contents with a wary eye. He tipped it back on the cork as the boy lay down on his back. They spoke light words of comfort, assuring Visah that they would be okay until she returned. Then the father turned the wet cork over and watched carefully until a single drop landed in Keth's mouth.

True to the promise, the boy fell asleep without another movement. Freyn watched his chest rise and fall until he was satisfied his son was safe. Then, rewetting the cork, he asked, "Why?"

"Why?" Dredek searched for a meaning to the question.

The Weaving of Wells

"Why threaten our lives, only to pay in kindness when you have what you need?" Pausing with the cork upturned in his hand, Freyn looked up with earnest eyes.

"No kindness was paid to my family at their end." Dredek looked him in the eye. "But, now they will live again."

Freyn looked back with wide eyes. A mix of awe and fear traced the rough face. He leaned back against the wall, lifting the cork. "I wish you luck. Please, if you succeed, show us mercy again." He touched the cork to his tongue and went limp.

"When I am finished..." Dredek bowed his head and took a deep breath. "I've made no plans for myself on that day."

The chamber was silent in spite of coughs, chains, and whispered words from the other cells. He had what he needed, and it was a disappointment. Dredek had expected to be reveling in his achievements, but instead it had brought back memories of loss and pain. He stood there in silence, watching Visah comfort her sleeping family. All he could do was wish he had been with Aeya, Chehl, and Tweggan, to offer them comfort on the day they were killed. He wished he could have died with them.

After a suitable few moments of punishing memories, Dredek looked up to see Visah standing at the door, ready to leave. He looked around the chamber and remembered that he had the room vacated and no guard was left to open the door. Taking a deep breath, he stood up straight and prepared himself to look the part of a leader again.

"Guards!" The door opened and light streamed into the room. "Bring the girl." Dredek turned and walked slowly to the door. Keys rattled in the lock, and rusty hinges squealed as the door to the cell opened. Visah cried out from rough treatment and he turned back to the men.

"No!" When he faced Aeya again, he wanted her to be able to recognize him. Before all this, he had been a gentleman. "You will treat her as a guest or I'll see to it you don't make it home to enjoy your gold."

The men gently motioned for Visah to follow. Dredek felt some small amount of pride in how quickly they changed tactics. He thought he saw the guard on the left offer an arm to Visah as an escort, but he had then decided against it and withdrew the arm.

"Get some lights up in the cells. Start cleaning and feeding the prisoners better. We're not animals!" He smiled as they passed by him, Visah leading the way to the well.

Chapter 17
Homefront

Toby looked out at the room. He hadn't expected there to be as many gathered in the room as there was. This was the first official assembly in the newly restored palace since the peace treaty ratification that was attacked over a year earlier. Voices echoed off of the stone walls; they were all passionate about the issues before them, and they were worried. Kenneth walked down the center of the room in his Vigile dress uniform, climbed the stairs of the raised dais, and took a seat at the far right of the table.

Quickly surveying the room, Toby noticed all five of his hains, his main advisors, were present: Desmond, Kirkus, Megan, Staut, and Trevan. In addition, the leader of the trade guild, Yessip, had taken time out of his very busy day to join the meeting. Then, of course, Kenneth was in attendance. And these were only the ones who could fit at the lead table.

Toby stood up, holding his hands out to silence the crowd. Only a few of the gatherers noticed the gesture, but they began to spread the word and conversations started to dwindle from a roar to a whisper. It didn't take long before he had the attention of everybody in the room.

"We all know why we're here. So, why don't we start this with a summation from our hain of treasury. Staut, please take the floor." Toby bowed and motioned him to step to the front of the table, then the ryhain sat back down. Staut stepped to the opposite side of the table, walked to center stage, and offered his hand to Toby, showing respect. Toby took his hand and bowed back, signaling for him to speak.

"Rowain's refugees have caused a significant strain to our already limited coffers." Staut opened the ledger he carried under his right arm.

"My home has been broken into three times!" A tall, skinny man stood up and shouted from the back of the room.

"I've got forty people sleeping in my fields each night. They've nearly eaten my entire crop of cabbage!" A woman stood up at the front of the room.

Osric's Wand

"Two of my horses are missing!"

"They've taken over my barn!"

"They tore apart two of my carts and are using them to build camp fires!"

The room erupted with a cacophony of voices. Who had made the complaints and what wrongs had been done were lost in the commotion. Otherwise kind and reasonable individuals were now shouting and shoving each other in an attempt to be heard. The Vigile guards at the doors looked nervously at each other and then towards Kenneth, who signaled for them to calm their nerves.

"Please, please!" Toby stood up, addressing the crowd. "We can't accomplish anything if we conduct ourselves in this manner!" Slowly, the volume began to decline until the Stanton citizens looked up at the table with concerned expressions.

"Hundreds flock to Stanton each day. Not only to our walls, but to other cities as well. They flee Rowain in an attempt to find new homes and safety. We see them. Not all bring mischief in their wake. Most are honest, hard-working families." Toby leaned on the table, earnestly speaking with the assembly.

"I need twenty-five new Vigile recruits, minimum, just to begin keeping peace in Stanton." Kenneth spoke up from his seat at the end. "I'll take you, if you want to join," he said, looking out at the crowd.

"Look, I realize that the resources of the city are stretched thin, and all of your concerns are valid. While I can't promise that there will be no more trouble from the refugees, I can assure you that I will find a way to keep our city safe and secure. Please." Toby gazed out at the assembled expressions of fear and anger. "Continue to welcome these people with the grace and generosity that has brought them here in the first place. The guard will be reinforced, and we will come through this time stronger if we stick together and keep our trust in others." Toby watched as his words lent a small measure of calm to the crowd. Some even smiled at the reminder that it was their good-hearted nature that made the outcast from Rowain seek solace in Stanton. He looked over to Kenneth and an idea struck him.

"How are the new walls, anyway?" Toby looked to Staut for an answer.

"Uh…" He adjusted his glasses. "The walls were finished three days ago, sir."

The Weaving of Wells

"Great!" Toby clapped his hands. "Yessip, I think we can do something to help speed things along, if you could help me?" He smiled.

"I am at your service, of course." Yessip bowed his best seated bow.

"I hear that there are still many positions that need to be filled in Stanton," Toby prompted.

"Yes, sir. With all the help lost in the palace collapse, plus the battle against the Kallegian, it's understandable that we haven't been able to replace the ones who were lost." The leader of the Trade Guild had his hands in many different businesses. He knew more about the business situation in Stanton than any other man.

"So, we have new walls and few to man them. And we have many merchants in search of help, with many positions yet to be filled in the palace. Then, we have hundreds flocking to our walls on a daily basis with no work. Why is it that all we can think about is the trouble that has been caused by these people, and have taken no notice of the aid they could bring to us?" Toby leaned forward in his chair.

"The walls were meant to keep them out. How could we let them in when we built the walls to keep them out?" Staut stuttered.

"We built the wall to keep out armies, like the Kallegian, not poor folks left behind by a sadistic leader." Kenneth laughed.

"But…" Nervously, out of habit, Staut looked to his books as he searched for something to say.

"Yessip." Toby turned his attention away. "In two days we will be holding a welcoming party for those who have turned to Stanton for a new home. See to it the market district is prepared to welcome them. Have the merchants that need help prepare. If we claim to be on the side of right, we need to be doing right by those that are left in the cold by those doing wrong."

"Of course, it will be done." Yessip nodded respectfully.

"I am sure there are many among those fleeing Rowain who have gold as well. Inviting them to join us could help to bolster our already strained economy." Staut looked up from his books expectantly.

"And the more appealing we can make Stanton appear, the better our chances to be the place they stay." Toby looked at him approvingly. "So if we can find any room to offer the markets some support, it could go a long way toward securing our town as their new home." He motioned for the two to work together.

"But what about our homes? We have been robbed on many occasions! Are we supposed to look the other way?" A large man stood at the front of the crowd with a child at his side. His homespun clothing and hearty build suggested he was a farmer.

"Kenneth, could you set a few Vigiles outside the walls to help our farms stay safe until we get things sorted? Maybe see if you could get a few volunteers." Toby looked to Kenneth at his left. Though those who inhabited Stanton knew that the Aranthians dwelled in their town, Toby knew that making the Aranthians a part of daily life could set a dangerous precedent, so he kept the implied favor between the two of them.

"I think I could spare a few men, and I am sure our mutual friend would be willing to give us all the help we need until I can train the new volunteers." He knew what Toby was indicating when he asked for volunteers, and it wasn't the town population he wanted working with the Vigile troops.

"Good." Toby nodded. "Now, I am sure some of you"—he looked back at the farmer—"could find suitable aid and the laborers you need from those outside the walls? You shouldn't have to put your children to work until they are finished with classes."

"I suppose I could use some help. I've been looking at purchasing more land. I've just been waiting until more crops were needed." He looked down at his son. "And I suppose he could put more effort into his schooling."

"Good, then it is settled. We will do what we can for the next couple days to negate the threat they bring, and then we will attempt to have many of them become a part of us. We can manage the threats that come afterward at that time." Toby stood up, signaling the guards to begin ushering the people out of the room.

The room's inhabitants began to funnel out the door at the back. The hains stepped down from the dais to join the others as Toby and Kenneth stepped to the side to confer.

"Do you plan to see Osric soon?" Toby stepped close and whispered softly.

"As soon as I leave this room. I'll try to get as many Aranthians as I can to help us. I am certain I can get a couple dozen of their finest for the next few days. They aren't planning anything sooner than that, as far as I know," Kenneth replied.

"That sounds great, but I was wondering if you wouldn't mind me accompanying you—there is a rather large favor I wish to ask of Osric, and I don't want to have it delivered as a message.

* * *

"I had him trusted early the morning before me and Serha..." Aridis shook, still unable to speak of the events that had happened. The old man looked shrunken and haggard from a week of drug-aided sleep and too little food. He wrapped his hands around his warm mug of rulha, but he hadn't taken a single drink. The dining hall in the Aranthian headquarters buzzed with quiet conversations, and Aridis struggled to maintain his focus on the question that Osric had asked. He had been struggling with most everything lately, but he silently chastised himself. Aridis knew that for events to unfold in the desired direction he must continue on his path, and if Serha had still been there, she would have insisted that he put his best foot forward. It took too much out of him to even discuss the particulars that had taken place before her death. Eight days had been little time to mourn, but his body had recovered so it was time to get back to work. Luckily, everyone understood the direction his statement was heading in, and Osric gracefully saved him from having to hear himself speak of it again.

"And Pendres, you believe, has information that could help us in defeating Dredek?" he asked, casting a quick glance at the hermit across the table.

After taking a few moments to gather his thoughts, Aridis said, "I believe he can give us a great deal more than just information." His answer was slow to the point of timid, and his old bones cracked as he squeezed his hands into fists. Serha's face was still fresh in his memory. Her large, watery eyes still haunted him as he remembered their last stroll into the woods outside Stanton. Focusing on the here and now was difficult, but somehow he managed it.

"I still don't understand what he thinks I can do, or if I will truly stay for long enough to offer my aid, but some of the words he said to me have me curious enough to see if what he says holds promise."

Pendres folded his arms across his chest—a defensive gesture, but harmless to those around him. His posture was a way to comfort himself in the presence of uncertainty; even Aridis could sense that without the Empath gift.

"And I'm at a loss as to how you could have been trusted in if you have no interest in helping us," Osric stated without malice. His implied question was sincere; he was genuinely curious.

"I have no interest in betraying anyone, so long as you are honorable in intent. Everything I have seen while I have been here suggests that you are all honorable, good people. My only issue is with your conflict—battle has done nothing but bring me misery and a very long life." His eyes were distant as he spoke. "A very long life to look forward to, and too many things haunt a mind when one is alone for that long."

"The Trust can attest to the fact that he would not betray us in any foreseeable situation. But I've brought him to you to attempt to persuade him to join our cause. I thought if you could tell him of what we have managed to accomplish, as well as what we are up against, he might see why it is so important for him to help us." Aridis's lip shook. It went nearly unnoticed, but almost nothing got by Osric these days. "If you could just start with the time you spent with the eagles, I believe that is far enough back to be useful.

"Okay." Osric shifted uncomfortably in his chair. "After the palace was attacked, we pursued the irua that left Stanton, thinking they were the ones responsible. While en route, the dragon we chose for transportation was mistakenly attacked by a young eagle."

"Mistakenly?" Pendres leaned in with a questioning gaze.

"Yes," Osric replied. "Eagles teach their young not to attack walkers." He looked up and sighed. "*Walkers* is the term they use for all land animals. They teach them to avoid hunting us because they want to avoid the tradition behind the hunt."

"Why would they avoid it?" Pendres asked.

"Well." Osric's brow creased. "They didn't tell us, but from what we witnessed, the only meat they eat is fish. I'm assuming they don't want to track down someone's loved ones after the hunt is complete." He winced and turned to Aridis with an apologetic expression. "Anyway," he continued, "we were brought to the cliffs where they live while we waited for Greyback to heal."

The Weaving of Wells

"Greyback was the dragon's name?" Pendres inclined his head questioningly.

"Yes." Osric nodded. "While we were there, the eagles told us about how wands were invented and about how the dragons were enslaved shortly after the caldereth were wiped out."

Pendres looked down at his hands with a mournful cast. Osric looked the hermit over. There was a great deal of regret in Pendres's outward shift. Aridis wondered if something in the story touched at some point in his past life, and he felt that Osric had the same thought.

"At that time," Osric continued, "it was decided that freeing the dragons would do more for the cause of avoiding a war than continuing to the Irua Realm. The irua were just too far ahead of us, and we had to wait for Greyback to heal after the eagle attacked us and wounded her.

"Through a great deal of planning, even more luck, the timely intervention of the eagles, and some courage from an enslaved race of dragons, we managed to free them from their captors." Osric shook his head slowly, remembering the day. "After that, we returned home to try to make sense of everything. We needed to get our bearings and figure out what to do next. Unfortunately, the Kallegian took an interest in Stanton due to our investigation." He drew in a long, slow breath as he related the story.

"The Kallegian took interest in you and you survived?" Pendres narrowed his eyes and his lips pressed close with distaste. He didn't believe what he was being told, and this was obvious to anyone close enough to witness his gaze.

"Oh, yeah." Osric turned his hands out to ward off any argument, showing that he understood the lack of acceptance. "But while they patrolled our streets, trying to find me"—one hand pointed back at himself—"Kenneth and I had been captured by Dredek and his men in Rowain."

"Dredek?" Pendres stiffened in his chair. "His name was Dredek?"

Osric looked up at the interruption. "Yes. Why?"

Aridis leaned forward, listening to the exchange. Something about the way Pendres held himself told him that there must be a connection between the two men. Though, why the name meant something to him was unclear.

"It's just"—Pendres shrugged—"Dredek was a common caldereth name." He looked suspiciously at Aridis.

"That's because he's a caldereth." Osric joined Pendres in questioning Aridis. "What did you tell him?"

"I told him nothing. I left everything for you to reveal." Aridis looked innocently between the two large men.

"Well, that's one of the things we learned about him in Rowain. I don't know how he survived, but somehow he has modified his appearance enough to appear human." Osric turned his attention back to the hermit. "Well, at least he is close enough in appearance to human to fool anyone who hasn't seen a caldereth. But he hasn't only modified his appearance; he has taken gifts from the living to give himself more power, all in an attempt to bring the caldereth back from the dead."

Pendres's eyes went wide and traced the grain in the table. He raised his right hand to his mouth and stroked the braid along the side of his blond beard.

Osric continued with a casual but somewhat cautious tone as he gazed across the table at the newcomer. "Since then, we defeated the Kallegian and very nearly stopped Dredek from capturing Angmar."

"A caldereth captured Angmar?" Pendres stood up with such gusto that his chair slid backwards, nearly tipping over when it caught the edge of the stone floor. He held a panicked expression as he breathed rapidly, looking to Osric for confirmation. There was genuine despair in every aspect of his stance. Pendres glared over at Aridis. "Your dragon told me the Turgent took the city."

Before Osric could confirm Pendres's fears, Gus burst through the door, followed by a very flustered-looking Eublin. Gus pointed a furry paw at Pendres, but his shouting was directed at Aridis.

"This guy can't be killed?! You're telling me we have been wracking our brains and training hundreds of men to die in the deserts of the Irua Realm and this guy can't die? Why don't we just send him over there to take on the entire army and wipe out Dredek for us? All our problems can be solved with one man, and you are in here sipping on your mugs and swapping stories!"

Eublin shuffled in, nearly bowing and alternating between adjusting his spectacles and tugging on his tunic. "Please note that I have no intention of requesting any such thing of our guest. Gus is

The Weaving of Wells

misconstruing everything that I said. I take no credit for his assumptions about Pendres, nor for his terribly rude and misguided outburst."

"By the strands, you old bookworm! You said this guy can't be killed. How could I possibly misconstrue that?" Gus screamed at him.

"You may have heard the words, but you are certainly misunderstanding their meaning," Aridis interrupted Gus's rant. "It is not that he cannot be killed; it is that he cannot die until the war is over."

"Yes, because there is so much difference between those two statements. Everything is clear now." Gus's sarcasm impressed no one.

"A great deal of difference, actually. Killing is an action that you engage in; being killed is that action taken against you. Dying is a finality, but not something that can be inflicted upon you. Would you ask Pendres to be killed, over and over, simply for his lack of dying?" Aridis asked, his voice gruff and strained by the threat of tears. Speaking of death was no easier just because the reference was to someone other than Serha.

Gus glanced over at Pendres a bit sheepishly. "I hadn't thought about it like that."

"That's because you didn't consider the burdensome implications of such a supposed gift. I did not bring Pendres here to ask him to suffer for us. I brought him here because he is the only man alive who is likely to understand why Dredek is seeking the Well of Strands, and maybe even how he intends to use it to raise his people. Maybe, if you stop yelling for a moment and listen, you will learn something too."

"The rat has a point." Everyone in the room turned to Pendres in surprise, though Gus's annoyance at the term *rat* was more apparent in his expression than his shock at being scolding by Aridis. "Maybe I should just go kill Dredek before he accomplishes his goal." Pendres was serious; the Empath ability was enough to convince Osric of that, but that didn't explain how he thought he might accomplish it.

"Is it true that you cannot be killed?" Osric's voice was low and hesitant.

"It is true that I have taken many fatal injuries in my very long lifetime. I should have died, I have died many times, but I didn't die. Aridis seems to think he understands why." Pendres paused, but it was clear he wanted to say more. "I am just as susceptible to injury as any other man, though I am better than most at avoiding it. I feel every ache and pain, every blade and arrow tip, every tooth and claw of the beast as it tears into my flesh. As Aridis says, I can be killed, I just don't die."

"In that case, I will not send you to Angmar to suffer the blows that Dredek will surely deliver. To answer your earlier question, Dredek has also usurped the Turgency of the Human Realm. The whole city of Angmar is overrun by the his army, by great hulking beasts that tunnel through sand and stone like garden worms and kill indiscriminately like paun, and by Dredek's very advanced and effective magic. I wish I didn't have to send anyone back there, but I certainly won't send only one man." Osric watched Pendres, using his abilities to determine the effects of his words. Though the recluse from a distant land seemed little impressed by the danger, the mention of the sand creatures had given him pause, and Pendres's level of respect for Osric increased significantly by the end of his little speech. Osric glanced away, feeling his cheeks burn slightly, as if he had overheard his own praises while using his gifts to spy on a private conversation. He needed to know if he could trust Pendres, but he didn't think he would ever be comfortable using his abilities to pry into the minds and hearts of others.

"I admire your commitment to your people, and your resolution to not put any one person in harm's way as a means to an end, but I fear you may not be able to make the hard calls necessary to win a war," Pendres said. "Still, I believe it will be worthwhile to aid you in your mission. Perhaps, if Aridis is correct, it will bring me some peace as well."

"It seems I will be bringing about your death either way. It is not a position I take lightly," Osric said, and Pendres nodded once in acknowledgment of the concern for his life. "Will you tell us what you know about the wells?"

Pendres thought back to his conversation with Aridis when he had first arrived in Stanton, about the spell that was cast upon him and his painful memories of who had likely cast it. "It is quite possible that the wells are why I am still here to speak with you today." He glanced over at Aridis. "No one could have cast the spell you spoke of without the aid of the well's power. But it was not the well in Angmar that she used." Memories haunted his eyes.

"Do you know how many there are?" Osric asked.

"No, I can't be certain, but there must be at least twenty. The one that Dredek seeks is the largest and most powerful. It is the center of the network, a direct line into the source of Archana's magic."

"What?" Gus interrupted. "What does that mean?"

"All of life, all magic, comes from Archana. Not only in a generative way, but literally from within Archana. Beneath the ground, perhaps at the core, I'm not sure exactly how it works. Just as our magic can be harvested from Archana, as any Wand-Maker would understand, so too our life strands and all the potential magic the world has to offer is stored within the ground beneath our feet." Gus glared at the man, as if this information wasn't obvious to him as a world-renowned Wand-Maker. "It is a closed system. When a creature dies, or a spell diminishes, the magic returns to the soil and to the source within Archana. The wells, for lack of a clearer description, are taps into that system. They open a vein into the heart of Archana's magic stores, and they allow the wizard to draw on the unlimited source of strands all at once. It is probably far more dangerous and terrifying than any of you have considered." All eyes were riveted on Pendres, staring silently at the implications of his words. Osric could not even formulate a question as he considered what it would mean for Dredek to have access to that much power. "Are you sure you don't want him assassinated?" Pendres could see Osric's fears written on his face.

"While I understand your desire to end the threat quickly, I do not yet believe that one man could manage such a thing. And I can't help but suspect that Dredek is motivated more by a devotion to the kin that he lost than by evil inclinations in grabbing for power and world domination." Osric thought back to the pain he had seen in Dredek's eyes, though he feared he was misleading himself in giving the caldereth such credit.

"You don't really think that a man who intends to bring an entire race back from the dead will relinquish the power that allows him to do so, do you?" Aridis was eyeing Osric like a specimen in an experiment.

Osric's Wand

"No, I suppose I don't. Regardless of his current goals, it would be devastating to allow Dredek to harness the power of the Well of Strands. We have to stop him, but sending an assassin would be futile. Even if you made it close to Dredek, he is too fast and too well versed in the use of his many abilities for any one man to take him out." Osric winced at the truth of his own words, remembering how Dredek had defeated him the last time they met in battle.

"When you say 'many abilities,' you don't mean…"

"Yes, Pendres, I do mean abilities. Somehow Dredek is capable of severing the strands that house a man's innate gift and taking it for himself. He has a half-dozen gifts, at least, and he knows how to use them with lethal efficiency."

Pendres's only response was a long, slow whistle as he leaned back in his seat.

"Pendres, do you know what the wells were built for? Was there a specific purpose in mind?" Aridis asked.

"As far as I can tell, they were built to end the war of all wars. In those times, every realm was at war with someone, and oftentimes we weren't even sure who we were fighting. We would start marching toward a battle with the injuk and end up in skirmishes with every town and tribe along the way. It's no wonder history has erased the names of so many peoples and forgotten so many of the atrocities of that hundred-year span. It was a terrible chapter for the Human Realm, and I have spent centuries wishing I hadn't been a part of it."

"Who built them?" Gus asked, humbled by the peaceful life he had taken for granted for so many years in the comfort of Stanton's economic and political stability.

"The Alliance," Pendres said. "A few hundred talented folks around Archana who wanted to see a unified world and more efficient uses of magic than violence and warfare. My wife was a member." He had to pause for a moment as memories washed over him and constricted his throat. "While I marched off to war, she was traveling the world trying to save us all."

Before Pendres could explain how the wells were constructed, Kenneth walked into the room with Toby right behind him. Osric noticed the arrival with surprise, as the Ryhain had come to the Aranthian headquarters only a few times since it had been founded. There would have to be a good reason for Toby to be there. Osric hoped his presence wasn't an ominous sign. He stood up to greet the two as those surrounding him took notice of the newcomers.

"Ryhain Toby, Contege Kenneth, this is Pendres. He is a guest of the Aranthians." The two men nodded with friendly smiles in greeting. "So, to what do we owe the honor of this visit? It's good to see you both. Will you join us for a meal?" Osric indicated the free chairs to his left.

"We at least have time for a drink. Don't worry, we won't distract you for long. We've come to ask a favor." Toby brushed his hands down the front of his jacket and sat down as a server approached the table. "A mug of mead each for the two of us, please." The server left with a nod of his head to get the drinks.

"You're a welcome distraction. What can the Aranthians do for you? We are at your service," Osric replied. "Ask what favor you will, and if it is within our ability you will have it." Osric kept the conversation official, avoiding their typical friendly banter. They had come on business, and the stranger who sat listening to them engage in the conversation was cause for a more professional interaction than usual. Toby's body language echoed his feelings on the subject.

"We need men," Toby said plainly.

"Men?" Osric cocked his head.

"Three, four dozen should work. I'll need them for several days. We have a situation brewing with all of the refugees coming to our town from Rowain," Toby continued.

"A situation?" Osric leaned in. "What kind of situation?"

"Well, the farms outside our new walls are being inhabited by"—Toby tilted his head, choosing his words carefully—"less than respectable individuals. We need to bolster the support from the Vigiles with Aranthian troops to see that our citizens and food sources are safe. I was hoping that, since you and Kenneth are old friends, you might allow us to borrow some of your troops."

"Of course. You will have them first thing in the morning." Osric looked at Kenneth, and then anxiously back toward Toby again. "Can I ask what you intend to do about the refugees? I don't want to send our men out if they are going to be a part of sending away the hungry and homeless."

"Actually, we are going to hold a welcome for the families and those who have an honest interest in making Stanton a home. In the wake of the attacks on Stanton over the last year, there are many jobs that need to be filled." Toby leaned back in his chair. "We need your men to help keep our resources secure until we can sort through the rabble that comes with them. It shouldn't be more than a few men in a hundred that we turn away, but we need to be sure we can protect our citizens."

"The Aranthians are happy to help. I'll spread the word that we are looking for volunteers, so you'll probably have more than you asked for by evening." Osric looked around and stood up, addressing the room.

"We're looking for as many volunteers as we can get to work with the Vigile force to secure Stanton's wall, as well as helping to secure our farms. There are many refugees of Rowain outside, and we need to treat them with respect while making sure our town's resources are kept safe. Spread the word to all of our members and meet us back here for dinner." Osric sat back down, looking to Toby for approval.

"I think that will do." Toby chuckled lightly. "But I don't think I'll be able to be here for dinner."

"No need, we'll have our men report directly to the Vigile office at the palace first thing in the morning." Osric looked to Kenneth with a smile.

"I promise I won't take them from you for too long. I have recruiters working full-time already. We have our training crews working every day right now." Kenneth nodded respectfully.

"No need to rush," Osric replied. "There may be some benefit to the Aranthians to get in some real-time patrolling the streets."

"It certainly did good for you." Kenneth laughed.

"Then it's settled." Toby stood up, leaning over the table to shake Osric's hand. "But, if I could have a word with you in private, I would appreciate it." His eyes drifted to the surrounding ears.

Pendres looked relieved to have a reason to excuse himself from the discussion of Stanton business and from all of the people gathering at their table. "If you don't mind my departing your company for a while, there are a few books I would love to locate in your library. I haven't laid eyes on a library in decades," Pendres said. Osric gripped his wrist and gave him leave to seek out the library. Pendres excused himself with a tight smile and a polite bow, and Eublin offered to escort Pendres to the library and help him navigate the shelves.

The Weaving of Wells

"I have to speak to my fellow sight-enabled fools about another project they have going. They seem to think they are about to create a tool that would allow the non-gifted to manipulate strands so they could make their own wands. I am not a fan." Gus jumped down from his chair with a feigned frown, failing to hide his newfound excitement, then scampered out of the room.

"I think I could use the solitude of a good book myself to divert my mind from our world. Could you offer me a few suggestions?" Aridis looked questioningly to Eublin. "Somewhat of an escape would be nice."

"Of course." Eublin motioned for him to follow them. "I've got just the thing. Have you ever heard of the grand epic *Saulsman's Journey?*" Their voices trailed off as they exited the room, leaving Osric at the table with Kenneth and Toby.

"Kenneth, you should stay so you know what I'd like to have happen." Toby looked around the room. "Would this be a good place to talk?"

"It's as good a place as any; every person within the protection spell has been trusted in. You can say anything you want and not worry about your words being used against you." Osric motioned for him to continue.

"Very well." Toby sat back down in his chair and thanked the server as their mead arrived. "I don't suppose we have time to sample some of James's famous cooking? I miss that damned cart he used to push around, and I haven't had a chance to visit the new establishment."

"If you have the time, I am always willing to partake in what he creates." Osric turned to the expectant face of the young man who brought the mead. "I'll have mead as well. Then, get a message to James. Tell him the Ryhain is here and would love to sample some of his restaurant food."

"Very good, sir. I'll let him know, straight away." He turned sharply toward the kitchen and became lost in the activity of the room.

"He's a good kid, but a bit too stiff," Osric said, referring to the waiter. "He's a new Aranthian who James brought in for the kitchen specifically. Too stiff to work in any environment other than a kitchen, that is. He is the best server in this place, though. Just wish I

Osric's Wand

could remember his name." He laughed. It was just the three of them now, so all pretense of formality quickly dispersed.

"I'm a bit envious of what you've managed to create here. The food alone, from what I'm told, is enough to make me want to abandon my post and enlist as an Aranthian." Toby relaxed into his chair, sipping his mead as the three men laughed.

"You might as well." Kenneth smirked. "It's not like they'd miss you all that much. Put a goat in the office and nobody would notice you're missing."

"A goat?" Toby scoffed playfully. "They'd never want me to come back if they did that."

"I don't know." Remembering some of the whispers he heard, Osric probed. "I hear people are petitioning to make you Turgent."

"Nah." Toby waved his hand. "There are always people talking, but that will never happen."

"Not when they get a taste of what the goat can do." Kenneth slapped him on the shoulder.

They laughed, slowly drained the mead from their mugs, and watched as the server brought in three wide-brimmed, small, white bowls. He sat one in front of each of them, then pulled silver spoons from his spotless white apron.

"Our first course is potato pillows and mushrooms in cream sauce," he continued, pointing with an outstretched hand to a second server placing a wooden carving board with a steaming loaf of bread atop it. "And rosemary salted loaf. Enjoy." He bowed and backed away from the table.

Toby listened expectantly to the description of the meal and closed his eyes while breathing in the aroma that rose in vapor trails above the dish. Then, he sighed again as the bread was placed in the center of the table.

"He didn't have anything like this on his cart." Toby shook his head in awe. Then, filling the spoon, he tasted the dish for the first time. The potato pillows had a soft, velvety texture. The mushroom flavor carried itself through the buttery cream sauce. Slowly savoring the taste, he sighed with delight and reached for the bread, tearing a large chunk off of the loaf. "I'm going to have to get a vat of this sent to my rooms."

The Weaving of Wells

"Can you have me reassigned to be your chamber servant?" Kenneth was already cleaning the bowl with his spoon.

"I'm sorry, the Vigiles need you. But I'll have you inspect my quarters for hidden threats on a regular basis." Toby's belly shook with joy as he dipped the bread into the bowl unceremoniously.

"That could take some time. It would go faster if I helped him." Osric licked the last of the cream off of the backside of his spoon and leaned back, watching Toby finish his portion.

It didn't take long for him to finish. Then he cleaned whatever he could out of the bowl with the remnants of his bread, looking to the kitchen with great eagerness.

"If that was just the first dish, I can't wait to see what comes next." Toby whistled.

They each nodded in agreement. Their eyes traced the dishes on the table for signs of remnants as they smiled contentedly. Osric placed a hand on his chin, trying to remember the reason for this unannounced visit. But something else came to mind before he could recall.

"So, what do you think is the reason behind the talk of you becoming Turgent?" Osric inclined his head.

"Well." Toby pushed his dish to the edge of the table. "The irony of all this is that our home has become more stable since the attack than Rowain." He shrugged. "Whispers come to us that the family of Bartholo have reasserted themselves in the leadership of Rowain, but have found their ledger balance is in the negative after Dredek sailed to the Irua Realm. They simply don't have the coin to operate effectively. Dredek bled the Rowainites dry. It will take some time for them to be effective in governing the realm. But when they do, I have no intention of challenging their claim."

They continued with the small talk as their next two courses came and went. The second dish was, as their server described it, "lemon chicken served over a bed of quinoa, kale, and a balsamic reduction," which left Toby speechless. The meal was finished with a simple yet delightful raspberry tart. They each leaned back and Toby patted his belly happily.

"I guess we've spent enough time with lax conversation. I must admit that I miss the time we had before each of us had so much responsibility." Toby's eyes looked lost in memories, but in an instant they refocused and he continued. "Still, responsibilities abound. There was a favor I wished to ask of you, and that's why I am here." He sat upright pleasantly enough, but it was clear that business was once again at the forefront of his mind.

"He didn't even tip the waiter. And look at him, he's already fled from the Aranthian paradise and returned to the drudgery of palace politics." Kenneth shot a jibe at Toby for the sudden shift in formality.

"Fair enough." Toby reached in his satchel and five gold coins spilled out onto the tabletop. He smiled back at Kenneth and winked. "I just felt I had been gone from the palace for long enough. I feel guilty leaving them for so long, but maybe I can bring back something for my efforts. I can only handle so much relaxing and being spoiled with phenomenal food, so I figured I should at least get back on track with this *brief* visit."

"We understand." Osric laughed lightly and nodded in agreement. "And I was honest when I told you earlier that we are at your service if there is anything else we could do for you. Did you have something in mind?"

"Well, I do have a concern that some of the folks outside our walls may not be entirely trustworthy, and I was hoping you might lend me three or four of your Trusts? I'd like to make sure that we don't invite anyone in who would only contribute to the problems we're having." Toby winced slightly in his request. It wasn't the normal function of a Trust, and he knew it.

"It's entirely possible that some who live in Stanton are not entirely trustworthy. Would you be asking them to leave as well?" There was a small amount of skepticism in Osric's tone, and he narrowed his eyes at the question.

"Now, I know a Trust is typically only used in small circles." Toby raised his hands, trying to calm any suspicions.

"And for good reason. A hungry man may have theft in his heart only as long as he is hungry and has no option to work for it. A Trust could only see his intent to steal, not that he would work for it given the chance," Osric replied.

"Now, that's not fair. You would have sole control of the Trusts, and I would invite you to join them, if you wish." Toby took a deep breath and leaned in, speaking with a reasoning tone. "I wouldn't ask to keep out all, just those who may have been sent with orders to cause mischief. We will be feeding them before they enter the gates, so I would think that they would go unused for most of the day. I've thought this through. Anyone intent on wrongdoings not directed at the palace should be allowed to pass. I have faith that the giving nature of our people would negate most of the other intentions by eliminating their need."

Osric relaxed somewhat with the explanation, but his own Trust ability, along with a strange surge in the Seer gift, indicated that it was something he should consider. If that wasn't enough, the Portentist gift had chosen that moment to reassert itself as a mature gift within his mind.

The reemergence of the gift was a welcome surprise to the uncertainty about which path to chose. He had been forced to make too many choices lately without knowing where the danger lay. Still, it wasn't only wondering about whether the choice held danger that held him up—this time, anyway. It was the morality of using the Trust gift to choose which of the many destitute men, women, and children to allow to make his home their own. Even knowing that three separate gifts indicated it was the right action didn't make the choice easier.

Osric sat there thinking silently as Toby and Kenneth looked at him, waiting. His head was in turmoil about having to pick between following magic's guidance and his own feelings on what was right. There was a large difference between testing someone to see if they would be a good fit to join the Aranthians and seeing if they were worthy to make a life inside Stanton's walls. Even the compromises Toby mentioned felt like too little, considering that turning people away meant that Aranthians would be responsible for endangering people.

He looked to Kenneth, searching for some clarity of thought, and noticed that the Empath ability was indicating that his childhood friend had been surprised by Toby's request as well, and that settled it. He knew that his answer would be no, but he was struck with another idea.

"I'll offer you a compromise." Osric looked Toby in the eyes, in all seriousness.

"Okay, I'm always interested in better ideas. If you have one, let me hear it." He nodded.

Osric's Wand

"It has come to my attention that we need to be more selective in which gifts we choose, as well as choosing those we can trust, to become an Aranthian. Up until now, we have chosen a bit too indiscriminately." Osric took a deep breath, knowing he was about to give himself more work. "We will send our Trusts outside the walls in search of more to join our cause. The Aranthian cause."

"Okay." This time it was Toby's turn to look concerned.

"I'll pair each of them with a Wand-Maker and set up recruitment tents to let people know exactly what we are about to do. Each will be examined to see which gift they have. If they have one that is desirable for what we are in need of, they will be examined by the Trust."

"I'm not sure how this plan will help me with Stanton's needs." Toby shifted in his chair.

"How many people are outside our gates?" Osric met his gaze.

"Last count, about four hundred" Toby shrugged. "Why?"

"Because"—Osric leaned in—"to a Portentist, this place would be like a magnet. I've had three Trusted in just over the last week. One said he could feel the portent radiating from Stanton all the way in Barlington. There will be a higher than normal concentration of Portentists in that crowd, and if Kenneth could spare a few recruiters of his own, we could help you bolster the Vigile numbers with a very useful gift."

"If we could get a few more Portentists in our numbers, that would make a world of difference." Kenneth smiled, nodding his head. A hint of a smile began to show on Toby's face as well.

"But here is the compromise." Osric tapped the table with his forefinger. "Every able, willing man and woman at that gate will be welcomed into Stanton, assuming they wish to make it their home. Any troubles we face after that should be as easy to handle as the ones we faced before all of this happened." After he said it aloud, it didn't seem like as much work as he thought it would be.

Toby hesitated only for a moment before he nodded, and then he began to laugh, rubbing his hands over his shaved head.

"Even though you refuse to work for me as Contege, I sure am glad you are here and on our side." Toby waved a hand in Kenneth's direction. "Not that I wasn't happy to name you to the post." Then he stood up, placing a hand out for Osric to shake. "But I believe you are meant for something bigger than that position anyway. I accept your terms and thank you for the meal. We should do this more often. Your council is very much appreciated."

"Thanks, and I appreciate your leadership of Stanton too. I think I get things wrong just about as much as I get them right, but I look forward to every moment we spend in one another's company. It seems to come too little these days." Osric stood up, stepped around the table, and shook the Ryhain's hand.

Chapter 18
The Other Seer

Chanda sat in an overstuffed chair surrounded by books, disbelief in her eyes. After her failed interpretation of Bridgett's vision, she had been set aside for so long without being called upon. Now, after months of tutelage under the revered Serha, and Serha's untimely death, she found herself sitting in a room with Osric, Aridis, Gus, and Eublin while they discussed matters that had worldwide significance.

True, Serha hadn't been the most gentle of instructors; yet in spite of that, Chanda valued the lessons she had learned. But after being placed under the direct supervision of someone so renowned for so long, she had a hard time understanding why she was being thrust to the forefront of the important matters involving Seer work. She had, after all, been the one responsible for nearly bringing an end to the very foundation of the Aranthians. She bore the guilt of that mistake the only way she knew how: Chanda kept it buried inside, as a reminder of her foolish past. She vowed to never repeat the mistakes that had led her to these humbling past few months.

"The books triggered some sort of response from Serha's gift. Maybe it will do the same for yours." Eublin looked up at her where she sat across from him. Then, he turned toward Aridis with regret. "I apologize, my friend. I should have spoken softer and with more consideration," he added.

Aridis nodded. "Her death will mean something if we can gain some knowledge from her experience." He reached over and placed a soft hand on Eublin's shoulder. "Please, don't apologize for bringing her light to this dark time."

"When the hunt changes, her name will echo through the ages." Eublin patted Aridis's hand with understanding and turned back to Chandra. "Are you willing to offer your assistance to this venture?"

"I am willing," she replied. Though, there was a great deal of fear keeping her from foolishly throwing herself into the role of a Seer again. "But I am sure that dozens of others are more suited to this task than I."

The Weaving of Wells

"Serha believed you would play a great role in the events of this time," Osric replied. His expression showed both his trust in her as well as his lack of sympathy for her timid nature. "So, let's prove her assumptions correct and get on with it."

"I already played a great role in our time. I nearly kept you and Bridgett apart," she sulked.

"I understand your lack of confidence. If I had bungled up that bad, I would have never been able to sell a wand. Luckily for you, we already know you will overcome your early folly." Gus stepped forward with a smile on his face. "Unless you lack faith in Serha's abilities?"

"No." Chanda shook her head. "She was the greatest Seer Archana has ever known, but even she berated me for my mistakes up until the very end. How can she be right about my greatness and my foolishness? I've been such a fool for so many years. It's hard to think of myself as anything else."

"Well." Gus stepped forward, sarcasm plain on his furry face. "I've been widely regarded as the greatest Wand-Maker of our time for most of my life. It wasn't until my inexperienced child taught me something I'd never thought of that I realized what an idiot I'd been all along. Life is so much easier when nobody has to prove to you that you're an idiot. Your understanding of that fact should be a blessing, not a curse."

Chuckles echoed throughout the library as the group gathered together by a few tables, with Gus wandering through the group in high spirits while Kenneth and Osric leaned against the end of a bookcase. Eublin pushed up his spectacles with a thin finger and a broad smile.

"We've all been trying to tell him he was an idiot for some time. Children have a way of getting the point across that surpasses any army's efforts." Kenneth nodded with a supportive glance.

"It's true. Everyone here has done their best to show me things I didn't understand at the time. I didn't understand them because they so fundamentally went against everything I thought I knew. Yet, there was one thing we all thought we knew, and a child taught us all that we were wrong."

"What one thing?" Chanda asked. Her interest was piqued. What could everyone have thought they knew, only to be proven wrong by a child?

"It turns out, after decades of debate on the subject, that unicorns can talk," Eublin interjected.

"Uni... What?!" Dumbfounded, Chanda shook her head as if something had become lodged in her hair and it had to be shaken out.

"My reaction was very similar to yours, only I leapt at my son and frolicked through the grass like an idiot for a long while." Gus nodded.

"They don't actually talk. They communicate telepathically. It seems their vocal ability is limited by their biology." Eublin stepped forward, resembling an instructor giving a lesson to his students. "Their bodies just aren't set up to allow for vocalization of thought. To add insult to our ignorance, they are a terribly proper community that insists upon etiquette. If you are thought of as rude then there is no chance any of them will speak to you."

"And you have too many of my sort attempting to study them, then teaching the rest of the world what we learn from those encounters. Wand-Maker's have never been too cordial in our dealings with others. Rather than offering our knowledge to further the craft, we debate who is right in an effort to stand out from the crowd and make a name for ourselves." Gus frowned playfully. "We may have been responsible for stifling the advancement of magical knowledge while attempting to do the opposite. We can save so many more lives with what we know now. Wars can be avoided with the crop advancements and water reclamation knowledge we have gained. Who knows how many sentient species have died unnecessarily, just because we didn't know unicorns could communicate and would let us look at their magic if only we would have asked first."

"How horrible!" Chanda took a quick inhale of breath and held her hand up in front of her mouth as the reality of it all set in.

"Indeed." Gus nodded with a smile.

Gus laughed. It wasn't a long laugh, but it was startling to the Seer who sat listening to someone admit to unknowingly being a part of something that set the world back by several generations. It was a heartfelt, short-lived, belly laugh.

"That's an odd thing to laugh at." Kenneth squinted with one eye.

The Weaving of Wells

"I'm laughing because I've only just learned how stupid I am. Life would have been so easy if I had known it a long time ago. Life is easy now. I don't have to fight with anyone who thinks I'm wrong anymore. Now, I assume I am wrong. It's so much more fun that way. So what if you're an idiot? The rest of us are too. You'll mess up along the way, no doubt. Just grab the book and see what happens. We'll all try to sort through it afterward." Gus's ear twitched wildly as he looked at her with eager eyes.

Chanda looked at Gus uncertainly. His argument made some sense, and she found a strange comfort in knowing they expected some failure to occur. From the way Gus was speaking, she suspected that their plans might even allow for uncertainty, but still she doubted herself while reaching ever so tentatively for the book on the desk.

"Did Gus just get away with calling us all idiots?" Kenneth looked to the other members of the group.

"I think so." Osric nodded.

"I believe he did too. And to tell the truth, I can't fault him for his logic." Eublin looked up with appreciation on his face while Aridis simply smiled, nodding in affirmation.

Chanda placed her hand on the book on the table she was seated at, holding her eyes closed in expectation of the coming vision, but nothing happened. She opened her eyes slowly, cringing. Osric placed his hand on her shoulder.

"It's all right. We don't really know if this will work, but it is worth trying. Will you keep trying?"

Chanda nodded, smiling up at him. She opened the cover and traced her fingers over the paper. It felt strangely warm and comforting, and she grew less hesitant and anxious. Chanda flipped through the pages, resting her hand briefly on the foreign writing of each page. She was a quarter of the way through the book and her frustration was building. Nothing was happening, not even the strong urge that she often felt and associated with her gift. She looked up at Osric, ready to give up, but he smiled and nodded encouragingly. Chanda sighed softly and turned the page again. As her fingers lit upon the parchment, she was transported to a strange and unfamiliar location.

Before her stood a small hill covered in lush green grass, an array of wildflowers, and two small stone chimneys protruding from its top.

Osric's Wand

Only a small patch of bare soil the size of a large shield stood out from the otherwise grass-covered hill. She stepped forward and seven symbols lit up above the grassless space.

As she watched, the soil began to fall inward, far too regularly and orderly to be natural. It swirled to the right in a circular motion, slowly expanding from the center as a hole grew and the earth faded. When the opening had completed its transformation, a dark oval-shaped opening stood welcoming her.

She stepped through the entrance, and candles began to light themselves along the walls of an expansive, round marble chamber. The room was far too large to fit inside the small hill she had stepped inside.

Along the outside wall of the chamber, the floor sank into large steps spiraling downward. She walked down the steps as candles continued to spring to life lighting her way, and when she reached the last step she sat down and gazed around a smaller circular chamber. Across the room from where she was seated, she noted a pedestal with a candle, a magnifying glass, a quill, a bottle of ink, and an open book sitting atop its flat surface. In the center of the room was a round depression in the stone floor, about three paces across, but from where she was sitting she could not tell how deep it was. As she stood up with the intention of examining the artifacts on the pedestal, she found herself again in the library at the barracks.

"Well, did anything happen?" Gus looked up at her.

"It's like remembering a dream," Chanda said, "but yes, I saw a great deal." In short order, she relayed what the vision had shown her and then looked at her questioning companions. "I'm not sure it's all that helpful. I didn't see any identifiable locations or markers. But I do remember the symbols above the entrance."

"You remember them? I can't say we expected that." Eublin nodded, impressed.

"The symbols were clear in the vision, but that's not the issue. How are we going to find the well from what I saw?" Chanda looked up at faces that showed no concern. She felt as though there were something she didn't understand hidden behind the eyes of everyone looking at her.

* * *

The Weaving of Wells

It felt wrong to search for more wells without Serha, but finding them was the first step in defeating Dredek. Osric knew that somehow they would play a part in their victory, yet the role they would play eluded him. How could relatively small fountains of magic scattered throughout the landscape of Archana help him overcome a man who would be tapped directly into the Well of Strands? It was a question that consumed most of his time these days.

He let go of Chanda's hand as she inhaled deeply with disbelief. It was a risk to let her bring him to the location using the traveling spell, so they brought nobody else the first time out. The shock of being transported instantaneously to an unknown location was plain on Chanda's face. The physical toll of the magic might have injured her greatly if the distance had been too far, but she seemed only mildly fatigued, so it must have been relatively close to their former location.

"This is the place, but how did we get here?" Confusion was more evident on her face than was the fatigue of the spell.

"The words you spoke as you pictured this spot in your mind, they were a spoken spell. The spell brought us to the place you envisioned. You no doubt feel tired now, but that will pass. If my gift had shown any ominous portent, I wouldn't have let you bring me here to begin with. That spell is dangerous if done improperly. We both could have died if there was a wall, a tree, a mound of dirt, or any other obstacle in our way when we appeared." Osric steadied her and helped her to sit in the grass.

He looked at the landscape surrounding them. Grass was scattered across the horizon, but over the ages the lack of tending had allowed weeds to slowly overtake it. Rolling hills littered the landscape, and atop every mound two small stone chimneys stood tall. Though some of them had toppled and been scattered by wind and rain, their purpose was clear. Stepping closer to the hill they had faced upon arriving, Osric could sense the power growing stronger with every step. Then a thought occurred to him.

"These were homes?" Osric questioned Chanda.

"I'm not sure." She shrugged. "This was all I could see in the vision." Chanda motioned to the hill on her left.

"Well then, let's get back." Osric held out his hand.

"I don't think I can do that again." She shook her head in protest.

Osric's Wand

"No doubt, it would probably kill you. But I can take you back quite easily, so let me help you up." Osric helped her to her feet again.

"Wait. Don't we need to inspect the interior of this one to see if it is anything like my vision?" Chanda pulled away.

"No need. We have the location as well as the way to access the chamber if we need to. And we know that there are no obstructions to hinder the traveling spell you just demonstrated. We know all we need to know for now." He held her hands reassuringly.

"But what are we going back for? Haven't we done what we were to do?"

"Not even by half." Osric smiled. "We need to see what else the book can show you."

He took her hand, and after a few words they appeared back in the library with everyone exactly where they had been when they left.

As soon as they appeared, Eublin excused himself politely and walked quickly from the room. He had been gone a few moments and no one had asked if they had been successful in finding the well.

"Is he all right?" Chanda asked.

"He's fine," Gus said. "He drank too much rulha and he's been squirming in his seat since you left. He'll be back in a moment, and then you can tell us all about your trip."

"Why didn't he just go while we were away? What if it had taken us a long time to find and explore the well's location?" Chanda was confused.

"There could have been danger that demanded an early retreat, or any number of other things that could have brought you back at an unexpected time. We have lost men from the use of that spell, so we take every precaution to keep things exactly the way they were when someone leaves. It makes it far more likely that someone who is scared or injured can successfully return with the traveling spell if they can just think of the room as they last saw it. Besides, it was funny to watch the brilliant little guy squirm." Gus shrugged playfully.

"You're one to call me little. I could still step on you with little effort, if the mood so inspired me." Eublin slipped back into his seat, and Gus jumped slightly at the sound of the gnome's voice.

"Ah, see. There he is now. We were just saying how much we missed you, Eublin, since we had to await the arrival of your empty bladder to hear about the well." Gus smirked, and Eublin's cheeks colored a pale pink.

"I apologize for the delay. How did it go?"

"We found it, just as I saw it in my vision, but we didn't go inside." Chanda sounded a little disappointed.

"She did a great job, but we have a great deal more to do before we can attempt to enter the wells that we find. Let's see if the book shows her any more locations." Osric held a hand out, indicating Chanda should sit back down and flip through a few more pages.

She sighed and sat down, still showing her weariness from the trip to the green hills. As she began flipping through the pages, Osric stepped out and brewed her a cup of tea. Bridgett had mixed the herbs specifically to aid in her recovery from travel fatigue. She sipped the hot beverage slowly and turned the pages of the book with renewed determination. Once past the place where the first vision had occurred, it took several moments before she found a second trigger. She sat silently for a short time, obviously occupied by her ability, before she sighed and returned her focus to the group of people in the library.

"What did you see?" Gus stepped forward with a great deal of curiosity on his face.

"This was much different than the last. There was no building or any ruins, just a large hole in the ground. There were no symbols or anything, but there was a long walkway that spiraled down into the hole." Chanda looked at the expectant eyes all focused on her, worried that she would disappoint them.

"We can't expect everything to present itself to you without a puzzle to solve—that wouldn't be realistic. It's obvious they hadn't finished constructing this one. Let's go and see how far down the walkway goes." Gus shrugged.

"There is ominous portent in letting her take me there, but not in my leading the way. I need to know if there is a way for me to see what you witnessed in the vision." Osric stepped forward and placed his hand on her shoulder. "Is there a way you can show me?"

Chanda looked at her trembling hands, fatigued by the use of her gift and of the traveling spell. She looked at him and winced. "I don't suppose you have a large water dish?"

"A water dish?" Gus frowned.

Osric's Wand

"I use a small basin of water to show people what I have seen in their futures." She paused, casting her eyes downward and pressing her lips together as guilt flushed her cheeks. "At least I did before I met Serha."

"Let's get this lady some water!" Osric shouted.

He smiled as several nooks and shadowed corners throughout the library erupted with movement. It didn't take long for five young Aranthians to come back bearing small vessels full of water, all of which were set on the table in front of Chanda. She pulled the largest vessel toward her and smiled at the rapid response to her request.

Once the five Aranthians had melted back into their previous positions in the library, Chanda took a small vial out of a side pouch and dropped a single drop into the water and looked into Osric's eyes.

"Sit down and look into the water." She had a serious expression on her face, as if she were in her element.

Osric did as instructed.

Slowly the ripples in the water faded and an image of a forest surrounding a large opening in the ground came into focus. A faint outline of the bottom of the hole could be made out, so it wasn't too deep. Circling the interior was a circular ramp that led to the right, directly in front of his feet, in a shallow decline to the bottom. He was disappointed by the simplicity to the vision as he found himself back in the library.

"Well, that one won't prove too much of a challenge. The issue is arriving at the right location because there were trees all around it. But I think I know just where to go." Osric recalled a large patch of dirt on the opposite side of the hole. It was no larger than his bedroom inside the Aranthian habitat, but it was the best location he could see from the brief vision. He grasped Chanda's hand and checked for portent as he whispered the words that would take them anywhere they chose.

Upon arrival, Osric could see the danger in letting Chanda utter the spoken spell. In the location that they would have appeared across the chasm, there were several new, young trees. It would have been a fatal mistake to appear where the trees now stood. The location he had chosen was only a year or two from yielding the same result to new arrivals—not from new saplings, but from dirt collapsing into the hole before them. It would have been a long fall, and only a few Aranthians knew how to keep their wits about them when in freefall.

The Weaving of Wells

However, from his new vantage he could see a trail that the vision hadn't offered to them. That would be the point of entry for any future visits, and he could feel the power emanating from the bottom of the hole. Osric looked over at Chanda with a smile.

"If we come back to this location, all future arrivals must choose that path as their arrival destination. Let's make sure they choose the open patch right there." Osric pointed to a location across the opening.

"Is this another danger to the traveling spell?" Chanda inquired.

"Yes. If you appear where something else is, then you're likely to be impaled on that object," Osric answered.

"Before this day is over, I may become a bigger fan of horse and cart." She shook her head.

Osric smiled at her, noting that her emotions indicated curiosity and excitement as well as mild anxiety for the spell's dangers. He suspected that she would be using the spell regularly, with just a healthy respect for the risks, in no time at all.

"Stay here for a moment. I want to see if I can identify anything more about this location."

Chanda nodded and Osric glanced around for a potential vantage point. He was surprised at how cold the air was after the mild temperatures of the fall weather in Stanton. He assumed they must be pretty far north, but there was nothing significant about the forest to indicate its location.

The trees were dense around the small clearing where the hole had been started for the well, and Osric could see no hills or cliffs to give him a better view. He couldn't use the traveling spell, but that didn't keep him from wanting to see the surrounding area. Finding a tall, sturdy tree that had lost most of its leaves for the year, he climbed carefully high into its branches. Soon, Osric could see over the tops of most of the other trees nearby, and he was both disappointed and impressed with the view. The forest stretched as far as he could see in every direction. He thought he saw the smoke of a few small fires, or perhaps an inn along a seldom-used path, but there were no towns or other landmarks in sight. It was an immense, flat sea of trees, but the beauty of the forest did little to dull the ache of disappointment about still not knowing where the well was located. He wondered if they were even in the Human Realm, and something at the back of his mind made him doubt it. He frowned and climbed quickly back to the ground, shrugging when Chanda looked over at him expectantly.

"No luck, but we should probably get back before any full bladders take issue with our absence." Osric took her hand and spoke the spell. "Eo ire itum."

"It's about time." Gus responded to their appearance from the top of a low bookcase next to their table. "I chased off several curious Aranthians who weren't here to read. I was tempted to banish them for spying."

"Don't do that." Osric looked over at the prairie dog. "They came in handy when we needed these." He motioned to the cups, bowls, and small basin full of water.

"It never hurts to have more hands to help, and we have no secrets in this habitat," Kenneth agreed.

"Fine. So, let's hear it. What did you find?" Gus hopped down several stacks of books to the ground, and his tone reflected his excitement to hear their report.

"Exactly what I expected. It was another well, but the construction was never finished. I could feel the increase in power in the area, but there was no wall keeping us out to require the symbols. Now let's see if the book gives up any more of them, shall we?" Osric gestured for Chanda to sit at the table again.

When all was done, thirty-seven wells were located with the aid of the book Serha had helped them find. Several were too small for any significant use, but there were at least twenty-four with larger than expected strand collection, though significantly smaller than the Well of Strands that Bridgett described. Osric still had no idea how they would utilize the wells, but portent showed that they were of vital importance.

The solution would come to him eventually, he knew. No doubt he would have to bring Bridgett and Trevar to each of the locations to figure a way to enter, at least for those where visions hadn't shown the symbols. The day's magical exertion of the traveling spell, Wand-Maker sight, and sharing Seer visions with Chanda had brought him a great deal of fatigue. Entering the wells would have to wait. The group's excitement had passed, and when Chanda finally touched the last page of the book, they were all looking forward to their beds. When nothing happened, she sighed audibly with relief, and the others nodded and began gathering their things to leave. Osric's mind was flooded with the images of the various locations, but he was too tired to sort through all that they had seen and learned. Osric slept heavily through the night, the constant portent ignition causing no more than slight stirrings in his slumber. It was the best night's rest he had had in days.

Chapter 19
Bubbling Black

Dredek ran the long bone through his hands. Did this femur belong to Aeya? He had lost track of her bones years ago, thanks to an encounter almost a decade earlier with bandits who had dumped the contents in search of coin. He knew they were in one of the chests he had kept safe, but which box and which bones were hers, he no longer knew. Centuries were too long to keep track of something so small, yet he handled each bone as if it belonged to the love he had lost so long ago.

He hadn't found her body with his children, and none of the bodies of the young were recognizable. Most had been trampled beneath the hooves of horses and were too badly broken to be salvageable, and he hadn't gone back to gather what he could until he had formed his plan years later. It was then that he had decided not to bring the children's bones at all. Someday, he was certain he would have to answer for that, but he couldn't help but wish his children could rest through the struggles the caldereth would have to face, until they had established themselves again.

He placed the bones neatly on the floor inside the well. He made sure each and every one was perfectly placed in the correct place to ensure as much success as possible. He hadn't attempted the spell with only bones before; there had always been some tissue remaining to hold everything in its place. Dredek knew it would be different this time, but with the power of the Well of Strands to aid him, he knew he could do it.

The bones had all been placed carefully in cloth years earlier. Each bone had been collected and wrapped, and then separated into individual bundles belonging to each of two hundred slain caldereth. It had taken him a great deal of time, sitting at the bottom of the well, to put just over half of the bodies in order. It would take him another few weeks to duplicate the effort. Weeks of verifying and correcting the placement of every tiny bone after his tremors forced his hands to shake so badly that he couldn't control where he placed them.

The Weaving of Wells

"Sir!" a shout rang out from above. A young man, thin yet muscular, in light chainmail that covered his hardened leather armor, leaned over the path leading to his location. "I'm supposed to tell you that it just turned black!" The voice was difficult to hear from the doorway above, but the point had been made. Dredek stood up and craned his neck to reply.

"Take it off the flames! Take it off the flames and ice it! Go! Tell them, now!" Dredek followed as close as he could, but he was cramped from hours of sorting on his knees, and he tripped over a set of bones at the foot of the stairs, swearing as he fell. "They need to throw the herb bundle in as soon as it hits the ice!"

The young man ducked his head back into the well and nodded before disappearing again through the opening. Dredek hoped they got it right. He had been expecting it to happen at any time, but sitting in the room and waiting would have accomplished nothing, and sorting through the bones was his task and his task alone.

The steep incline of the stairs leading out of the well was difficult to climb after spending so much time crouched on the floor of the well, but he found it easier if he used his hands to aid himself as he circled the shaft in a sprint on all four limbs. His natural caldereth speed could easily be a danger on the stairway, so he was careful to stay close to the outer wall. Once he reached the door, however, he could safely and quickly cover the distance to the chamber where the potion was brewing.

Still, the chests that carried the remaining caldereth bones hampered him in the hall leading away from the well. He wished he had planned for the moment better, but there was nothing for it now.

As soon as he was past the obstructions, he sprinted on limbs meant for speed. He would pay for the exertion with aches and fatigue, but the next few moments counted toward his being able to revive his people, so he was willing to endure the suffering. When he could finally use the thick, black liquid, the small amount of discomfort he was about to face would seem insignificant anyway.

In the distance he could hear the voice of the man who had brought him the news shouting instructions with short breath. *At least they sent a competent man to fetch me*, he thought.

Moments later, he was entering the room. Three men had already placed the pot in the ice bath he had prepared, and the herb bundle

Osric's Wand

was tossed in as he entered the room. The herbs were only necessary to mask the horrific taste of the potion so he would be able to choke it down, but he was glad they had followed the instructions before the heat of the black liquid lowered and was unable to draw out the flavor from the mint leaves. He smiled at the men, nodding his gratitude for their efforts. It would be a while before it would be cool enough to drink, but the hard part was over. In a few days, he would have his physical strength back, along with the full use of his magical potential.

Chapter 20
Trained but Deadly

Osric stepped into the cave, knowing the paun would still be where he left them. It had taken time for him to find them after his long period of unconsciousness following his battle with Dredek, but once they had been located he moved them back into the cave he had met them in. They had taken to training faster than any dog he had ever known, but teaching them to eat all of their prey was the most daunting task he had undertaken.

Cooking the meat of the animals they brought back had been the solution to the problem, though they still ate the internal organs and eyeballs before bringing their hunt to the cave. Osric felt that it was nearly time to bring the two out to meet his friends. He had kept his nightly routine secret from all but Bridgett, but she hadn't been eager to meet the beasts. He understood her worries, but he was convinced that the paun could be valuable companions. He had been bringing the two pups along with him to different towns to expose them to human contact for some time, albeit he made sure they remained invisible the entire time. He felt that they were ready to join the rest of the world, though he was nervous about how they would react if everyone who saw them screamed and ran away.

There had been no doubt in Osric's mind that they were intelligent, as he could get them to drop their invisibility on command and he had witnessed them using magic to start fires and bury their possessions. Though what the paun saw as possessions was laughable to most humans; they seemed to form odd attachments to different rocks they had discovered in their wanderings. The larger of the two adolescent paun would even spell the area where he buried his rocks to protect them.

As he entered the room, the two became visible and approached him playfully. A fire was burning and the cave had been cleaned of any evidence of last night's meal, though there was the last quarter of a doe waiting for him to cook.

"Looks like you two have been busy. Good job!" He patted them on their backs, feeling strange to treat larger-than-human animals as pets. It had taken him time to get used to the act, but they didn't speak. However, they responded very well to verbal instruction, learning dozens of commands during his first week of visits.

He took out his large hunting knife and began to prepare the doe. Most of his actions were habitual, muscle memory from the time he had spent training Happy and a lifetime of hunting. He knew he couldn't bring them back to the Aranthians without names. Though genitals were not evident on either of them, the smaller size and narrower chest of one led Osric to assume she was female. He called her Vesh. The larger of them was dubbed Kane, because he had taken a liking to the flavor of raw sugar, and Osric often found scraps of sugarcane scattered around outside the cave. He had no idea where the paun found the plant, but the two often wandered far from the cave to hunt and play while Osric was away.

Osric was in awe of the paun body, and he took time to study their structure and movements every chance he got. They were lean, and their heavily muscled bodies would put even Kenneth's dense musculature to shame. Yet, it wasn't only their muscles that gave them the strength and speed he knew all too well. The paun had many more muscles than a human body has, with muscle attachments at more points along the adjoining bones. That wasn't the only thing remarkable in their makeup; each limb had an additional joint that allowed for even greater speed and flexibility of movement.

Kane and Vesh both could, at times, choose to stride at a normal human pace to walk alongside Osric. Yet, they could run at astonishing rates by recruiting more muscles and extending the joints of their limbs to the full extent. The length and sharpness of the claws, however, seemed to be dependent upon how much use they received while hunting and taking in prey. Vesh had clearly been superior to Kane in the hunt, and her razor-sharp claws had grown significantly longer than her brother's. There was nothing else like them on all of Archana.

In the time he had spent with them, he continued to marvel at the speed with which they grew. When Osric had been forced to fight it the day Orson died, the third of their group had been about the size of the two pups combined. Now, both were not only taller than the paun he killed, but even Vesh was wider and bulkier than that paun had been. Kane was also significantly larger than the first paun Osric had

The Weaving of Wells

encountered in the forest. He wondered if they were yet fully grown, but he had no idea how large a paun could get, as so few had ever been seen. Both of them easily dwarfed him in size, but they showed no sign of making him their next hunt. And the only thing he ever sensed from them was import from the Portentist gift and a sense of calm curiosity from the Empath gift.

For lack of any other explanation, he attributed their growth to the change in diet he had introduced. How long the paun had lived only eating a small portion of their prey was unknown, so feeding them all of the animals' meat after cooking, no doubt, had contributed to their size.

"Do you two think you're ready to take a trip? I have some friends I'd like to introduce you to." Osric spoke calmly as he watched them strip the last remaining scraps of flesh from the bones. He had tried to speak with the paun using the Telepathy gift he had gained from his proximity to Thamas and Legati's magic, but the two pups showed no signs of recognizing the mental prodding. However, they did respond to audible commands, calming down noticeably at the sound of his voice. They knew they were going to be leaving soon.

Osric looked at them for a long moment, and they twitched with eagerness. He was nervous, but every previous day had been leading to this. Both pups sensed his anxiety, whining slightly, but they continued to show their readiness to leave with quick nods in the direction of the cave's exit. He had come early in the day this time, choosing to reveal the proof of their existence to the Aranthians in the light of day, rather than at night. Too many nightmarish stories were told to children about the paun to bring them to the barracks without light to dispel the myths. The story of his first and second encounters with paun did not help to inspire trust of the creatures either.

Osric, however, knew the truth of the matter, after the time he had spent with the pups. They were not evil, inasmuch as it was said; they were simply carrying out their version of a hunt. It would take some effort to convince his brethren of the truth of the matter. He stood up, motioning for the paun to gather at his sides.

"Well, let's do it then. Delaying won't help the matter." He was speaking more to himself than to the paun, but they moved close to him, knowing that contact was how he brought them to new places.

Osric's Wand

After they took a place on either side, he spoke the spell and soon arrived outside the barrier to the Aranthian home. They moved as if to run and play, but Osric halted them with a word. It wasn't easy for them to restrain themselves, but they did.

A merchant screamed in terror at the sight of the three of them in the road, but to their credit—and to Osric's great relief—the paun looked at the man in alarm but held their place at his side. Osric attempted to calm the merchant down with a smile and a friendly greeting, but there was nothing he could do. The man, in tan breeches and a dirtied yellow tunic, fell off of his cart in an attempt to run away and sprawled flat in the dirt. It took only a moment for him to regain his footing and dash off in the opposite direction, looking back and screaming with every breath.

It wasn't the start he had hoped for, but more or less it was the one he had expected. The merchant's horse reared in fright, nostrils flaring and eyes rolling in panic. Osric hurried to calm the horse down with a few pleasant words and no small amount of magic, and then he held the reins tightly while watching the calm yet curious gaze the paun aimed at the man fleeing from them. They paid little attention to the horse, as Osric had not given them the command to hunt. Once he was sure the horse would not bolt and injure itself, Osric tied its reins to a nearby post and returned to the paun.

"He'll come around. You'll see." Osric sighed with relief that the paun were behaving so calmly, patting them each on the head to reassure and praise them. "I bet he adopts the first paun litter we raise."

"Whoa!" a playful voice interjected.

Osric looked up to see Pebble peeking out of the window of his wand shop. It was a bit early, but Pebble had taken his role as a world-renowned Wand-Maker very serious. The only surprising part about his being at work this early was that Gus wasn't there with him.

"Pebble," Osric shouted as he led the paun toward the old forge, "come say hello to my friends."

There was no doubt Pebble was nervous, but his curiosity won out and he jumped down from the open window and slowly approached the massive creatures.

"You sure they won't eat me?" Pebble looked up at Osric with more question in his expression than insecurity.

The Weaving of Wells

"Honestly?" Osric returned the expression.

"Uh-huh."

"I'm not sure they won't try, but I would never let that happen to any of my friends." Honesty was best in these types of situations, and Osric felt that Pebble deserved it.

"Oh." Pebble took a nervous step back to look at the two hulking beasts. A serious, piercing gaze crossed his face and then he looked back to Osric with a shrug. "I'm too small to feed 'em. They won't bother with me. And portent says nothing bad is coming, so I trust 'em."

"Portent?" Osric looked down at Pebble with surprise. "Congratulations. I forgot that you had gifts developing still. How long has it been?"

"Since I opened the shop." Pebble pointed at his store. "'Bout twelve days, I guess."

"And how long was it before you could tell if there was danger?" Osric knelt.

"Couple days, maybe. I saw you do it so much, it was easy."

"I suppose you did." He smiled at Pebble's matter-of-fact explanation. "So, where is your father? I was hoping he would be here to meet Kane and Vesh." He looked around, searching the landscape.

"He's out gettin' me some sticks. He don't like me making wands outta everyone's stuff they bring me," Pebble replied.

Osric laughed, remembering earlier conversations with Gus about what was suitable material for wandcraft. Gus had always been rather particular on that subject.

"Well, do you want to introduce yourself properly, or should I take them to the Aranthians for their introductions?" Osric teased. He felt great about the way this meeting had gone, so he was more than ready to move onto the next one.

Pebble stepped forward. He was still a bit timid, but there was a determined effort in his stance. Then, looking up at Osric's smile, he grinned and approached quickly with a defiant swagger. The two paun had taken a sullen stance side by side, clearly uninspired by the long chat, and they only took notice of the fat prairie dog when he drew close enough to touch them. Osric crouched down so Kane and Vesh would see that Pebble was welcome, and he gave the hand signal to wait patiently. For good measure, he held his fist out in the signal that

Osric's Wand

meant an object was not food, and he kept it there as Pebble stood before them.

"Hi," he began. "I'm Pebble. If you wanna play, me, Trevar, and Happy are the only ones 'round here who play. We'd love to show ya."

The two paun looked at him with curiosity, nostrils flaring as they sniffed the air. They leaned down and nudged him with curious prodding snouts. Osric reached out and ran his free hand over Pebble's soft, well-groomed coat, attempting to show them how to demonstrate affection.

First, Kane slowly reached out a clawed front foot and rested it lightly on Pebble's head. He pulled the foot back quickly, casting a look of disbelief at Osric. Osric smiled and repeated the gesture.

"See, he is a friend." It was a motion they were used to experiencing, though usually on the receiving end. Osric hoped he could instill in them the same sense of gentleness that he had shown for them.

Kane reached out again timidly, then pulled back again. Then, Vesh pushed him out of the way forcefully. She stepped up to Pebble and placed her left forefoot on the pup's head. She looked up at Osric in shock, but didn't remove her foot. Her gaze fell slowly back to Pebble and her head tilted slowly from one side to the other as she studied the fur beneath her touch.

"She has pretty eyes." Pebble giggled as the tip of a claw tickled him on his side.

Vesh continued her stroking, and soon Kane stepped around her and joined in the activity. Pebble began laughing and squirming about. Out of curiosity, Osric used the Empath gift and found that the two paun were completely enthralled by the prairie dog pup, and he could sense a bond of affection growing in them.

He let them study Pebble for some time, and Pebble certainly didn't mind the attention. It was an interesting sight, watching an animal built to kill petting and tickling a gentle, plump, and ticklish prairie dog. He lost himself in the rarity of the moment, smiling at the accomplishment.

"Get!" The gruff, scared voice sounded from the distance. "Get away from my son, now!"

The Weaving of Wells

Osric spun on his heels and saw Gus standing with an outstretched wand. He reached out his hands in a calming motion. It wasn't the introduction he had hoped for, but he should have seen it coming.

"Gus, don't worry." Osric looked back to check the paun, and they had ended their playful exploration and were looking with interest between the two who were speaking.

"Don't worry? You've got two paun pawing at my boy. What's to worry about?" He stepped to the side, looking around Osric to see his son.

"I've been training them for some time. They won't harm anyone." He made a point of not pulling out his wand. If it came to it, the paun would make themselves invisible and move several feet to either side of him—at least, that's what he had trained them to do.

"How comforting, but maybe you could experiment with some humans first? We have plans that don't involve death today." Gus's scowl intensified.

"Pa, they been tickling me. Portent says they don't wanna eat me. It's okay," Pebble said with more authority than either of them had expected. Gus even looked at him in shock.

"Let those older than five years old discuss the issues of the day, boy," Gus replied, but it was a much weaker reply than his former.

"Now that's not fair, Gus." Osric took a step toward him, intending to correct him for the insult, but Pebble stepped quickly in front of him.

"Which of us is master Wand-Maker now? I am." Pebble stood up and stuck his chest out authoritatively. He wasn't being disrespectful, and there was no doubt that Gus respected him for it. "I am because I know when to watch and look. I know how to see what you taught me to see."

"We're not talking about wands, boy." Gus was a bit ashamed of himself, looking down and kicking the dirt by his foot.

"I teached you about the unicorns not wanting to make him too powerful too. I knew 'bout Osric's wand and that's why they don't wanna get too close to him. I imitate the unicorn wands with my own as well. These is all things I seen when you didn't. I see they is okay to trust too." Pebble walked back to the paun and patted one on the foreleg.

Osric's Wand

"You remember the last paun we met?" Gus replied, but Osric just watched, in awe of Pebble's speech and maturity. "That paun would have ate us all. The last one Osric saw killed Orson and he had to fight off three of them."

"Actually, these two are two of the three you mentioned," Osric corrected him. "I've been training them since the day Orson died."

"They're what?" Gus shouted, dumbfounded.

"They're trustworthy. If you come here and look at them, even you could see that the Trust gift shows they is tame." Pebble pointed at the two paun with fearless impatience.

"Trust gift?" Gus looked at his son in disbelief. "What makes you think the Trust gift will work on these things?"

Pebble rolled his eyes and then looked to his father with a blank expression. "If you pay attention to what the gifts are saying, you would know." There was no small amount of a child's condescension in the tone.

"Do you believe this boy?" Gus turned to Osric.

"Don't look at me. I'm half tickled to see someone so young getting the best of you for a change." He laughed.

"Next time you want some time alone, you can count on me bringing a dozen Wand-Maker's to study your gifts." Gus scowled at Osric.

"Pa." Pebble pointed at the paun again. "Look!"

"Am I that obtrusive when I know something others don't?" Gus looked up at Osric with little hope.

"You're downright insulting. At least he's cute about it." Osric waved to Pebble.

Gus strode impatiently toward Pebble. The young Wand-Maker was still standing, impatiently pointing at the fierce-looking animals. Vesh and Kane only looked with pacified faces at the two prairie dogs moving at their feet. Gus looked uncomfortably at the toothy snouts that were far too close to his son for his liking.

"See, the Trust gift shows you the intentions of them." Pebble said enthusiastically. "If their intentions was to eat us, we could see it. And, the Portentist gift would tell us they was dangerous. And, the Empath gift would tell us they feel hatred or hunger or something." Pebble patted Vesh on the leg. "They feel curious and loyal, and like they might want to eat the cows. Osric, you should keep an eye on the cows."

Gus looked up at Osric with frustration. The gaze indicated his distaste not only for his son lecturing him on new gifts, but also for having paun study the two small prairie dogs as Pebble carried out his explanation.

"Gus, don't you see. If they become aggressive toward any one of us we can just withdraw the invite from our habitat, and I've already faced several paun. I could defeat them again, if I had too. So," he continued, "Pebble is right that all of our gifts are sufficient to determine that the paun are tame. Well, as long as I don't let them too close to the cattle."

"Well, if they kill us all and build a paun-hunting hub out of the Aranthian headquarters, it would be a great leap forward in paun social development," Gus grumbled with a shrug and a shake of his head.

"That's highly unlikely." Pebble frowned at his father's words.

"Okay. If the two of you think the gifts are showing us they're trustworthy, who am I to argue?" Gus shrugged, walked to the two paun, and patted them on the legs. "Maybe I could stick close to them and provide them with a small snack the next time they are hungry."

"That's the spirit." Osric tousled his hair. Sensing the excitement, Vesh and Kane stood on trembling legs as he spoke. "Kane, Vesh, you are decisively invited into our sanctuary."

The scene changed in the familiar, shimmering way. Though the grounds of the old Vigile barracks had been tended to, the one that stood inside the barrier was still much more impressive. Sprites danced in every which direction and bodies moved to and fro in the lively surroundings. Yet, to Osric's surprise, the paun continued to look at him expectantly, waiting to depart. The change in visual stimuli was too little to signify to them that they were in a new location, and they looked a bit disappointed after a few moments had passed and they still hadn't headed off on a new adventure.

Even more impressive was the fact that Aranthians moved about in their daily routine, taking no notice of the pale beasts that stood in their front yard. Dumping a pot of water on his herb garden outside the window to the kitchen, James took notice of Osric, setting down the container of water and approaching with a casual smile.

Osric's Wand

"Osric, I was hoping I could have a word with you." He spoke in a friendly tone. His eyes darted to Gus, Pebble, the two paun, and then back to Osric. "We've got more meat than we need for the Aranthians at this time, and I was wondering if I could donate a hundred pounds or so to feeding the new arrivals that Toby is reaching out to. Our hunters have been outperforming expectations, and we…" He paused in his approach, taking notice of Kane and Vesh again.

James scratched his head slowly, craning his neck. "What are…" He looked at Osric, who was ready to laugh at his expression. "What are…" His face drained of color and he took two steps back.

"That's about the best greeting any paun has ever received." Gus laughed a short, humorless laugh.

Osric joined Gus in the humor of the moment. "It's okay, James. These paun are trained well and they pose no danger to any of us." He stepped between the two of them and gestured to the right. "This lovely lady is Vesh, and her larger friend with the bored expression is Kane. I've spent a lot of time with them since Orson died, and every one of my abilities and instincts indicates that they are not a threat to us."

After a moment, James replied, "You trained two paun? That's incredible!" He approached with a wide grin.

"It was much easier to train them than I thought it would be." Osric ran his hands down the backs of the two creatures.

"Amazing! I had a hard time believing they were real, even after hearing the stories of your two encounters with them."

"Most people would be dead after one encounter, and Osric can find trouble better than most," Gus chimed in with a disapproving tone. "But he has a knack for surviving his unfortunate luck," he sighed.

"That raises a good question." James spoke enthusiastically, lifting Vesh's foreleg while examining her. "Why do you suppose you have run into paun on multiple occasions while most folks are fortunate enough to still believe they're a myth?"

The Aranthians out training on the grounds had begun to take notice of their activities. Trainers and students began to drift slowly closer while the conversation continued. The forge had emptied and loud whispers carried over to the group as the paun became the center of attention.

"I've given that a great deal of thought." Osric shrugged. "The only thing I can think is that it has to do with the amount of travel I've done over the last year. And based on what I've seen, I don't think there is a large population of paun on Archana."

"Really? Based on their bodies, they would be perfect hunters. They are muscled like nothing I've ever seen, and I don't see any pores, so I doubt they have an odor—or a very slight odor, if so. Without an odor, they'd simply smell like whatever they come into contact with while walking through the forest. They should have no trouble finding food to sustain a population." James continued to examine them, not breaking eye contact to have the conversation.

"I hadn't noticed their lack of odor," Osric replied. "But then again I've only had these two with me in cold weather, so I guess the lack of smell didn't seem strange to me. They don't live in large groups, though. At least the four I've encountered don't share much company, and these two were much smaller, probably just babies when I fought the paun they were with. I guess having no particular odor could be one of the causes of a low population. If they can't find each other, they can't mate."

"The fact that we've only come across them in large, unpopulated regions could show that they avoid busy roads and cities as well." Gus furrowed his brow, thinking.

"So they like to be alone, or in small groups, and they don't sweat." James spoke mechanically. "I don't see any visible, external genitalia either. What made you introduce this one as female?"

"Oh, well." Osric scratched his head. "To be honest it was the shape of her. She's less bulky when compared to Kane, and her personality is a bit less forceful. I know it's little to go on, but considering I had to come up with names to train them, it was as good a guess as any."

"Evidence does suggest that you were correct in your other assumptions, so let's just assume you're right until we know more." James ended his examination and moved to stand in front of Osric. "Now, the only question I have is this: Why did you bring them here?"

"Ha!" Gus exclaimed.

Osric shot an angry glare at the prairie dog. Then he met James's gaze with a shy smirk. "I brought them here because I couldn't just leave them out there. If I left them alone, they would just go back to what they were: feral creatures that kill anything they come across. And some mix of the gifts I have… Some pull that I don't understand leads me to believe this was the right move. But beyond that"—he winced—"I have no idea why I brought them with me."

"Great!" Gus rolled his eyes and addressed the paun. "Just don't kill the rest of us while he's learning to interpret his gifts."

Chapter 21
Fire

"I can't believe you trained two paun." Toby shook his head. "I mean most of us have nightmares about them, hoping to never see one and that the stories about them are just that: stories. But you spent enough time with them to train them?"

Osric frowned. This was, no doubt, another example of words being spoken about him that turned into wild rumors about his unbelievable magic and heroism. The whole thing wasn't half as impressive as it sounded—the paun had just taken to his training. They had shown a tremendous amount of devotion to him immediately following his battle with their mother in the cave, so it only made sense that they looked to him as the head of their pack. Their easy training was a natural outgrowth of that instinct to follow him, nothing more. Unfortunately, it was almost impossible to convince others to see it for what it was.

"People have been questioning my sanity for years." Osric attempted to play it down. "Gus brings it up almost daily."

"Well, if there is any truth to it, we're lucky that your skills in evading the grave exceed your mental deficiencies." Toby relaxed into his chair, studying Osric with a smirk.

"Indeed," Osric replied.

"So, what are you going to use them for? I don't think they will be very effective as gardeners or midwives."

"Actually, I've given this some thought, and I think they would be of great use in helping us keep our people fed." Osric leaned in with a serious expression.

"You don't mean you want to eat them?" Toby's face contorted, signifying his distaste for the idea.

"No." Osric closed his eyes and shook his head. "I mean I think I could train them to join with the Aranthian hunters. With all of the new arrivals to Stanton, I think we will need another food source soon. We have several rooms available in the old Vigile barracks that could be easily modified into a butcher shop, maybe even another dining hall."

Osric's Wand

Toby's face took on a worried expression. It was gone in a flash, but Osric knew why he was worried.

"I know, I know. You're worried about me letting them venture out alone, but I would never do that. And I wouldn't let them out of my sight in a population without knowing for certain they wouldn't try to hunt our citizens."

"That will be a tough promise to keep. Some of Stanton's citizens live outside the city proper. Some of the animals that live in the woods would consider themselves Stanton citizens as well. How will you guarantee to keep them all safe?"

He had given that very thing a lot of thought. Part of his struggles had to do with the way the hunt operated. Osric needed to give all of it a great deal more thought before it was put into action, but how they would help in the hunt without complicating the trend in its reformation was easy.

"I can guarantee they won't be in danger because the paun will only be taken on deer hunts." He met Toby's gaze. "There won't be any need to honor last wishes when their prey are lower animals."

"That's a great idea." Toby looked a bit surprised by the idea. "But I don't think you'd have to limit it to just the deer. There are many animals outside our walls that have no magical sentience."

"No." Osric shook his head. "I'd like to keep the prey limited to one species of animal, to eliminate any mistakes that could take place by making the paun uncertain what they are supposed to attack. It just makes more sense to keep the targets limited, at least until I can be sure they can differentiate between what they can and can't kill."

"I can see you've spent some time thinking about this. I'm impressed." Toby bowed his head in a gesture of respect.

"I have. The more time I spend around the Aranthians, the more I am reminded that every choice has a consequence. Never have I felt the weight of my responsibilities more than with these paun."

"They are deadly animals," Toby replied.

"Gus almost had a fit when I brought them in." Osric smiled.

"Gus has fits over lots of things, but I hear that barking prairie dog learned how to laugh and play?" Toby leaned in with great interest.

"Oh." Osric was taken aback. "With everything that has been happening, sometimes I forget who to tell these stories to." He chuckled. "Yes, it seems that Gus does have a softer side under all of

The Weaving of Wells

his razor-sharp words. It was the damnedest thing to see his ears twitching wildly, and then he just started tumbling around the training grounds with Pebble, giggling and laughing as if he were a young pup. I didn't notice a hint of his limp or hear a trace of his normally gruff demeanor."

"No?" Toby looked at Osric with skeptical eyes.

"I swear. The old codger is changing. He seems to walk with a bit of a spring in his step. I can't begin to tell you how often we all hear him bragging about his famous son. These days, it's almost difficult to find him without a smile on his face." Osric met Toby's gaze.

"I never thought I would see the day." Toby just shook his head.

"Never tell him I told you this," Osric said, "but I found him playing with Trevar and Pebble in the wand shop a couple mornings back. They were playing with the spelled rocks from one of the vendors in town, and they weren't trying to figure out how they worked either."

"He was actually playing?" Toby was dumbfounded.

"Actually playing. A rock pulled him halfway across the room before he saw me. He tried to tell me he was helping the children cope with the recent loss of two friends, but you should have seen him laughing and shouting about how unfair it was that he weighed so much less than either of them. They seemed to get a perverse pleasure out of tossing him about the room with the help of those rocks." Osric smiled. Then, something caught their attention.

Raised voices sounded from the hall outside the office. More than one person shouted, but it didn't sound like an argument. One of the voices was looking for the Ryhain and shouting to gain entrance while the guards insisted he had to wait until he was out of his meeting. Both Toby and Osric stood up, looking at the door.

"Are you getting anything on this?" Toby looked at Osric for some hint of what was coming.

"There is portent. Not immediate danger to us, but there is danger somewhere in the news." As quickly as possible, Osric summed up what he sensed.

Toby nodded and stepped out from behind his desk. Two long steps carried him to the entrance and he flung the door open to reveal the scene. At the opposite side of the hall, the two guards were holding

Osric's Wand

another man up against the wall. He was a young man, a messenger, and he looked at Toby with pleading eyes.

"Sir, I've been sent with news. Rowain was attacked by dragons!"

One of the guards raised a club threateningly to silence him and the messenger covered his head in anticipation of a blow.

"Stop!" Toby ordered the men. "Give him some space."

The club was lowered and they stepped aside, allowing the messenger to gather himself where he stood.

"Who sent you with this news?" Toby inquired.

"Your spies reported in as the attack was underway. They are still talking to the scouts via wand and I was sent here to bring you news, but the guards don't know me. I'm still new." His words came breathless from his mouth.

"Take me to them." Toby motioned for the lad to lead the way.

The young man turned and headed down the hall. The boy looked nervous, turning anxiously to be sure the Ryhain was following him.

"I recently arrived in Stanton from Rowain. I just started a couple days ago, but this was my first task," he mumbled as he led the way, while Toby and Osric exchanged uncomfortable glances.

"You did good to find me and report quickly. Now, let's get to the office as fast as possible. We need to know what has happened." Toby interrupted the boy's ramblings and they traversed down the stairs to the main floor in silence. As they rounded the corner, they found the men running the scouting operation talking in the halls.

"We need to soften the blow. There are going to be a lot of worried people as it is, and it will be chaos if we tell them the truth."

"What truth is that, Jacobs?"

"Ryhain Toby," the short, slender man replied from behind a set of wire-framed, half-moon glasses. He fidgeted nervously at being overheard as he searched for his next words. "The damage is much more than we thought it would be, but the attack is over. We are still waiting to hear a final count, but it seems that the palace and all surrounding buildings are a total loss."

"Get word to the late Turgent's family that we are sending aid. Osric, could you spare a few more men for security, until we can get men there to help rebuild?" Toby began issuing orders in a methodical and ordered tone.

The Weaving of Wells

"We can spare some men, and I'm sure Kenneth could spare a few of his better-trained Vigiles. I think he has men to spare since recruiting so many of the refugees that have been streaming into Stanton." Osric nodded.

"Good." Toby turned back to the troops. "Get on your wand and let them know we are sending Aranthians and Vigiles to aid in security. Also, let them know that we will be checking in with other areas to see how much food and coin we can spare, but we will send everything we can." Their expressions had turned to panic as they looked back and forth between Toby and Osric.

"I'm not sure you understood, but there is no one to talk to. The palace and all surrounding buildings have been leveled, burned beyond repair, including the Turgent's palace. We're not even sure any of the Turgent's family has survived to claim the throne. There is no communication coming from Rowain that doesn't come from our scouts."

The truth hit Toby hard, and it took him a few moments to gather his thoughts. More time passed as he considered the appropriate course of action, and his gaze quickly turned to Osric.

"Could you get us to Rowain and back tonight?" Toby's question had more to do with the amount of power it would require for Osric to use the traveling spell over such a great distance than anything else.

"I could have you there and back a dozen times, if needed. I've got everything I need with me, so just tell me when," Osric replied, knowing that his power growth hadn't slowed in recent months.

"Let's see if we can lend a hand wherever possible." Resignation blanketed Toby's face. "Maybe we can find a few survivors." Osric nodded and placed a hand on his shoulder as the corridor of men and women watched. He spoke the familiar words and they vanished.

Fire danced into the dark, windless sky of Rowain. Osric had taken them as far into the town as his memory would allow without too much risk. The streets were nearly vacant in the aftermath of the attack, except for a few slow-moving merchants packing gear into wagons.

Through the ash-filled air, cries for help drifted like echoes in the vast, empty streets. On top of the pleas, low grumbling moans of discomfort carried like drum beats far off in the distance. Even from their position, a half-dozen streets from the palace, they could hear the creaking timbers heaving as their burden became too much to bear. Stone broke in loud, violent collisions upon weakened foundations, as endless shouts of horror rang out.

Osric and Toby followed the sound as quickly as their legs could run, each keeping pace with the other. Blue flames licked at the sky as Toby and Osric rounded the last corner and came to a sudden stop in front of a horrific scene. A flaming figure of a woman approached them, begging for release in pained, garbled shrieks. They looked at her in horror as they realized she was carrying what had once been two infant children in her arms.

Nothing could be done for the woman, or her children, and they fell in a lump of melting flesh at their feet. The screaming faded to a whimper as flames crackled and sparked, dragging along with them the last hopes of a young family. Osric drew Legati to end the suffering of the three, but Toby stopped him before he could.

"No." He shook his head once as a tear ran down his cheek.

"I can't let them suffer," Osric replied, attempting to hold back sobs of his own.

"I know." Toby motioned to Legati. "But you will carry this moment with you a lot longer than I. Let me do it." He pulled out his own sword and Osric looked away.

Two portions of the palace's eastern wall stood as markers to the dead and dying amongst the rubble. The scent of burning flesh made them both cover their faces with their sleeves. Though it wasn't safe, they began to climb on top of the rubble and survey the wreckage for signs of survivors

They took separate paths, careful of each step, trying to avoid bringing down some small opening that could house survivors below. He searched dozens of hidden locations with no luck before a few men dressed in Rowain guard attire joined the search from the opposite side of the rubble. Then, looking over at where Toby was, Osric saw the Ryhain digging frantically in the broken stone.

In a moment, Osric appeared beside Toby. He could see immediately why the Ryhain was digging where he was. An ash-covered hand was reaching out of the ground below them, and panicked shouts, though muffled, wafted out of the same hole.

"We're here. I'll get you out. Just stay calm." Toby dug with his bare hands, careful not to let any of the rubble slide inside the widening opening. "Keep anything from falling in, and by my bones don't let me fall in either." Toby looked Osric in the eye, the sweat trickling down his brow leaving streaks in the ash smeared across his face.

With both Legati and his new Pebble wand in hand, Osric held Toby from falling in and kept even the smallest rock from finding its way inside the hole. It was delicate work, but with both of them working together, soon Toby was helping a man out of the opening. And then a woman, a young girl, and a bewildered-looking black cat exited the rubble. Without missing a beat, Toby lowered his head inside to examine the expanse for more survivors, but there were none. From the look of their clothes, they were servants who had been lucky enough to be in the right place when the attack occurred.

"Do you know where the Turgent's family would have been?" Toby asked the three dazed evacuees. The older gentleman pointed towards the deepest part of the smoldering stacks with a shaky hand. Then he withdrew the gesture with terror still covering his face. His eyes darted from point to point as if searching for more signs of danger. When he found nothing but the burning wreckage of the Rowain palace, he covered his eyes and a high-pitched moaning escaped his lips. He fought the breaths of panic for a few short moments before his eyelids slammed shut. Unconsciousness took hold and he crumpled to the ground.

Toby stood up quickly after seeing the three tended to by another who had just joined the search, and he and Osric made their way as quickly as they could to the center of the former building. They began to dig—with their hands when they were able and with wands when pieces of rubble were too heavy for them to lift. The sun had traveled across the sky and slipped over the horizon before they paused, and even then it was only for long enough to drink a few sips of water. The dark of the night had taken over and several Aranthian troops joined in the effort to find survivors. Neither Osric nor Toby could remember summoning them to help, but more appeared to carry away debris or cast light on the efforts as the night grew long, but for all of their efforts the progress was slow.

Many of the men and women who worked on the Rowain palace that day had been in Stanton when that palace had collapsed amidst mysterious circumstances, and they knew all too well the fear that the families of those who worked in the palace would be feeling as they waited to learn if their loved ones had survived. This knowledge seemed to fuel those who labored all night in search of anyone still breathing in the wreckage. More continued to be unearthed, but disturbingly only from the outer regions of the complex walls.

As fatigue began to set into the bones of everyone engaged in rescue operations, the sun began to slowly rise in the east. Toby looked weary in his fine clothing. The ash that still rose from their surroundings had covered everyone and everything in thick black soot, which mixed with dripping sweat. So much of it had covered each body working the scene that no distinguishing characteristic could be detected on anyone except for vivid white eyes tinged with red and the shape of their body against the grey backdrop of the sky.

Until these recent events, no recorded history or fire-telling spoke of attacks like these taking place anywhere on Archana. It was a stark picture for anyone to observe as black, soot-covered figures fought against rock, smoke, and fire that would not yield, to rescue those who had little chance at life. But a little chance was still a chance to anyone still clinging to life beneath the rubble, and every successful rescue brought to the surface more shocked faces of buried men, women, and children who had expected to die. The rescuers worked to a point of physical fatigue and emotional numbness as they uncovered twenty corpses for each single survivor.

By noon the next day, the word had gotten out at the Aranthian headquarters and hundreds of people were working alongside Osric and Toby. In spite of their efforts, the central mass was disturbingly difficult to uncover, and so far not a single survivor had been uncovered from the area. Also, very little progress had been made in carrying out walls due to the instability in the way the walls sat upon the next layer below. They had to uncover nearly the entire outer structure before it was safe to begin digging in the middle—a fact that became obvious a short time into the search when every attempt caused a small cave-in.

Yet, with the experience of the Aranthians to bolster the efforts, by nightfall on their second day, significant progress had been made. After only a short rest, both Osric and Toby had gotten back to their efforts and they found themselves, with the help of five Aranthians, lifting a large section of wall away from the Turgent's living quarters.

The Weaving of Wells

"Keep your side higher than ours!" Toby shouted above the smashing boulders that fell on his side of the wall. "Let the rubble fall to our side!"

"Higher!" Osric urged them on, stepping out of the way as debris fell toward him. "We need to keep the survivors safe. Don't let up!"

"Over here!" A small man who worked as a healer in Rowain had arrived early in the morning to help, and he led a small band of workers under the raised stone wall to inspect the area. "We have bodies!" he shouted as the seven who lifted the wall passed the burden onto the next dozen workers to carry it out of the way. Most of the rescue workers were far too fatigued from using magic to levitate stone slabs and put out smoldering fires to even attempt a simple spell. The only option remaining was to work together and use the strength of their arms and backs to lift the vast chunks of rubble.

Osric and Toby lowered their wands and ran to help with the inspection and to prepare the floor to be moved for the next layer to be opened. They led the digging, but when it came to this part there was no substitute for a local healer, so they let him lead in the rescue. At a quick glance, five bodies lay before them. It didn't take a healer to know that at least four were beyond any hope, but the fifth, a young girl in her early teens in what looked like a soiled yellow dress, could possibly pull through if she was still alive.

"Dead." The healer swore and threw a rock into the air. His tan robes were stained with smoke, and dirt heaved with silent sighs where he knelt on the tilting, cracked floor.

"Is it the Turgent's family?" Toby knew it was too soon, but he needed to continue working to rescue them, if there was still a hope of finding them, so he pressed the issue. "Well?"

The robed man wiped his face with the soiled rags of his clothing and looked around. "This young woman was his only daughter." He stood there, examining each of the bodies with a horrified expression. "This was his wife, but these three bodies are too badly burnt and crushed for me to tell if one of them was his only son. I just don't know."

"These two wore armor and stood near the door." Osric pointed to the two mangled bodies by the outer edge of the floor. "This one's dress suggests servant status. Would they keep a chambermaid?"

Osric's Wand

The old man surveyed the bodies again, and a hint of recognition reflected in his eyes. Slowly he began to nod and then he barked out, "Yes! The boy was eight years old and quite a bit smaller than those two as well. They couldn't be him."

His search began again, and he moved in the direction the bodies had fallen. The wardrobes and bed had created a hollow underneath the wall, but survival would have depended a great deal upon how they fell when the palace crumbled, and if they were near anything that still burned. An overturned wardrobe lay on its face, cracked and ready to come apart.

"Get this up and see if the boy took refuge." The Healer looked up at Osric and Toby with longing eyes. "Let's hope, for his sake, the sight of a dragon drove cowardice into his young heart."

The wardrobe was unusually heavy, and it looked to be made of quartz. As Osric, Toby, and two of the townsmen lifted the stone panel off of the back of the wardrobe, it became clear that it was designed for more than just clothing. Eight swords of different lengths and styles, four staffs, and a selection of daggers filled a narrow chamber.

"It's a false back. I bet many of these are magical in nature." Toby looked to Osric for confirmation. "Probably gifts from different dignitaries."

"The staffs are actually wands, and the one with the ruby set in the carving has a flame charm set in it." Osric confirmed Toby's suspicions. "There's nothing magical about the rest of them, but they look a lot like the ceremonial swords I've seen over the years."

They spoke fast and began to remove the items from their resting place, making sure to preserve them for the heir they hoped they would find. When they had placed the items on the remains of a charred bed, the men returned to lift the next stone panels from their case. Upon inspection, the hidden door was in three separate panels. It took several long moments before they figured out how to open it and allow them to see inside.

"It's a spell that opens it. Look, here," Osric said out of habit from having Gus around, and then he realized none of those around him were Wand-Makers. "All we have to do is"—he held out his wand—"trigger the locking mechanism."

The Weaving of Wells

A click and a whirling sounded from within the stone walls at the sides. The panels to either side sunk in and the middle raised, then the three stone plates moved together to the left side, disappearing into the sidewall. The odor of sweat, urine, and vomit rose up from the small figure that lay on top of the clothing.

"Elgon! This is the Turgent's son." The healer knelt by the side of the wardrobe and gently felt for a pulse. "He's alive. Water, bring me some water. Quickly!"

Osric and Toby stood back and watched closely as the older man worked, issuing orders to men and women moving the boy from the mounds of rubble to a safe, clean location within a building not too far away. They had Elgon carried out on a blanket by two Vigiles, stepping slowly over the remaining rubble that was left of the palace. Dozens of men and women had come to help secure the heir to the Turgency, and they watched with worry and relief plain on their features as the two men handled their burden with gentle, careful hands.

There was still work to be done, and the two leaders from Stanton knew it, but they stood there for a moment to watch Rowain's people care for their helpless young leader. Then as the second day's sun was setting, they turned back to the work that had summoned them and set themselves to finishing the task. After another full night of work, they uncovered the last of the survivors. In all, seventeen men, women, and children survived the dragon's attack.

Chapter 22
Old Friends

"I don't think you can appreciate how much damage was done." Shrad looked across the table with weary eyes. His hand shook as he lifted a cup of rulha to his mouth. "We could tell a lot about what used to be there by what was left."

Osric brought a tray of cheese, sausage, and bread to the table. Weeks had passed since he had sent Aron's defectors to the Elven Realm to check on them after Bridgett informed him of the dragon attack on the Elvenwood. He had been waiting for the report, but recent events had taken precedence over previous curiosities—until Rowain. It was only a day after he and Toby had returned from Rowain—horrible timing, since they were still sending relief for that effort, but the attacks in the Elven Realm were among the first and they might give him some idea of what they were up against if he could hear the accounts from the survivors.

"But what took you so long to report? I almost forgot that we sent you." Osric topped off the steaming cup.

"Well." Shrad took a piece of cheese. "Even though many of the smaller villages are in ruins, the spells concealing them are largely in place. It was seventeen days into our search before we encountered any elves who would let us in to get information. We had been close to the spells and they interfered with communication, but we didn't know why until later. And once we were inside, we couldn't just gather information and leave. I doubt they would have let us leave either."

"Okay, then how were you able to leave and bring us the information without raising their suspicions?" He poured himself a glass of water and sat down.

"By the time I left, they had no reason to be suspicious of any of us. We've been gone all this time because we got swept up in the events of De'assartis. The one redeeming thing to come out of these attacks is that De'assartis has been nearly unscathed through it all, though few of the smaller elven communitites can boast the same." Shrad paused, reflecting.

The Weaving of Wells

"If De'assartis was left alone, what events could you get caught up in?" Osric questioned him gently.

Shrad sighed heavily. "The first thing was the way the trees seemed to speak. At first it was almost musical, seductive even, but the closer we got to the source, the more it seemed to bring on waves of emotion. We were saddened beyond any rational explanation. Our whole group wept for days on end. That was what got us discovered, but we couldn't control ourselves; the forest's call was unlike anything I'd ever experienced before."

"When they found us they kept saying that the mother had told them where to find us, that help was on the way. You see, they worship the trees. They thought that their mother, the trees, told them we would help, and I suppose we did. At first we were only allowed to help with some small things, like packaging fruit and bread to be sent to groups of survivors. We collected water in corked husks of a fruit the elves use as canteens. We spent days bundling bandages and medicines together, and then they began sending us to help, once they felt they could trust us."

"You should have reported to us. We could have sent more help." Osric leaned in. Shrad's emotions were starting to affect him, and Osric could sense the most intense emotions were yet to come.

"Like I said before, we got swept up in everything that was happening. We traveled with them to several small villages that were almost completely destroyed, but part of the mother was always near the survivors." Shrad shook with some hidden memory.

"We saw families weeping over unrecognizable, burnt bodies. Lines of them were laid out, hastily wrapped in linen. They just kept bringing more and more bodies, some alive and some not, from different places across the realm. I remember one boy; he was burned beyond recognition on his right side and only a small, blistered, black nub hung from where his arm used to be. The smell was just…" His face contorted in horror.

"I think I've heard enough." Osric motioned for him to stop. "Is there anything we can offer? There must be something we can do."

"Right now, what they need are healers, and medicine, and food. But the elves have a strictly vegetarian diet, which may seem strange but it actually tastes pretty good. With that in mind, I don't think sending them things that we eat will be of any help, and it may actually hurt in the long run."

"They fear that many of the things that we grow and eat in our climate may infest their grounds, taking over ground cover and choking out much of the natural vegetation that grows in the area. They have many plants in that area that are essential to their way of life, and their habitat is very fragile." Shrad emphasized his final words.

"So, what should we bring?" Osric was beginning to understand how difficult the relief effort could be.

"They need manpower. It's really that simple. We could send medication and healers straight away. But they would need to train our people on the proper ways to gather many of their more fragile crops. Then, they also have many cultural beliefs surrounding the mother that extend into cultivating and farming of crops as well. It would take several days, or longer, for them to trust us to send our own men out to perform the tasks. This is no small project we would be getting ourselves into."

"Do you think they would allow me to come and see things for myself before I commit our overwhelmed resources to the cause." He didn't know what he was doing, but portent was leading him in this direction. If they were to face Dredek with the five hundred dwarves Machai was supposed to be bringing back with him—and he had already sent Aranthian troops to help bolster the Vigiles in Rowain, and even more to the Elven Realm—he wasn't sure there would be enough men for them to be able to stop Dredek. In spite of Osric's misgivings, his Portentist ability hadn't misled him yet. He was inclined to follow the pull from the gift out of sheer experience, with or without the support of logic.

"I'm certain they would," said Shrad. "One thing they would frown upon is dozens of our men showing up at once. There are very few elves available to train them in gathering food, so the fewer the better the first time we go."

"I'm not sure how many we can offer, but there will be help sent." And then Osric had a thought. "I think Bridgett and I will accompany you to the city. We can decide from there what to do with the rest of our efforts."

The Weaving of Wells

"Great, sir." Shrad stood up with relief and drew his wand. "I'll let them know we are on our way."

"I'm sure I won't have to talk Bridgett into going back, but I don't want to speak for her. We'll depart later this morning, after I talk to her and see to some things here." Osric nodded and stood up to leave the room.

* * *

After a short wand conversation with Landin, enough to give Osric his bearings for the traveling spell, the three Aranthian troops arrived under a canopy of trees. A cool mist was in the air, as if a storm had recently passed through the area. Gad, Landin, and Asram stood in front of them with a dozen elven archers training their bows in their direction. Osric could sense it was purely for security reasons and none of the elves intended them harm, though their nerves were understandably on edge. He smiled at seeing the three men again, entirely ignoring the weapons surrounding them.

"Shrad, it's good to see you've brought help." One of the many warriors stepped out from the shadows, suddenly becoming visible behind the rest of the elven archers. "And the High-Wizard, if I'm not mistaken?"

"Yes, this is Osric. I think you'll find he is everything we told you he is." Shrad inclined his head and motioned to the other three men.

"I'm Elisad, commander of the eastern gates." He was tall, with dark hair, a spotless brown and green tunic to match his breeches, and he trained a vivid pair of silver eyes on Osric as he stepped through the crowd and held out his hand in greeting.

Osric stepped up and grasped his arm just before the elbow. "I sent some of my best to discover what was happening after Bridgett departed, and I hear things are dire for much of the Elven Realm."

"I am sorry to report that the stories are true. One mighty, black beast of a dragon has burned seven of our villages to the ground." Elisad's voice was low and heavy with remorse.

"Velien, is Velien still alive?" Bridgett strode forward with a confidence that commanded attention.

"Velien?" Elisad stuttered. "I'm not entirely certain."

"He worked this gate before the dragon attacks. He's half a head shorter than you with wide, curious eyes and the same color hair as you." Bridgett held his gaze firmly with her own.

"He's served with me before. I know who he is. It's just that..." Elisad measured her with skeptical eyes.

"You don't know where he is at? Or you don't know if you should answer?" she continued with forcefulness.

"Bridgett, what are you doing?" Osric held his hands out, trying to calm her down.

"I am attempting to get some answers," she replied.

"I'm just not sure if he's still alive, and having an outsider question the well-being of an elf surprised me. Guard groups shift sites and commanders on a regular basis, and things are more irregular than normal these days. He could be on one of the relief crews, or be watching the western gate. Then again, he could be dead. They started sending troops to outlying villages when the attacks began. I just don't know." A mournful shrug echoed Elisad's grim expression.

"And now the Aranthians are here to aid you. I'm sure the answer will be known in no time." Gad injected the pride of his station into the conversation.

"We'll lend whatever aid we can." Osric nodded, but the elves shifted with unease at the words, so Osric continued. "And along the way we will observe any customs you wish us to. I am here to get a feel for the kind of help we could send, and what magics they may need to know in order to assist you as quickly as possible."

"Well..." Elisad winced, preparing his reply. "You should know that speed could lend itself to the improper execution of our tasks. We appreciate any help you can send, but our problems will not be solved overnight, no matter the magic you bring."

"That is why he is here." Shrad stepped forward with a calming gesture. "Trust us. There are many new magics. I'm sure we can find some that can help to speed relief without causing concern for the elves."

"And"—Osric stepped forward with open hands—"we won't attempt anything without the knowledge and permission of your people." He took a breath. "But we must attempt to speed relief, if we are to offer it. The Aranthians are in the midst of battle and cannot promise a long, protracted arrangement. But rest assured that we will

The Weaving of Wells

attempt to ensure that none of our actions violate your customs and beliefs."

"Attempt?" Worry filled Elisad's eyes as he held Osric in his gaze. He was clearly concerned, but Osric could sense that curiosity at his honesty was the driving force behind the question.

"There are many unknowns with the magics we bring," Osric spoke openly. "We are still learning what consequences they have, but we will use caution in selecting which to use, as well as your council."

"Could you not simply send us scholars? I see no use in more warriors filling our forests." Elisad continued to probe, but an underlying sense of respect began to fill his mind.

"Many of our warriors have the minds of scholars, and many of our scholars have the skills of warriors," Landin said, taking his place beside the group.

"The ones that don't possess both skills tend to pass away in the early days of becoming an Aranthian." Gad joined them, swelling with pride.

"New magics test one's mind and body. Mistakes lead to an early grave if we do not possess a keen mind and stout body." Asram stepped to their side.

Osric was surprised by their display. He was proud of what the Aranthians had become, but he had never heard any of them speak so highly of it. He had hoped they would become worthy of such praise, yet hearing his own men speak so highly of the infant organization made him realize how far they had come. He swallowed hard, regathering his thoughts to form an argument. Then Elisad spoke.

"A lesser man would tell us he could guarantee everything we wished. He would say he could observe all our customs and beliefs while delivering speedy healing and food stores. He would say this thinking he could uphold the bargain, but would eventually fail in such a way that would see him, and his people, banished from our walls forever. But you bring no promises?" Elisad's question was directed through the men displaying their pride in the Aranthian name and directly at Osric.

"We don't lie." Landin completed the four-man formation.

"Pride in who we are aside"—Osric parted the group and extended his hand—"my father always taught me not to oversell yourself. He taught me that honesty yields better results than false promises. I can offer you aid. I cannot promise that we can stay within your guidelines at all times, but we will try."

Elisad took his hand. "Let's get you to De'assartis and see what help you can offer." He turned to lead the way, then stopped and turned back. "I know you have a way to cover great distances with magic. The trip there with such magic would not violate any of our accords and would speed things along greatly."

Bridgett stepped forward with a sorrowful expression. "There are too many unknowns with that spell and this many people. If we arrive in a location with new growth—or worse yet, another living being—both the person and the unseen obstruction would die. We take precautions at our base to avoid these issues, so we cannot attempt it here until we have a chance to prepare. It was already a danger for us to arrive here without the protections in place. For the time being, we will have to walk in order to ensure that we all arrive safely."

"As you wish." Elisad turned and led the small group of six into the trees.

As they walked, Osric began to sense the emotions behind Bridgett's uncharacteristic display. He was in awe at the way trees grew together, as if they were all one tree, but Bridgett was filled with relief at their sight. Inclines were adorned with steps formed by rectangular roots, perfectly placed and measured, with sharp corners and no sign of workmanship or cuts from saw blades.

As they walked further, ever closer to the city, more signs of life emerged. Osric began to sense eyes watching them from somewhere in the canopy of trees. He kept looking to his left to see Bridgett smiling at his observation of the world they had entered. Then he witnessed the most amazing thing. As they entered the city, entire homes appeared to be grown out of a single tree, and the handrails on the walkways that crossed the expanses between homes were grown from a single branch. There were no signs of intertwined branches or workmanship of any kind. It was as if both trees on either side were the source of the extending branch, and the footpath was the same. In between the rail and the path, vines connected and acted to stabilize the structure, but once again there was no indication that tools of any kind had manicured either of them.

Bridgett was filled with even more relief as they entered the city. Not only was the relief evident in waves of emotion from the Empath

The Weaving of Wells

gift, but her shoulders also began to relax and her walk was less rigid, less pressing, and less forceful. As she took his hand, Osric knew that the fear that had prompted her outburst at the gate had faded, though there was still the persistent worry over Velien, whom Osric had heard about many times. He hoped Velien had survived. He felt he owed him for looking after her while she was in De'assartis, and he wished to thank him for what he had done.

The heart of the city was far from the veiled canopy of life and hidden eyes peeking from the shadows that he had seen on the outskirts of De'assartis. As they began to climb the perfectly grown steps at the center, Osric began to see just how densely populated the elven city was. Hundreds of wounded elves rested along the mountainside under the shadows of the Mother's leaves. Healers were tending to many, and others who were capable were lending a helping hand by bringing food and water or cleaning another's wounds with clean cloths. Osric's stomach twisted into knots when he saw how many elves were suffering injuries from the dragon attacks.

As they went higher up the mountainside, a low, sad sound filled the air, growing louder the further they traveled. It was almost a hum, and Osric thought it sounded as if an endless breath were playing some wind instrument. *Was this the mother singing? The Mother in Bridgett's stories?* Osric quickly shook off the thought. There was too much emotion behind the tone for it to be controlled by a tree. Whatever it was, it created a somber feeling in the air itself. The music was colored by sorrow and mourning, and Osric felt the emotions welling up inside of him as the sound reverberated in his mind.

They continued up the mountain. A mist followed them as they traveled, lending its aid in disguising the tortured elven figures along the sides of the path. Some were merely blistered, but many others were burned beyond recognition, littering the hillside. Osric started to get an idea of the type of people he should send in their first wave of relief. He did his best to look at the path and the trees, but the music continued to draw his attention to those surrounding him. Bridgett and the other three Aranthians made no such attempt, and tears fell freely from their eyes as they took in their surroundings.

As they walked, Osric noticed that many of the people tending to the wounded were not elves. They were a much shorter race of elvishlooking creatures covered in a layer of tan fur. No doubt they were related to the elves in some way, but whatever had caused their lineage to yield this result was beyond him. His first thought was there must be some ancestor that shared both dwarf and elf parentage, but they had traits that looked distinctively catlike as well. Osric recalled Bridgett describing the girl who had served at the inn she stayed in, and he realized these creatures must be the nieko. He wondered why he had never heard of them before in the Human Realm.

As they walked, Osric made a mental list of the resources that seemed to be lacking, and he agreed with Shrad's assessment that manpower and supplies for the healers should top the list. He attempted to keep his emotions in check so that he could focus on the daunting responsibility before him, but even without the Empath ability, it would have been nearly impossible to block out the tragedy surrounding them. Osric kept his thoughts busy with the preparations that would be needed to supply men and women with the necessary items once he knew exactly how he could help the elves the most.

They continued up the mountainside until a large hall was visible before them. A steady light filled hundreds of windows. Osric was beside himself wondering how such a building could be grown, but there was the telltale lack of planks, panels, carvings, or joints—anything that would indicate work done by hand or tools. The building appeared to be a large, hollow trunk, with many different levels. The size of the entire dwelling rivaled that of any castle or palace he had ever seen. Bodies moved in the windows as elves went about their routine, but on the bottom floor stood dozens of red-haired figures with somber faces. They wore long black robes that covered all but their faces. Osric looked to Bridgett and she shrugged.

"They were chanting when I was here last."

"We have no songs when the mother is in mourning. Now is the time to reflect." Elisad hung his head for a moment and then ushered them into the hall.

When they entered, the line of robed figures remained in solemn pose with their heads bowed and hands tucked inside their sleeves. Signs of life were everywhere, from pillars to walls, ceiling to floor—even the steps leading to the raised dais crawled with vines. On twelve thrones adorned with vines sat eleven imposing figures looking down

The Weaving of Wells

on them with pleading eyes. The central figure stood up and stepped to the edge of the platform.

"Osric, I presume?"

"I am. To whom am I speaking?" He inclined his head.

"I am Lord Aveloc. The High Lord is away." He bowed to each side, showing respect for those who sat to his sides. Each of the figures who sat on the dais bowed their heads in acknowledgment of the gesture.

"Lord Aveloc, it is a pleasure to meet you. I can assure you that allowing us to aid you was a good decision." Osric reciprocated the respectful bow.

"Of that we have no doubt. We had a visit from a Seer after Bridgett departed. Our concern is that our culture may suffer from a large influx of outsiders." Lord Aveloc stood stoically at the edge of the platform.

The news was unexpected for Osric, but the presence of a Seer failed to trigger his Portentist gift, so he continued. "I can understand your concern, but I assure you that we will try to minimize the interference. I was thinking we could send a couple of healers first. We have been able to make some impressive gains in magical understanding of the healing process. They shouldn't cause any interference in your culture with the magic they practice."

Osric had only recently been caught up on the advances that the healers in the Aranthian crew were making. Though he didn't have knowledge of healing himself, Bridgett had assured him that they were significant advancements in instances of disease and tissue damage. All of these advances would be useful in aiding the elves in their current predicament.

"The healers' help would be welcome. We could also use help securing our borders and gathering food, if you could spare the resources for such a venture." Wide eyes looked at Osric and his crew with uncertainty.

Osric was taken aback by the swift admission that the elves needed help securing their borders. How much damage had the dragons done?

"I'm not sure how many we can spare, but we will send what we can offer." Then Osric hesitated, looking to his companions and back again at the dais. "I suggest we send in six-man teams to be trained alongside your men, at first. Then, after a few days we can send in twelve to be trained by our men and work alongside yours. This would allow you to supervise all of the training that takes place, and to be able to see that the instruction is up to your standards. All of this with the understanding that we are currently battling a superior force and we may have to withdraw the majority of our men at any moment." He wasn't at all sure how the proposal would be received.

"A wise step in the right direction. I can see that you have given some thought to meeting our needs." Aveloc nodded with approval. "And I can assure you we are well versed in your need for men at this time. Any help would be appreciated."

"I share your concern for your realm, and I am happy to offer any aid that is within our means." Osric attempted to express his surprise that the elves were so openly and tactfully admitting their need for help. "I'm glad that you are willing to accept the assistance of our people."

"We were not confident that you would offer aid, High-Wizard. After all, our last meeting with Bridgett did not end well, as we were less than receptive to your needs." Lord Aveloc looked to his chaired compatriots. "It is necessary that we be cautious in our negotiations with other realms. Yet, our encounter with the Seer has reassured us of the prudence of this alliance."

"There is no evidence that your decision to deny aid in our time of need has caused us additional hardship," Osric replied. "If you had granted our request, your situation may be even more dire today. We can be forgiving for the mistrust of yesterday, and grateful that prophecy has paved the path for our future negotiations."

"Kind and wise words." He bowed. "Now I will leave you to plan with your men, and I will see to arrangements for the arrivals." Aveloc turned toward his throne, pressing his forefinger to the emerald on his headband.

Osric turned back to see surprised faces on all four of the men who had been living with the elves for some time and a searching gaze on Bridgett's face as she surveyed those gathered. He could feel the nervousness coming off of her in waves. Then, he remembered why.

"Lord Aveloc." He whipped back, interrupting the telepathic conversation made possible by the headpieces they wore.

"Yes, Lord Osric?"

The Weaving of Wells

"I am no lord," he said, correcting the mistake. His men snickered behind him.

"My apologies, High-Wizard. What can we do for you?" Aveloc arched an eyebrow in annoyance.

Osric realized he was testing Lord Aveloc's welcome by interrupting and correcting him, but Bridgett's peace of mind was worth pushing the boundaries of political formalities. "We wish to know the fate of an elf by the name of Velien. He looked after Bridgett on her last trip here. Could you tell us, is he still alive?"

"Velien?" Aveloc gazed down at Osric with narrowed eyes. "I have no knowledge of his death, but you have more urgent matters to concern yourself with at this time, do you not?"

"Of course. Please forgive my inquiry, but his well-being is of particular concern to myself and Bridgett." Osric squeezed Bridgett's hand in his own and held Aveloc's stare.

"He is at the western gate. I received a report on their status just this morning." A woman on the left side of the dais stood up and rested her fingers lightly on Lord Aveloc's arm. Her long blonde hair was adorned with the same array of delicate leaves as the rest on the dais. Her smile lent an air of elegance to her slight features. She wore a long green dress that cascaded down her throne and lay perfectly across the floor before her.

"Is there any reason he couldn't be brought back to work with us? Familiarity goes a long way toward establishing trust among humans." The request was more for Bridgett's benefit, but Osric earnestly wished to thank him for the time he had spent with her.

"His rotation is nearly complete. I will bring him back to serve as our liaison to the troops reinforcing our borders," the woman affirmed with a nod. Aveloc raised his brow, waiting to see if Osric would be satisfied or ask further favors of him.

Osric looked to Bridgett with a slight smile and turned back to the dais. "Thank you," he said. Then as the group walked back out the door, Osric reached for his wand to initiate the communication spell and summon the first of the three men, but he wanted some space to talk freely. They continued down the path to a large open space free of trees and prying eyes. There were still some magics he didn't want to share at this time, and he didn't know who might be watching or listening.

Osric's Wand

Before he could initiate the spell, dust billowed from the rock-strewn ground as two eagles landed in a rush of wind and feathers. The eyes of the larger eagle peered at the group with dignity and respect. The smaller one, with brighter, black feathers and white atop its head, looked to the other with searching uncertainty.

"Ero!" Bridgett shot out from the group and ran across the distance.

Osric, surprised to see his wand outstretched in a defensive posture, lowered and resheathed the newly created treasure. His heart thumped vigorously but it took only a small amount of effort to regain his control after being startled.

"Bridgett." Ero's gaze let loose no small amount of joy with his greeting. "It is good to see you again. And Osric..." He looked to the four men standing a short distance behind him. "It is good to see you all."

"I haven't had the chance to thank you properly for what you did for us in the battle for Stanton." Osric stepped forward with a nod. To his surprise, Gad, Landin, Asram, and Shrad stepped out from behind and approached Ero.

"And we have never had the chance to tell you how sorry we are for our part in enslaving your cousin flyers." Shrad took the lead, referring to how the four of them had served as guards at Braya.

"It was wrong of us to do so," Landin echoed.

"We should have fought to see them freed." Gad stepped closer.

"But we were foolish cowards until the Aranthians showed us a better way," Asram added.

"We submit ourselves to your judgment. We are certainly to blame for the dragon attacks on Archana," Shrad finished as the four men bowed to Ero.

Empathy told Osric that the speech had been rehearsed, but the emotions behind their remorse were genuine. Ero looked to Osric questioningly, and Osric held out his hands, shaking his head to signify he knew nothing.

Ero looked down at the men before him and blinked slowly. "Should I drop you from the sky to fall to your death?"

"That would not be effective." Landin looked up and shook his head. "Aranthians have experience falling great distances, and we could save ourselves."

"Do you wish to be punished?" Ero looked back to Landin.

The Weaving of Wells

"It is not for the offender to decide if they should be punished." He spoke in earnest.

"Then what gives me the right to serve as punisher?" Ero replied.

The other three men looked up with uncertainty. They each looked to the other for answers until Gad spoke in an unsteady voice.

"You fought to help free them, and we opposed you."

"Osric and his men fought as well. Did they not bring you into their fold?" Ero looked them each in the eye as if they were children.

"Well, yes," Gad replied.

"Then if they chose to ally with a former foe, why would you think I would dole out punishment? Do my feathers look like scales to weigh your value as men?" Ero looked down at his own chest.

"A nice gesture, gentlemen." Bridgett began helping each of the men to their feet. "But prophecy brought you to us, and neither the eagles nor dragons argue with prophecy."

Embarrassed, each of the four men took their place behind Osric.

"They are good men. You chose well in recruiting them." Ero did what he could to restore their confidence. "Not many men would willingly submit themselves to punishment. Even fewer would inform the jailer which punishments would be futile."

"We choose only the best." Osric nodded, happy to have the uncomfortable moment behind them. "Do we have business to discuss, or is this just a reunion of sorts?"

"How did you get into the elven city?" Bridgett interrupted. "There are spells protecting this place from airborne intruders."

"Eagles do not intrude, my lady. The eagles have lived in communion with the elves for centuries. We come and go as we please, and we are welcomed upon arrival. We bring aid to an old ally under siege from the fire above." Ero looked insulted by the words.

"No disrespect intended," she replied. "I never knew you were allies to the elves. My apologies."

"But how can you be allied with both dragons and elves at this time?" Osric inclined his head.

"Those that attack the walkers are no cousins to the eagles." Ero's voice was adamant but controlled. "The offending dragons are led by a massive, black-scaled beast named Calx. Though it appears that only the dragons that never felt bound to the elders are involved, we fear more may join him if things do not change."

Osric's Wand

"What do you mean?" Osric stepped closer. "What needs to change?"

"The change isn't on the part of any walker, but rather on the part of dragonkind. Something dark has awoken in the minds of many since the battle at Stanton. After partaking in such violence against humans, some dragons withdrew and began seeking solitude. Once they found it, too long left alone and without touching the minds of other dragons, they would likely feed the anger and resentment. We suspect that Calx has sought them out, attempting to seduce them into taking action against walkers."

"And emotions once seeming shameful seem righteous when you find someone of the same mind." Bridgett nodded in understanding. "The anger grows in the company of anger."

"Yes. It grows to the point that grace and kindness no longer hold power over it when left too long without." Ero bowed his head. "It is possible that the dragon threat will grow."

"Why can't the dragons that are still allies of the eagles speak to their wayward kin?" Bridgett shook her head with a worried frown.

"That part is a bit more complicated. Many of the dragons are still struggling with their own feelings on the subject—I don't think you realize how much that one battle affected all dragonkind. Many of them have been avoiding walkers because they too feel the stirrings of bloodlust. While I am confident that most of the dragons will never be a threat to walkers, it will take time for the relationship to be restored. It is also likely that they fear communication with any dragon who is engaged in the attacks. The dragons have the stability of their herd to worry about."

"Does Stargon have any plans to deal with the situation? With all the destruction they've caused, I would hate to have the Aranthians go up against a group of angry dragons." Osric's tone was somber and worried. An earnest desire for the dragon attacks to cease without sacrificing more lives fueled his plea.

"That is a complicated question," Ero replied.

"Why is it complicated? If anyone can stop the bad dragons, it's the good dragons." Gad stepped forward, and Osric could sense his need to trust in the compassion of the dragons that had saved his life near Braya.

The Weaving of Wells

"Yes, they are doing something, but their efforts may prove to be less than successful in the end." The eagle's expression was sympathetic, but it carried some small hint of warning too. Ero wasn't about to tolerate rude questioning. "Unfortunately, the defecting dragons had already gained knowledge of the traveling spell before they parted ways. Locating their hideout—or hideouts—is turning out to be a more daunting task than any could have guessed. And then there is the final issue." His last words were suggestive and unsure. He looked at Osric, searching his eyes for a few moments.

Osric's brow was creased with concern. "There is something more, something worse?"

"It seems there always is these days. Stargon and the other elders have reason to believe that the attacks are not just random rage-filled dragons seeking treasure or sating bloodlust. It is possible that they are being coordinated, that the dragons are taking orders. Stargon suspects that a single mind is behind this chaos and destruction."

"Have you attempted to use your Chronicleer gift to see where they are, or who is behind it?" He wasn't even sure if it was possible, but the idea made sense to Osric.

"Unfortunately, these events are much too current for my gift to be of any use. The timeline becomes clearer the further away in time we are from the events. Perhaps a Seer could be of more assistance, as my gift is reliable only for events that occurred perhaps five years ago or more."

Osric nodded in agreement. "Now the clarity of the fire-telling in the Caves of D'pareth is making more sense. So, what do we do? How do we help the dragons find them?"

Osric was starting to feel overwhelmed by the amount of work he was volunteering the Aranthians to perform. They were still working on bringing Dredek to justice, and they had just offered to help the elves in their recovery and defense. As if that weren't enough, they were supposed to help the dragons find flying beasts from the ground? How they were going to accomplish the current goals was a big enough challenge. Adding a nearly impossible task to their limited resources could prove to be a fatal mistake.

"I'm not sure what would be a good course of action. I'm here to offer aid to our elven brothers. I'm sure Stargon would be more than willing to discuss options, if you can offer assistance." Ero's shrug held more than the uncertainty of his answer. There was a sorrowful cast to the eagle's body that showed how truly difficult it was for him to not be able to provide the insight that Osric needed.

Osric knew he would have to have another meeting. The next would be with Stargon, but when he would have the time for that discussion was another problem altogether. He felt a terrific weight settle on his mind as the different obstacles ahead revealed themselves to all of the gifts he still fought to understand. There had to be some relief on the horizon, or the Aranthians might feel their might buckle under the weight of it all.

Portent was the gift that centered him, but even with that familiar tug telling him that these were the right choices, he began to question if something had gone wrong with the gift. Had the gift grown back corrupted, or was some other gift changing the way it worked? His mind reeled with the possibilities as he began to dread facing another choice that put lives on the line.

Chapter 23
The Iron Valley

The march from FireFalls to the Iron Valley had been long, but with the combined abilities of the large group it hadn't been terribly difficult. Those like Machai and Lers, with the Fire Elementalist gift, had been able to keep everyone warm with hovering fireballs that traveled alongside the company. Several members of the group had worked out the spell that kept a very thin layer of air between the boots of the dwarves and the icy ground, preventing slips and falls as well as keeping their feet dry and warm. Since they weren't trudging through snow or scrambling over loose gravel, the rough, icy terrain was not nearly as exhausting as it would otherwise have been, and they made exceptionally good time. Most of their supplies were carried in wagons pulled by hardy mountain mules, and the hovering spell was cast on the wheels and hooves of each team to allow for easier travel. Many of the party members kept their wands out, maintaining shields around the group to keep the icy wind at bay and trap the warmth from the fireballs. Others used Stone-Sight to watch for weaknesses in the stone of the trail, avoiding rockslides. Those with the gift of Hearing listened for the distinct cracking of ice and shifting of snow that signaled an avalanche, and those with the gift of Sight looked far ahead from each elevated point with good visibility to identify the easiest trails. Some members of the company used gifts less suited to the strategies of an army to keep spirits high on the long trek, singing traditional war chants or bawdy tunes while others accompanied them on wooden flutes, small stringed instruments, and handheld drums.

The party headed northwest through the mountains until mid'day on the second day, when they reached the river. From there, they followed the Diutinus River due north to its headwaters. The source of the river was a network of springs bubbling up to the surface in a cluster of caves. The party reached the caves just as the sun fell behind the peaks on the third day. Machai sent the Stone-Sights ahead into the first cave entrance they came to. They reported back quickly that a recent rockslide had closed off the access to the springs, but they could clearly see a better way in just beyond a curve in the trail. Machai urged the men on, promising a hot soak in the healing waters of the hot springs, and the party moved forward in good cheer. The path hugged the side of the mountain, climbing steeply and often narrowing, allowing only one or two to walk abreast without being too close to the dizzying drop-off that overlooked the river frothing over the rocks far below. It was fully dark before the entire party was able to file into the cave system, and once they were inside, a thick fog made it even more difficult to see. The warm waters collected in dozens of small pools, and contact with the cold mountain air caused dense clouds of steam to gather in the natural stone corridors.

The trail-weary dwarves held their wands aloft, using a simple spell to ignite the tips and cast warm light through the mist of the caves. Water droplets clung to their skin and clothes, and dazzling rainbows danced through the billowing steam as light came in contact with the fog. Much of the party wandered deeper into the caves, seeking the warmest pools of spring water, Machai among them. A trip to the hot springs was a rare treat, and Machai had only made the trek a few times before. He had led their party slightly out of their way, adding perhaps half a day to their journey to the valley, but it would be well worth the extra distance they would have to march to soak in the healing mineral waters. When he was young, he had heard a legend that when the mountains were formed a dragon had been trapped in the ice and stone, and his angry breath had heated the water as he thundered and thrashed in his prison deep underground. Machai had always laughed at the story, thinking the idea of a dragon being caged by mere stone and ice was absurd, but after seeing the dragon elders imprisoned at the Braya Volcano, he found no humor in the tale.

Machai held his lit wand out before him, seeking to penetrate the dense steam and make his way safely on the slick stone floor. At the edges of the caves, thick ice had built up in rippling waves against the cold rock walls and across the high ceilings, and the light from his wand made it appear that he was walking through a tunnel of flowing lava. He thought about the view from the top of his clan's mountain. When the sun was sinking into the horizon, the snow on the trees and mountainside were awash in flame, providing the name of his home: FireFalls. He wasn't sure he would ever get to see it again, and the beautiful spectacle of the cave system was bittersweet.

The Weaving of Wells

Machai reached the end of the chain of caves he had been walking through, dead-ending in a small, high-ceilinged chamber with a circular pool in the center. It was hard to believe that the whole network of caves and pools was formed naturally, but he had never seen or heard any convincing evidence to the contrary. As he began stripping off his cloak, gloves, chainmail, boots, and tunic, Machai was joined in the deep chamber by Kablis, Lers, and Krind, the kiln master from FireFalls. Before wading into the pool, Machai and Lers formed and placed a few small balls of fire around the perimeter of the pool to lend light and diminish the fog. The four men moved slowly into the water, allowing their aching muscles time to adapt to the heat of the mineral-rich water. Krind, being impervious to heat as his natural gift, sank more quickly and sighed comfortably as the water rippled over his shoulders.

"This water be almost hot enough to be warming me frozen fingers and toes," Krind said with a smile.

"It be nearly hot enough to be boiling me blood," Kablis responded, "but it be feeling like paradise after that cold march."

Machai closed his eyes and listened quietly as his companions discussed the journey from FireFalls, the most exciting parts of the gathering, and the organization of the army once they reached the Iron Valley and the troops from seven other clans. Although Kablis and Machai had both fought alongside dwarves from SnowStand and IronAnvil in skirmishes with bandits and battles with earth elementals, in Machai's lifetime, no more than two or three clans had banded together in battle. As far as he knew, this would be the largest army assembled by the dwarves since before the nine clans had separated.

After soaking for a good part of the night, Machai felt rejuvenated and eager to resume the march toward the valley, but he needed to check in with the men and make sure morale was up, even though they had all left their homes behind and wouldn't be able to return. The fiery ice of the caves would have reminded them all of the view from FireFalls too. Machai dressed quickly and scooped up one of the fireballs in his hand, holding it out before him to light the way. Many of the men had already climbed out of the healing waters and dressed, and they were quickly readying camp and taking stock of the company's supplies for the rest of the journey. Others, mostly the oldest and youngest of the dwarves who had followed him, were still luxuriating in the warm waters. Machai spoke with as many as he could, thanking them for their commitment to the war and reassuring them that he would value each of their contributions and skills in the coming battle. For the most part, spirits were high and Machai was confident that no one regretted leaving their home. Still, many eyes were cast upward with longing and sadness at the light dancing across the ice. There would be much grieving in the coming seasons, but Machai hoped that the Aranthians would welcome his men with eager friendship and the barracks would quickly become their new home.

Once supplies were accounted for and warm meals had been cooked and distributed, the dwarves spread quilted pads out on the stone near the warmth of the pools and crawled under heavy skins to sleep for as long as they could before starting out again in the morning. Only a handful of guards were needed to watch the entrances to the cave system and to keep an eye on the mules and wagons. Machai scheduled the watch shifts shorter than normal so that all of the men could get as much sleep as possible. Just as the sky was beginning to lighten, they all awoke refreshed and completely healed of the aches and pains from the long march. The rest of the journey to the valley would be easier, as it was downhill and a shorter distance, and the songs that were sung were jolly tunes about dancing gals and fruitful hunts.

As the party worked its way down the rocky slopes of the mountains and into the wide, sweeping valleys, the snow grew deeper and softer. The spell that kept a thin layer of air between the snow and the boots, the hooves, and the wheels was less effective on such powdery terrain, and every now and then the spell would fail and a dwarf would tumble down into the snow. Machai assigned several men to maintain a stronger spell on the wagons and mules to prevent a broken axle or leg and the loss of time and supplies. Maintaining the spell for so long was fatiguing, so the shift had to be rotated out frequently. The last thing Machai wanted was one of his men to collapse with the fever and fatigue that can come from using an excessive amount of magic in a short amount of time. Like Osric, Machai had somehow developed the Enduro gift that allows a dragon to use magic to fly for extended periods without growing fatigued, but he wasn't nearly as strong as Osric was in the number of gifts or the ability to use them. Machai wished he had the strength to travel his

The Weaving of Wells

entire army safely to Stanton with the spoken spell, but it would likely kill them all if he tried. He would have to find another way to get them there swiftly or just be satisfied with the time it would take to march over land. The journey from the Iron Valley to Stanton could take nearly a month, and Osric didn't have that much time to wait. Once he had gathered all of his troops in the valley, Machai would contact Osric and determine the best course of action for moving the men.

The further from the mountains that the men traveled, the warmer the air grew. The Iron Valley had long been a meeting area for trading and training for the nearby dwarven clans. Machai didn't know who had first discovered the strange warmth of the valley among the icy slopes and cliffs of the surrounding mountain ranges, and each of the clans tended to claim the ancestor who manipulated the terrain which led to its name, but no one knew for sure who it had been. Machai had his doubts that it had been a dwarf at all, since other peoples had been living in the region before the severing of the clans. Still, as the snow melted away to reveal lush green grass and flowering bushes, Machai began to grow anxious and excited about assembling nearly one thousand troops. He eyed the beauty of the landscape, attempting to ease his mind and his stomach and content himself to wait and see what would happen once all of the clans met together in the Iron Valley.

As they moved deeper into the valley, eyeing the vast walls of stone that jutted up on either side with awe, the FireFalls dwarves grew quiet and contemplative. Veins of quartz striped the valley walls with bright white lines, and the flora grew denser and more varied. Soon, the walls swept out and away from each other, allowing the valley to open and flourish like the desert flowers under a full moon. The wide, sweeping fields of lush grass and wildflowers welcomed Machai and his men. As they came into the widest point, where a gurgling brook bubbled up over moss-covered rocks, Machai caught sight of several dragons sunning themselves on large rocks along the west wall of the valley. Over the buzzing of bees and the chirp of small, yellow-spotted frogs, Machai could hear the sound of gruff voices and weapons clanging in combat. The men picked up their pace toward the far end of the valley, and Machai hoped that he would find the other clans only sparring and not truly engaged in a fight.

Osric's Wand

"How many be here, ye be thinking?" Kablis came up beside Machai as they came into sight of the gathered dwarves.

"It be not all, certainly, but it looks to be five hundred at least. It be quite a sight for a banished betrayer." Machai grinned over at Kablis, though his words stung his own ears with a certain ring of truth. Kablis only shook his head and flashed a return grin.

"Be ye ready to be leading 'em all?" Pavyn asked from Machai's left.

"Nay, but we be having no choice. Pavyn, be seeking out the commanders from each clan to be meeting in me tent. Kablis, be having the men set up camp and then they can be joining the others to be training and making acquaintance. We be needing all the dwarves to be fighting as one beast, and clan divisions willn't be helping 'em. See what ye can be doing to be merging them as one clan, will ye?"

"Aye." Kablis headed back into the line of dwarves from FireFalls and Pavyn moved off toward the gathered dwarves further down the valley. Machai eyed the dragons, envying their stillness as they soaked in the warmth of the sun. But he knew their idleness was deceiving and that the massive creatures were watching everything with patient eyes.

Shortly thereafter, Machai was seated on a wooden bench at the head of a large table inside his command tent. He was used to traveling alone or in small groups and sleeping under the stars, so the thick woven fabric was unfamiliar and unwelcome. Machai felt trapped by his role as commander, but he was determined to provide Osric with the troops he needed so badly. Machai forced his gaze away from the pale walls of the tent and back to the intimidating and argumentative group of dwarves who sat with him at the table. After listening to them bicker about whose weapons were the finest and whose shields were the strongest and whose journey to the valley was the most dangerous, Machai finally slammed his fist down on the table and gained their attention.

"We all be fighting together, so this be not a competition. Ye be among the best dwarves of all the clans, and now we be united by purpose. We be not divided by clan name, so ye be stopping yer fighting and be saving it for the field with yer swords. I be needing to know who be here, and where we be with supplies." Machai stared across the table and waited for a response that did not involve boasting by a specific clan.

"I be here with five grids of sixty from IronForge," Festil said. "We be supplied for a lengthy battle or a short siege. We be having little to be sparing of fare for a long march."

"Thank ye, Festil." Machai nodded in appreciation.

"We be two grid of fifty strong, but we only be supplied for one. BlackAxe be hit hard, but we be making the trek with what we could."

"We be expecting the shortage, Jom. Thank ye." Machai nodded and then glanced over at Prex from IronAnvil.

"Fifty hardy and well-trained dwarves that be well supplied." Prex tugged on his beard with narrowed eyes. "Perhaps we be well enough supplied to be easing the shortage a wee bit for BlackAxe."

"That be excellent, Prex," Machai said. "Ye be aiding me greatly if ye be able to assist with gear."

The final member in their meeting was the representative from SnowStand, and Machai did not recall having met him before.

"Me name be Rubin of SnowStand clan, and it be me pleasure to be leading one hundred willing fighters to be aiding ye in yer fight. Old Rhemt be among me men, and he willn't stop telling the story of yer gathering to any dwarf who be listening."

"Rubin," Machai said, "we be pleased to be having ye here with us. Be ye well equipped and ready for battle?"

The SnowStand dwarf was slow to respond, and his white beard nearly hid a hesitant expression. Piercing blue eyes sat deep in creased skin and he was missing several teeth. He shook his head slightly as he began to speak.

"I willn't be lying to ye, Machai. Me clan only be sending the members who be volunteering. Me men be young and eager, but they be not as well trained as I be liking. They'll be throwing all they be having at yer enemies for the glory and power that be trailing behind yer name after the gathering, but they be not weathered warriors. I cannot be saying if they be ready, but I'll be doing all I can to be preparing 'em."

"I be grateful for yer candor, and there be plenty of seasoned fighters to be working with yer younger additions to our army. If they be as eager as ye be saying, then they be as welcome as any battle scarred dwarf among us." Machai nodded and stood up from his seat at the bench. Before he left, he said, "There be seven hundred and fifty including our two hundred from FireFalls. That be more than we be seeking when we first be setting out from Stanton, but the more there be the better. Be there any word from the other clans?"

"SteelBorne be due in the morning, and BillowBluff be not far behind." Pavyn reported from his position behind Machai. "There be a storm in the mountains that be delaying both clans, but last report be saying they be making up time well. There be no word from StoneStar or IceIsle."

"Aye, we be not expecting any from IceIsle unless they be reporting on the dragon attack. I be hoping that Legin be pulling through though. Inform me immediately if ye be hearing anything more."

"Aye." Pavyn nodded, and the other dwarves stood up and moved toward the flap of the tent.

"Let us be seeing our men, and perhaps we can be getting them to be fighting together instead of fighting each other." Machai led the way out toward the open field at the end of the valley, where men from the five clans were sparring and training together.

Machai was pleasantly surprised to see how well the five clans were integrating their fighting techniques and working together on organizing their ranks. Several of the clans had brought experienced combat trainers along, and they were hard at work to find the strengths of each group. They were also systematically identifying weaknesses that could be accounted for and countered by the abilities of others.

By the end of the day, everyone had at least adequate gear and had been assigned to one of twenty-five units. Each unit had at least one leading member with experience in both combat and training.

As the dwarves settled in for the night around campfires, with hearty stews simmering over hot coals and heady liquor being passed around in clay jugs, Machai moved slowly around the edges of camp looking for trouble. He walked with Kablis and Irto, and several others whom he trusted were among the men listening for indicators of the intentions behind each dwarf's presence there. Tagel, who with his innate ability could hear a whisper from across the valley over all of the other noise, had climbed a tall tree at the edge of camp and was listening to the variety of hushed conversations and mumbled curses from the less eager members. Machai needed to identify those who

The Weaving of Wells

had been sent to the valley to spy on him or gain use of his spells rather than to help the Aranthians defeat Dredek and save the Irua Realm. He knew he would need Trusts before sending the men on to Stanton, but if he could identify the dwarves who were only loyal to themselves or their clans, rather than to the realm or the world, he could send them elsewhere to prevent them from compromising his mission.

Only a handful of men had been identified as potential spies, but several more had been picked out of the crowds as suspiciously unsupportive of Machai and his purpose with the Aranthians. Those dwarves were casually reassigned so that Machai could work with them closer in the morning and have them easily at hand when he was able to call in a Trust from Stanton. Machai knew he had likely developed the Trust ability, but if it was fully matured, he didn't know how to use it. He could have one of the Charm-Makers look for it, but he didn't feel like he could rely on it even if he knew it was present, and he would prefer to avoid having any of his men scrutinize him with the ability. He understood how uncomfortable it must have been for Osric to constantly have Gus peering inside of him when the gifts first started developing.

The next morning, Machai and the other leaders were gathered around the fire enjoying a meal of oats and fruit when one of the men on watch approached to report that the members from SteelBorne and BillowBluff had been sighted nearby and they would be in camp soon. Machai finished his breakfast quickly and walked to the end of the valley to greet the newcomers. Furtl led fifty volunteers from SteelBorne, and Orgom led one hundred and fifty dwarves from BillowBluff. Hern was not among them, but Machai was not surprised by his absence. The rest of the morning was spent assessing all of the new arrivals and moving them into appropriate units based on experience, fighting style and weaponry, and commitment to the mission. Out of around nine hundred and fifty dwarves, Machai had weeded out twenty-seven who he knew would not be a good addition to his army. He requested that one of the dragons transport those twenty-seven to IceIsle to provide aid and extra arms after the recent dragon attacks. Then, he contacted Osric to arrange for transportation of over nine hundred new recruits to the Aranthians headquarters.

Osric's Wand

"Osric, be ye available? I be needing yer help to be fattening yer ranks." After a brief moment, the connection was established with Osric's wand and the image of the High-Wizard appeared in the display of light from the tip of Machai's wand in his outstretched hand.

"Machai, it's good to hear from you. Any luck?"

"Aye, more than we be expecting. It be taking too long to be floating us all down by river. Can ye be helping me be getting me men to Stanton?"

"How many were you able to recruit? I was beginning to lose hope that you would come back with any men at all." Osric waved someone away, but Machai couldn't see who was vying for his attention.

"Over nine hundred." Machai grinned at the look of astonishment on Osric's face. "Can ye be sparing some men with the stamina to be making the leap by spell with some of me dwarves? There be seven dragons here to be helping, but they can only be safely flying with a handful of passengers."

Osric was silent for a moment as he considered the amount of men it would take to transport so many dwarves with armor, weapons, and other supplies safely. Only a few members of the Aranthians that had worked closely with him the longest had developed the Enduro ability, and he wasn't sure it was safe to send anyone that far without it. Then, he smiled and nodded at Machai.

"Actually, I think I can do even better than that. Can you give me a good view of the landscape with an open area please?"

Machai turned and moved his hand to the side, providing Osric with an unobstructed view of the valley behind him. He found a good angle where Osric could see the rock formation that the dragons were lounging on and the open field of green grass and wildflowers that surrounded it. A moment later, the wand connection was severed and Machai glanced up to see Osric standing near the closest of the large rocks. The two men greeted each other warmly, Machai reaching up to grasp Osric's wrist.

"It be good to be seeing ye again, me friend. Be ye planning on traveling a thousand dwarves all by yerself?"

"No." Osric laughed. "I need to speak with the dragons briefly, but I believe we can get you all back to Stanton much faster and safer than if we used men. Give me a moment and I'll let you know my plan."

The Weaving of Wells

Machai watched as Osric leapt up onto the rock, which was just above the High-Wizard's head at its lowest point, and moved quickly over to the dragons. It wasn't long before he came scrambling back over the rocks and jumped down to the soft grass, returning to Machai with a triumphant smile.

"I will be taking one of the dragons back to Stanton with me, just to show him exactly where the others can travel to, and then the rest can follow. It might take a couple trips, but we should have you all back to town and setting up camp by mid'day."

"Ye be sounding sure, but it be muddy to me. How do ye be suggesting we be sending so many per trip on a dragon's back?" Machai asked.

"They won't be on dragonback. The men don't need to ride because the dragons don't need to fly. We will have them travel from the ground, so you just need as many dwarves as possible to be in contact with the dragon when it initiates the spell. There is plenty of space in the fields between Stanton and Lothaine, and then it's just a short march to the city. The dragons will need to travel one at a time, with enough time between them to allow the field to be cleared before the next group arrives, but it shouldn't take long at all. Have your men gather their gear."

Machai grinned and shook his head, grateful for Osric's quick thinking and pleased to see his friend again. "Aye, ye be growing wise while I be away. It be a good plan." Machai turned and headed back to the troops to explain the plan and to answer questions from confused and skeptical dwarves, who had not yet seen the impressive feat of traveling by spoken spell. The incentive to learn the spell for themselves should be motivation enough to override any fears that would prevent the men from keeping a hand on the dragon. Still, after the first group disappeared, Machai had to reestablish communication with Osric so that the next group could see that everyone arrived safely in the open field. Soon, nearly one thousand dwarves were marching across dry grassland toward the trading city of Stanton, half a continent away from their dwarven homes.

Chapter 24
Reinforcements

Osric sat with his back to the window in the dining hall of the barracks. The morning sun warmed him, but the pressure of the current situation dulled his senses, keeping him from enjoying the sensation. The sun's warmth may have escaped his notice, but the clanks of silver on plates and the quick, dry scraping of quill on paper filled the room.

The room was full of Aranthians discussing Legati, the paun, and a myriad of other topics surrounding accessing the wells and defeating Dredek. It was a typical morning for the crew, with the exception of the several hundred men and women who were kept from their morning meal, assigned to other tasks around Archana.

For the Aranthians, it was becoming an unspoken honor to be selected for the relief efforts. It made them feel like they were contributing to something, rather than spending all of their time training. They volunteered to go on any new assignment that presented itself, and it seemed that Osric alone felt the pressure of the dwindling numbers. Indeed, it was the numbers that caused him to sit alone in the room surrounded by scholars and magical experts on subjects that were of no use on current deployments.

Even though they hadn't been sent to operations outside of the headquarters, they still carried on with their duties. New magical discoveries continued to occur on a regular basis. In addition to the new discoveries, Osric had given himself time every night to practice with several new gifts he could purposefully channel. But, much of that time had been spent alone and in solitude—even Bridgett, with her Empath ability and her keen questioning, couldn't fully grasp the complexity of his emotions due to what he had been going through. Still, Gus had felt the need to keep company with him every morning, droning on about news and events of importance, and this was yet another one of those mornings.

"He inflated the strands!" He stared at Osric for several dull moments before waving his hand in the air and then probing an exposed shoulder with his wand. "Pay attention, Osric! That was an important revelation in wandcraft!"

Osric shook himself, returning to the subject at hand. He hadn't intended to ignore Gus, but since the old Wand-Maker's playful moment with Pebble outside the barracks, Gus's words didn't seem to carry the same disturbing quality of their former days.

"What was it you said?" Osric wasn't as embarrassed as he would have been a short time ago, but he had missed the beginning of the conversation.

"I said he snipped strands off of the stuff he got from Archana and joined them in a circle. Then, in a stunning display of ingenuity, he inflated them by means I have yet to glean, creating loops of independently adjusting resistance to flow. Add that to what we know of the magics contained by what the wand took from Bridget's amulet and you have a wand that can channel as much magic as your sword, plus a sword wand that bestows the power it takes from those around you on you whilst simultaneously giving those powers to everyone around you. The fact that Pebble mimicked the wand so completely is just astounding. Albeit, without the addition of the magical gifts, but still an amazing feat of ingenuity!"

The kitchen erupted into motion and the two of them looked up as David, James's most trusted kitchen attendant, waved his hands frantically and issued orders as a man leaned in and spoke in his ear. Osric laughed quietly as he watched the chaotic scene, noting how well the noise-containment spell worked on the kitchen to prevent shouting from reaching the diners. The busy scene was, no doubt, in preparation of dinner service. Throughout the kitchen, the cooks began firing burners and placing pans on the flames. It was a frantic display of efficiency, and Osric enjoyed the show, as he hadn't been in the dining hall at this time of day in a long time. He spent a brief moment appreciating how well James ran his kitchen, and then he turned back to his conversation with Gus.

"It's a potent combination," Osric echoed, knowing that the truth behind all that he had experienced in the last year was due to his sword having been crafted into a wand by the unicorn at the Ratification Ceremony. He still wondered why they had chosen him, and why that moment to do it. At least the unicorns' reticence to allow him anywhere near them made sense, considering the accident that killed Willam. He had needed the time to let the gifts mature naturally, rather than have the gifts instantaneously mature and kill him, and too many too fast may have yielded the same result. "Do you know why he didn't make them with the same magic that is in the sword's rings?"

"Not entirely, but I'll have to speak to the amulet and charm makers and see if they can offer some insight into that." Gus was surprisingly open to the thought of consulting with the rival users of his innate ability.

"I never thought I would see a day where you were comfortable with the idea of a sword wand. You tend to be less than enthusiastic about anything other than a stick wand." In spite of Osric's worried mind, this small harassment of Gus brought a smile to his face.

"Well, yes. If I had chosen the medium it would have been a stick, but I've come to realize that I have been far too closed-minded about a lot of things. It's a bad habit and far too much a part of the Wand-Maker trade." He shrugged off the question easily and smiled back at Osric.

"I have to admit, it is strange to talk to you so openly. Without your bad attitude, I feel like I am talking to a stranger, rather than someone I've gotten to know over the last year."

"And I feel like I am a new man." Gus laughed lightly before concern furrowed his brow. "But you used to be a carefree man with an open, though sometimes overeager, mind. Though it caused me much frustration at that time, it was many of those traits that brought about the most significant evolution in magic since the wand was invented. Now, even our culture seems to be evolving into something better as a result. Eublin has a great deal of support for changes in the way the hunt is performed. None of that would have happened if it weren't for you."

"And your point is?" Osric felt a bit uncomfortable being reminded of how foolish he had been at the beginning of their adventure, but Gus seemed genuine in his query.

"What happened to that man?" he replied.

"People started dying as a result of my actions and discoveries." Osric stared down at his hands, guilt squeezing his throat around the words.

The Weaving of Wells

"But death happens all around us, everyday. Many more would be dead if you hadn't been the man you were then. It's not all bad either. Look at all the advances we're making in the healing arts. The strand-sight device could lead minds better suited to healing to finding different ways to cure many of Archana's deadlier diseases. The uses could be enumerable." Gus's tone was both rational and reasonable. There was no hint of flattery or blame in his voice.

"It's different when the deaths are directly related to what I have exposed them to. Now, I have most of our men committed to actions outside of our main objective with no idea how I am going to get enough men to replace them. And even if I could replace them, Dredek is going to complete his task long before I could get the men trained in the new magics, let alone dual wielding." Osric spoke in an emotionless monotone.

"Then why don't we focus on the things we can control?" The look on Gus's face suggested he had an idea.

"What can we control?" Osric leaned forward, his interest piqued.

"Well, let's look at the first prophecy we received on the dragon platform. What was the first line of that prophecy?" Gus arched an eyebrow.

"Victory cannot be achieved until the wand that is not a wand is known by all on their path? What can we do about that? We already know the wand."

"But do we? I don't think the prophecy is telling us that we need to know what the wand is; I think it's telling us we need to have all of us use it, touch it, hold it and have those powers shared by all Aranthians. We need to *know* it. If the Aranthians are going to be what we want them to be, then we can't let only a few of us hold your level of power." Gus turned his paws over in a pleading gesture.

"No. Absolutely not." Osric was quick to his reply.

"Why not? I've seen you change the outcome of a prophecy, but you've never ignored it altogether." The prairie dog's reasonable tone continued.

"This sword killed a man because he accidentally cut his friend's hand. You want me to put it in the hands of more, only to lose them in foolish accidents?"

Osric's Wand

"Yes. Only now it will be different because we will all know the risks involved." Gus attempted to calm Osric's reaction, miming surrender by raising his paws.

"And who should we give it to first? Maybe Pebble, or Macgowan? Surely we could live without them if an accident occurred. Perhaps we should give it to Eublin so you have one less person to argue with? I'm certainly not giving it to Bridgett or Kenneth. Or here, I have an idea." Osric took Legati out of the scabbard and laid it on the table. "Here, you can have it. That will be one less frustration to deal with on a daily basis, should something happen to you."

Osric's hostility was countered by a sympathetic tilt of the head from Gus. "Now, I have been a terrific pain in your backside for over a year, so I'll ignore that last part. But you did say something that bears a bit more consideration."

The lack of confrontation gave Osric pause. It wasn't like Gus to back away from a fight, and the fact that he had skillfully sidestepped several opportunities was eye-opening. Osric sat back for a moment and let the words settle in his mind. He wasn't ready to yield, just yet, but maybe he could at least listen to the ideas rather than immediately resist them out of habit.

"We both know that Kenneth is farther along in inheriting gifts than anyone else, so I propose you let him have it for a few days. I am positive he would be safe since most of your gifts are already growing naturally inside him. Then I think he should train with us every morning, and the sword should remain within our grounds at all times. If and when we need it to be used in battle, you carry it as always."

"Why would we leave it here?"

"Well, not only would it be easier to control the danger you are rightfully concerned about, but there is another benefit to leaving it in the hands of someone here." He motioned for Osric to look at the wand with the Wand-Maker gift before he continued.

"These strands right here. They dance to and fro, stealing small amounts of the magic in our gifts and grafting them onto the wand. But here you can see the yellow wisps that keep reaching out from the third ring of the wand and then swatting back at the pommel? These are the ones responsible for giving gifts to those around you. Keeping the sword within our boundaries would help us to expose even more minds to the possibilities you could potentially unlock. You were a

The Weaving of Wells

Vigile, and look at the evolution in magic you inspired. Just think what could be done by a healer, a chemist, an armorer, a gardener, or even a chef!" Gus was getting excited as he spoke, and some of that excitement had managed to seep into Osric.

"Every background has unique experiences that change the way they think about things. I could see the benefit of that plan. Keeping it exposed to Aranthians would help us to control the risk, and eventually they would be far enough along to not risk death with a simple accidental cut." There was a great deal of danger in the beginning of the plan, but Osric knew the risk would diminish with time. It was a good plan, and the fact that some progress had been made in dealing with the many situations that had come about because of him gave Osric a modicum of relief.

"It just occurred to me that Jane may need an examination by a Wand-Maker too. She spent a great deal of time with that blade, making it into the piece of art it has become. I would guess that anyone who worked with her in her blacksmith shop could have inherited a great deal more than they know. We may have a second set of Aranthians who could safely use Legati. We wouldn't have to limit exposure to Kenneth, if I am right," Gus said, smiling.

"Kenneth does have other duties. I can see how having more hands to hold Legati could be useful." Osric nodded in agreement. "But my abilities have changed as new gifts have developed. It will do little good to have dozens of people with dozens of gifts if no one can use any of them."

"That's true, but it shouldn't be difficult to shift some training time toward learning to use the new abilities. Most of the gifts granted by the sword should be represented somewhere in the Aranthian population, so we just need people to spend a little time teaching the use of their own innate abilities. Eventually, we could train everyone in all of the gifts." Gus's ear was twitching as he grew more excited about the idea.

Osric grinned, the possibilities finally lifting some of his pessimism. "All right, Gus, you make a good case. Now, if we could come up with a plan for helping Eublin, creating more troops for our battle with Dredek, or dealing with the dragon situation, I would consider this one of the best meetings I have had in a long time."

Osric's Wand

Gus patted the blade. "I'm still not sold on changing the hunt, and the dragon issue is a priority." He motioned for Osric to put Legati away. "But I think it will have to wait until we finish with this Dredek business. And as for recruiting the troops we need for our upcoming assault—"

"For that, ye be needing me and me kin."

As they looked up from the sword to see who had interrupted Gus, a grin greeted the two.

"Machai!" Osric rejoiced as the thought of over nine hundred dwarves filled his mind. They would be familiar with both dual wielding and close-quarter combat in tunnels below ground. He couldn't imagine a greater moment for his old friend to arrive, but there was so much to catch him up on. He stepped around the table to greet him properly. "I can't begin to tell you how happy we are to see you."

"I have to admit, even I am thrilled to see your grisly-bearded face." Gus laughed.

"I be glad to be seeing that smirk on yer face hasn't fled." Machai ruffled the hair on Gus's head and then held his hand out to Osric. "And I be seeing ye be busy during me absence. Ye still be looking as strong as ever, but there be far fewer men than when I be leaving. What trouble be ye placing me students in?" He smiled and grasped Osric's wrist in greeting.

"Actually, the boy has been rather wise in his allotment of men, given the current issues he's been dealing with. Even you would be proud of the way he has been handling things." Gus nodded respectfully.

"Aye, I be always proud of the High-Wizard's command of me Aranthian brothers. Be ye having many new problems arising?" Machai spoke the word *Aranthians* with pride, letting it linger on his tongue a bit longer than the word would normally elicit in conversation. "Who be earning our scorn this day? Me kin be longing to be part of the Aranthian fight."

"Our men are out on duties that extend beyond battle," Osric replied.

"Aye, then it be relief efforts that be taxing yer mind? We be seeing dragon attacks even on the shores of me realm." Machai's guess was correct.

The Weaving of Wells

"Yes. I've just committed nearly all of our healers and tradesmen to helping the elves. Though some are still trickling in due to cultural requirements," Osric answered with a quick nod of his head.

"Aye, demand for aid in dragon attacks be causing a bit of frustration for me as well." Machai grinned. "Do ye be having plans for me brothers in arms already? Or be we having time to train in spells?"

"Well, I'm afraid that the assignment of Aranthian troops doesn't end there." Osric's expression was apologetic. "We have also sent all but a few remaining healers and tradesmen to Rowain to help them deal with a dragon attack that nearly destroyed all lineage that could take back the Turgent throne. We are taxed beyond our breaking point. If it weren't for your nine hundred, I fear we would have no chance at defeating Dredek. Even now I fear it may not be enough."

"Perhaps ye be underestimating me determination to be easing yer burden. Me troops be gathered on the ground. Will ye be kind enough to be greeting 'em?"

"I don't see why not. We're finished here for now, right Gus?"

"I think so, and I've had my fill of James's fine soup. Let's see if more of his kin have the same scraggly beard, why don't we?" Gus almost swaggered when he jumped down from the table and headed for the door, looking back at Machai with a mischievous grin.

"Ye be testing me patience, ye cuddly rat." Machai grinned as he traded insults with Gus.

"Ah, patience shouldn't be a problem for you, dwarf. You move so slow on those stumpy legs of yours, surely you have developed great patience over the years," Gus replied, picking up the pace as he scampered on four legs.

Gus continued to lead the way, scurrying up the stairs. He chose a path that led to the balcony overlooking the training grounds in front of the barracks. Osric knew it would be an excellent location to view the recent arrivals and discuss the ways to use the troops wisely, without the interruption of Machai's men wishing to meet him and discuss whatever rumors had been circulating in the Dwarven Realm. He had had enough of that sort of talk in Stanton alone, and Osric knew how the dwarves were famous for telling stories. Human legends paled in comparison to the drunken stories told by dwarves.

Osric's Wand

Osric gazed out over the balcony railing, taking in the sight of the mass of dwarves gathered in the yard. He had expected a large group, but the crowd filled the entire training grounds, the field surrounding them, and the path that led to town. More were appearing every moment as the Aranthians who had been sent to retrieve the dwarves traveled into the protective spell that secreted the headquarters from the outside world. Over a dozen wagons were lined up along the west boundary of the property, loaded to the brim with weapons, armor, supplies, and large casks of what Osric assumed was mead. The scene overwhelmed Osric.

"Machai," Osric said, "I don't know how to thank you for coming through for us with so many men. Honestly, I wasn't sure you would be able to recruit the five hundred you went for. I know there was tension between you and Thenar the last time you were home. How did you pull it off?" Osric gazed out at the ranks of well-armed dwarves with renewed hope for their cause.

"Aye, tension be an understatement, but I be telling ye ye could be counting on me." Machai grinned widely, but Osric could tell that the expression masked much darker emotions. The smile faded quickly from the dwarf's face. "It be a difficult task to be accomplishing. Me kin, from FireFalls, willn't be returning home after yer battle. Thenar be banishing us from the clan walls. Ye be gaining nearly two hundred new recruits for the Aranthians."

Osric's eyes went wide at the news, and he looked between Machai's sorrowful expression and Gus's astonishment. "I'm so sorry, Machai. I never intended for you to lose your home."

"Aye, but I cannot be following a clan leader that be turning his back on the needs of Archana in bitter greed or wretched pride. This be me home now, and ye be the man I be choosing to follow." Machai's gaze was on his kin gathered below them, but when Osric gripped his shoulder in appreciation of his loyal words, he nodded.

"There has to be at least seven hundred ugly buggers down there." Gus attempted to break the solemn mood, though both men largely ignored his attempt at humor.

"Nearly nine hundred, once they all be arriving, from seven different clans. We'll be telling ye the story of the gathering once we be settled in." Machai looked out over the gathered dwarves with bittersweet hope. Many of them may not make it out alive from the

The Weaving of Wells

battle with Dredek. His own clansmen would not be going back to the Dwarven Realm at all.

"I don't have the words to tell you how grateful I am for this." Osric looked down at Machai with a weak smile.

"Let's just be hoping we be having time to be preparing them before we be moving out. They be able fighters, down to the youngest and weakest of the bunch, but they be not a fighting unit. A bit of motivation from the High-Wizard may be a good start to uniting 'em and readying 'em to be fighting for ye." Machai looked up at Osric expectantly.

Osric looked out at the men gathered and realized how difficult it must be traveling that far from home in the blink of an eye. Many of them would never lay eyes on their loved ones again. That alone lent an air of finality to their fate. But he would ask them, in due time, to accomplish an impossible task that could not be accomplished by any other means. Machai was right, they deserved to be welcomed into the place that they had given up everything to be a part of. He looked out over the crowd and couldn't help but wonder if their sacrifice would bear fruit.

"Welcome, Aranthians!" Osric began, but his voice broke under the weight of what they had to forfeit to be where they stood.

Osric dropped his head as he attempted to regain some strength and composure. It took him longer than he had hoped because of the emotions that escaped the crowd of dwarves as they gathered closer to the balcony. He nearly shut off the Empath gift to escape the flood of uncertainty from their minds, but slowly other emotions began to overwhelm the initial doubt. Hope, pride, and an unyielding desire for justice assuaged his despair. Not only did they want to help deal justice, but in many of them there was also a desire to accomplish their task in the quickest, safest manner and then return home victorious. And Osric could sense a keen intellect in most of the minds standing below him.

"I realize how much you have sacrificed to be here today, and how much you have pledged to sacrifice in the coming war. It would be arrogant and inconsiderate of me to attempt to equate your commitment with my meager words, but I cannot do more than tell you how grateful and humbled I am that so many of you have arrived to fill out the ranks of this army. You have been Trusted and welcomed into this arena of hope for the future, and I wish for you to know that you are welcome in every sense. While you are here, this is your home and your family, and we will accept you here as equals and as an integral part of the system we have designed. What is ours is yours. For those of you who choose to stay, these terms will remain for as long as you call yourselves Aranthians and reside within our boundaries. For those who choose to leave, after the war is over, know that you will always be welcome here if you wish to return. I cannot begin to express my gratitude, and I vow to commit myself to your safety and well-being, just as you have committed yourself to the well-being and security of Archana. If you will follow me to the ends of this world to secure the future of Archana, I will do my best to lead you well. For now, however, I imagine you are hungry. If I am correct, our kitchens are well prepared for your arrival. Would you all do me the honor of joining me for a meal?"

Loud cheers rose from the crowd, and as the crowd began to move toward the large doors of the barracks, Osric caught the trailing words of one dwarf: "He be good at talking, but we'll be seeing if he be good at drinking."

And the retort: "Aye, I willn't be following a man who cannot be holding his drink." Osric smiled and prepared himself for a raucous evening welcoming his new troops.

Chapter 25
Broadening Options

The night had been filled with a great deal of extraordinary food. The dwarves were so impressed with the kitchen's ability to turn out fast, delicious food that they offered the kitchens the entirety of the stores they had brought with them. David had been so overwhelmed by the effort of cooking for the lot and attempting to find a place to store the vast quantities of supplies that he called James out from the duplicate dining hall outside the barracks to aid in the effort. It took nearly the entire staff of both facilities combined to undertake the task of properly storing the resources, and they were forced to use the supply rooms in both kitchens to accomplish the feat.

They ate and drank well into the night. Osric listened to all of the stories about the gathering a dozen times, and each time it took on different attributes that became more flamboyant as the night progressed. Machai humbly objected each time the teller recited his version of the final speech that swayed the last remaining opponents. Yet, even he bowed his head in sorrow when they arrived at the part of the story when hundreds of dwarves were forced to choose between honoring the outcome of the contest and being able to ever return home.

In spite of the solemn outcome that had brought them to join Osric's troops, shortly after the storytelling had ended, the mood quickly returned to joyous celebration and drinking. The dwarves truly understood what it was to commemorate a moment in time with a gathering of their own. As they indulged, they filled the dining hall, all of the halls throughout the barracks, and even large parts of the training grounds. They stood on tables and sang lighthearted chants about beautiful women, legendary weaponsmiths, epic battles, and drunken revelry.

They were a rowdy bunch of miscreants half bent on gluttony, but in spite of their jubilation, when all of the drinking had ended for the night not a single glass was broken, not a chair or table sat askew. They were a respectful crew, and though many rested in tents until suitable arrangements could be made, the only complaint about their behavior came from a new cook who insisted the food needed no alteration when one dwarf seasoned his own food liberally from a personal stash of spices. It was as great of a first meeting as Osric could have hoped. He even received several comments about how well he could drink. By the time he tumbled into bed, he was beginning to doubt the wisdom of drinking with dwarves, but he felt they had all built a rapport and trust that would unify the troops as they began training together for the coming battle.

It was far later than he had planned to wake up the next morning when Osric forced himself out of bed, his head pounding and a horrible taste in his mouth. However, after a warm bath and an herbal concoction that Bridgett laughingly called "too-much tonic," he was more or less functional and ready to go. Despite the residual throbbing in his head and a slightly upset stomach, Osric was still in a surprisingly jolly mood from the night of jubilation, and he trudged on to meet Pendres in the hopes of finding a way to utilize the wells. When Osric arrived at his office, the old recluse was waiting patiently, engrossed in a large book he had borrowed from Eublin.

"Anything of interest?" Osric asked, squinting at the bright light pouring in through the window.

"Immensely interesting, but likely not very helpful for our current plight. How are you feeling?" Pendres eyed Osric with an amused smirk. He had indulged little the night before, having instead sat back and watched the revelry.

"I've felt better after battling an ancient caldereth wizard, but I'll recover." Osric rolled his neck in protest to the pain and stiffness.

"Perhaps a month of lying unconscious led you to believe that wasn't so bad, but I know just the thing to purge the sickness from your mead-soaked muscles. Why don't we conduct this meeting in the training arena. I can give you some pointers on your bladework, and the exercise will clear your mind. Maybe then we can figure out how to counteract Dredek's intentions with the well."

"Have you even picked up a sword in the last hundred years, old man?" Osric couldn't resist the verbal jab, but he grimaced at the idea of sparring. Osric had been the best swordsman in Stanton since before he accepted the promotion to Contege.

"I'm sure I can find a blade lying around here somewhere. How hard could it be?" Pendres only grinned at Osric's unspoken challenge. He left the book resting on Osric's desk and led the way out of the barracks.

Osric felt the anticipation of having a sword in his hands rising in spite of the residual headache, and his step quickened as they walked outside and crossed the grounds to the armory near the practice arena. As they stepped inside, they were greeted by the welcoming scent of oil, leather, and steel. Both men selected well-balanced short swords and small wooden shields. They belted the sheaths quickly and quietly, both thinking about their strategies for sparring with an unfamiliar opponent, and their feet stirred up small clouds of dust as they walked side by side into the enclosed circular arena. Dozens of dwarves and the familiar faces of many Aranthians gathered to watch, but none looked all too ready to join in with the swordplay.

Osric and Pendres traded a few strokes, warming up and getting a feel for the other's technique. It took only moments before Osric was engrossed in the activity, focusing completely on his sword and his opponent and forgetting all about his headache. Pendres was far better with a blade than he had anticipated, and soon Osric found himself on the defensive. He countered the attacks with practiced precision, reading Pendres's intentions through the patterns of movement and the angle of his head, and with the Portentist ability, among other tactics.

Allowing the Hunter's ability to guide his sword with perfect accuracy, Osric anticipated each blow with the Portentist Gift and monitored the emotions of his opponent with the Empath ability. He waited for just the right moment when Pendres was feeling confident and preparing for an aggressive attack. As Pendres paused for the briefest amount of time, drawing back his sword, Osric dropped his shield and drew his wand, rapidly buffeting Pendres with several concussions of air. Dust flew up into the elder man's eyes, startling and disorienting him. Osric followed the air attack with a spell that snared Pendres's feet, rooting him in place and knocking him off balance, and then Osric lunged at him with his sword. Pendres fell backward slowly, his arms windmilling and his mouth open in surprise. Just before Pendres would have hit the ground, Osric halted his attack and used his wand to direct a cushion of air under his opponent's body. The air caught Pendres mid-fall, and he lay splayed out, a hand's breadth from the dirt, as Osric released the rooting spell.

Osric's Wand

Osric returned his wand to the pouch at his belt and offered the man his hand to help him to his feet.

Pendres took the proffered hand, hauling himself into a standing position and eyeing Osric with respect. He brushed the dirt from his clothing and spit the dust from his mouth, nodding and smiling.

"Good. After I heard about your last defeat, I was afraid you didn't know how to fight. It isn't your skills with a sword that are lacking," Pendres said, walking toward the crowd of onlookers at the edge of the arena.

"It wasn't my swordsmanship that lost me that fight." Osric gritted his teeth, thinking back to the battle with Dredek atop the sand dunes in Angmar.

"So, what was it?" Pendres asked. Osric was silent for a moment, remembering the battle in flashes of anger and desperation.

"Inferior control over my magical abilities." Osric stared at Pendres, wishing he could claim that he had learned enough since his defeat to be sure of victory in the future. He had worked hard to develop the coordination between his gifts that had allowed him to best Pendres, but he still doubted it would be enough to beat the experience and power that Dredek wielded so easily.

"Maybe," Pendres said. "Or perhaps it was a lack of foresight in how to engage your enemy." Pendres moved so swiftly that his limbs were nearly a blur. He spun around, grabbing a young irua off of the fence that surrounded the arena and pinning the startled recruit's upper body with one massive arm, holding his sword across the trembling youth's throat. Pendres stared across the ring at Osric, locking eyes with the startled leader as dozens of wands and weapons were being aimed at his back. Pendres ignored everyone but Osric, watching the High-Wizard carefully. "What do you do?"

Osric raised one hand, preventing any interference from his men gathered around the arena. Osric could feel great importance in the moment with his Portentist gift, but he sensed no conflict with his Trust ability or any other gift that would indicate that Pendres was actually a threat. It was disorienting to see one of his men being held hostage by what appeared to be an armed enemy and yet have his gifts all tell him that Pendres was a trustworthy member of their group. Luckily, no one made a move against Osric's silent orders to stay their hands, but all eyes were locked on Pendres in anxious anticipation.

The Weaving of Wells

"What do you do," Pendres repeated, "when the enemy has the power to destroy your men, your friends, your loved ones? What do you do when he wields power over you that you cannot counter with your wand or your sword?" Pendres never took his eyes off of Osric.

Osric swallowed hard, trying to keep the reassurance of his gifts in mind to calm the anxiety raised by what his eyes were seeing. He knew that Pendres would not actually hurt the Aranthian, and thus there must be a reason that he was risking the retaliation of all of the gathered men and women around them. Osric thought about the question Pendres had asked. If he couldn't fight with his sword or his wand, what else did he have at his disposal? He could use any number of his gifts to attack Pendres, possibly saving the Aranthian's life but more likely causing his death. Every idea that came to mind resulted in the same risk: if he wasn't faster than the enemy, his men would die. Osric realized that he could not fight the situation, he couldn't fight Pendres and guarantee the safety of his man, so there had to be something else he could do to take control back from the enemy. A calm surety washed over him as he committed to his course of action.

Osric slowly slid his sword into its sheath and raised his hands, sensing Pendres's emotions with the Empath ability. The man holding the irua hostage smiled subtly, emitting confidence that Osric was heading in the right direction as well as a glimmer of fear that the demonstration would fail. Osric straightened, holding his hands out to his sides, and engaged his invisibility gift. Osric smiled as Pendres's eyes went wide and he looked around the arena. Osric moved slowly and silently, approaching Pendres at an angle. He drew his wand, careful not to draw attention to his location. He waited until Pendres was feeling unsettled and his attention was monopolized by looking for Osric.

Osric worked quickly but quietly, drawing magic from Archana and isolating single strands. Osric very carefully anchored the strands to Pendres in strategic locations—the hand that held the sword, the sword blade, Pendres's head, shoulders, legs, feet, and torso. He walked silently around the two men, making sure he could see their bodies from every angle and verifying that he had not made a mistake. When he was sure that he had isolated Pendres with the strands of magic, and that no strand was touching the irua at any point along its length, Osric returned to his previous position. He took a steadying breath and disengaged the invisibility spell. Pendres's eyes locked on Osric immediately, and Osric sensed a worried questioning from the old hermit. Osric raised his wand and aimed it at Pendres. He focused his mind and all of his power on using the wand to maintain contact with each of the strands he had attached to the old hermit. He could feel the frustration that Pendres was experiencing as the man realized he could not move any part of his body. Osric used the same ability that had allowed him to catch Pendres before he hit the ground to cast a dense layer of air between the blade of Pendres's sword and the Aranthian's neck. If his plan didn't work, he needed to be sure that the blade wouldn't accidentally behead one of his men.

Osric crafted the cushion of air at an angle, so the man's head would bend backward and slide under the blade as his body moved, just in case. Osric focused his mind on isolating the two bodies, and when he was confident that he could focus on the irua while maintaining the strength of the strands on Pendres, Osric used a spell to summon the Aranthian to him. At the same time, Osric channeled the summoning spell through the strands so that Pendres was summoned separately and perfectly immobilized by the anchoring strands. As the spell was initiated, Osric focused on separating the mass of the two bodies, and the magic of the spell allowed the bodies to arrive at two different locations—the Aranthian on Osric's left and Pendres on Osric's right. As the spell was completed, and the two men stood on either side of him, Osric released the breath he had been holding. A roar of cheering burst forth from the crowd, and Pendres's eyes narrowed as he realized he still could not move. Osric waved his hand, using his ability as a Wand-Maker to manipulate the strands and allow them to fall back and be absorbed into Archana, freeing Pendres. The irua Aranthian ran off toward the gathered onlookers, eliciting further cheering, and Osric turned toward Pendres.

"How did you know that would work?"

"I knew if I tried to fight you, you could most likely kill him before I could defeat you," Osric said. "You held that power, after all. My only option was to find a way to take that power from you." Osric held his gaze steady, but his hands were trembling. "If it hadn't worked, then it would have been me who killed him. I was sure it would work because I can only use the power I can control to fight

The Weaving of Wells

you. My mind, my body, everything within me will fight with every ability I have to fight myself. It was instinct not to kill my own man."

"So, you had no idea it would work?" Pendres's tone was soft and compassionate.

"No, not really. I took precautions in case it failed, but I also had to accept that I cannot control every aspect of a situation and that sometimes my abilities are more aware of how they work than I am. I had to trust the magic." Osric headed toward the armory. "But it did give me an idea of how to counter the Well of Strands using the smaller wells."

Pendres hurried after Osric, nearly breaking into a run to keep up with him.

"What sort of idea? What are you thinking?" Pendres asked as they entered the barracks. Osric rushed down the halls, around corners, down stairs, and through doorways, and Pendres soon felt lost and disoriented. "Where are you going?"

"I need to find Gus and Eublin. We also need to find Gareth."

"Who is Gareth? I don't recall meeting him," Pendres said.

"He's the most experienced Stone-Sight we have in residence, and he has spent most of his life mapping out Archana. I need his maps."

"There are dozens of books in Eublin's collections with maps of Archana. What is so special about the ones Gareth makes?" Pendres followed Osric down another flight of stairs. He thought they must be several stories below the ground by now, and he hadn't even realized there were floors beneath ground level. Osric paused as he tried to remember exactly where the Stone-Sights had been working most recently on the excavation and construction of the lower levels. He turned to Pendres, breathing heavily.

"Gareth is a Stone-Sight, Pendres. He hasn't been mapping the surface of Archana; he has been mapping everything beneath the surface. He has collected years of specific documentation of the layers of earth, stone, caves, waterways, and lava flows beneath the ground. I need those maps, because I think I can use them to map the volume of the flow of magic that feeds the wells." Osric almost turned left, then he stopped and turned right instead. He passed two more branches in the corridors and finally turned left into a large natural cavern. The floor was bare stone, the walls were bare rock that climbed several stories into the air, and Pendres could see small points of light where

Osric's Wand

the ceiling was not completely closed. He wondered where they were in relation to the barracks, if there was access to the cavern from outside. He hadn't remembered seeing any holes in the ground, so he assumed they must be a good distance from the main path and various walkways on the grounds.

On the far side of the cavern, three people were standing together facing the wall and speaking in hushed tones. A petite woman in dusty brown robes was pointing at something high up on the wall, but Osric was sure it was nothing they could see with their eyes. The shorter of the two men was nodding as he listened to her speak, and he turned quickly at the sound of Osric and Pendres approaching. He smiled and interrupted the discussion about the wall, and he politely introduced his companions to Osric.

"High-Wizard, welcome. This is Dorim and Elana. They are both incredibly talented in the use of our gift, and they have become invaluable to my work. Dorim can see further through the stone than any Sight I have met, and Elana catches minute discrepancies in the stone that even I miss. We have made excellent progress on the excavation of the new levels recently. Are you here to inspect our work?"

Osric introduced Pendres as well and greeted the two Stone-Sights warmly.

"Actually Gareth, I was hoping I could speak to you. I have a great need to utilize your maps. Would you mind if I borrowed them for a while?"

"I don't normally like to lend them out, seeing as the project is not completed, but of course I will make an exception for you. Is there anything I can assist you with?" Gareth asked.

"Yes, I believe there is. Can we speak for a moment alone?" Osric smiled at Dorim and Elana. "Would you excuse us for a moment? I don't want to interrupt your work here, and I won't keep him long." Dorim and Elana nodded silently, slightly awed by Osric's presence and the mystery of his visit. Gareth followed Osric and Pendres back across the cavern and then led the way to a small, empty room just down the hall. A door had not yet been put in place for the chamber, but no one was around and Osric nodded that the space would do. The three men entered the room. Gareth stood more than a head shorter than Osric, and he was more than twice as old. His black hair was

The Weaving of Wells

salted with grey, clipped close to his head, and his greying beard was trimmed short and even. His dark skin crinkled around sharp, dark brown eyes when he smiled.

"Gareth, I am hoping I can use your maps to determine the flow of strands within Archana. In order to do this, I need to figure out if there is a correlation between the density of strands and the material it flows through. I will need you to work with me, help me, but first I need something else." Osric paused, his brow wrinkled with hesitancy. "I need some of your blood."

Gareth and Pendres both stared at Osric, mouths slightly open and eyes narrowed.

"My… My blood?" Gareth stammered.

"I know it is a strange request, and I can't really explain everything to you as to why, but I would ask that you trust me. It's complicated, but I assure you it is of dire importance. I wouldn't ask if I didn't think it would make a difference in the outcome of this war." When Gareth nodded his consent without reservation, Osric was relieved. "Thank you. I am glad that you have Elana and Dorim here working with you. They are going to need to take over the project for a day or two. I will need you with me as a teacher and a guide while I learn how to identify the flow of strands. After mid'day, meet me at the front entrance to the barracks after your meal. I will explain what I need then."

"Of course. Um…" Gareth paused for a moment. "How do I, um…"

"The blood, of course, sorry." Osric glanced around. "Pendres, may I have your water skin please?" Osric took the pouch of water from him and unscrewed the cap. He held his right palm upward before him and slowly poured a thin stream of water from the skin. As it pooled in his palm, Osric used the Water Elementalist ability to form the water into a small ball, continuously swirling in on itself to maintain its shape. He drew his knife from its sheath on his belt and handed it to Gareth. "Just a few drops will do."

Eyeing the blade in his hand with distaste, Gareth drew it across his forearm and made a short, shallow cut. He allowed a small amount of blood to well from the wound and then scraped the blade across his arm to collect it. He handed the knife back, and Osric slowly passed the blade through the swirling globe of water. The blade came out

Osric's Wand

clean and the water turned a light shade of pink. Osric sheathed the knife and drew his wand. He cast a small shield around the water globe, keeping it intact and in place, hovering at chest height in the air before him.

"Let me see your arm." Osric held Gareth's wrist in his hand, activated his Wand-Maker ability, and drew a single strand up from Archana, much as he had when binding Pendres in the training arena. "I'm not sure if this will hurt, but I hope it won't." Gareth nodded, and Osric quickly used the strand to sew the small cut closed on Gareth's arm. Osric stitched the wound tightly and then anchored the ends on either side of the wound to Gareth's skin. He glanced up at Gareth's face with a questioning expression.

"Didn't feel a thing. What did you do?"

"I stitched it closed with magic, just as a healer would with thread. It should heal quickly and cleanly and avoid infection. Thank you for your sacrifice to our mission." Osric released Gareth's arm.

"If that is all the blood I shed for our mission, I will be luckier than most. It was little to ask when so much is on the line." Gareth smiled. Osric nodded and turned to leave, using his wand to guide the shielded globe of blood-tinged water along at his side.

"I will meet you on the grounds just after the mid'day meal. Keep up the good work down here." Osric and Pendres made their way back up through the winding corridors and stairs to the training grounds. Osric was fairly sure he could find Kenneth sparring with his Vigiles at this time of day. The sun was growing warmer as it climbed higher into the sky, and Kenneth was standing bare-chested and barefoot in the center of the arena. Three Vigiles stood around him in offensive stances particular to DuJok, a form of unarmed combat that all Vigiles trained in from an early age. Osric approached the railing, where several new recruits were watching the sparring match, and he located Elmeric, a seasoned veteran who had helped train Osric when he first joined the elite group of Stanton's defense force.

"Do you think he can handle all three of them? He has gotten older and a bit wider since I last saw him spar." Osric laughed as the surprised and outraged expression on Elmeric's face quickly morphed to amused laughter when he saw who had made such an accusation against the Vigile Contege. Elmeric slapped Osric's shoulder familiarly.

The Weaving of Wells

"If those three can't take him, then I'm not training 'em hard enough." Elmeric laughed. "What brings you out to watch the sporting?"

"Actually, Kenneth has my sword, and I find myself in need of it. Do you know where his things are?" Osric asked. Elmeric nodded and pointed at a neatly folded tunic and a pair of unlaced boots lying next to the door to the armory. Osric's sword was in its sheath, leaning up against the wall next to the clothing. Osric smiled in gratitude and walked over to retrieve his sword. He grabbed his sheath in his free hand and stepped into the armory, carefully guiding the levitating water globe with his wand. He closed the door, not ready to explain to his men what he was about to do, including Pendres.

Osric pulled Legati from the sheath and slowly drew the blade through the bloody ball of water. By focusing carefully, he could discern the moment when the Stone-Sight gift merged with his other abilities as a fully formed and functional gift. He knew that with the new ability, the amount of power he had to channel the strands of Archana's magic also increased, and he briefly felt awash with a mixture of euphoria and revulsion. How easy it would be to allow himself to be overwhelmed by the power, by the ability to gain more and more power by taking more gifts from others. The revulsion came from the method of acquisition: the blood of another person was feeding his power, and Osric's stomach twisted at the idea that he could feel euphoria from such an event.hen it was done, Osric was surprised to see that the globe of water was no longer tinged with the pink of Gareth's blood. It seemed the sword had absorbed it somehow, taking the substance itself from existence in order to bequeath its innate power to Osric through the magic of the unicorn horn. Now the water was only water, and Osric was something more than he had previously been. He shook his head in wonder, dried the sword on his breeches, and slipped it back into its sheath. Osric stepped through the door and returned the sword to its resting place near Kenneth's clothes. He still kept the ball of water hovering at his side as he returned to where Pendres and Elmeric were standing. Osric leaned against the railing and watched his oldest friend beating three men at once in combat. It was an impressive sight.

Osric grinned and glanced at the water globe. He began twirling the tip of his wand in a small circle, causing the ball of water to spin and

Osric's Wand

swirl rapidly. He used his Fire Elementalist ability to slowly draw heat from the water until it grew slushy and then gradually more solid. When it was ready, he waited for the opportune moment. Kenneth had one man in a complex headlock that Osric had always had trouble breaking free from whenever his friend managed to secure the hold. The other two were looking a bit dazed and catching their breath with their hands on their knees. When it looked as though they had mostly recovered, Osric launched the ball of snow into the arena and it splattered against Kenneth's back, dripping from his long, black braided hair. The heavily muscled man was so stunned by the attack that he lost his grip on the Vigile and turned to seek out his attacker. The other two Vigiles used the opportunity to orchestrate a collaborative attack and managed to flip Kenneth onto his back, pinning him securely. Osric burst into laughter as Kenneth caught sight of him in the crowd and scowled, though the angry expression soon turned to raucous laughter, and he congratulated the men on using their resources wisely.

    The sun was almost directly overhead, and Osric waited for Kenneth to don his tunic, lace his boots, and belt Legati around his waist. The two of them headed into the barracks with Pendres and Elmeric for the mid'day meal. Osric's stomach had settled and was now rumbling, looking forward to the delicious meal that was surely awaiting them in the dining hall. He wasn't disappointed; the aromas that greeted them as they entered the large room promised herb-roasted chicken, wild rice, and fresh-baked bread. The four men enjoyed a leisurely meal while discussing Kenneth's chilly defeat. Nothing was mentioned about Osric's request for a man's blood or his ambiguous claim to have found a solution to the use of the wells, though Osric noticed Pendres eyeing him curiously several times during the meal. When they had finished eating, Kenneth and Elmeric excused themselves to head to a scheduled training exercise for the Vigiles in the woods east of the palace. Osric and Pendres made their way to the main entrance to meet Gareth.

    While they waited for the Stone-Sight to arrive, Osric gazed at the stone bricks that made up the bulk of the barrack's construction in an attempt to activate the new ability. He stared at the wall, focusing intently on the small cracks and crevices in the stones, but he could not detect anything unusual or different from what he could see with

The Weaving of Wells

his eyes only. He turned around when he heard Gareth's voice behind him addressing Pendres.

"What is he doing?"

"Honestly, I'm not sure. He's just been standing there staring at the wall," Pendres responded. Osric smiled, slightly embarrassed, and indicated that they should walk with him as he headed up the path toward the main road. As the three men crossed the boundary of the enclosure spell around the barracks, they were startled by the drastic change in the temperature of the air—and the change in scenery. Within the protection spell, it was perpetually early summer. The bright, warm sun was perfect for growing crops in the massive gardens in the barracks courtyard. Outside the spell, Stanton was chilled by the light winds and low clouds of late fall. Their breath formed small puffs of steam and they picked up their pace to stay warm. Osric used his wand to cast a silence shield around them, ensuring that no one would overhear their conversation as they walked past the palace and headed west toward the rocky hills just outside of town. Along the way, Osric explained his plan briefly.

"Gareth, the drops of blood that you provided allowed me to acquire the Stone-Sight ability." Both men glanced at Osric with surprised expressions, but neither interrupted him. "I need you to teach me how to use it. Once I have control over the gift, I am going to try to identify a correlation between the substance underground and the volume of magic that flows through it. If I am correct, I might be able to use your maps to identify the currents of magic that supply certain areas of Archana with a greater concentration of strands. If I succeed, your maps will be the key to our success in this war." Osric looked over at his companions, pausing for a moment. "If I am wrong, I will have to start all over on thinking up a solution to our problem. So, let's hope I am correct."

"So that's why you were staring at the wall when I arrived. Were you able to use my gift?" There was no hint of resentment in Gareth's tone, but Osric again felt revulsion at having stolen another person's gift, even if he hadn't hurt him badly to do so.

"Unfortunately, I was not. I'm hoping you can help me trigger the ability. Simply staring at the stone didn't seem to accomplish anything other than you two thinking I have gone daft." Osric smiled and the two men laughed with him.

Osric's Wand

"I've never really thought about how I use my gift. Every Stone-Sight I've ever met knew how to use it, even if they weren't very good at it." Gareth frowned as he thought about how to teach the High-Wizard to use an ability he wasn't born with. "Regardless, we will find a way for you to gain the knowledge you need. I will not be the reason your plan fails." Osric nodded and they continued in silence, allowing Gareth time to think of the best method for instructing Osric.

The land grew more uneven as they passed by the palace grounds and continued on away from Stanton. Pendres wondered if the chamber they had been in with the Stone-Sights was somewhere beneath them, but he was sure they were too far away from the barracks for that to be the case.

"Osric, the corridors beneath the barracks, do they extend out this far? I noticed the ceiling in the chamber was unfinished, but I don't recall seeing anywhere on the grounds with holes in stone."

"Gareth and his crew are studying the effects of the protection spell on the surrounding area. We still don't know much about how it works, which is why I have his team focused on that chamber. The space is located outside of the protection spell, but the majority of the corridors are directly below the area within it." Osric tried to think of an explanation for what the Stone-Sights and the others working on the construction had discovered so far. "If you enter the old barracks, the building that is on the property and accessible if you have not been invited into the protection spell, those lower levels do not exist. The construction is technically occurring in the past, since the protection spell isolates the area inside of it from the passage of time. Yet, we don't know how far down the spell extends. We are still trying to determine if that chamber that is being constructed outside the perimeter of the spell is somehow contained within it, because we have yet to locate the chamber outside the circumference of the spell. We know where it should be, but it doesn't seem to be there. We will need to do a lot more research before we fully understand it." Osric looked over at Pendres, as if he were going to say more, but he remained silent and returned his gaze to the rocky terrain they were walking over.

"So, if you are altering that area of Archana in the past, wouldn't that cause the area to be altered from that point in time forward? I don't understand." So stunned by the idea of Osric using magic that removed space from time, Pendres forgot to put one foot in front of the other and stopped walking. It sounded too much like the magic that had been used on him, severing his life from time and causing him to lose everyone and everything he had ever loved.

"That's what we wondered originally, when we began the construction, but it is as if the old barracks and the new barracks are the same space existing simultaneously in two different times. We have only altered one, and the other remains unchanged, so we can only assume that the spell completely separates the new space from the old."

"What happens if the spell fails?" Pendres sounded curious about how such a spell could work, and he didn't seem to realize the implications of his simple question.

Osric hesitated to answer, but eventually he took a deep breath and spoke.

"From our past experience with this type of spell, we believe that the new space would disappear if the spell were no longer active. Then, only the original barracks would exist. That is part of the reason we are trying to learn more about the spell's extent and effects, and why we are expanding the area beneath the barracks. We aren't sure what would happen if the spell were to falter and people or objects were to exist in the same place in the old and the new space at the same time."

"Oh, bloody blades, it could be an instantaneous massacre!" Pendres's eyes were wide and he was silent for a while. Then he glanced at Osric with narrowed eyes. "You said from 'past experience.' What do you mean? You have used this spell before?"

Osric sighed, remembering his choice to use the protection spell around the Grove of the Unicorn to end the battle with Aron. He cringed at the recollection of the fear and anger he had caused the Maiden of the Unicorn and the other residents of the grove, including the desperate terror Bridgett had felt when she found out the grove had vanished.

"I modeled the spell on another, and that one is no longer there. We don't know exactly how the spell failed, or if it could ever be erected again, but… it's gone now." Osric's voice cracked and Pendres stayed silent, respecting the emotion bared in Osric's tone and ceasing his questioning. Gareth had remained quiet throughout the whole exchange, and Pendres wondered if he knew what Osric had been remembering when he spoke of the spell. Pendres had forgotten how much pain a single lifetime could contain.

As they walked, Gareth pointed off to the hills that rolled across the open land to the north. A small stream trickled down between the mounds of earth, and large boulders broke through the hardy wild grasses and late-blooming flowers. A brown crust was the only evidence of the plush moss that had thrived on the broad stone backs of the mostly submerged rocks earlier in the year.

"Just beyond that hill there," Gareth said, indicating the tallest of the hills that were closest to them, "is a small cave. Let's go there and see if we can get this gift working for you."

Osric and Pendres followed him through the knee-high grass, stirring up the fragrance of drying flowers and annoying small insects that flew up into their faces as the men disturbed the grass. Osric was very familiar with the area, including the cave that they were heading toward. He had often played there as a boy, and he liked the small shelter for hunting rabbits. The vegetation along the spring was tender and fragrant, and rabbits were well fed and plentiful in the area. Pendres, on the other hand, had ventured little from the busy populace of the Aranthian barracks within the protection spell. He had not had the pleasure of exploring the land that surrounded Stanton, and he was enjoying the soft rolling hills and the bright-green grasses and plants, so much more teeming with life and thriving than the rough terrain of Inasis, where he had been living before Stargon sought him out.

The cave was shallow, more an outcrop of stone where wind and water had carved away the soil than an actual cave. There was room for all three of them to stand comfortably a few paces under the rock ceiling, and the ashes of some hunter's fire was lying in a cold circle of stones on the dirt floor. Gareth indicated that Osric should stand facing the back wall, and he placed his hand against the stone.

"When you look at a lake, you can see the reflection of the sky and the trees on the surface. Because of the light that reflects off the water, you have to focus your vision beyond that image in order to see the fish darting among the rocks down below. It's a bit like that." He waited for Osric to nod before continuing. "The stone that you can see is merely the surface, the part of the stone that the light reflects off of. To use the Stone-Sight, you must look beyond the surface. Instead of

The Weaving of Wells

fish, you will see the various densities, flaws, cracks, and layers of the stone. It might be easier at first to try looking all the way through the stone, looking for the space beyond it as if you were looking for the bottom of the lake. Give it a try."

"It sounds a lot like using the Wand-Maker ability, but it isn't the strands that I am trying to see just yet. What will it look like if I manage to see through to the other side?"

"Much like the land behind us, but lacking the distinct lines and color." Gareth's hand still rested against the stone, and his face was soft as he looked through the solid substance.

Osric gazed at the stone wall in the dim mid'day light that found its way to the back of the cave. His eyes could see the rough texture, the grey hue, and he tried to think of what he was seeing as merely a reflection on the surface. He stared harder, willing the rock to be transparent and allow his vision to penetrate deeper. At first, he just felt that he was making himself cross-eyed. His vision became less focused and he grew frustrated. Then, suddenly he could see shapes and lines in the stone that hadn't been there before. He noticed a long crack about waist high, and it took a moment for the disorienting sense to pass before he could distinguish that the crack was several paces beyond the wall of stone he had been looking at. Again he refocused his eyes, seeking layers even deeper in the rock, and then his sight slowly sank through the rock until he could see the vague colorless image of waving grass.

Osric squeezed his eyes closed, the strain of focusing so hard causing a throbbing behind his eyes. When he opened them, once again he could only see the rough, grey surface of the cave wall. It took several more tries before he could control the speed and direction of the sight within the stone, but the sun was still high overhead by the time he felt he could use the ability with some modicum of control. Then, he tried using the Stone-Sight in combination with the Wand-Maker's ability. If he couldn't get the two gifts to work together, his whole plan would have to be discarded and he would be back where he started.

The first time he tried, he lost control of the Stone-Sight as soon as he tried to focus on the strands. Rather than the layers of stone deep beneath his feet, Osric found himself staring at the dirt in front of his boots. The second time, he had more success, but both abilities wavered and he couldn't determine the density of the strands flowing through each layer of stone. It was as if the abilities both relied so much on the vision of his eyes that he could not use both of them simultaneously, but instead his eyes would prioritize one sight or the other to process.

Osric was encouraged by his ability to gain control of the Stone-Sight gift so quickly, and he worked tirelessly to bring the two gifts into harmony, rather than succumbing to the frustration of his failure. Most of the day had passed and the air was growing colder when something finally settled into place and the two gifts began to enhance each other, rather than fighting one another. Osric sighed audibly when he felt the abilities synchronize, and Gareth smiled, understanding that some crisis had passed, though he did not know what Osric had been battling with all evening. Finally, Osric could determine where the strands were flowing through the various layers of stone, and he grew even more determined to find a pattern.

"Gareth, can you tell me what I'm looking at here?" Osric didn't take his eyes off of the stone in front of him. Pendres, though fascinated that Osric had acquired and was now learning to master an ability that he was not born with, stretched out on the fragrant grass outside the cave to wait. When he looked at the rock, he could see nothing but the stone wall, and he couldn't offer any help to Osric. He remained alert and listened with interest to the conversation inside.

"On the surface, here, you can see the minute imperfections where the wind is eroding the rock. It isn't smooth the way it appears when you look with your eyes. You see?"

"Yes, I see what you mean."

"Then deeper, here, you see this crack? That is a weakness in the stone. When the cave erodes this far, this area will go faster, causing the crevices in the rock like this one over here. Then about four times further in, you see how the color is deeper, a darker shade of grey with the sight?"

"Yeah. Down there?"

"Yes, that rock is more dense and solid. It will erode slower and remain after the surrounding softer stone is gone. There, that area another five times deeper and to your left, where it looks foggy?"

"I see it."

"That's water. There is an underground spring. You can follow it and see where it disperses into small sinkholes. That water is forming a cave system deep below the ground. Do you see the areas that look white?"

"I do. Are those the hollow spaces, the caves?"

"They are. It's a fairly small system. There is a much larger one near the barracks. We have almost reached it, but we need to make sure we approach it properly in order to keep it as stable as possible. Once we are in, it should provide about three times the space you currently have in the existing structure. Do you see that pale stone near the largest cave, where the water is accumulating?"

"It's difficult to distinguish the stone from the water there."

"Yeah, it is. It gets easier with experience. That area will likely crumble sometime in the next few months and cause a rockslide that will connect those two caves. The water is eating away at it quickly. Those types of areas are what we must avoid, and we are taking the proper steps to reinforce and circumvent any that we locate. A few more days and we should have our first access point to the caves."

"That's fantastic, Gareth. I can't tell you how grateful I am that you were able to devise and execute this plan to ensure the safety of the Aranthians."

"Thank you, sir." Gareth cleared his throat. "So, can you tell me what you are seeing, in addition to what I can show you?"

"Well, there is very little distinction in the amount of strands moving through this stone. It is slightly more than what flows through the soil on the surface. But that area where you pointed to the denser stone, that area has a little higher concentration of strands. There are essentially no strands at all in the water and the hollow space of the caves." Osric was silent for a moment. "There. Ten times further down than the cave or so, that band of dark stone that snakes off to the north, there is a much denser flow of strands there. What type of rock is that?"

"Ten times further than the caves? Are you sure?" Gareth sounded concerned, and Pendres got up and returned to Osric's side.

"Yes, well, it is difficult for me to judge distance, so I cannot be completely confident in my assessment. It's possible that I do not have sufficient control over the ability to know for sure. However, I have sought out the area with the Stone-Sight several times and my calculations have been consistent. Each time, it is about ten times further down than the caves, straight down. Why?"

Pendres cast a questioning look at Gareth as the Stone-Sight stared open-mouthed at Osric. It took him a moment to reply.

"Osric, I cannot see the band of stone you are referring to." Gareth was gazing at Osric with wide eyes, and Osric withdrew his sight from the stone and turned to look at the older man. "I can't see even half that far, and I can see further than most. Not even Dorim can see nearly that far, and his distance is why I chose him for the project. Your power, considering you only became a Stone-Sight today, is baffling. I am awed by you, sir." Gareth gave an awkward bow and Osric had to stifle his laughter.

"Gareth, my power is worthless without men like you to guide my learning of its use. You have been incredibly helpful, and I believe we have been successful here today. If you can continue teaching me, particularly in reading your charts, I think I can strengthen our position against Dredek significantly."

"Of course, sir. I would be honored. Perhaps we can evaluate some of the stone in the lower levels as well? You may be able to see something that we wouldn't see until it is too late to avoid without altering all of our construction plans. Your ability can ensure that we select the best route for the greatest amount of space and stability in the cave system."

"I would be happy to help. Anything to make the Aranthian headquarters a safer place to live and work. Thank you, Gareth."

Osric spent the rest of the evening surveying the stone around the large chamber where he had first found Gareth and poring over Gareth's maps to try to identify the various types of rock that they charted. Osric was able to locate two small sections of the same dark stone that had high concentrations of strands close enough to the area for Dorim to see, and he confirmed that it was the hardest type of rock in the region. As far as Osric could tell, the denser the stone, the denser the flow of strands, but he wanted to research it further instead of just relying on his theory.

The next day, Gareth continued to instruct him in identifying the various layers within the stone. Osric found areas where there were higher concentrations of strands, and then Osric and Gareth would work together to identify the corresponding stone and locate it on

The Weaving of Wells

Gareth's charts. Throughout the morning, Osric became more confident that he was correct, and after the mid'day meal he retired to his office with the maps. It was nearly morning again when he finished, but he emerged with red, tired eyes and a victorious grin. He was certain he could track the flow of magic across most of Archana, easily identifying potential sites for the smaller wells that they may not have already located, and he had a plan for using the information to thwart Dredek's use of the Well of Strands to raise his army of the dead.

For the first time in a very long time, Osric actually felt optimistic about the future of Archana, and he wanted nothing more than to find Bridgett and tell her the good news. He jogged through the corridors with rolled charts in both hands, drawing questioning looks and shaking heads from the few Aranthians who were awake before the sun rose. Osric smiled at each of them as he rushed past, slowing only when he arrived at the door to Bridgett's chamber.

Osric burst through the door, breathing heavily from running through the corridors. He nearly knocked a vase full of fresh-cut flowers to the floor, but he managed to drop one of the charts he was clutching and catch the crystal vase awkwardly in one arm before it crashed to the rug. Bridgett emerged from the doorway to her bedchamber with tousled hair and eyelids heavy from sleep, startled by the noise. When she saw Osric leaning against the wall embracing the large vase, she smiled and he grinned back at her like a child caught playing too rough in the house. Osric carefully replaced the flowers on the stand near the door and rushed over to Bridgett, sweeping her up in his arms and kissing her passionately. She stood in the circle of his embrace, breathless and bleary-eyed, and Osric could only stare at her for a moment. Each time he held her he was still amazed that she was there with him, and he couldn't help but feel a twinge of the fear and pain that had gripped him so terribly when he thought she was gone forever. The relief that he could touch her, kiss her, was so potent that he found it difficult to speak before he caught his breath, and it had nothing to do with the exertion of running to her rooms. Bridgett turned slightly in his arms and looked down at the roll of parchment in his hand and the second one lying on the floor near the door. She glanced up at him with one eyebrow raised, and he released her to retrieve the dropped maps. Osric crossed the room and began to spread the charts out on the table near the window. Bridgett followed and looked down at the maps with lines and circles drawn in light all over the strange-looking charts. She waited for Osric to explain what had brought him to her door with such excitement so early in the morning.

"I've figured it out. I know how I can draw more magic from Archana than Dredek can access at the Well of Strands."

"What are these?" Bridgett's voice was still husky from sleep, but her eyes were bright and curious.

"These are charts of Archana. Well, more accurately they are charts of what lies beneath the surface of Archana. I was up all night working it out, but I did it."

Bridgett looked at Osric with a wide smile as his excitement radiated toward her, and she couldn't help but be affected by it.

"What did you do, love?"

"I mapped the flow of magic across Archana. I can identify where the greatest amount of magic comes close to the surface, so I can find all of the wells. Now, I just need a few of the world's greatest Wand-Makers to help me manipulate the strands, and a few of the world's greatest Earth Elementalists to help me manipulate the stone, and I can link all of the wells. If I can pull it off, I will be able to use all of the smaller wells at once to magnify my power, and it should be enough to outweigh the power that Dredek has in Angmar." Osric's cheeks were flushed and his eyes were fierce as he gazed down at her. "I can defeat him, Bridgett, from half a world away from the Irua Realm!"

"Osric, that's incredible!" Osric would not be battling Dredek in direct combat again, and Bridgett was as elated about this as she was about the prospect of undertaking such an amazing feat of magic. Osric grabbed her hand in his and began dancing her across the room, twirling her in circles, and Bridgett laughed as the room spun around. She felt lighter than she had since she had stepped through Chandra's beaded curtain what seemed like a lifetime ago.

Bridgett collapsed into Osric's arms, giggling like a little girl, and he kissed her again. For a moment, only his lips and his arms existed, and if she could have had her way it never would have ended. Osric released her reluctantly, but he quickly rolled up the maps and kissed her on the cheek.

The Weaving of Wells

"I have to go find Gus. We have a lot of work to do today." Osric rushed to the open door, leaving Bridgett standing in the middle of the chamber with a soft smile on her lips and the room spinning slowly around her.

Chapter 26
Weaving Wells

Gus and Eublin stared at Osric in silence. Gus's ear was twitching steadily, and he opened his mouth a few times as if to say something, but then he closed it and continued staring in silence. Eublin kept pushing his spectacles up his nose even though they weren't sliding down, but his mouth remained closed. Osric sat in the chair, his feet propped up on his desk, waiting for the response. He had expected Eublin to be bouncing with excitement, and he was sure that Gus would launch into one of his classic tirades about the irresponsibility of using magic they didn't understand. While he was explaining his plan to the others, Bridgett had slipped into the room. She stood against the wall with an expression somewhere between worry and anger, but she too remained quiet. Honestly, Osric was growing quite anxious as all of them just stared at him. He dropped his feet from the desk and propped his elbows on his knees, staring back at them just as intently. Eventually, one of them would speak, and then they would come up with a plan and Osric would try to end the war once and for all. Eventually. Eublin finally broke the silence.

"We knew that the wells could tip the balance of power in our favor, but what you are suggesting…" Eublin shook his head. "Are you actually suggesting what I think you are suggesting?" Before Osric could respond, Gus's twitching spread from his ear to his entire body and he began stammering and then yelling.

"Boy," he shouted, "either you are suicidal or you are a plain idiot. Channeling that much power could kill you!"

"Gus, I…"

"Let's ignore the fact that nothing like this has ever been conceived before. Let's just ignore the fact that no one in the history of Archana has ever attempted to use a fraction of the power you want to tap into and survived. Let's also ignore the fact that what you are suggesting would be a hundredfold greater than the powerlock you experienced with two wands!"

"How do we know that?"

The Weaving of Wells

"What? Are you as foolish as I thought you were when you refused to believe me about that wand I made? I was right then too, by the way. I'm great, but I didn't make the prophecy wand. I know my limits, and you don't!"

"Gus, how do we know that nothing like this has ever been conceived of before? The wells are evidence that we know next to nothing about magic, even with everything we have discovered. We don't know that no one has ever used this much power before, because we can't even begin to understand what it took to create the Well of Strands. We don't know what I can handle either, because we don't fully understand how my power growth works. For all we know, I can channel a thousand times the magic in that powerlock, but the point is we don't know." Osric didn't allow Gus to interrupt him. "What we do know is that Dredek is attempting to raise his people from the dead by using the greatest amplifier of magical power that exists in this world. What we know is that if we don't find a way to combat him with at least as much power as he has access to then he will succeed, and we cannot even begin to contemplate what the consequences will be. What we know—what *I* know—is that if we don't do this it will be our fault because we didn't try, and if it kills me then you will take up the reigns of the Aranthians and keep working to make this world a safe place, a good place, for our people, for all people."

"And you expect us to help you do this?" Gus was still yelling, but his ear had stopped twitching.

"Yes Gus. I expect you to help me—you and many others—because I can't do this by myself. You may not have made the wand of the prophecy, but you have been making magnificent wands all of your life. There are very few people in this world who can do at all what you do effortlessly, and I need that talent on my team, because you are right that we don't really know what we are getting ourselves into. I might be the one who will be channeling the power when we're done, but we have to pull this off first, and I think with your help we can do it. What do you say?"

"Stop trying to flatter me into agreeing to this crazy scheme and tell me exactly what your plan is."

Osric pointed back at the maps spread out across his desk. He indicated each of the circles of light scribbled on the parchment.

Osric's Wand

"Each of these is a potential site for a well. We need to confirm which of these areas have ports and which don't, because that will determine if the terrain can be altered without causing significant risk of a rupture in the stone." Next he pointed to the lines drawn in varying directions between the circles. "These are the segments with the highest concentration of strands near enough to the surface. We need to connect as many of these areas as possible, while isolating the well in Angmar if we can. Once the net of strands is complete, I should be able to utilize all of the wells by accessing only one of them. From that well, I will have more power than Dredek has."

"So we need to get someone to each of these locations. But once we identify the feasible sites, how will we connect the strands?" Eublin was standing on his chair to better see the charts on the desk.

"Well, with the help of the Earth Elementalists, we will align the stone that channels the most strands between the sites. We need to make sure there is no interruption with less productive stone, water, or other substances that interfere with the density of the strands. To avoid unforeseen consequences, we need to change the ground as little as possible but just enough that we have a continuous system of high-density strand flow connecting all of the wells. The wells themselves should serve as an outlet for any power or pressure that otherwise might cause an explosion, eruption, or other complication. Can you help me recruit the best Elementalists and Wand-Makers for the job? I want to have it done today."

"I was wrong. You aren't just going crazy; you have long since arrived there. This whole idea is absurd," Gus said, pacing back and forth along the edge of the map on top of the desk. He mumbled to himself while Eublin leaned forward on his chair to scrutinize the charts closer and Bridgett's expression slowly grew less worried and more angry. Gus's eyes darted back and forth, searching over the map as he moved. Then, Gus suddenly stopped pacing and threw his paws in the air, looking up at Osric with narrowed eyes, "But I can see that you are going to attempt it with or without my help, so the least I can do is try to keep you from killing yourself. I can't do that if I am not with you, so I will help. Tell me how many Elementalists you think you can gather, and I will seek out as many with the sight for strands."

"Look at the charts," said Osric. "These, the most feasible and most necessary wells, are the ones I want to focus on. We will need at least two dozen of each to link the twelve wells that I believe I can link. If we can come up with more, there are a few more potential sites here and here." Osric pointed at two outlying circles on the map.

"Where will you be? Where will the primary well of your system be?" Bridgett finally spoke from across the room, and her voice was even and low. She approached the desk, looking only at the maps rather than at Osric. He watched her for a moment, and then he placed his finger on the map.

"Here, in the elven ruins by Braya. It has the highest concentration of strands, and it is located closest to Angmar. It's the best location."

Bridgett nodded, then turned to Gus.

"Then that is where we shall be. Go find twenty-two more Wand-Makers, Gus."

Osric rose from his chair. "Bridgett—"

"Gus and I will be at your side," she cut him off before he could protest. "We will help you with the strands while you direct what must be done with the stone."

"I don't know what will happen. What if—"

"Osric, you don't know what will happen. None of us do. You can't protect me, and I can't protect you. Come what may, I will be by your side." Bridgett's voice never quavered and her hands were not trembling as her anger carried the words from her throat. "If you succeed, it will be with me at your side. If you fail, we fail." She stared up at him with only a hint of a smile and fear in her eyes. "Don't fail."

Gus scampered from the room, turning right and heading for the stairs that would take him to the Wand-Maker's workshops on a lower floor of the barracks. Though many of the Aranthians had been spending extra time in the arena training in weapons and combat, he hoped to find at least half of the crew he needed for Osric. The wizards who had been studying and perfecting the crafts of wand-making, amulet construction, and charms all had the ability to see and manipulate the strands, and Gus had personally helped recruit many of the best with the gift on Archana. He would need more, but by the end of the day he would find the people that Osric needed, no matter what it took. He would even be willing to persuade Eni to help them if he had to, even though his rival Wand-Maker had not been Trusted into the Aranthians. Osric believed that this was the only way, and Gus had a gnawing feeling that they were quickly running out of time.

Bridgett continued to stand against the wall, silently watching Osric sort through that myriad of emotions that he never had to voice because she could feel each one acutely as her own. She didn't know when it had happened exactly, but she could no longer distinguish between his feelings and hers. When he laughed, she felt joy. When he worried, she became slightly nauseated. When he was scared, her heart raced and it was difficult to breathe. Her Empath ability had either strengthened as she acquired some of his gifts, or he had become so much a part of her that she couldn't tell where she ended and he began. His heart-wrenching fear that she would be killed if she was with him when he tried to channel more power than he could logically contemplate was crushing her chest too. Her anger that had kept her voice steady when she thought she might fall apart was a burning rage that he would risk something so likely to kill him. She was furious that he had left her head spinning and heart fluttering with a kiss on her lips in her chambers, dancing around in his excitement about his new discovery, just to find out that his discovery would allow for such a dangerous endeavor. He hadn't even intended to tell her what he was planning, as far as she knew, because he had run from her rooms with a smile on his face and left her dizzy with happiness. She had wanted to know more about what had inspired him to wake her, and now all she wanted to do was set the maps on fire and pretend that Dredek didn't exist.

But pretending that he didn't exist wouldn't make him go away. It wouldn't keep him from slaughtering the irua people because he wanted to use the Well of Strands to raise his people from the dead. It wouldn't keep Osric from taking extreme measures to stop Dredek either. So, Bridgett put all of her effort into shutting down her gift, into blocking out Osric's fear in an attempt to shut out her own. She stood against the wall, willing herself not to feel, because she was going to do everything she could to make sure that Osric was successful. Either way, she would be there.

* * *

The Weaving of Wells

The ruins were a forest of white stone, crumbling and quiet in the early morning sunlight. They rose up out of the forest like ancient trees, overgrown with moss and vines, covered in leaves and in several places soil. Trees had grown up between the stones, pushing aside large sections of the roads and walls and completely toppling some of the structures. Osric and his companions picked their way carefully through the remains of what were once grand, beautiful buildings. There was still evidence of intricate carvings and graceful arches on most of the walls and entranceways. The ceilings had collapsed on many of the larger structures, but it was clear that most of the smaller enclosures were designed with no roof, or perhaps they were made of a material that had disintegrated over time. The tropical region was subject to an immense amount of sunlight and rain almost year-round, and fibrous materials such as cloth or thatching would not remain long once the city was abandoned.

Osric halted their progress frequently to inspect the area using the Stone-Sight to determine the greatest concentrations of strands in the stone far beneath their feet. Their path seemed sporadic to Aridis, who had roamed these ruins for longer than Osric had been alive, but he trusted that they would end up where they needed to be. He had told Osric that he could show him where the area with the greatest power amplification effects was located, but he had no way of knowing if there were factors other than a well contributing to the strength of his Obcasior ability in various places. When Aridis had heard that Osric was planning to execute the finale of his plan from the well in the old elven ruins, he had finally understood why he had been able to see so much of the future's potential in these crumbling stones. He had never known why he was drawn to the ruins to practice his gift, but the presence of a smaller version of the Well of Strands would explain it. He suspected they would eventually find their way to the dome where he had read the stones so many times, but he had no idea if a structure like the one Bridgett had described might lie below the stone floor.

Aridis was correct in his assumptions about their destination, and he ran his hand along the familiar curve of the stone wall that was still standing in the structure. Much of the dome had collapsed long before he had first seen the ruins, but enough of the building was intact for him to identify its likely purpose. Openings in the stone were perfectly aligned with certain stars and with the sun and moon on days significant to the elves, and he had always suspected that the structure was originally constructed as a site for rituals and specific spells related to the seasons and celebrations. Knowing that a well was somewhere nearby didn't change Aridis's opinion, but it did make him wonder if it also hid the power source somewhere beneath them. In all of the years that he had lived near the ruins, Aridis had never attempted to excavate the ruins and see if the structures continued below ground. It was possible that a network of tunnels or preserved rooms with elven artifacts of magic extended beyond the surface ruins that he had explored.

Osric stood at the center of the domed room, gazing down at the stone at his feet and studying the array of magical strands that were woven into the rock and the mortar. The high concentration of free strands was not obvious near the surface, which explained why no Wand-Maker had even taken notice of the wells around the world. However, if he utilized the Stone-Sight ability to peer deep down into Archana, he could see the dense, swirling pool of strands. The floor of the structure had a significant amount of magic in it as well, although it was not the free strands that a Wand-Maker would be used to working with when creating wands. It was a varied and unfamiliar display of protection spells, like the ones he had seen on the island well they had discovered first with Serha, but Osric was not afraid of the spells now as he was then. He stood there silently, closely studying the spells and how they were woven into the stone. Ideally, Osric wanted to find a way into the well without severing the protection spells. It would be easier to leave them intact to keep others out of the site than to attempt to create new ones strong enough to do the job, but they had never discovered the key to deciphering the majority of the book that Trevar and Bridgett had found. Although they had been able to identify a few of the wells and the symbols Trevar needed to enter them, they had made little progress on the secrets the book contained. It was possible that every well's location and symbols for entrance were recorded in the book, and Osric had brought it with him in hopes that identifying the locations with Gareth's maps would aid them in sorting out the book's contents, but Osric wasn't confident that this would be fruitful. It was more likely that he would only be able to get inside if he could deconstruct the well's defenses.

The Weaving of Wells

There was certainly a hollow space beneath the floor of the domed chamber, but the area couldn't be seen with the naked eye. Osric couldn't tell if the space was filled with water or air, or even some other substance, but his Stone-Sight told him it was not solid stone or the rocky soil that surrounded and covered much of the ruins. He suspected that the spells on the stone, which were designed to hide the well, were interfering with his ability to use the Stone-Sight gift with accuracy. Yet, he still had enough control over it to combine with the Wand-Maker ability and view the strands on the far side of the thick stone. Directly below them was the well where the strands were most concentrated but somehow contained by the bowl-shaped structure that Bridgett had described to him in vivid detail. He must find a way inside, and he was not willing to begin by trying to harm the ruins or by damaging the intricate web of protection spells that had been cast at the time of its construction. He couldn't just use the traveling spell, because he had no idea what the inside of the well looked like.

Luckily, the wizards posted at the other well locations didn't actually need to get inside in order to alter the stone and thus the flow of the strands. Osric, on the other hand, would not be able to utilize the amplification power of the wells for his spells unless he could get inside of the protection spells.

Osric paced back and forth on the stone floor of the half-crumbled building. He thought back to everything they had learned about the wells: their origins, their construction, and the means of entering one of them. Nothing seemed to point him in the direction of how to enter this one. They had the book that contained the symbols for all of the wells, but he had no way of identifying which section in the book correlated to a specific well. Chanda's visions had been triggered by some of the pages, leading them to several of the wells, but this one was not one of them. If he could identify which page in the book belonged to the Braya well, he would be able to use the symbols to open the portal.

Osric stopped pacing and sat with the book in his lap. He ran his fingers over each page, hoping to trigger his own Seer ability, but none of the pages caused a vision. Many of them caused his Portentist ability to flare up, but it was impossible to accurately read the ability's meaning because it was not only triggered by one section of the book. It was clear that there was still a great deal he could learn from the

Osric's Wand

book if he could decipher it, and most of the Portentist signals he was getting were mild warnings or subtle hints of importance that didn't seem urgent. None of them indicated that what he needed right now was on any page in the book. Still, he knew it had to be.

Osric tried examining the book with his Wand-Maker vision, trying to see if the patterns of strands attached to the book could give him some clue about the contents. All he could see were some basic protection spells, mostly to keep the book from weathering with time and moisture, and a few unfamiliar chains of strands along the binding. Osric assumed the chains were another type of protection spell, but he couldn't tell what it did just by seeing the pattern of the strands. As far as he could tell, it was merely reinforcing the binding of the book to make it more resilient over years of use. In frustration, Osric looked up at his companions. Bridgett was watching him with a quiet, concerned expression softened with a subtle, loving smile. Aridis was sitting down across the room, leaning back against the cool stone wall with his eyes closed and humming softly to himself. Gus was staring up at the stone ceiling. Osric watched the prairie dog, needing to distract himself from the frustration of the book for a moment, and he noticed something he had never noticed before.

When Gus activated his Wand-Maker ability to look at the strands woven into the structure of the domed ceiling, Osric saw a visible surge of magic course through the green orbs that resided in Gus's eyes—the root of the Wand-Maker gift. Osric blinked, wondering if he had imagined it, but he could still see the steady stream of magic flowing through the orbs as Gus utilized his ability. Osric wondered why he had never noticed it before, but it was subtle and he hadn't been looking for it. The realization of the gift's activity made Osric wonder if the other abilities would do the same thing.

"Hey, Gus," Osric yelled out with feigned urgency. Gus turned quickly, losing his focus on his ability causing the Wand-Maker sight to deactivate. When he noted the stream of strands cease flowing through the green orbs of Gus's gift, Osric smiled. Osric picked up a small stone and threw it at the prairie dog, causing Gus to shriek in surprise and scuttle to his left. Osric smiled even wider, as he had seen exactly what he had hoped to. At the back of Gus's skull, the small purple orb of the Portentist gift had flared up to warn Gus of the

The Weaving of Wells

danger, and Osric had detected the nearly imperceptible flow of magic through that gift as well.

"Hey! What did you do that for?" Gus yelled, his gruff voice echoing off the partial domed ceiling.

"Sorry, but I think you will forgive me when you see what I just saw. How come you never taught me this before?" Osric was only teasing somewhat, as he genuinely couldn't believe that Gus had never pointed out how magic was channeled through natural abilities just as it was channeled through a wand. "Come over here."

Gus shuffled his feet, watching Osric to be sure he wasn't armed with more rocks. When he was close, Osric knelt down on the ground.

"Use your Wand-Maker sight, and watch the orbs for my sight very closely. Are you looking at them?" Gus merely harrumphed in response, but Osric took it as an affirmative. Osric activated his ability, looking at the strands in the stone just as Gus had been. "Do you see it? Did you know that's how they worked?"

Gus's ear was twitching rhythmically as he stared at Osric's eyes, and it took him a moment to form words.

"I must give you more credit than you deserve, you idiot. You think if I had ever seen that before, I would have failed to mention it to you? I taught you everything about your Wand-Maker gift that I could while we were trying to solve the ultimate wand mystery! This is not something I would have left out."

"It's the same with the Portentist ability. That's why I threw the rock at you, to check it out. Uh, sorry."

"You are obviously forgiven, although you could have chosen a more gentle means of triggering it, don't you think?"

"It was the first thing that came to mind." Osric deactivated his Wand-Maker sight, and Gus gasped with glee.

"It turned off! How is it that I've never seen this before? Surely I have been examining you while you used one of your abilities."

"Maybe the exponential growth of power that accompanies the new acquisition of gifts has strengthened our sight to the point where we can see it now, and before you just couldn't have noticed it?" Osric couldn't see any other explanation. It seemed obvious that the gifts must have always worked this way, but he had never noticed it before either. However, Osric wasn't sure if he had ever studied the orbs of the innate gifts closely enough in someone while they were active that he would have noticed it.

"Yeah, that might explain it. It's phenomenal, although I'm not sure if it was worth throwing a rock at my head. What good does it do us right now? We gotta get you inside this well, not sit around ogling each other's gifts."

"Well, that depends," said Osric. "I think it might help a great deal, but I will need to conduct an experiment first. Are you up to letting me manipulate one of your abilities?"

"You are out of your gift-riddled mind, boy. I'm not gonna let you experiment with the magic that makes me up. What if you break something? I might never be able to use my gifts again!" Gus began backing slowly away from Osric, back toward the other side of the structure. Osric laughed, although he wasn't confident enough that Gus was wrong to attempt the experiment against the old Wand-Maker's will.

From across the room, Aridis's voice drifted softly under the oppressive heat of the mid'day sun. Storm clouds were gathering overhead, and the distant rumble of thunder nearly drowned out his words.

"You can do your experiment on me."

"Aridis, are you sure?" Bridgett had been following the conversation closely. "Osric, do you think it's safe? Is Gus right to worry that it might interfere with the ability's function?"

"I don't believe so, although there is always a risk when we attempt new uses for or new methods of doing magic. Aridis knows that." Osric hesitated to make any guarantees, but he really wanted to try what he had in mind. He was fairly confident that there would be no adverse effects.

"It's all right, Bridgett. I trust Osric to know when my mind cannot take what he intends, and if it will aid our mission then it is a necessary risk." Aridis rose from his seat against the wall and walked over to Osric. "Go ahead."

"All right." Osric nodded, formulating a plan as he assessed Aridis for gifts. In the time the old man had spent with Osric at the Aranthian headquarters, Aridis had formed a few fully functioning gifts, and he had several fledgling gifts that would still take a while to become mature. One of the fully developed gifts that Osric recognized and felt

The Weaving of Wells

comfortable with for his experiment was the Air Elementalist ability. The gift was rooted in a small white orb in the back of Aridis's throat, and there were no other full gifts located nearby. "Aridis, I want you to come stand over here and face away from Gus and Bridgett. I will be right next to you, and I just want you to relax." Osric led the old man out to the crumbling stone road between the buildings. Gus and Bridgett remained inside, but with one side of the structure completely collapsed they could watch the experiment while staying out of the way.

Aridis stood still, gazing out at the forest that surrounded his home not too far from where they stood. His shoulders were relaxed and his back was slightly curved, and he leaned his weight comfortably on his walking stick. If he had any trepidation about the experiment, it was not evident in his posture. Osric focused his mind on that small white orb, concentrating on the origin of Aridis's ability to manipulate the air. Carefully, channeling as little magic as possible in an attempt to minimize the risks, Osric pushed strands through Aridis's ability the same way he would channel magic through his wand. It was an exercise in intent, and most people on Archana thought little of the mechanics of using a wand. Osric, however, had studied the function and process of wand-casting in great detail, striving to understand everything he could about how wands work and how to use one more effectively. It was one thing to channel magic through an object that was designed for it, but Osric was attempting to channel magic through something that he did not understand—and that something was located inside his friend's body. He could not be too careful.

As Osric channeled the strands through the orb, the dirt at Aridis's feet swirled up into a small, twisting cloud, but it lasted only the length of a breath and then settled back to the ground. Aridis swayed slightly, but he steadied himself on his walking stick quickly and glanced over at Osric.

"That was mildly unsettling. Did it work, whatever you were trying to do?"

"Yes, it did," Osric said with a grin. "Would you mind if I tried it again, with a bit more oomph this time?"

"Once more, but if the discomfort is proportional to the oomph, as you call it, then once more will be all I can handle," Aridis said, bracing himself with both hands on his staff.

Osric's Wand

"I will try not to overdo it." Osric focused again, narrowing all of his concentration to the small orb in Aridis's throat. This time, he channeled a steady stream of strands through the orb, though it would only be enough power when using his wand to perhaps levitate a small stone or to light a candle. The response was significantly greater than he had expected, though. The air was still behind Aridis; not even a breeze drifted through the ruins or lifted Bridgett's hair from her shoulders. Yet, in front of the old man a gust of wind burst forth, kicking up small rocks, laying grass flat along the cracks of the path, and stirring up the closest edge of the forest as leaves swirled around and then drifted down to the ground. Startled, Osric cut off the stream of magic and rushed over to Aridis with concern.

"Are you all right? I didn't expect it to be that strong. It is definitely not proportional to the power used with a wand to cast spells." Osric put his hands on Aridis's shoulders to help steady him, but the old man looked over with a smile.

"It was no worse that time than the first, though I still don't know what you did. We should be hurrying, though, because it sounds like the storm is moving in quickly, and we don't want to be caught out in these ruins in the dark either." Aridis walked slowly back to the ruins of the dome, humming softly to himself. Osric followed with excitement in his steps.

"Aridis, were you aware that you could control the air?" Bridgett lent him her arm as he stepped back up onto the stone floor of the building.

"What? What do you mean?" Aridis looked at her with a furrowed brow.

"The ability that Osric tested his theory on was that of the Air Elementalist, and it was your ability he used. Did you even know you had it?" Bridgett asked. Aridis shook his head, glancing over at Osric for confirmation.

"It's true. And now I think I know how to get us into the well. You were brave to let me try it, and I really hope it pays off." Osric rushed over and picked up the book. "Gus, did you see what I did? Did you see how it worked?"

"Yeah, boy, I saw it. You sure know how to put on a show when you have an idea." Gus was shaking his head, but he gazed at Osric with something approaching awe.

"Good, because I need you to do it, only to me this time. I want you to trigger my Seer ability so I can try to identify the proper symbols for this well's entrance."

"Why don't you just bring a Seer out here like you did with Chanda for the other wells?" Gus asked, although he was already approaching Osric with his Wand-Maker sight activated trying to locate the little blue orb of the Seer gift among all the others near the back of Osric's head.

"Because there is no way to know if her gift will be triggered. This way, we know for sure it will be and we just have to try to control what it shows me. I will sit here, directly above the actual well that contains the strands, and we will hope that it uses that to determine what I see when you trigger the gift. You are just working as a catalyst. I need a true vision with the ability in order to trust what I see." Osric crossed his feet in front of him, sitting comfortably in the exact center of the structure. He laid the book on his lap, although he kept the book closed in order to prevent the vision from focusing on a specific page in the book—that could lead to seeing a different well instead of getting him into this one.

"Okay, here we go." Gus stood behind Osric, focusing on the blue orb. He channeled the magic, but he knew immediately that he was being more aggressive with his strands than Osric had been, and he let it calm down before continuing. It took Gus only a moment to get control of the flow of strands and to feel confident that he could keep it steady and slow, but he had no idea if it was working. Osric was sitting quietly with his eyes closed, and there was no outward indication that he was having a Seer's vision other than a very subtle, rapid twitch of his left eyeball beneath the lid. When the twitch spread to Osric's left hand and foot as well, Gus ceased feeding the steady stream of strands into Osric's gift and began to fear that he had done permanent damage to the man. After several moments of tension and anxiety for everyone present, Osric opened his eyes and spoke.

"Wow, perhaps I didn't think that through very well before I let you try it."

"Are you all there, boy? How's your head? Did I scramble your brains? What were you thinking, letting me do that? And what in strands was I thinking not giving you my standard 'we can't be toying around with untested magic without considering the potential dire consequences' speech? We're both idiots!" Gus was rambling, but Osric was grinning from ear to ear.

"Gus, remember how I described the power lock with Legati as being so euphoric it was almost unbearably painful?" Osric waited for Gus to stop mumbling and to focus on the fact that Osric was speaking an intelligible sentence and thus his brains were intact.

"Yes."

"Well, this was not like that." Osric laughed as he watched Gus's brow furrow and his ear begin to twitch. "It was incredible and unexpected, though, and you will have to try it sometime. How long were you triggering my gift?"

"Not long, maybe ten breaths. Why?" Gus was moving slowly around Osric, gazing at his head and each of his gifts with his Wand-Maker sight, looking for any signs of damage from the experiment. He began to calm down when he had reassured himself three times that everything looked as it should, considering how strange it is to see more than one gift in any one person.

"It felt like half the day. I had flashes of so many different visions it was impossible to keep them straight or to even attempt to analyze or interpret them."

"Did you see anything about the well? I don't think I want to try that again," Gus said.

"I'm not sure. I did see a strange symbol in many of the visions that stood out to me as important. It was as if my Portentist ability was triggering for the tiny amount of time that the symbol was visible. It was really disorienting, but maybe the symbol means something?"

Gus jumped up on the book in Osric's lap and threw his weight in order to pull the cover open. He stood on Osric's leg and began flipping through the pages.

"Do you see the symbol anywhere in here? What did it look like?"

Osric lifted Gus up, moved him off his lap, and then set the book on the ground between them. He gazed down at the pages, looking for a familiar image from his visions.

"It looked like a circle with three dots inside of it. It was small, and almost always in the lower left corner of my sight. It never quite seemed to belong."

"There are so many symbols in this book, how can anyone make any sense out of it? I can't tell what is writing, what is a key to get into a well, and what is just a kid scribbling in a book!" Gus crossed his arms over his small chest and growled down at the pages.

"It's okay, Gus. I will look through it. I'll let you know when I find something," Osric said. Gus stared up at him with a look of angry refusal to sit idle while Osric looked through the book. "Hey, I have an idea." Osric took out his wand, held the image of the circle firmly in his mind, and then cast a summoning spell on the book. To his delight, rather than having the book flip up into his hand, the pages started turning rapidly on their own. When it stopped, in the lower left corner of the page, Osric saw the small circle with three dots from his visions.

"Looks like your crazy experiment worked after all. Not that I think it was a good idea or anything."

"Looks that way." Osric smiled, letting Gus go back to grumbling about the irresponsible nature of Osric's magic use. He scanned the page, looking for something recognizable other than the small symbol, but he couldn't make sense of it. Bridgett walked over to see what he had found with the spell, and he looked up at her hoping she would enlighten him, or kiss him, or both. At least she wasn't glaring at him anymore the way she had when he divulged his plans.

"Trevar was able to determine that each section of the book is organized the same way. If this page is the description of this well, then this here should describe the location." She pointed to a section of symbols on the top of the right page. "This should have something to do with its origin—we assume so, anyway. We don't really know." She pointed to the bottom of the left page. "And this should be the sequence we use to open the door." Bridgett rested her fingers lightly under a line of seven symbols near the bottom of the right page. Shall we give it a try?" She tossed the small stick of stone she had borrowed from Trevar into the air and caught it again with a smile. Osric scrambled to his feet and glanced around, excited to be making progress.

"Trevar didn't mind, did he?" Osric asked.

"I didn't exactly tell him that I would be taking you into the well. He still hasn't been able to explain why someone is allowed into the well and why another isn't. It has something to do with an extra strand, but he doesn't seem to know what will happen if you try to go inside. Although we should be careful, I assume that there is nothing preventing you from entering, other than the traditions of the guardians of the well. Still, I thought it best to borrow the stone rod rather than bringing Trevar along to try opening the well. He would try to stop you from entering."

"Bridgett, you know I have to get inside, right? This will all be for nothing if I can't get into the well."

"I know. I won't try to stop you, but please be careful. I would hate to get the door open just to lose you as a result." Bridgett reached out and touched his cheek with the back of her fingers. Osric closed his eyes briefly, relieved that she seemed to have forgiven him for risking his life in this plan and grateful that she was there to help him. Still, he would prefer if she were safe in Stanton instead.

"Where should we write the symbols?" Osric asked. All of the wells that he had been to had been accessed from the side, but everything he could see with the Stone-Sight indicated that the entirety of the structure of the well was beneath them. He had no idea how to open a door without first having a wall.

"Hmm, I'm not really sure. Maybe we should try the floor, er the ceiling?" Bridgett's smile faded as she considered the possibility of falling through a hole in the stone in order to get into the well. It had little appeal for her, but even less for letting Osric do it. He was never careful enough for her liking.

"Why don't we just dig down and find the wall?" Gus was no longer scowling or mumbling, and he looked up at them both as if they had no brain between them.

"That would likely cause the ruins to crumble further and bury us all. I suggest we don't disturb the stone if we don't have to, and that includes removing the soil that is holding it all in place." Aridis sounded tired, but he spoke with authority. He knew more about the ruins than any of them, and Osric nodded, indicating that he would find another way in. While Gus and Aridis argued about the fragility of the ruins, Bridgett began drawing the seven symbols from the book on the floor of the circular room close to the section of wall that was still standing. Just as she finished the seventh, Osric noticed what she was doing. He screamed and grabbed wildly as Bridgett slipped into an oval-shaped hole that had appeared suddenly beneath her. He managed to catch her wrist, and her weight pulled him toward the opening. Combined with his momentum from lunging to catch her,

The Weaving of Wells

Osric was helpless to stop their motion and he fell forward to his knees. He grimaced in pain as his chest hit the stone and his arm was nearly pulled from its socket, but he held tight and did not allow her to fall. He was calling her name as she clung to his wrist with her free hand when Gus and Aridis realized what was happening and rushed to Osric's side. Aridis was crawling toward the hole, trying to find a way to help when Bridgett shouted out that she needed a wand.

"Osric! I'm okay. You caught me, and I'm okay. Hand me a wand before you pull me out of here. I seem to have dropped mine." Aridis handed her the requested wand, and Bridgett wasted no time in lighting the tip to shine light into the dark stone trap that she had fallen into. "Let go!"

"What? No."

"Osric, look." Bridgett's voice was calm and sure, and Osric looked down past his outstretched and aching arm, past her dangling feet. A stairway was just below her, and Osric reluctantly released her hand and watched as she fell less than her own height to land lightly on a step. Osric could see that the curve of the stairs followed the wall, and if she had drawn the symbols on the other side of the room she could have stepped down onto the stairway without any risk of falling.

Osric watched as Bridgett skipped down the stairs and disappeared from his sight around a bend. He glanced over at Aridis and Gus, wondering if Bridgett was right about Trevar's concerns only being rooted in tradition and ritual. Before Osric could muster the nerve to enter the well and find out, Gus scampered over to the edge of the opening and dropped down into the hole. Osric gasped and looked down into the opening, fearing he would see Gus lying on the stairs with a broken neck—or worse, caught in the grip of the protection spells. Instead, Osric glanced down in time to see Gus landing lightly on the step, his wand in one paw casting a flow of air that slowed his fall.

"It seems the lovely lady was correct. I have come to no harm by crossing the threshold. Get down here, boy. What are you waiting for?"

Osric glared down at Gus, both angry and touched that the prairie dog would risk his own life to test the protection spells before Osric entered the well. He wasn't sure if he should yell at Gus or thank him, and he wondered if Gus yelled so often because he was really just worried. Osric shook his head in dismay and leapt down into the hole. He scooped Gus up off the stairs and settled him onto his shoulder, giving his furry head an extra pat in gratitude. Osric lit his wand to provide light and rushed down the stairs to catch up to Bridgett. As he descended, Osric could feel the concentration of power growing, and his whole body was throbbing with it by the time he reached the bottom. The glow of the pool of strands in the center of the floor was so bright that he didn't need his wand as long as his Wand-Maker vision was activated. The whole room was pulsing with a bright white light from the magic of Archana, and the sight took his breath away. He heard Gus's sharp intake of breath in his ear as the prairie dog took in the vision of more strands than he had ever seen in his life.

Only one small table sat a few strides from the bottom of the stairs, and a bowl sat in the middle of the room; the rest of the room was bare. Osric just stood for a moment near the edge of the bowl, allowing the power of the space to seep into his being and purge all aches and vestiges of fatigue from his body. It was the most incredible feeling he had ever experienced, including the euphoria of the powerlock with his wand while trapped under the rubble of the Stanton palace.

"Isn't it beautiful?" Bridgett's voice resonated with the power of the well, drawing Osric back to his purpose. Before he considered how to begin shaping the stone beneath the well, he pulled Bridgett into his arms and hugged her.

"It is incredibly beautiful." Osric's gaze was locked on her eyes, and they both laughed when Gus flicked Osric's ear.

"Put me down before you go all lovey-dovey!" Gus nearly leapt from Osric's hand before he could lower him to the stone floor. The old Wand-Maker's eyes were wide with awe as he stepped close to the round bowl full of swirling strands. "Do you think I could dive in and swim in it?"

"And he yells at me about untested magic and irresponsible behavior," Osric said with a grin. "I would advise against it, Gus. We don't know what would happen, after all. Perhaps you would sink like a stone and drown in the strands. Actually, maybe you should try it."

The Weaving of Wells

The sarcastic, though obviously unrealistic, suggestion was enough to bring Gus's attention back from the well and into the necessity of their mission.

"So, what's the plan? What are we doing here?" Gus's voice was back to his normal gruff seriousness.

"We need to contact the others so we can initiate the alterations. I need to be able to guide the entire process, and I won't know what I'm looking at until we can hear from every well. This will take some coordination, but with the right angles I should be able to see everything I need to see. Are you two ready?"

"Ready." Gus and Bridgett nodded and spoke in unison. Gus held up his wand and initiated the communication spell. After a brief moment, the image of Irgon appeared in a beam of light above the tip of his wand. Behind the burly half-giant, Osric could see the chimney-topped hill that Chanda had helped him find.

"Irgon, have you located the stone I told you about? Is it there?" Osric asked.

"Yes, sir. It's deep, but I can see it. We are ready for you."

"Good work. Bring up the next site please." Osric waited as the Wand-Maker at Irgon's location used his wand to link communication with the next well. Osric checked in with each of them, using wand communication from one site to another until he could speak with every man and woman he had recruited to aid him in this undertaking. When he knew that each of the Stone-Sights had located the proper swath of stone to identify the depth and trajectory of the concentrated strands, he spoke to the entire group.

"Stone-Sights, you will need to trace the flow of the strands using the density and makeup of the stone. Follow the stone until you can no longer locate the proper stone. That's when you guys come in, Elementalists. You are going to have to work closely with the Stone-Sights to alter the rock because you will have to work deep without compromising the safety of the surface. We need to avoid rockslides and creating air pockets that could cause cave-ins later on. Keeping the integrity of the terrain intact is an utmost priority. We also need to maintain communication at all times, so if anyone gets into trouble I can come assist you.

"Wand-Makers…" Osric heard an awkward throat-clearing from one of the many wand displays. "Excuse me. Strand-Seers, it will be your responsibility to ensure that the concentration of strands is consistent from your origin well all the way to the next vein of stone as the others work. If anything interrupts the density of the strands, you need to let them know immediately so they can account for it and make any necessary adjustments before moving on. Stone-Sights, make sure to keep to the path of least resistance, and guide the Elementalists carefully and accurately. This will make the project take less time and require less alteration to Archana's underlying structure. The less we do, the better." Osric waited as a chorus of affirmatives was channeled through the wands and he was sure that everyone understood his or her role in the effort. Before he sent them all to work, he reminded them again of the monumental task before them. "Remember, the further you get from the well, the faster you will grow fatigued from expending magic. This will be a long, grueling task, and it is incredibly important that you return to the well to recover before you are too tired to do so. Watch out for each other, and if you need help do not wait to say something. As long as the wand-communication is intact, I can reach any of you almost instantly if I know where to go. Speak clearly and specifically so I can find you quickly, and hopefully nothing will go wrong. I will be moving among you all, helping where I can, but I can only be in one place at any time. Whatever you do, do not allow the wand conversation to be interrupted or we will lose the whole group. Is everyone ready to begin?"

"Ready!" The cacophony of responses echoed from the stone walls of the well, and Osric gave the signal to begin their work. It was going to be a very long day.

Chapter 27
Killing Time

Dark rock and moist clay covered the wall. Dredek was beginning to enjoy the scent that greeted him each morning. Not just the damp, sweet, mildew odor that permeated most of the corridors throughout Angmar, but also his room, which was strategically close to the well's entrance, as well as the garden. It was strangely fragrant located between the two, and waking with a deep breath of the mingled scents helped his mind to focus on the tasks ahead.

He let his right leg fall over the edge of the bed, allowing himself to wake slowly in the early morning hours. This was the day he had been waiting for, but it would do him little justice to rush the process with the day's work left in front of him. Dredek reached to his bedside table, retrieved his wand, and triggered a spell to warm the water in the tub he had brought into his room. Then, with a second wave of his wand, he lit the candles mounted on walls and tables throughout the room.

He lay still, letting his senses grow more alert. As his excitement grew, he took many deep, calming breaths, stifling the rise of emotions. It was a process he would have to repeat many times as the day wore on, but a necessary step in avoiding mistakes.

When he could smell the humidity rising up off the warm bathwater, Dredek sat up and stripped his clothing from his body, seeing in the mirror the foreign human figure he had transformed himself into so many years ago. This would be the last day he would be forced to live with the disguise.

He let himself slip slowly into the warm bath and dipped his head under the water, holding his breath to calm himself once again. It was an odd feeling, being so close to being reunited with his people. He wasn't sure what to expect, since the only attempts he had made before were with recently deceased animals, with most of their flesh, tendons, and innards intact. But the physical parts of the spell weren't difficult anyway. The magical issues were the ones that made him hesitant, but he had been just shy of the power needed on his last try. Since his last attempt to bring life back to Archana, he had grafted two more gifts into himself and knew he had enough now to perform the needed magic.

He lifted his head out of the water and exhaled sharply, and then he inhaled. He let the water cascade off of his face, reaching for the soap and running it over his head. He continued to bathe, forcing himself to relax and savor the scent of the lavender soap.

When he had washed, dried, and clothed himself, Dredek boiled some water and added a small amount to a bowl of oats, nuts, and berries, stirring it softly while the water cooked and absorbed into the meal. Once again, he made it last. He purposefully took small bites, noticing the different textures—savoring them as if it were the first time he had experienced them.

Then, Dredek took a walk. He had awoken early, so he promised himself it would be a long walk, but the further he wandered from the well, the greater the sense of panic that filled his mind. So, instead of a long walk through the tunnels, he settled for a long morning pacing the chambers immediately surrounding the access door to the Well of Strands.

This alternative was much duller, as he had wanted to walk the gardens, but he felt a great deal more comfortable keeping his wandering to a relatively small location. His soldiers patrolling the halls were alarmed at the number of times they encountered him in the closed quarters. He issued small orders that meant nothing, more to provide a sense of normality than to accomplish any specific goal.

When the wait was more than he could bear, he walked back to his room. It was nearly lunchtime, and he had wasted half the day ambling back and forth, but now it was time to eat and begin what had taken him several decades to plan.

For his mid'day meal, Dredek had chosen something more substantial because he didn't know how long he would be occupied. While on patrol in the tunnels of Angmar, his men had discovered rats nearly the size of dogs roaming around the lowermost levels in packs. Dredek had grown accustomed to a changing diet in his early years, even before the battle that took away his family, so there was no hesitation before devouring the meal.

To occupy the little time remaining, Dredek focused on the pull from his new Portentist gift. He let his mind trace the pull, letting the way his senses heightened with its prompting make his mind drift. It

The Weaving of Wells

was a trick he learned after the first time he took a gift from another being. But the Portentist gift was altogether different than the others.

His only innate gift, Wand-Maker, had always been initiated with conscious control. Though he had never been truly great at the craft, it was relatively easy to master the depths of visual control he had while observing magic.

The elemental gifts were the first he had adopted, and they too proved to be easy to master insofar as the conjuring aspect. He could summon flames of different sizes, manipulate them into different shapes while he held them suspended in the air above his hands, and even keep himself warm on the long snow-filled nights he spent mourning the loss of his people. The Water Elementalist gift had proved equally useful in staying cool in the years he spent in Rowain.

Earth and Air Elementalist gifts were similarly mastered, though uninteresting for much more than trivial amusement. Even with his number of gifts, there wasn't enough power to move a sufficient quantity of air or earth to make the gifts worthwhile.

But each and every gift he had was activated by his own will—until the Portentist gift. He had few opportunities to study its pull, and each time it activated it felt a little bit different. It always heightened his senses, true, but it was moments like these, sitting in his room alone with the sensation, that helped him to understand what was happening. This pull was one of importance, and it drew him to the bottom of the well where the bones of his people were lying.

Though, truly understanding the pull was almost unnecessary since he found that instincts, mingled with the speed that was so natural to the caldereth, caused his body to act in response to the gift's leadings. Mastering the Portentist gift would be a feat unlike any of his other gifts, and he envied Osric's skill with it.

He found that he could almost feel the direction of the pull, like the way his young son used to tug at his clothing to get his attention. It was subtle, and he still felt as if he was imagining it more often than not, but he was learning to give into the sensation and allow it to guide him. He knew he shouldn't resist the sensation, but he was used to being in complete control of his abilities. This new gift was intuitive, though, and he felt his body wanting to lean or push away from the direction of the prompt. Sometimes it was mesmerizing, and other times it was a warning, but each time it accompanied either a pull or a push. When the gift activated, it was very briefly disorienting, like something was overwhelming his senses. He felt his vision and hearing sharpen, his muscles tense, and the hairs along the back of his neck and arms stand on end.

He knew the reason behind this pull from the depths of the well. It was nearly time for the most important event in recent years. Others may have pointed to the attack of Stanton or the defeat of the Kallegian as the most important event of their time, but the truth was that they were all distractions or events that had to happen in order for this day to occur. Raising a nearly extinct species from the dead was the culmination of it all, and nothing could stop it from happening.

Dredek stood up from the chair and willed his mind to acknowledge and then dismiss the pull of the Portentist gift. He forced his focus to return to his chambers. It was time to begin.

He opened the wooden door and stepped out into the hall, turning right and quickening his step. He could no longer completely resist the urge to press on with speed. For the first time that day, he let his excitement grow, though not to the extreme that it threatened to achieve. Nevertheless, when he ducked through the archway into the well, the full force of his anticipation hit him—he would see his mate today.

Looking around the expansive distance in front of him, he wondered which set of bones was hers. A tear slid down his cheek, and he let it fall untouched. Then, he stepped carefully down the ramp, avoiding any contact with the carefully laid-out bones. As he passed, he looked into the skulls of each skeleton face, empty and void of life. They were shells of former beings, but soon he would see them made whole.

Upon reaching the bottom of the well, Dredek felt the same surge in energy he had felt on all previous visits. Being surrounded by so much power and having it surge through him, showering the entire space in a visual spectacle, was empowering. It was even more empowering to realize that only those with the Wand-Maker gift could witness the spectacle of magic that cascaded in vibrant colors. Vivid wisps of every color shot from the floor beneath him. Below the floor, torrents of the ever-changing, flowing power surged and pulsed.

Dredek raised his wand and began to weave new flesh back onto the bones. It was a familiar spell based on the same principles ingrained in every young mind that learned to heal wounds. Although his was a bit more involved, bringing mass quantities of flesh, muscle, tendons, blood, and organs back to carefully displayed bones. Luckily, the bones still held enough of their previous lives to ensure the flesh formed as it had been the day they died. In a matter of moments, he brought every physical aspect of life back to the multitude, but it was the thread of life that would test his mettle.

He could feel the magic building in intensity below his feet. He cast his gaze down, watching the twisting mass of strands that flowed up in a swirling column from below and pooled in the massive bowl on the floor of the tower. He hoped his calculations were correct, but based on the pull of the Portentist gift, he was sure that his timing was perfect. He suspected if he were wrong, the gift would be triggering a warning. Dredek anticipated the moment that he would be supplied with sufficient power to enact his spell and fill his people—his wife—with life.

When the moment was right, he would have only the shortest time to fulfill his plans and give life to the caldereth bodies. A surge of power would lend him the magic that he needed, but it would not decrease the difficulty of forging life strands for his people. Still, everything was going as planned, and Dredek knew he would be successful. Joy bubbled to the surface of Dredek's mind as the impending reunion grew ever closer.

He found that being reunited with the caldereth wasn't the only thing raising his spirits. He had been too long at killing, and although it was necessary, killing had never been a task that he longed to perform. Now, his days of ending life were over. Decades of murdering innocents that stood in his way were at an end. He laughed and let the tears stream down his face as a weight lifted from his chest. In his mind, he was finally able to take back some of the death he had caused, and it felt good.

Osric's Wand

Chapter 28
Wielding the Wells

Osric stepped toward the swirling pool of strands that the Aranthians had labored tirelessly to create. Bridgett had used the seven symbols repeatedly to create a larger opening in the stone above them, allowing the light of day to pour in and illuminate the cylindrical space. The golden sunlight was a welcome reprieve from the dark of the night and the insufficient glow from their wands, and they continued their work until nearly mid'day. But now, with the work finished, Osric and his three companions basked in the creation of a true wonder.

The chamber still looked very much the same as it had before they started. Earthy tan and light-brown stone surrounded them from the walls, and the crumbling dome of the ruins could be seen through the gaping hole in the ceiling. Daylight spilled down the stairs and across the floor, brightening the area and allowing Osric to clearly see the bowl in the center of the circular room.

Bridgett had described the Well of Strands in detail over the long night. From the description they knew that this was a very similar design. The sloped stairs led up and out of the hollow to the right, but there was one difference that Osric thought he could use to his advantage when the time came. Though the Well of Strands was massive in comparison, once the strands reached the top of the bowl they erupted into the air and cascaded in a bright display, climbing the walls and stairs and spreading out over the large space. Here, in the much smaller tower, the strands were so dense as they swelled up from the bowl and poured down from the walls that they pooled in the room and remained concentrated and collected.

The only significant differences between the appearance of the room before their alterations and now were the several veins of quartz, granite, marble, and limestone that jutted from the outer wall below the stairs and from all sides. The strands that flowed along these dense veins of rock poured into the well like vibrantly colored waterfalls of light and now filled most of the room to the fifth stair. In the center of the room, the wide bowl of stone still held the densest concentration of strands, as if the concave surface were designed to keep the strands contained. There, the mass of strands swirled and entwined so tightly that it was impossible to discern individual strands.

As the pool deepened, the mass of strands in the bowl swirled faster. Soon, Osric could see a whirlpool of strands forming as Archana attempted to regulate the influx of magic in the location. Osric held his breath, fearing that the stone floor may crumble beneath them to allow the strands an exit, but it wasn't long before the system balanced out. Rather than striving to contain the strands, the stone of the central bowl softened as Osric looked on with amazement and relief. The softer stone allowed the strands to pass through more easily, and it quickly reversed the slow flow of strands in the center of the room. Where magic had previously bubbled up into the bowl, now the strands slowly seeped out through the floor. For now, the strands were spilling into the room from the stone veins in the walls faster than it was leaving, but Osric knew he would need to use this incredible source of power soon if he was going to succeed in stopping Dredek from using the Well of Strands.

Osric stepped into the pooling magic. The moment he entered the flow of vividly colored strands, he could feel the entire night's fatigue drain away. The feeling reminded Osric of standing below a waterfall as the cool water washed over his skin. Not only was it a revitalizing sensation, but he also found that the flow that washed over his legs bordered on being visible to the naked eye.

"I think this may be a larger flow than the Well of Strands. It's hard to say, since it doesn't shower down on us like it did at the Well of Strands." Bridgett sat watching with awe.

"I…" Gus looked on, ears twitching and eyes wide.

"You've said that for the last span. Could you come up with something original?" Osric looked over at Gus, wagging his legs in the pool from where he sat on the stairs, with a smirk.

"I understand your lack of words, Gus." Aridis sat upon the steps looking down into the chamber. "Though I do not fully understand what you are seeing when you look upon this stone, I can feel the incredible influx of power. Whatever you have managed to do this night, Osric, you have truly altered the flow of magic from Archana. I am catching flashes of the paths of the future without even having to wet the stone, though it is almost too overwhelming to read."

Osric's Wand

"It's too bad you can't see this, Aridis. It's truly the most beautiful thing I have ever seen." Bridgett smiled widely as she cast her gaze around the room.

"I just can't get over it. That has to be one of the most remarkable things I have ever witnessed. You actually moved the soil below our feet to create a larger well." Gus looked up at his three companions, amazed.

"Actually, he moved the veins of stone that ran below the soil." Bridgett joined Osric at the center of the room. A soft white glow was visible around them where they stood. She leaned in and kissed him. "A far more impressive feat."

"I love the enthusiasm that all of you are showing." Osric took Bridgett's hand and turned toward Gus. "But all I did is direct the ones who could perform the task. Most of my labors were spent bringing the tired back to a well to recover from their efforts." He shrugged in an attempt to dismiss their elaborate praise. "Our Elementalists did more than their share of the work last night."

"You know, sometimes your humility can be truly annoying. I am not known for compliments, so when I hand them out frequently someone should take notice." Gus chuckled, then jumped down into the pool and took in a deep breath. The breath was more a reflex of his senses than a necessity. Once inside the flow of strands, Gus relaxed and regained his composure. He hadn't dove feet first into water, after all, but he had sat for so long gazing at the pool of swirling strands that his body had reacted as if it were liquid that flowed over his head as his paws hit the floor. "Even if you didn't do the work, I can think of no other mind that would have thought of such an absurd undertaking."

"Absurd?" Osric looked down at Gus with a hurt expression.

"Well, it was absurd, but I'm still impressed." Gus paused, and then he added. "Extremely impressed."

The sun was nearly directly overhead when Gus smiled with a quick nod of his head, then panic rose as all three looked to the northeast. Portent had flared dramatically from far away, and the strands that pooled around them flowed through their gifts and amplified the reach of their abilities. There was no doubt what had been the cause of their sudden awareness of important events so far away. Dredek was attempting to bring the caldereth back from the dead.

With a quick flick of the wrist, Osric had his wand out and Machai's image hovered above the tip. "Machai, it's time to attack Angmar. Gather the troops and go. He's already initiated the spell to bring the caldereth back!"

"There be several hundred properly trained in the traveling spell. All me dwarves and every able bodied Aranthian'll be there faster than ye can be drawing yer wand."

"Good. Move fast. You try to stop him from inside and I'll try to stop him from here."

* * *

Machai lowered his wand and looked out at the field. Since the Aranthian base wasn't yet large enough to train nearly a thousand dwarves effectively, they had been training wherever they could find an opening in the forest outside of Stanton. Looking at the swatch of forest that had been cleared for them to train in, he knew that he could mobilize the dwarves quickly.

"Gather ye wands, gather ye blades!" His voice echoed off of the surrounding trees and every face turned. "It be time to be stopping a crazy necromancer!"

The units of dwarves moved quickly and efficiently into place, joining the Aranthian troops that were also heading into battle in Angmar. A few wide-eyed youngsters still had fearful expressions as if they had no idea what to do, but they moved with their units and ended up in the proper position with little intervention from their leaders.

A thin man in a blue robe moved through the ranks blowing a pinch of a tan powder in the faces of the troops. The alchemists had finally stabilized the formula for the stuff, promising Osric and the others that the powder would stave off the exhaustion brought on by the excessive use of magic. It was no Enduro gift, but it would allow a man to travel as far as Angmar by spoken spell, with four or five others in tow, and still be in good enough shape to fight all day. For those less experienced fighters, it would let them utilize their innate abilities, their wands, and their blades all at once throughout the battle without the typical nausea, headache, or blackouts associated with strand-fatigue. They had been testing this blend for the past month, and the only side effect reported was severely aching muscles after it wore off for those who used far more magic than they normally could have tolerated. The effects lasted anywhere from two to four days depending on the person, and the muscle aches lasted up to a week. Machai just hoped that they wouldn't end up in a long engagement with Dredek's army, or his men would be in trouble when the powder wore off and they still had to fight. Whatever Osric was doing, he needed to do it fast and well. Machai waved the young blue-robed alchemist past, knowing the Enduro ability would give him the same benefits without the side effect.

Once everyone had been dosed, Machai instructed those who had been trained in the traveling spell to hold the location image firmly in mind and to link hands with the men they had been assigned to transport. Each man knew his place in the sequence, timing the spell so that the arrival location was never dangerously full. The execution of the plan went off perfectly, and soon over one thousand dwarves and well-armed Aranthians were standing on the hot sand near the capital city of the Irua Realm.

The army had chosen the location because it was close, but not so close that they would likely be in sight of any enemy troops when they arrived. Machai sent scouts out immediately to determine the positions of Dredek's men, but a strong wind was blowing sand horizontally across the desert. Gritty sand stung Machai's skin, forcing him to squeeze his eyes shut. He pulled a thin piece of fabric across his face, but it was still difficult for him to see his own army; he feared that his scouts wouldn't fare much better at seeing the enemy guards over such a great distance.

He was right. The scouts came back with little to report, for the most part. One of the recently recruited Aranthians had more to say, however. He was an Air Elementalist, so he could keep the wind and sand from touching him. He had gone further than the other scouts, and he reported that the entrances were heavily guarded but there were few troops outside of the protective shelter of the doorways. Machai thanked him, and he spent a few moments trying to decide if it would be better to use the storm as cover and attack while the army was under shelter, or if they should wait until the storm settled so that his men could see. He decided it was likely that Dredek's men were packed into the tunnels just inside the entrances, and there wouldn't be a better time to catch them unaware. He worried that it would be dangerous to attack during the sandstorm, but he also knew that Osric needed him to get to Dredek and the Well of Strands as swiftly as possible; they just couldn't wait for the winds to calm.

"We be marching on foot or we be dying!" Machai shouted to his men. "Grab what courage ye may. There be no traveling today! Their gates be guarded by many men, but none be matching the spirit of the Aranthians, and none be matching the cave experience and might of me dwarven kin!" As the words flew from his mouth, he hefted his axe above his head and motioned for all to follow as he turned in the direction of the entrance and sprinted on short legs.

Above the whipping winds and abrasive sand on his face, Machai could hear the sound of more than a thousand warriors at his back. Their march, muffled by the coarse sand below, still carried along with their battle cry. Blade clanged against blade as his brethren pounded one sword against another to instill fear in their enemy. The uproar sent chills of excitement through Machai as he led the way.

He crested the first dune and sand assaulted him with even greater vigor, but the thrill of battle—either death or survival—urged him to continue at a quickened pace. His feet continued to kick through the softened upper layer of sand until he could finally make out the shape of the entrance through the storm. At least a dozen soldiers stood around it with a mixture of fear and fortitude in their eyes.

By the time he had gained his vantage on the entrance, many of the Aranthians had overcome his position and had engaged the enemy with surprising deftness. They wielded both wand and blade with such skill that many of the enemy faltered, watching with mouths agape.

Machai turned, sensing the pause, and addressed his kin. "Don't be letting 'em steal all the glory!" He turned back and, with a shout, charged headlong into the fray.

Humans had nearly always been easy opponents in battle. Machai had watched them battle dwarves on many occasions. Predictably, they would swing for the head of any dwarven opponent, attempting to end the fight at its start. Humans had rarely respected his kind for their prowess and had rarely fought them as equals, but rather they had seen dwarves as inferior due to their stature. Whether it was luck or some kind of prophetic intervention was a question one never asked on the battlefield, but Machai's first foe was one who hadn't learned from the folly of others. Machai easily ducked under the attempted beheading.

With a quick spin and heft of his axe, Machai removed the legs from below the fool. The man let out a scream as Machai turned to face whatever was before him. Before he could swing his axe for a killing blow, two men stepped forward with the tips of their swords held low, but they were wary and careful in their approach.

Machai smiled, as these two respected him for both his stature and his skill. They wore worried expressions as their eyes followed him. Holding their swords low would keep him from rushing in like he had with the last soldier, but he knew more tricks than just dodging a fool's sword strike.

He held his axe as if he were going to smack a rock across a field and whispered the traveling spell under his breath. Machai appeared between the two men, and he could see the shocked looks on their faces as their guts spilled out with one well-timed sweep of the axe.

He had dispatched three of Dredek's men, and as he turned he could see dwarves rushing into the entrance just a few strides away, with several of Dredek's men and one of his brothers lying dead in their wake. He allowed himself a moment's regret for the dwarf who had fallen a short distance away, but then he followed the line of soldiers into the vast empty dark that lay ahead.

The main corridor led down at a slow slope but continued its descent for a great distance. As they proceeded down the tunnel, their eyes adjusted quickly to the lack of sunlight, and dim globes of light bloomed brighter along the wall as more men approached. The stone floor and walls were smooth, forcing the Aranthians into combat in the tight, unfamiliar quarters. After seeing the efficiency with which Osric's men fought, the FireFalls dwarves took up a deep, rumbling chant. "Aranthians, Aranthians, Aranthians." Machai smiled through his blood-splattered beard, cheering as his men embraced their new position among Osric's ranks. Most of the dwarves from other clans joined in, and the chant grew louder. The sound echoed from the narrow walls of the passage and became a thunderous roar that preceded them down the tunnel. By the time they reached the bottom, where the tunnel widened out and joined other passageways in a large,

The Weaving of Wells

high-ceilinged chamber, Dredek's soldiers were struggling to maintain their positions as the wave of intruders crashed into them.

Although their training together had been incredibly brief, the discipline of both groups allowed the Aranthians and the dwarves to fight together more effectively than Machai could have hoped. Pendres led the Aranthian troops with firm efficiency, calling out single syllables that translated into elaborate orders which could be yelled back through the ranks without interfering with a fighter's focus. The dwarves had picked up the code quickly, and all of the units moved together to keep the enemy contained as they pressed firmly into the depths of Angmar. Machai stayed close to Pendres, awed by the man of myth who fought as well in life as he did in stories.

Pendres moved like a machine, his face clear of all emotion and his grip perfect on his sword and wand. His blade carved a smooth arc through the air, only making contact often and long enough to immobilize his target. He never allowed the sword to get caught up in the armor of the enemy. He used small spells from his wand to clear his path—a blast of air here, a tangle of roots from the ground there—and he kept himself shielded to help deflect the few stray blows that made it past his own blade. Many times Machai thought Pendres would be struck down, but the limber old man moved or blocked attacks that Machai thought it was impossible for him to even see coming. The worst he suffered was a few shallow cuts that he didn't bother deflecting.

Meanwhile, Machai was just as enveloped in the battle off to Pendres's right. He wielded his axe with deadly efficiency, surprising the enemy with his deftness at fending off the blows of much longer blades from much taller foes. Machai used his stature to his advantage when he could, moving inside the enemy's defenses, and he used his wand when he couldn't to even the match.

Many of Dredek's soldiers were also dual wielding, attacking or defending with a wand while battling with swords. However, they had only been practicing for the short time since they had last battled the Aranthians, and Machai had been training in the technique for his entire life—all of the dwarves had. The floundering humans quickly realized how much harder it was to utilize the skill in a chaotic battle with experienced troops than it had been in training, and many of them dropped their wands or took fatal strikes from swift blades before they could get a spell off. Still, they were skilled with their swords, and the battle was far from decisive in the early moments of engagement in the open chamber.

The Aranthians and dwarves were outnumbered, and even as they cut through the ranks of Dredek's men before them, two more were waiting in the tunnels to the sides of the room to replace each one that fell. Pendres was hard at work trying to determine the best strategy to get the upper hand, and his mind raced as he considered how many men Dredek could have in the extensive network of tunnels and rooms beneath the desert floor. They needed to get to the Well of Strands as swiftly as possible, and then they could only hope that Osric's plan would work. None of their men, including the old war hero, would be a match for Dredek if Osric couldn't stop him from afar. Then, Pendres and Machai noticed their opening at the same time, and the two communicated with a quick nod to each other as they started calling out orders to shift their troops.

A small group of Aranthians, the men and women who had remained in Angmar to aid the irua after the last battle there, had managed to fight their way up one of the tunnels to join their comrades in the main chamber. Having seen them arrive, Pendres and Machai shifted the drive of the battle toward that tunnel. It took several moments, but a unit of dwarves and Aranthians led by Ergon from Stanton broke through the last bunch of Dredek's men who blocked the way, and suddenly Pendres and Machai were following the unit through the gap to meet their men.

"Well met! Be there any chance this tunnel be leading to the Well of Strands?" Machai asked the man leading the group who wore the dirty but still recognizable uniform of a Stanton Vigile.

"Not directly, but we should be able to come into the tunnel we need from both ends and clear it out. I will lead you there, but it would be best if we weren't worried about being followed."

"Go now. I will make sure you have the men you need and you aren't followed," Pendres said, heading back into the large chamber where the battle was still raging. He barked out several orders, guttural syllables that would sound only like grunts or war cries to the enemy, and he was pleased to see his men falling into place according to his calls. One unit pressed forward, pushing back the enemy troops

The Weaving of Wells

to widen the path to the tunnel. A second unit, still nearly intact with only a couple of losses, sifted quickly through the area, taking out all stray enemies that had been fighting behind the main line of combat. Pendres called out more orders. A line of troops funneled through the narrow opening created by the others, and Pendres waved them into the tunnel behind him. He fed just over one hundred men through the opening, and then he ordered the others to clear the immediate area and to press the attack harder. As the men melted away from the opening of the passage, Pendres stepped away from the arch and watched as the last of the men headed down the tunnel behind Machai. Pendres held his wand up before him and began a simple cooling spell. He widened the spell's target area to span the stone several paces around the archway. The spell was quite basic, the sort of thing a child could use to cool his soup so he didn't burn his tongue—but Pendres was no child.

Pendres watched closely as frost formed on the stone all around the opening. He continued cooling it until the air before him caused his breath to fog out in a white cloud when he released a controlled and focused exhalation. When it was done, cold enough that any flesh brushing against the stone would be burned and blistered instantly, Pendres swung his sword in a great arc and struck the top of the arch. A loud crack echoed throughout the chamber, startling men on both sides of the battle, followed by the crashing of large chunks of stone and the raining of crumbling rock. Pendres felt his head pounding from the extensive use of magic, but he pushed the pain down and ignored it. He looked at the space where the archway had been, and now there was only a wall of massive rocks, rubble, and sand. He still held his wand out before his body, and he took a deep breath before his final spell.

Rather than merely halting the cooling spell, Pendres channeled a great deal of magic into reversing the spell. The air in the huge chamber cooled rapidly, chilling the sweat on the skin of the fighters and sending a deep ache into their joints, but the air around Pendres grew so hot he had to shield his face with one arm. The many minerals in the stone liquefied as heat replaced cold, and the pile of rubble was sealed tightly. It wouldn't just be a matter of moving the chunks of stone aside; the blockage of the passage was nearly as solid and strong as the stone surrounding it, and there would be no worry of the enemy soldiers following Machai into the tunnels. Pendres turned and waded his way back into battle, ignoring the pounding of his head and the burning of his skin, and his men cheered him as he swung his sword into the next enemy.

* * *

Introductions were brief. The leader of the Aranthian group in the tunnels was named Elidin. He had been with the Aranthians since the beginning, and he had served under Osric as a Vigile before the attack on the palace in Stanton. Machai had trained him to dual wield, although he did not hold it against the dwarf at all that he didn't remember him.

"I'm a head-down, work-hard, stay-out-of-trouble kinda guy. It's served me well here in Angmar, and we have been able to get quite a few of the irua out to safety, not to mention the headaches we have caused Dredek's men when the opportunity presented itself. Although, we never want to risk too much, so mostly we spend our time making sure the irua we can find are fed, sheltered, and out of sight of the soldiers who patrol the tunnels. Most of them have gone to other irua cities, but we send the ones who want to keep fighting back to Stanton to gain strength and training. I never realized how peaceful the irua are as a race; I guess I only met the ones who leave because they aren't at home here."

"Thanks for yer commitment to be seeing this through to the end, Elidin. Ye be coming in just when we be needing ye." Machai followed him through the tunnels at a jog, reassured by the sound of one hundred men moving steadily along with them.

"We knew something was happening when all of the soldiers started mobilizing at once. They were all heading toward the main chamber at a run, fully armed and stinking of nervous sweat. We figured either the invasion had begun and the Aranthians were here or Dredek had done something horrible with his creepy magic and the tunnels were about to flood with fire, or poison, or worse. Either way, we wouldn't have been safe or helpful hiding out in secret rooms deep in the tunnels. We were glad to see it was you when we finally got that tunnel cleared."

The Weaving of Wells

Elidin turned a corner, and they startled a group of five men running toward them. Dredek's soldiers recovered quickly, but they hesitated when they saw how many people followed Elidin and Machai around the corner. The five heavily armed soldiers paused, raised their swords, then their eyes went wide and they spun around to run the direction they had come from. Likely, there were more men back that way, and Machai threw out his hand before they could get far. A wall of flames sprung up, blocking their escape, and they barely had time to spin around before the Aranthians cut them down. Machai waved his hand to quench the flames, and the column of troops continued down the tunnel with Elidin in the lead.

"Let's go find their reinforcements, shall we?" Elidin asked.

"Aye. Where be the tunnel we be needing for the well?"

"Just ahead, we will send half our force down a side passage. Juri here will lead them, as she knows that section of tunnels better than any of us. This tunnel will dead-end at the intersection of the passage we want, and she will bring the rest around to the other end. It's a main tunnel between the armory and the chamber we found you in, so it's likely to be full of Dredek's men headed up with fresh weapons to relieve the others. We will have to sandwich them in and clear it out in order to get to the only tunnel we know of that will lead where you want to go. Their troops are getting pretty good at fighting in these close quarters, so I doubt we could overtake them without making them fight on both fronts. Let's just hope we brought enough men and their ranks are thin."

"Aye, let's be hoping," Machai said.

* * *

Dredek watched as the last of the flesh grew on the caldereth. All of the months of experimenting on recently deceased animals had culminated in the picture-perfect forms that lay before him. Though he had been successful in reviving the dead once, with a deer in the forests of the Elven Realm, the upcoming spell to reattach gifts and life strands was the one thing he hadn't yet perfected.

He had, however, had decades of experience to tell him how to proceed and what would yield the results he sought. It was the lack of

Osric's Wand

power that had kept him from establishing the connections needed in all previous attempts.

His people lay naked on the bare stone floor inside The Well of Strands. Dredek looked down and could feel the surge in the flow that would bring him the power he needed. He had located his mate, Aeya, while her flesh was still growing. Now, he looked at her as tears began to fall. She was lifeless where she lay on the lower portion of ramp that led out of the well to his right, but soon she would be breathing again.

He couldn't help but stare at her where she lay. It wasn't the lack of life that kept him from tearing his eyes away; it was that this was the first time he had laid his eyes on her since gathering her bones. If he didn't know better, he would have sworn she was asleep.

Her long black hair splayed out softly against the stone below her head. Her bare, pale flesh looked damp in the light of the well. Dredek longed to reach out, take her hand, and whisper the words he had held for so long. He rejoiced at seeing her body whole again. Seeing her broken and covered in dirt and blood was a memory that he would be happy to part with. Soon he would have the chance to bid farewell to all of the bad things that the last hundreds of years had forced upon him. Whatever cost the vast use of magic and the unspeakable crimes he was forced to perform to bring about this day would demand of him, Dredek was prepared to shoulder the burden so long as Aeya and the caldereth would live again.

A chill ran up Dredek's spine as he prepared himself to channel the power necessary to revive the caldereth scattered throughout the Well of Strands. He stilled himself for the task and the fatigue that would come from it, even though he was so close to the source that surged around him.

Gooseflesh covered his body and his senses heightened. As his pupils constricted, he could feel portent pull him in the direction of the well's opening far above. Even through his limited experience with the gift, he knew something bad was coming. He could hear fighting coming from the halls outside the well. How had they known to attack now?

Dredek wished he had the ability to close the door to the well, but the irua girl was locked safely in her cell. He had no time to go and get her, to force her to lock them in and let him complete his task. It had come down to a race against the intruders, but as he looked down he knew they had come too late. The power of the well was increasing, ever so slightly, but it indicated that the time for his success was almost upon him. The surge in power that would allow him to bring back the caldereth was moments away. They could have him once he completed his task, but haste was a necessity now more than ever.

* * *

Osric stood thigh deep in a pool of magic, strands rushing around him like writhing snakes seeking an exit. The strands twisted and coiled around each other and around Osric's legs, climbing up every surface they came in contact with. The walls of the well were alive with brightly colored strands, and Osric felt the magic lending him strength and feeding his power. It was exhilarating, and a bit terrifying, as he wasn't sure he could control his abilities with so much source magic feeding them. Every part of his body was tingling, and he could feel his dozens of gifts all on the verge of activating due to the density of the strands around him. Rather than having to exert effort to use his abilities, it was as if he had to strain to keep them idle.

Still, some of his abilities were too well developed and too passive for him to restrain. Osric could feel every emotion of his three companions assaulting him, and he struggled to dampen the Empath ability so he could focus on his own thoughts and feelings. His Portentist ability was in full flare, heightening his senses and drawing his attention toward the Irua Realm and to the streams of strands flowing into the well, but Osric was so familiar with his birth ability that he was able to ignore its urgings once he acknowledged them. Heatless flames sprang up along his fingers even as water condensed and dripped from the ceiling, slipping through the intangible strands and splashing up from the floor. The stone beneath Osric's feet transmitted a mild vibration, and Osric put more effort into shutting down the Earth Elementalist ability until he needed it, fearing that if he couldn't keep it under control the whole structure might crumble around them. Bridgett's hair swirled around her face as air currents washed out from Osric's position in the center of the well, and he could still sense her emotions like they were his own: fear that he would be harmed, pride that he was trying to save so many lives, awe at his power and the incredible display of magic before her, overwhelming love and desire for him, and many others.

In addition to the distraction of Bridgett's intense feelings, Osric could also feel Gus and Aridis's emotions so strongly that it was as if he could read their thoughts. The prairie dog's excitement at seeing the well and watching as Osric's gifts fluctuated and pulsed with the power of the strands was palpable, and Osric wasn't surprised to see Gus's ears twitching so fast he might have taken flight if they were bigger. Aridis was also awed by what he was witnessing, but his anxiety was not for Osric's safety. The old Obcasior was worried what altering the terrain of Archana might do for magic use in the long run, as all magic required drawing on the strands that flow from the ground. Osric hadn't allowed himself to worry much about the eventual side effects of his plan, other than his constant attempt to do as little damage to Archana as possible while still accomplishing the feat of weaving the wells, and now he tried to keep Aridis's anxiety from feeding his own. Osric reasserted his focus on his gifts, striving to shut down the Empath ability, and he turned his attention outward to the overwhelmingly difficult task ahead.

From the strong urging of his Portentist ability, Osric knew he only had moments to use the power of the well to interrupt Dredek's spell at the Well of Strands. He had been formulating a plan for days, training and honing his various gifts in order to find a way to stop the caldereth wizard, but he had no idea if he would be able to pull it off. Bridgett and Gus had asked him a dozen times what he was planning, but he had deflected their questions for fear that they would try to stop him. What he was planning to do was risky at best, downright stupid at worst, and it would probably kill him. But he couldn't think of any other way.

He had actually come up with the idea before he orchestrated the reorganization of the flow of strands beneath Archana's surface, inspired by the way he had separated Pendres from his Aranthian hostage, but he had let them think he was still trying to think of the best plan of attack. He had told them he had a few spells in mind, but he would need to test them on a smaller scale. In reality, he only had one idea, and in a way the reforming of the stone veins had been the small-scale test. Now, he had to do something similar, but he had to do it much faster, and much more forcefully, and from a much greater distance. His hands were trembling and the flames flickered out as he finally gained control over his Elementalist abilities.

Osric had been working hard to master the use of the Stone-Sight and Earth Elementalist abilities. He downplayed his role in the reconstruction project because he didn't want Bridgett and Gus fretting over the amount of magic he had been using over the past few days. Really, he had done a great deal of the work himself trying to perfect his aim and his control of the gifts. Though the Enduro ability kept him from fatiguing quickly, and his vast amount of abilities made each use of magic tax him less than it would a normal man, he was still feeling the toll of everything he had done recently. His head pounded slightly, his stomach wouldn't settle, and he couldn't quite get his hands to stop shaking. Osric brushed his palms against his pants to dry the sweat and still the tremble, and then he cast out his gaze with the Stone-Sight in the direction of Angmar.

Gus and Bridgett both gasped softly as they watched the strands react to Osric's magical intent. Neither had ever seen anything like it, and Gus had been studying strands for his entire long life. They saw Osric's eyes narrow and his brow furrow, but his expression was unreadable.

Osric had been able to peer much further into the stone than any of the most skilled Stone-Sights in the world due to his multitude of gifts and their associated power linked to his life strand. Still, he had been terrified that he would not be able to amplify that power enough, even with the altered well, to be able to see as far as he must. As he pushed his sight further—across the span of water where the Darib Sea spilled out between the Irua and Elven Realms in treacherous currents, under the humid swamps near Catrain, and even further under the burning sands of the desert surrounding Angmar—Osric felt the strands from the pool surge toward him in response to his demand for more magic.

The strands flowed into him, absorbed into his body through his skin and flowing through the various gifts that riddled his anatomy, an endless supply of magic to feed his abilities. The rush of adrenaline that coursed through him in response to the influx of magic was incredible, and Osric had to consciously slow his breathing and his heart rate to keep himself from overheating and passing out. His mind felt both euphoric from the experience and strained from the demand as he tried to compartmentalize his thoughts to control the Stone-Sight gift while reining in all of the others. He already felt that he was testing the limits of his body's tolerance to such intense magic, and he was only beginning his task. He still had a great deal more to demand of himself, of his gifts, and of his magic source. He hoped that the pool of strands would be sufficient and that he would be able to keep his body intact for long enough to accomplish his goal.

Osric's vision swam through the stone beneath the surface of the Irua Realm, delving through sandstone and underground rivers, seeking the dense rock that he knew must feed the Well of Strands. Most of the terrain was loose sand, soft stone, and small stretches of hard rock. Nothing that was as large or as dense as what a flow of strands the size of the one in Angmar would need. Osric's heart beat faster as he began to worry that he would not be able to find the stone in time, but he kept looking anyway. In a moment of clarity, he realized that the reason the strands spray up inside the well as Bridgett had described was likely that the vein of rock was nearly vertical as it approached the well. He directed his vision deeper into the ground, seeking the stone that he still believed must be there.

Osric felt that time was rushing by him faster than the current of the strands surrounding him. He knew that he must hurry, and the pressure of Dredek's impending spell was distracting him from calmly searching for the vein of strand-carrying stone. He took the briefest moment to assess his body, consciously slowing his breathing and heart rate until he was able to regain control and block out the noise of his mind that kept telling him he was taking too long. Osric refocused his attention on the Stone-Sight ability and continued seeking his target. Finally, after what seemed like far too long but had actually only taken the span of a dozen breaths, Osric caught sight of a vertical column of incredibly dense stone. The vein was so wide and so compacted that it didn't resemble any natural stone Osric had seen under the surface of Archana. The wizards who had created the Well of Strands must have altered the stone vein that feeds it.

Osric gazed in awe at the immense flow of strands running up the column of dense stone. It had to be nearly as big around as the entire tower they were standing in. If he weren't aware of just how large the network of stone was that they had built by altering the course of the veins underground, Osric would have felt that his plan was hopeless.

The Weaving of Wells

He couldn't believe how much power the Well of Strands supplied, and he felt a wave of icy fear wash over him when he considered what Dredek could accomplish with such a source of magic. He had to remind himself that it was likely that they had networked three times that much power, and now he just had to hope that they had successfully molded the stone veins so that Osric could draw on it all at once. The pool of strands he was standing in was large, but it was only a portion of what was available if the network of strands stayed intact when he began drawing on its full potential of power.

As Osric prepared to initiate the Earth Elementalist ability, he once again felt the emotions of Aridis, Gus, and Bridgett pressing in on him. They were worried—very worried—and Osric couldn't help but glance back at them to assess why they were so concerned. Aridis was staring down at the stone beneath his own feet, watching what Osric could only assume was water tinged by the old man's own blood. The look on his face was a disturbing mix of shock and horror, but Osric had no way of knowing what Aridis was reading in the stones. Gus and Bridgett were both staring down toward Osric's feet, and he looked down to see that he had depleted nearly half of the pool of strands. He hadn't expected the extension of his Stone-Sight to require this much magic, but he didn't have time to wait for the stores to build back up. He could only hope the strain of his spell wouldn't cause the whole network to collapse.

Desperately, Osric lashed out with the Earth Elementalist gift, condensing the stone where it had softened in the center of the depression in the floor. Archana had altered its own terrain to maintain a safe concentration of strands in the enclosed space, but Osric needed to keep the system intact by making sure the pool did not empty completely before he initiated the final spell of his plan. He needed strands flowing in from every vein that they had anchored in the tower or he wouldn't be able to draw strands from that leg of the system. If he drained the pool completely, all would be lost.

Once again, strands were flowing upward from the center bowl in the floor, and the fountains of magic were still pouring strands into the structure from the various veins of rock along the wall. Soon it was clear that the level of strands in the pool was rising, but Osric could feel the tremor in the stone beneath his feet. He did not believe the structure would hold for long, and he was concerned that the stone would soften again and reverse the flow in the center. Osric hurried to complete his task, honing in on the column of stone under Angmar with his vision and preparing to activate the elemental gift. Just before he unleashed the ability, Osric caught sight of a surge of strands flowing steadily toward the Well of Strands. He had no idea what had caused it, but he knew he couldn't allow all of that magic to reach Dredek. He suspected the caldereth had somehow summoned it, and his Portentist ability confirmed that this was the moment of urgency that his gift had been warning him about.

The wave of strands was moving faster than Osric had first calculated, and he released his Earth Elementalist gift just as the surge of power was traveling up the column of stone to the well. Osric drew as much power as he could from Archana, feeling an incredible rush as strands flowed into him from all over the world. Each of the fountains of magic was supplying him with strands from spans of stone beneath the surface of Archana. Rather than the strands cascading down into the pool, they flowed directly to him in a long arch from each vein of stone. From Gus and Bridgett's perspectives, it must have looked like Osric was the source and the magic was radiating outward from his torso.

As the strands built up inside of Osric, threatening to tear his body apart, his muscles trembled. His breathing became rapid and strained, and his vision blurred. When he could no longer tolerate the pain, Osric gritted his teeth and cast out his hand, visualizing the complete destruction of the stone that carried the strands to the well. He released his restraining grip on the Earth Elementalist ability, and a concentrated beam of strands shot out from his hand. It took all of his focus and energy to maintain the beam's density. His teeth vibrated and his vision wavered, but he did not relinquish his control over his gift.

The ray of strands was so dense, much like the beam of light that erupted from Legati during that first fateful powerlock, that it bore a hole through the stone all the way to Angmar. The heat from the concentrated power melted sand as it passed, and the shallows boiled and burst forth with large plumes of steam near the shore of the sea. The closer it got to Angmar, and the further from Osric's position near Braya, the harder it was for him to maintain control over it. The beam widened, and tremors could be felt on the surface. Where there was little stone in its path, the sand above trembled and then sank, folding in on itself and sucking in anything on the surface with it. As the beam reached the column of stone, Osric spread his fingers wide and released his hold that bound the strands so closely together. The power burst outward, smashing through the column of dense stone just as the surge of strands was passing through.

There was an intense flare as the front wave of the surge rushed upward above the point where the column was severed. As the dense burst of strands shot upward, it narrowed and coiled around what looked like a central strand. Rather than slowing when the stone broke apart, the small surge gained speed as it climbed, as if it were being drawn upward by the initiation of a spell. Osric held his breath and waited, not knowing what effect his spell would have on Angmar, not knowing if he had acted in time to stop Dredek's spell.

* * *

Dredek gazed down into the Well of Strands, watching the swirling strands with hungry eyes. He could sense the massive surge of power moving closer, and he focused all of his attention and ability on the spell he would use at the exact moment that the surge arrived. He had spent the last two hundred years preparing for this day: cultivating his identity, gaining power, gathering his kin's remains, and seeking out the secrets of Archana. He knew how much power he had, and after all of his experimentation, he knew exactly how much he needed. The well was a wealth of power, a greater concentration of strands than he had ever hoped to find in one place on Archana, but it wasn't quite enough for what he needed. All of his planning, all of his carefully orchestrated lies and deceptions, all of the death and destruction he had dealt had led him to the well at this exact moment. Now he knew why, and he was sure that he was meant to succeed. The surge of power hurtling toward him from deep underground would be the tipping of the scales in his favor. It was enough, and he knew it would only last a brief moment.

Dredek had spent days trying to find a way to increase the well's power. Just the slightest increase in the amount of strands would be sufficient, but he could find no way to influence the flow of the strands. The only one of his abilities that he had tried that had any effect on the strand density had been the Earth Elementalist gift, but when he tried softening the stone to allow the strands to pass through more easily, it had actually decreased the amount of strands streaming into the well. Out of a great fear that he would compromise the well completely, Dredek had avoided using that gift again anywhere near the well.

Then, the Portentist ability had made him aware of the impending urgency of his preparations. In an attempt to determine the exact time that the gift was indicating his success, Dredek had studied the well carefully, and he noticed a gradual fluctuation in the amount of strands held in the bowl of the well. He posted three Wand-Makers in the well, ensuring that someone was watching it carefully at all times. Their orders were simple: watch the well and notate any changes in strand density. It had taken several days to identify a pattern, and then Dredek was able to create careful calculations of the opportune time to attempt his spell. The first day, the men recorded a slight decrease in the strands, and the second they reported that the strand density had increased a little. The next day, the levels dropped even further than the first, but climbed gradually until it was the highest Dredek had seen it. He studied the well himself at the times when the strand density was lowest and highest, and he discovered that the increase was exactly proportionate to the previous day's decrease.

Yesterday, the well had briefly fallen nearly three times as far as usual, and his realization that it would peak three times higher had made his decision for him—now was the time for his spell, and the surge he had predicted was nearly upon him.

Dredek took one last look at his beautiful wife's face, so pale and so still, and then he began the spell that would return her to him.

He held a wand in each hand, and he pushed all thoughts from his mind. His intent had to be unsullied by any image or idea apart from his spell. With the greatest of effort, Dredek used the wand in his left hand to establish a connection to each of the caldereth bodies that lay carefully arranged on the tower floor. He had successfully assembled the bones of each one, laid the foundation for flesh with a complicated concoction that had taken over one hundred years to perfect, and then watched as muscle, sinew, organs, and skin had grown over the skeletons. But their bodies were still empty husks devoid of life. Now, he must reconnect their bodies of flesh to Archana and establish the life strands that would truly bring back his people.

Dredek's arm trembled only faintly as he watched the last connection form between his wand and the caldereth bodies. The strands that stretched out from the tip of his wand to the head of each person were stable and vivid, and Dredek felt the first hint of fatigue seep into his mind and body as he held the spell perfectly steady while dividing his focus to initiate a second spell.

Dredek lifted the second wand and aimed it at his own chest. Without allowing his focus on the first spell to waver, Dredek delicately began manipulating his own life strand and its accompanying strands that coiled around the life strand with each new gift he introduced into his body. With extraordinary delicacy, like paring the color from a flower petal without damaging its veins, Dredek slowly separated a nearly microscopic length of his own life strand. Using the second wand, he painstakingly peeled a portion of his life away, while carefully slipping the piece of strand from the intricately winding supplementary strands. He had to be extremely careful, as one tiny slip could sever the strand completely and kill him.

Over the years, he had collected nearly a dozen gifts from other men, and while he didn't relish having to kill them, their sacrifices were worth the weight he felt on his conscience. By grafting the gifts into his own body, he had added to the breadth of his life strand. But the strands were still separate, still individually linked to the functions of his body, rather than actually expanding the single strand that anchored him and his power to Archana. They were tightly wound together, but he was able to distinguish the boundaries of each strand with careful observation. Removing the sliver of his original life strand from the center of the coiled strands was much harder, and sweat beaded heavily on his brow as he focused on his task. He hoped that he had begun the cut low enough that if he were to make a mistake and totally cut the portion of strand from his body, it would not cause too much damage.

In truth, he had no idea how much damage it would cause, and he kept his hand perfectly stable and controlled until he had separated a great enough length of the strand for it to reach the pool of Archana's strands in the bowl of the stone floor. Once his life strand had made contact with the main pool of magic, Dredek's hand trembled fiercely at the pain coursing through his body. First he felt relief at the success of this first step in his spell, but once the intensity of the moment passed, his body was able to process the stimulus from within. The pain hit him like icy water pouring through his chest. It was sharp and stabbing where he had begun the cut, and it spread quickly like fire downward through his body along the path of the life strand. Had the pain been isolated to the core of his body, he would have been able to keep his hand still, but it radiated outward like boiling tar through his limbs and all the way out to his fingers. He could no longer feel the wands he was holding, and he had to glance at his fingers to reaffirm that he was still grasping both wands in his hands.

Dredek consciously slowed his breathing, gritting his teeth to keep from biting his own tongue, and after a few moments he was able to gain enough control over the pain to manipulate it. With all of the tweaking he had done over the years to his own body, finding a way to alter his appearance to look more human and grafting in new gifts, Dredek was no stranger to pain. He had gained mastery over the nerves in his body long ago, though there was no way he would be able to rid himself completely of the ache in his chest.

The feeling came back to his fingers slowly, and soon he could keep his hands steady and his grip on the wands firm. Luckily, he could still see that the connections he had formed to each of his people were intact. With the pain relatively managed, Dredek turned his focus from his breathing to the portion of his life strand he had allowed to mingle with the Well of Strands.

The next step in his spell was the most difficult one, and it was the portion that he had failed in each time he had attempted this spell in the past. Most of his test subjects had died when he first began trying to resurrect the dead. He had never been able to link a life strand back into the bodies, restoring the connection to Archana and fully granting life and magic into the subject. In his two most recent attempts, though, with the lion and the deer near Braya, he had come very close. The lion had been first, the day he had come up with the idea to use a life strand from another being. The member of his personal guard had not been sedated heavily enough, and he had twitched while Dredek was stripping the life strand within the man's chest. The strand was

The Weaving of Wells

severed completely as he linked it to the dead animal, and he was too drained from the attempt to try again with the lion's corpse.

The deer, however, had been a masterpiece. The deer was the proof that his spell would work. He had selected his donor life carefully—a young elven boy whose life strand was strong and bright within his body. He had drugged the boy heavily, then for assurance he had severed the boy's spinal cord so he couldn't move as Dredek split his life strand. By the time he made the connection, the deer was already growing cold, and seeing that creature's barrel chest rise for the first time after lying dead for most of the day had been a moment of clarity and euphoria for Dredek. Before the deer could scramble to its feet, Dredek severed the life strand fragment from the boy. It had taken all of the power that Dredek could summon to pull enough strands from Archana and connect the life strand to the deer, but it hadn't been enough. Shortly after it got its hooves beneath it, the life strand in the deer began to fade. Dredek knew it wouldn't last, as the fiber of the strand was too thin and too poorly linked to Archana to be sustained, but the deer had fled into the woods with his heart beating and his lungs full of the breath of life. Dredek knew it would die within days, but he also knew that with enough power he could successfully restore life to the dead. The boy would have lived, but he was weak and paralyzed, and Dredek had no intention of allowing the child's body to be discovered and initiating a war with the elves before he could find a way to raise his kin. The last thing he had wanted then was to give the elves a reason to help Osric and his band of rebels.

Now, he had all of the power he could possibly need from Archana in the Well of Strands. He also had complete control over the life strand that he was using. He wanted the caldereth people to have caldereth life coursing through their bodies, and he wanted to make sure there were no mistakes.

Dredek began drawing strands up from the bottom of the stone bowl, gathering a greater concentration of strands for him to pull from. He would need the surge of power that was rushing toward the well to complete the spell for so many people at once, but he needed the connection established first. When he was sure there was enough, Dredek began channeling the strands into his body through the life strand segment. He had discovered that the life strand could function much like a wand through focused experimentation, but the effect it had on the channeled strands was completely unexpected. Once he had discovered it, he realized he could raise all of his people at once with enough power, rather than one at a time.

As the strands coursed up through his body from the well, Dredek sent the power back out through the wand that held a connection to each of the caldereth bodies. His life strand not only channeled the strands; it altered them. Dredek didn't understand it, really, but he didn't question it either. Perhaps it was because both types of strands were so closely linked to Archana. Maybe it was because the life strand had to have come from the source of all strands, and so all strands from Archana sought to be like the life strand. It didn't really matter, because Dredek was going to use the mysterious phenomena to resurrect his family, regardless of its explanation. He didn't need to know how it worked.

As the millions of individual strands passed through Dredek's life strand, they took on characteristics of it. Moving through him and his wand, they coiled around the anchoring spell that connected Dredek to each of the bodies, the strands binding tightly to each other until they were as dense and vibrant as a life strand. Then, as they passed into each of the corpses, new life strands began to form where the original ones had been severed. Dredek stood perfectly still, inundated by the strength of the strands flowing through him, staring at Aeya's body. His eyes were glued to hers, waiting to see the first spark of life enter her pale orbs.

Though, even if the emotions coursing through him hadn't rooted him in place, he could not have moved had he tried to. It felt as though every cell in his body was slowly burning, and he feared he may be torn apart by the magic he was struggling to control. His shoulders ached worse than he could ever remember experiencing. His eyes were dry and stinging, as if his body temperature were significantly higher than was safe. His skin was hot and dry, cracking in places so badly that blood began dripping from his fingers and soaking into his robes. He wasn't sure how much longer he could maintain the spell, but the thought of Aeya once again breathing air kept him holding on, kept his hands held aloft and outstretched from his body, kept the strands flowing through him.

Just when Dredek thought he was going to fail, when he was sure he could not continue for another breath, he sensed the oncoming

The Weaving of Wells

surge of power nearing the access of the Well of Strands, and he knew he was almost done. Once that vast rush of strands passed through him and into his kin, their hearts would beat and their lungs would breathe and Dredek would hold Aeya again. He held on a little longer. The life strands were nearly whole, and Dredek could taste his impending success.

It began with a flicker, the twitch of an eyelid, the hesitant and gentle rising of her chest, and Dredek watched every movement with hungry eyes. Aeya took a breath, then another, and she opened her eyes. The other caldereth around her also breathed, blinked, and began to stir. The life strands were whole within their bodies, powering their hearts and nerves. The caldereth could feel for the first time in hundreds of years, and Dredek found himself wondering if the process he was putting them through was painful. He could no longer feel his own body, but he hoped that Aeya felt no pain as the blood quickened through her veins.

Dredek could not feel it, but he saw the wand tremble in his grasp as his numb fingers failed to sustain his grip. He could not drop the wand and sever the spell before the life strands of his people were able to form completely and establish a direct connection to Archana. As it was, they were too much like the deer. They were alive—more alive than the deer had been with so little power to form its life strand—but they were not yet like they once were. They would be left helpless, unable to protect themselves without access to Archana's magic. He couldn't fail them now that he was so close to saving them.

Dredek dragged another breath into his lungs, the air feeling so hot that he was sure it was searing his body as it passed into him. The surge was close.

Just as Dredek allowed himself to feel a small measure of relief that the blinding pain would soon be over and he would be reunited with his love, a bright light erupted beneath his feet. His eyes locked with Aeya's, and recognition lit her face as the blast of light and strands surged upward and engulfed him. He felt his link with Archana severed, and the stone around him trembled and began to crumble. His wands fell dark and lifeless from his hands.

Dredek crumpled to the ground.

* * *

Machai and Elidin headed deeper into the passages with sixty troops behind them, while Juri took the rest down the side tunnel to bring the attack in from behind Dredek's men. Machai wanted to run down the tunnel, rushing forward to defeat the enemy and come through for Osric, but Elidin held them back at a more reserved pace to allow Juri time to position the others.

Just as Elidin had said, the tunnel soon terminated and they paused to scout the intersecting passage. To the left, a small chamber opened up off of the tunnel and Machai saw large crates with unfamiliar markings on the sides. Noticing the curious look on Machai's face, Elidin explained, "It's iat, one of the few things the irua import in large quantities. With the proper additives and spells it makes a lightweight building material that won't crack in the dry air, and when cooked it becomes nearly edible. The longer it cooks, the more it expands and the worse it tastes, but it is filling and it's inexpensive."

"What's it made of?" Machai asked.

"It's a plant, grown on an island out east, I believe. If we live through this, I'll boil some up for you myself and you can try it."

Machai grinned and turned his attention to the tunnel where it led away from their position to the right. "How far be it before we be encountering Dredek's men?"

"They'll be just around that bend, up ahead. The tunnel to the armory isn't far from here, and we won't have much time to maintain a surprise attack once we get close to that curve in the tunnel. We will need to move fast. Juri should be nearly there now, so we should be getting to it," Elidin replied.

Machai gave the signal and led the group forward, indicating that they should be swift but silent. He felt more at ease with his axe and wand in hand within the tight stone tunnels than he had up in the exposed stretches of gritty sand thanks to a life in the dwarven tunnels. He was still glad he had such well-trained men at his back when he rounded the corner. A steady stream of well-armed men was pouring out of a tunnel up ahead, and the passage was thick with the Turgent's colors.

They heard no sounds of battle from the other end of the tunnel, and Machai hoped that Juri hadn't run into trouble along the way.

The Weaving of Wells

Hopefully, they wouldn't have to wait long before the other army was forced to face them on two fronts.

The passageway was fairly broad, as it served as a main thoroughfare to the armory and other important regions of the underground city. Machai called out commands in the guttural code they had been taught by Pendres, and his men tightened their organized ranks. They moved forward five wide. Machai was in the front row, centered between four other dwarves. Dredek's men responded quickly to the surprise attack and formed up into rows with weapons held ready.

Machai sent a wave of flames across the stone floor. The flames licked at the walls and washed toward the soldiers quickly. Someone with the same gift was able to still the fire, and it burned out before reaching any of Dredek's men, but it served as an excellent distraction as Machai and his men closed the distance down the tunnel to the soldiers. The two dwarves immediately beside Machai were tasked with maintaining shielding spells, providing the first layer of protection for the entire unit. As Machai and the dwarves on his far left and right in the first row hurled balls of fire and blasts of air toward the enemy forces, the row just behind them cast spells over Machai's head. Deeper in their ranks, several men armed with bows shot arrows into the midst of the clustered men. Machai continued pressing forward, keeping the Aranthians on the offensive and limiting the chance that his men would be forced back into a corner. Soon, they were in striking distance of the soldiers.

Machai did not hesitate to swing his axe, thereby initiating the close-quarters combat. Dredek's men were larger, and they wore heavy and restrictive armor, so they stood only three wide in the stone tunnel. The Aranthians' tight ranks served them well, providing them with a denser face and giving them the extra hands to establish and reinforce shields by spell. The armor also made it harder to find an opening in the fight, however, and it took Machai a moment to fell his first enemy. He kept his strokes conservative and controlled, seeking only to incapacitate the men rather than kill them. They were the Turgent's men, after all, and Dredek was no Turgent of the Human Realm. Once the usurper was taken down, Machai did not want any more blood on his hands than was necessary. These men were loyal to Dredek only because they could not see that he was an imposter to the title. Once Dredek was gone, these soldiers would serve the new Turgent just as diligently as they now served the caldereth wizard.

Machai's axe slipped through the first man's defenses, severing a tendon at the shoulder and leaving the man's sword-wielding arm useless. The second man he easily knocked unconscious with the flat of the blade. The soldier's helmet was still reverberating from the impact like a deeply toned bell when Machai had to block a stroke from a long sword. Unfortunately, the battle plan of the Turgent's men was well organized and ruthless. Machai found himself up against highly skilled foes, and it was nearly impossible to navigate through the battle without inflicting fatal wounds. When he realized he could not fight them and protect them at the same time, Machai shifted his goal to killing them swiftly rather than leaving them to bleed out slowly on the stone floor of the corridor.

Machai swung his axe with deadly efficiency while his wand was busy sending small but effective spells into the soldiers' ranks. Dredek's men seemed innumerable, but they were slow in their heavy armor. Machai's men, on the other hand, were densely packed across the passageway and well shielded with magic. So, they were armored lightly and much more mobile. The Aranthians and dwarves moved together as a cohesive unit, blocking and casting spells for each other. They formed an unstoppable wedge in the corridor, pushing Dredek's men back, though it took everything they had to keep the enemy from picking them off and destroying their advantage.

Luckily, it wasn't long into the battle before Machai and his men heard familiar battle cries echoing toward them down the tunnel. Dredek's men were distracted by the addition of another threat from the other end of the corridor, and their lack of focus turned the fight further in Machai's favor. The Turgent's troops fell before the dwarven blades, and with each moment, the Aranthians moved closer to the entrance of the Well of Strands.

Machai heard a low rumbling growl, like the distant echo of thunder through the mountains around FireFalls. The sound was terrifying even in its familiarity, for Machai knew the devastation that could come from a force capable of producing such sound, but he had no idea what would be the source under the deep tunnels of Angmar. Small pieces of stone rained down onto the floor in front of his feet, and Machai scrambled backward from instinct. He glanced up at the ceiling of the tunnel just as the rock split open and a large chunk of stone landed where he had just been standing. Troops from both sides of the battle scattered, the current fight forgotten for the moment as Aranthians and Dredek's men retreated side by side from the new threat.

A terrifying creature squeezed its bulk through the hole in the ceiling and dropped down to the stone floor. It was the size of a bull, but it squatted on short hind legs and braced its weight on long, thick arms more like a gorilla. The arms ended in huge claws, and the small head held eyes set wide above an elongated snout. Machai glared in surprise at the brown, wrinkled skin encasing rigid muscles and the row of sharp teeth snarling at him from only a few strides away. He had never seen a creature like it, but he had heard legends of beasts that burrow through stone with sharp claws. Some tales said the things were attracted to the sounds of battle, but the older stories—the stories whispered by ancient wizards when the fires were dying low and the ice was settling over the mountains—claimed they were drawn by vast outpourings of magic. Machai suspected the latter was the truth, and therefore he feared the beast that blocked the passage before him. If those legends were the true ones, then these creatures would be far more dangerous than the best soldiers that the Human Realm could pit against his dwarves. If this was a stone slayer of legend, then there were more of the ravenous creatures on the way to Angmar; legend said they traveled in packs.

"Do not be using magic!" Machai called out to his troops, but it was too late. A fireball was hurtling through the air past Machai's head as he yelled, and the beast leaned back on its hind legs and took the blast fully in the chest. Most creatures would have crumpled and blistered into a mass of charred flesh from such an onslaught of magical fire, but the stone-tunneling monster merely shook its snout rapidly and snarled. The fire dripped harmlessly to the stone floor, sloughing off of the creature's hide and fading away without a trace of smoke.

The beast raked its claws across the floor, leaving four long indentations on either side of its body in the otherwise smooth, well-worn stone of the passage. It snarled again and then hurled its mass toward the crowd of mingled troops.

Osric's Wand

"No magic! Brawn and sharp blades, me brothers!" Machai hefted his axe and shouted as he shifted his weight. His blade caught the hind leg of the beast as it rushed past him, rending its flesh and spilling thick blood across the stone. The creature never twitched from the wound, as if it hadn't even noticed the bite of the blade in its leg, but Machai was reassured to see that his weapon could inflict an injury in the stone-like skin of the beast.

His optimism faded in the blink of an eye as he watched a dwarf and two human soldiers get ripped apart by the creature's fierce claws as it encountered the bulk of the crowd. Soldiers screamed and scattered on the edge of the crowd, and Machai muttered insults about cowardice as he rushed toward the monster with his axe gripped firmly in both hands. Three Aranthians were holding the thing at bay with their swords, and Machai launched himself up onto its back while its focus was on the other men. He landed on its spine in a crouch, but the beast twisted its torso viciously in response to the threat. Machai nearly tumbled to the ground, but he swung his blade down and caught the monster's neck with his axe. Keeping a firm grip on the handle, Machai was able to pull himself up onto its back as he pulled the weapon free. With another solid swing of the axe, Machai took its head off, and his men yelled out a mix of cheer and battle cry.

As Machai slid off the heap of muscle and bone, he grimaced to see two more of the creatures drop out of the tunnel's ceiling. He adjusted his grip on his axe and called out encouragement to his men.

"Our blades be more vicious than be their bite. Be sinking in yer teeth, brothers."

His troops had gathered themselves into a tight unit, forming a solid wall of steel across the tunnel. The Aranthian archers took their places behind the dwarves, arrows nocked and ready to launch. Dredek's men had separated themselves from the Aranthians, reforming further up the tunnel and eyeing both the rock monsters and Machai's men with violent intent. Machai called out an articulate grunt, ordering a few men to watch the soldiers and prevent an ambush. It seemed the cowards were content to let Machai and his men battle the sharp-clawed beasts, but Machai worried they would be fighting on two fronts if the soldiers decided to take advantage of the situation. He kept his attention on the monsters, counting on his men to give adequate warning from behind if necessary.

The Weaving of Wells

"Fire!"

The archers let loose the arrows, but the majority of the projectiles glanced off the thick, wrinkled hides like toys. A few found their mark, and the enraged creatures sprinted toward them with shafts bristling from their faces and torsos. Machai resisted the temptation to launch fireballs, knowing they would only absorb the magic and feed their rage. He fell into line with his comrades and readied himself for the battle.

The creatures came on fast, claws slashing and teeth gnashing, tearing into the frontline. His men held out well, those in front defending themselves and each other with shields while the row behind stabbed and slashed with blades. It wasn't a perfect fight, and several of his men took wounds that would require rapid, intricate healing to save their lives, but the beasts fell with agonizing roars.

Just as the animals cried out in death, Machai heard the warning cries of his men indicating an attack from Dredek's soldiers. The unit responded quickly, resuming the fight with the elite human troops. Wands were drawn, and Machai allowed the magic to rush to his fingertips. He launched three fireballs in quick succession, clearing the heads of the dwarves and slipping past the other Aranthians. Fire blasted the frontline of the soldiers, enveloping half a dozen men in flames.

Machai ordered the charge, and he rushed headlong with his men into the fray. He swung his axe methodically, no longer concerned for the lives he had to take to reach his destination. While the troops were loyal to the Human Realm, which Machai still saw as an ally, Dredek had established the Aranthians as enemies, and his soldiers wouldn't stop fighting to keep Machai from the Well of Strands. He cut through the troops swiftly, pushing toward the end of the tunnel and the promise of fulfilling his mission.

Finally, Machai struck out with his blade and there were no more soldiers to fell. He glanced around for the doorway, and he barely heard his men cheering behind him to celebrate their success. Machai rushed down the tunnel, past all of the bodies and his own men, until he found the entrance that he needed.

The archway loomed before him, a small break in the smooth stone wall of the tunnels. He hurried to it, ducking slightly to slip through the opening, and he slid to a stop on the platform inside. Looking

Osric's Wand

around quickly, he noticed a wide ramp leading down into the darkness off to his left. Before he could descend, he needed to know what he was rushing into. Machai moved slowly and quietly to the edge of the stone ledge on his hands and knees and peered down into the well. His breath caught in his throat at what he saw.

Dredek stood in the center of the well. Scores of bodies were strewn about on the stone floor around him, and Dredek held a wand in each hand. Machai was surprised to see that the bodies were whole, not the bones and decaying flesh he had feared he would see, and if he didn't know better he would have thought the caldereth were merely sleeping. Dredek began to tremble, but he kept his arms aloft with the wands gripped tightly in his hands. Sweat gleaned on his pale skin, and Machai could only imagine how much magic he was channeling through his body while standing in the Well of Strands.

Machai pushed himself back from the edge and tore his gaze from the wizard. He hoped that whatever Osric had planned would happen soon, because the bodies that filled the well looked as if they could awake and rise up at any moment. Machai knew that if Osric failed, no one other than himself would be standing between Dredek and an army of caldereth. He gripped his axe in one hand and his wand in the other and headed for the ramp.

Machai stayed close to the wall, wanting to get as close to the bottom of the well before Dredek could have a chance to see him and lash out with his magic. He hoped that the wicked caldereth wizard would be too deeply engaged in the spell he was casting to notice a dwarf sneaking down the ramp toward him.

Before he had made it a third of the way down the ramp, Machai encountered the first of the caldereth bodies laid out on the stone. It seemed that the floor of the well had not been large enough to contain all of the caldereth corpses that Dredek had brought with him. Machai stepped around the head of the body, pressing his back against the smooth stone that encircled the well. His progress was slow, as he feared that disturbing any of the bodies was likely to draw Dredek's attention. He placed his feet carefully, stepping over or around each of the still, dead caldereth as he made his way deeper into the darkness. He could see nothing but shadows and the faint outlines of the bodies near the wall at the bottom of the well. Had he been able to get a clear view of a safe place to conceal himself, he could have just traveled by spell and waited for the opportune time to attack Dredek, but the only way to stay out of sight of the wizard was to stay far enough toward the wall that his height and the ramp concealed him from view.

Machai was two-thirds of the way down the ramp when he froze in midstep, his back pressed against the wall. He could see the top of Dredek's head if he leaned forward, and if he descended any further he would be exposed, but that was not what made him stop. The caldereth at his feet, a pale man with thinning hair and sunken cheeks, took a shuddering breath as Machai stepped around his feet. Machai stood rooted to the stone, scared to move or even to exhale, and the man took another labored breath. The other bodies above and below Machai on the ramp also began to breathe. Their muscles twitched beneath their glistening skin, their fingers moved against the cold stone, and their eyelids fluttered open. It was happening; Dredek was bringing the caldereth back to life, and Osric hadn't stopped him.

Machai stepped forward from the wall, risking discovery by Dredek, but he could not just stand on the ramp in the midst of an undead army and wait for them to notice him and call out. From the edge of the ramp, Machai could clearly see Dredek still standing in the well, but he saw nowhere that he could travel to that would put him close enough to strike at the wizard without Dredek seeing him coming. Some of the caldereth along the ramp and on the floor of the well were beginning to stir, trying to push their long-dead bodies up from the cold stone. Many of them clutched at their chests, groaning or grimacing in pain. Machai finally saw what he was looking for; a large wooden chest sat open in the shadowy recess where the wall met the underside of the original stairs that Dredek had covered with the ramp. Machai could not tell if the chest was empty, but he spoke the traveling spell out of desperation. "Eo ire itum."

Machai appeared inside of an empty chest that smelled like fresh-turned earth. As he peered up over the rim of the chest, he felt a deep rumble in the stone beneath them. The ground shook, knocking Machai down into the chest. He heard the sound of stone rending, a cracking boom so loud that it made his ears ring. Then, the stone stilled and all fell silent. When Machai pulled himself back up and looked out at the well, Dredek lay in a crumpled heap in the bowl at the center of the room. He saw a caldereth woman with long, black hair crawl across the floor to the wizard's body with tears spilling down her cheeks and a forlorn wail emitting from her lips.

The caldereth were rising from the floor all around the well, but Machai leapt from the chest brandishing his wand and axe. Dredek might have fallen, but he had succeeded in raising his people before he had collapsed. Machai needed to make sure the wizard was dead and keep the caldereth people from continuing his reign of terror against the irua.

Before Machai could cross the distance to Dredek's body, caldereth surrounded him. They were naked and unarmed, but they stood more than twice his height and they had a severe advantage in numbers. Machai cast shielding spells around himself, trying to stay alive for long enough to fight his way through to Dredek. He swung his axe in a wide arc, forcing several caldereth to fall back a step to avoid the blade. In response, three of the caldereth cast out their hands toward Machai, and the expressions of confusion and dismay on their faces told Machai that they were as surprised as he was when no magic abilities lashed out at him. He wasn't sure what the caldereth had tried to attack him with, but he was relieved to see that they were not capable of using their magic. When repeated attempts yielded no results, the cladereth who surrounded him began to look worried and hesitate in confronting him and his large axe.

Machai formed a ball of fire and sent it spinning slowly through the air in the direction of Dredek's body. Machai followed it closely, and the ring of caldereth shifted to allow the fire and Machai to pass. The woman was clutching at Dredek's robes, sobbing loudly against his chest. When Machai approached, she scrambled back in fear of the fierce dwarf with his weapons and fire. He reached down and placed two fingers against Dredek's neck, but he could find no pulse. The wizard was dead, and the caldereth were alive but somehow incomplete. Machai didn't know what had happened, but he knew that he must keep the caldereth contained until Osric arrived and the Aranthians could form a plan to handle the new situation.

Machai gripped Dredek's arm and whispered the traveling spell, appearing with the body on the platform at the top of the ramp. He would take Dredek's corpse to Osric, but first he must contain the caldereth. Machai moved to the edge of the ramp and looked down, smiling at the sight of over one hundred caldereth staring wide-eyed at

The Weaving of Wells

the center of the well, where he had just vanished from sight. Machai cast a spell over the bowl in the center of the floor. If the caldereth recovered their magic, he did not want them to have access to the amplified power of the well. Then, he laid a line of flames across the top of the ramp and sent them slowly spilling downward toward the bottom of the well. He heard the caldereth gasp when they saw the flames moving toward them, and soon all of the caldereth were standing together on the floor of the well. Machai stopped the flames from spreading, but he left them burning on the ramp. He didn't want to hurt anyone if he didn't have to, but he would not allow the newly risen people to move freely out into the world. He would keep them contained here until Osric could be found.

Machai grabbed Dredek's robes behind the wizard's neck and dragged the body through the archway and out into the tunnels of Angmar.

* * *

With the spell completed and the Well of Strands cut off from its source of magic in Archana, Osric cut off the flow of strands and lowered his hand. His arm ached in the joints but felt numb and disconnected everywhere else. The muscles in his chest and shoulder were spasming, causing his arm to twitch and his hand to tremble. He could feel a sharp, searing pain in his neck and he feared that the strands had torn through his nerves the same way they had blasted through the rock and sand of Archana. His head was throbbing with his pulse, causing his vision to waver with every beat of his heart. Osric staggered over to the steps and sat down, cradling his head in his hands. He hadn't felt fatigue like this from the overuse of magic in a very long time.

Bridgett rushed over to him with concern creasing her brow and waves of worry washing over him as the Empath ability regained its active state. Osric didn't bother trying to temper the gift's effect, but he had little energy left and he barely noticed the emotions of his companions. His own feelings were muted and vague, his exhaustion settling over his spirit like a dense fog.

Bridgett worked quickly and silently, using a variety of her new gifts to evaluate his condition as she administered care. She dabbed a sweet-smelling oil on his temples and another with a heady floral scent to the pulse on his neck. She mixed several different herbs and a bitter, black paste into a small tin of water, heating it with a spell until it began to steam.

"Breath the steam for seven breaths, then drink it down. And don't make that face you make when don't like something. I know how it tastes, but it will make you feel better. Your grimace will only make you drink it slower."

Osric smiled at her words, amazed that she could speak so harshly, but her tone and her kind touch made it feel like she was whispering endearments in his ear. She had come to know him so well since they had first met—standing with a hornless unicorn between them as Osric muttered awkwardly, awed by her beauty and her... well, everything about her. He took the warm mug from her and obediently inhaled the vapors rising from the dark liquid. At first it smelled sweet like honey wine, but the sweetness took on a spicy note like cloves that warmed the lining of his throat. By the seventh breath, it smelled like the acrid smoke that rises from red-hot coals when apple cider spills over from the mulling pot. Osric quickly choked down the liquid before it could grow any more bitter from the steeping herbs. He handed the empty mug back to Bridgett, who smiled in appreciation of his cooperation. She reached out and wiped some of the herbs from his lips, laughing.

"I'm sorry I didn't bring a strainer along. You may want to rinse your mouth with water and clean your teeth," Bridgett said. Osric grinned playfully, displaying his teeth full of greenery.

Gus made a rude sound that combined clearing his throat and scoffing at their silly charades.

"I realize you likely feel like you were just crushed by a rockslide after that impressive display of magic, but you should probably come look at this."

Osric struggled to his feet and shuffled the few steps to where Gus was standing on the small table. The hole that Osric had blasted through the wall was just above the tabletop, and Gus jumped up into it without much difficulty. The tunnel left behind by the blast was just large enough for the prairie dog to stand at his full height, and he scampered down the small passage until he reached the point where

The Weaving of Wells

the mountainside fell away and Gus could see out across the rocky expanse of land north of the ruins that stretched out to the sea.

Although he dreaded the cost of using more magic, Osric grudgingly engaged his Stone-Sight ability and cast his gaze out through the stone to see what damage he had done with his spell. He heard Gus's voice echo back to him through the tunnel.

"You made a new lake, over there, where those hills are." Gus pointed his small paw due north, though he was obscured from view by the expanse of stone between him and Osric.

Gus was right. The land rose up into jagged hills just before it reached the sea, and Osric's ray of strands had bored a hole right through them. Seawater was pouring out from the hole on this side of the hills, pooling in a small valley and forming a shallow lake where the land was lowest.

"How far did that beam of light go, boy?" Gus came running back to the tower and hopped back down onto the table. Osric was leaning heavily on the top of the narrow table, lacking the strength to support his own weight as he projected his vision back across the water toward Angmar. He expected to see a hollow tunnel through the stone on the south end of the Irua Realm, but instead he saw a perfectly round underground river. Water flowed into the passage on that continent too, and Osric grew more anxious as he pushed his sight further to see where the water was flowing to and what damage it might be doing.

At the point where the solid stone ended and the sand began, Osric was stunned to see that the water was flooding the sandy terrain. Several animals were already stuck in the resulting quagmire, slowly sinking into the soft, sucking sand. Osric's vision showed him that the area of saturated sand was growing quickly, and he gazed at it in horror. He had completely altered the terrain of a large portion of the realm, and he had no idea how extensive the damage would be to the ecosystem. Thousands of people and animals could potentially wander into the region before it became widely known that the desert was now essentially a swamp. Osric cut off his Stone-Sight and closed his eyes, unable to face the hazard he had caused. He needed to get some men out there to reinforce the land or to at least build a safely traversable road. He would be cleaning up this mess for years, if not decades, to come.

Osric's Wand

In halting, emotionally choked words, Osric explained what he had seen. Gus just stared at him, speechless, and Bridgett wrapped her arms around him and held him tightly. She didn't know what to say, and she only hoped her embrace would convey her support for him. Osric let her hold him for a moment, allowing his whole being to focus on her warmth, on her solid, physical form, which could distract him from the rest of the world. But he couldn't stand in the well, an ocean away from his war, and ignore his responsibilities. He took a deep breath, smelling the faint aroma of lavender that clung to her skin and her hair like wildflowers on a mountainside. He still felt shaky and weak, but an army was depending on him—half of the world was depending on him—and he couldn't live with himself if he didn't try to come through for everyone who needed him.

"We have to go to Angmar. Bridgett, do you think you can take us there? Is there anywhere within the tunnels you think it would be safe to travel to? Somewhere that is likely to be empty even with the tunnels overrun by fighting soldiers? We need to get as close to the Well of Strands as possible, because I don't know if I can fight my way through from the outside." Osric looked down at her, her arms still wrapped around him, and she felt the burden of his responsibilities pressing down on him with crushing force. Tears filled her eyes, but she held them back and nodded.

Osric glanced over at Aridis, expecting to see a congratulatory smile on the man's face, but he was greeted instead with red-rimmed eyes and the same look of shock that he had worn when Osric sensed his intense feelings of worry.

"Aridis, what is it? Is everything okay?"

The old man was trembling, obviously supporting his weight on his heavy staff, and his skin was more pale than usual.

"I could not resist the opportunity to use my gift with such a great deal of power to feed it, but I fear it was a grave mistake to do so."

"What do you mean? What did you see?" Bridgett stepped over to him and slipped a concerned arm around Aridis's trembling frame, offering him support and compassion.

"I don't think I can explain the potential devastation that I have witnessed, as I am not sure I will be able to sort through the various paths or their origins with any accuracy. Rest assured, darker times than any caldereth conjuror can summon are sweeping toward us, and

The Weaving of Wells

that shall have to be enough for you to understand at the moment." Aridis began climbing the stairs slowly, his staff striking the stairs, causing an echo in the well that sounded like a battering ram colliding with stone.

"Aridis, wait. Where are you going?" Osric started up the stairs, reaching out for the old man's arm to stop him, but his hand froze at the icy expression Aridis turned on him when their eyes met.

"I will not be accompanying you to Angmar, High-Wizard. There is much I must see in the stones if I am to make any sense out of what I was shown here this day."

Osric's hand dropped to his side at the cold disapproval on his friend's face. Aridis continued up the steps, leaving his three companions staring after him in confused alarm.

"I don't know what's gotten into him, but shouldn't we be making sure that that blast took off Dredek's head?" Gus stood there for a brief moment, glaring at the retreating form of the cryptic Obcasior. Then, he glanced back at the hole in the wall and shook his head, grinning and muttering about magical marvels.

"You're right, Gus. I wish I knew what Aridis saw, but we must hurry to Angmar and ensure that this fight is finished." Osric gripped Bridgett's hand and drew her attention back to him. "Bridgett, do you think you can travel that far with the three of us?"

"I can, but where do you want us to arrive? I don't feel confident that any location in the tunnels I am familiar with will be clear of fighting."

"We will just have to hope that Machai or Pendres can be reached, and they can let us know where it would be safe to travel to." Osric pulled out his wand, but after using his Stone-Sight again so soon, even the small amount of magic required to link wands for a conversation seemed daunting. Gus shook his head and smacked Osric's hand.

"You have done all any of us could ask you to do, today. The least I can do is call the dwarf and let you rest, my boy." Gus drew his own wand, and Osric nodded gratefully and sank back down onto the bottom step of the small well.

* * *

Osric's Wand

Machai stomped through the tunnels of Angmar, dragging Dredek's limp body behind him. He moved through the passages quickly, stopping only to display the remains of the caldereth wizard to any of the Turgent's troops that he encountered. He had no intention of killing anyone else now that the threat was eliminated, and he was relieved to find that all fight fled from the soldiers when they saw that their leader had been slain.

Soon, Machai had made his way back to the main tunnels, turning into wider and more well-worn passages whenever he encountered them. He had no idea where he was, but he was gradually moving upward and toward the sound of clashing arms. His footfalls were still angry and forceful when he rounded a curve and the tunnel opened up into the main chamber where he and Pendres had first encountered Elidin. Machai stepped into the cavernous room and dropped Dredek's corpse onto the stone floor. He glanced around the room at small clusters of fighting and dozens of injured Aranthians, dwarves, and Rowain troops along the outer walls. It seemed that no one had noticed his entry, nor one more body lying dead on the ground, and Machai's anger flared anew.

Fueled by the rage of seeing his comrades bleeding throughout the room, Machai launched a massive fireball straight up into the air. The speed behind the burst of flame caused a roaring whoosh to drown out the sound of the battle. As the light and noise drew the attention of the gathered troops, the fighting stopped and everyone looked to where Machai stood over Dredek's body with his axe gripped in his fist. Pendres caught his eye and crossed the chamber to stand at Machai's side.

"I take it the High-Wizard's plan went well?"

"I cannot be saying what Osric be doing, but the ugly bastard be falling down dead, so this war be over." Machai scowled down at Dredek's pale face. "Let's be putting an end to this fighting."

Pendres nodded and called out brief but effective orders in the guttural code that the Aranthians had been trained in. His troops, including the dwarves, reacted swiftly and fell into organized units with expectant faces turned toward Machai. The Rowain troops stared in awe at Dredek's dead body—most with looks of shock and confusion, but many with expressions of relief.

The Weaving of Wells

"Aranthian troops, ye be fighting valiantly today, and ye all should be proud of yer contribution to making Archana a safer place to be living." Machai nodded respectively at his kin and other members of the Aranthian army. Then, he shifted his gaze to Dredek's men. "Ye, soldiers of the Human Realm, ye be honorable and loyal to the Turgent." He stepped to one side and let the blade of his axe fall toward the body at his feet, swinging like a pendulum above Dredek's neck. "This imposter be not yer Turgent of the Human Realm. Ye be fighting for him out of loyalty, but he be a liar and a murderer. And now he be dead."

Pendres waited for the cheering from the Aranthians to subside before contributing to Machai's speech.

"The Turgency will be reinstated to the proper members of the reigning family, so those commanders of the Rowain army that are still alive should be gathering your troops rapidly and making arrangements to return to the capital city of the Human Realm. Once the documents of surrender have been negotiated and signed, the Aranthians will, if necessary, assist with transporting the injured and the dead. I will speak with whomever has the authority to negotiate those terms now." Pendres turned and walked through a low doorway into a small room with no door off of the chamber, and a soldier with one arm in a sling and a gilded helmet under the other arm limped after him through the archway. Machai was grateful that Pendres would be handling the political aspects of the resolution of the war; he was far more concerned about contacting Osric and then sorting out the implications for the Dwarven Realm.

Before he could join his kin and fully feel relief that the fighting was over, he felt the distinct surge of power through his wand that indicated a communication link, and he heard Gus's voice vying for his attention.

"Machai, pull out your wand."

Machai glanced one more time at Dredek's body and then stepped over toward the melted mass of stone that Pendres had left in the wall. He rested his axe against the wall and held his wand out before him. The diaphanous image of Gus hovered above the tip of his wand.

"Gus, the battle be over." Machai could see Osric sitting just behind Gus, and the High-Wizard looked haggard and beaten. The dark circles under his eyes and the trembling in his hands were clear,

Osric's Wand

even in the small depiction via the wand connection. "Osric be looking a bit bleak."

"Well, he pushed more magic through his body in one spell than I have probably ever used in my life, so *bleak* doesn't begin to capture how he must be feeling. But he survived, and there's a hole blasted through half of this world to show for it." Gus was grinning so wide his furry cheeks looked as if they were stuffed with nuts. "The question now is: Did it work? Did he defeat Dredek?"

"Aye, Dredek be dead, and his troops be laying down their arms. Pendres be discussing the terms of surrender now."

"That's great news. We want to head to Angmar immediately, but we needed to know we wouldn't get our heads chopped off the moment we appear. Can you give us a good location so Bridgett can get us there safely?"

"Aye, can ye be giving her a good view of this fused stone behind me? It be a clear landmark, and I can be keeping the space open to ensure yer arrival." Machai held his wand high to show a clear image of the rippling stone. In the tower beneath the elven ruins, Bridgett moved closer to observe the location that she would be traveling to. After a brief moment, she nodded and stepped back toward Osric.

"We will be there in a moment," Gus said, eyeing Osric with worry as he wrapped up the conversation with Machai. "Keep the area open for us. And Machai, if there happens to be a healer nearby, it wouldn't hurt to have someone around in case our fearless leader doesn't recover quickly from his spell fatigue."

Machai nodded curtly and tucked his wand into place on his belt. He motioned two men out of the way near the fused stone wall and called one of them to his side.

"Be finding a healer immediately—someone who be having a great understanding of the sickness from using too much magic." Machai sent the man running off into the tunnels, and he turned around just in time to see Bridgett appear with Osric leaning heavily on her arm and Gus perched on her shoulder.

Osric's skin was pale and clammy, and his eyes rolled upward slightly as the effects of the traveling spell washed over him. He stumbled forward a step, but Bridgett's hand was firm on his arm and helped to steady him. After a moment, he was able to stand upright on

The Weaving of Wells

his own and approach Machai to grasp his wrist and thank him for a successful battle for the Well of Strands.

"It be me honor to be fighting for ye, but I be suspecting ye be responsible for the fall of the dreadful wizard. Dredek be collapsing in death with no man taking a weapon to him." Machai kept hold of Osric's wrist, counting the rapid pulse of the High-Wizard's heartbeat to reassure himself that the man was not in danger of collapsing. Color was returning to Osric's cheeks slowly, and his eyes were already looking clearer. Once Machai was confident that Osric's condition was not likely to overcome his ability to heal and recover quickly, he released his grip on Osric and motioned for them to follow him along the high wall of the chamber. Machai walked slowly, not wanting to tax Osric's body too much after what must have been a terrible ordeal, and the three new arrivals followed him closely. Machai stopped near the body of Dredek, still lying on the stone floor of the chamber, allowing Osric a moment to take in the sight.

Seeing the corpse of the powerful wizard flooded Osric with conflicting emotions: relief and revulsion, a small amount of pride, but mostly regret that he had once again taken the life of another. He knew that he had spared the world from Dredek's reign of death and destruction, and he had likely saved many lives by ending the life of the caldereth wizard.

"I wish this hadn't been necessary," Osric muttered to himself softly. "And I hope I'm not wrong to think it *was* necessary."

Osric took a shaky step away from the body and turned his full attention back to Machai. "What became of the caldereth bones? We should give them a proper burial, and Dredek too. Though many of his means were wicked, he was motivated by a love for his people and a deep sense of regret." Osric's hands trembled and his brow was creased over red eyes.

"The caldereth be well contained." Machai thought about his flames spilling down the stairs and trapping the newly risen people at the bottom of the well, and he was surprised by the compassion in Osric's voice when he spoke of burying Dredek's body.

"Wait, do you mean that Dredek was successful? The caldereth are alive?" His voice raw with dread and defeat, Osric feared he had killed Dredek for nothing if the caldereth had been able to raise his people from the dead before Osric's spell had killed him. He had destroyed the greatest source of power ever discovered on Archana, and it had all been for nothing if the caldereth wizard's spell had been completed before Osric severed his power supply.

"Aye, the caldereth be risen from the dead, but they seem to be having no magic. At least, they be having no luck in attacking me with it when they be trying." Machai wondered if the disappointment in Osric's voice was due to his fatigue or to the news of the caldereth's lives.

"If they have no connection to Archana," Bridgett said, "then they could not wield magic as they were once able to. Aridis said something similar about the deer that I encountered in the forest."

"If they can't wield magic, they will be of little threat to any of us." Osric cradled his head in his hands as he thought about the implications of the day's events. "Though, it means they will be incredibly vulnerable to anyone who may wish them harm. I had intended to stop Dredek from bringing them back to life, and I failed. But we set out to stop the slaughter of an entire race, and I'm not about to perpetrate the same upon the caldereth. It is not their fault that Dredek undertook this path, and I will not punish them for existing at the hands of a dead madman."

"Where are they now?" Bridget asked, eyeing Osric with worry.

"They be trapped in the depths of the Well of Strands. I be shielding the opening of the well to be keeping strands out—in case it be a fluke that they be failing to assail me with their spells."

"Trapped?" Osric glanced over at Machai. "How exactly are they trapped in the well?"

"I be spilling some flames down the steps. I be needing a quick exit with Dredek's corpse to be stopping the fighting, and I be needing to know they willn't be following me up the stairs and into the tunnels. If they be having their magic, it be likely that I be dead now. It'd be a hard fight to be taking on hundreds by meself when one hand be gripping the dead wizard's robes."

"I'm glad you made it out safely, Machai, but we can't just leave them down there. Do you know who is in charge of the irua now?"

Bridgett shuddered silently as she recalled the raspy voice of the Nagish condemning her to death, and worse, the lustful eyes and curved blade of the tan-robed irua who planned to carry it out while she was lashed to the stone slab in the center of the main chamber that

The Weaving of Wells

they had just appeared in. It had not been her only brush with death, nor her most recent, but it was the one experience that still caused the hairs on the back of her neck to stand on end and left her reaching for a weapon at her belt.

"The last leader, the Nagish, died in Dredek's initial invasion. Surely by now they have another in the position. Though, I guess I know little of the traditions and politics of the irua. Do you know how a Nagish is selected?" Bridgett asked Osric.

"If my memory serves me well from my time as Contege of the Vigiles, the Nagish will not be named until three full moons after the last is laid to rest. It is not a familial progression, nor is it an election, but I do not know more than that about the selection process." Osric's eyes were still red rimmed, but they looked brighter after the brief time he'd had to rest.

"Then they are a leaderless people, for now." Bridgett tried to shake her memory of the irua with the long, curved knife. "We should be seeking out the sect that is charged with protecting the well. They wear the tan robes, and those of highest rank have gold embroidery along the collar."

"That is probably the best place to start. Machai, can you see if you can find an irua of that description?"

"Aye." Machai turned and disappeared into the crowd of celebrating Aranthians.

"Osric, be cautious. Not all members of the sect will welcome us here." Bridgett shuddered slightly once more, and Osric nodded, needing no verbal explanation for her reservations—she had told him of her experience, and he could sense each of her emotions as if they were his own.

Machai returned quickly with an irua in long, tan robes with elaborate gold embroidery covering the entire length of the fabric. Bridgett was surprised to see so much of the gleaming thread stitched into the robes, and she wondered if the man who had tried to kill her had been of much rank at all. Osric greeted the man formally but warmly, hoping to form a quick alliance.

"Thank you for meeting with us. With the Nagish gone, we were unsure who would be able to make decisions concerning the irua people."

Osric's Wand

The golden-robed irua stared at Osric with narrowed eyes and lips pressed tightly together. His skin was pale, almost bluish in tint, and heavily wrinkled with age. He stood as tall as Osric, with thin limbs and long, straight hair that hung in a narrow braid over one shoulder.

"Are you responsible for the damage that has been done to the Well of Strands?" His voice was high-pitched and raspy, as much air as sound, but his words held more authority than accusation.

"I am." Osric would not deny his role in the destruction of the source of strands, but his tone displayed no pride or arrogance for the feat. "I regret that the Well of Strands was damaged, but there was no other way that I could see to defeat Dredek and stop him from executing his plans."

The irua's expression did not shift as he listened to Osric speak, but he seemed to be weighing the High-Wizard with his eyes.

"You did defeat him, but did you stop him?"

"No, not entirely. I suspect that I interrupted his spell before it was completed, as his people are alive but apparently unable to use magic."

"This is true," the irua said. "The caldereth people will never be able to touch Archana." Osric felt as if the questions were more of a test than a request for new information. It seemed that the protector of the well already knew of everything Osric said. "Is the damage you have caused irreparable?"

"I cannot say that the well could not ever be restored to a functional strand source, but I believe it would be naïve to say that it could ever be as it was. I have a great deal of work ahead of me to try and repair the world where magic has altered it. I will do whatever I can to bring balance back to Archana."

The irua did not respond for a long while, and Osric only just managed to remain still and patient as he considered his own feelings about the spell he had sent halfway across Archana and the extensive damage it had done. Finally, the irua in the golden robes ended his scrutiny of Osric and turned his attention to Bridgett.

"Can you forgive this man for the damage he has done?"

Bridgett's eyebrows arched upward and her mouth parted slightly in surprise at the unexpected question.

The Weaving of Wells

"Of course I can. He did what he did to end a war and save the irua people, among many others." Her brow creased in confusion. "I never felt that there was anything to forgive. I do not feel that he has erred."

The irua nodded slightly, watching Bridgett carefully. "You cannot feel the despair of the earth you tread upon? You are what is needed for the wells—your bones should ache with Archana's pain."

"I don't understand. What do you mean I am what is needed?" Bridgett looked up into the old irua's face and shook her head softly.

"It is not wrong that Trevar trusted you, but you are blind." The irua opened his mouth as if he would say more, but then he shook his head and said, "It is not only trees that sing songs of sorrow." He turned back to Osric. "What is it that you want from me, High-Wizard?"

"The caldereth were contained within the well, but that is a temporary solution. I wanted to consult you on the fate of the caldereth people."

"They are already being moved to a portion of the tunnels where they can be cared for and watched until we understand what it is that they are. The irua do not wait for warlords to hold councils when there is work to do beneath our sands. We will take care of Angmar. You are welcome to leave our city at your soonest convenience." The irua turned to Bridgett. "If ever you wish to learn to see, you are welcome to return."

Although it was not said, Osric heard the implication that he would not be welcomed in Angmar with her if Bridgett did return. The damage his spell had caused reached far beyond the terrain of Archana, and Osric wasn't sure he would ever be able to restore the alliances that had been so nearly established at the Ratification Ceremony. Perhaps it was foolish to think that their world could ever exist in peace between all races.

* * *

Aeya's cheeks showed dirty streaks where her tears had streamed down her face. The scraps of clothing that the irua had provided her with before locking all of her people into a small region of the tunnels covered her naked body, but they were damp from her tears and anxious sweat. She had wailed in agony until her throat was raw and her voice was hoarse.

Now, she sat in silence against the wall with her knees pulled tightly toward her chest. Her body ached, and her muscles twitched and spasmed painfully as they became accustomed to living and moving once more. Her long, thin fingers were wrapped around a smooth stone, but her eyes were gazing off toward the images her mind replayed of waking to see Dredek once again—only to see him fall to the ground in death. Still her fingers clutched at the stone as they had clutched at his robes, begging for him to rise and breathe once more, pleading to find a beating heart rather than a cold stone buried in the fabric of his robes. Aeya's lips moved as if she were whispering to him, and her fingers clawed at the rock, but her eyes were still and staring; no amount of compassion or companionship from her people could console her.

Chapter 29
A Vision of Death

For the Aranthians, the last few months had been remarkable. Indeed, the fledgling organization had begun exploring magic in ways that couldn't have been dreamt of before. They had grown from a few members who were thrust together in a time of turmoil to hundreds of volunteers who could sustain their growing population for the foreseeable future. They had toppled formidable forces, solved magical mysteries, and freed an enslaved species from cruel cages. Gus sat on the edge of the balcony overlooking the inner gardens of the Aranthian habitat and took it all in.

However, it wasn't only the Aranthians' success that caused him to pulse with pride. It wasn't the stumps being pulled out of the southeast corner of the grounds or the eight men and women making it happen that caused his heart to swell, a smile to crease his face, and tears to dampen the fur of his face. It was the plump, jovial ball of fur directing them all on where to leave the wood they pulled out of the earth that made a laugh escape Gus's mouth.

He was so lost in the moment, watching his son command a group of acquiescent humans, that he didn't hear the door open behind him, but a soft familiar chuckle brought him out of his solitary observation.

"I wonder what our friends would think if I told them I found you in here alone giggling to yourself. We all thought you practiced bickering with people when no one was around." Osric stepped up to the balustrade and let his feet slide through the rails, joining Gus in his good mood.

"Let them think what they will. I am happy!" Gus smiled up at Osric, slapping the stone floor of the balcony for emphasis.

Moments drifted by in silence as they both listened to Pebble shout barely audible orders in a cheerful tone. Even though he was working, the young prairie dog still bounced in his typical manner as if he were playing.

"He's a good kid." Osric turned his gaze back to Gus and nudged him playfully with his left hand.

Osric's Wand

"Yes he is. I'm starting to wish Eublin could have his way and that we would find an alternative to the hunt." He nodded.

"Gus! You too?" Osric was so startled by the revelation that he leaned back, looking at Gus with new eyes.

"I know. I know. But I can imagine no better life than watching my son's. With his mind, can you imagine all the marvels he could discover, or create? He just had his fifth birthday, and he understood everything about the wand and your power nearly a year before the thought of it entered any of our minds. This is exciting!" Gus was grinning.

"Yes, but you've been one of the harshest critics of Eublin's ideas about the hunt."

"I don't even fully understand this change in me, but I am fine with not understanding it." Gus shrugged and then leaned toward Osric with wide, serious eyes. "I haven't belittled a hunter since you woke up. Do you know how odd that is for me?"

"What?" He tipped his head to the left and looked Gus in the eyes, confused.

"You haven't noticed how I treat hunters? Most of my life I've been trying to anger them enough that they would hunt me out of spite." Gus looked up at Osric, a bit ashamed of the admission.

"That's crazy, even for a supporter of the hunt." The thought of someone trying to force another person to kill them, for any reason, seemed absurd to Osric. Why would someone try to incite a man to kill and eat him?

"Well, I agree, but it seemed better than the alternative. Now, I think the alternative might not be as set as I once thought." Gus's eyes grew distant, but hope radiated from his mind, mingled with worry.

"What could be worse?" Though Osric was genuinely curious, he did suspect he knew which direction Gus was going. He suspected that he was about to learn something that many had jokingly speculated about but that Gus himself had never revealed.

"Rotting alone under an avalanche of stone, fire, and mud in a place where no one can find me, for one." Gus sighed deeply and his shoulders sank.

"What gave you the idea that that would happen?" Osric encouraged Gus to continue, knowing that Gus needed the relief of sharing his fears even if Osric already knew the answer.

The Weaving of Wells

"It was a vision I was given by a Seer during my first year away from home while studying wandcraft. The words he delivered told me of fame, fortune, and mastery of my craft, but an ultimately undesirable end. I watched as flame and stone showered over a much older version of who I was then. The fire or the stone killed me, I don't know which. But then I could see through the stone, and I watched as time passed and my body decayed. I was horrified to watch what was left of my fur peel away, sticking to the rocks surrounding me with the help of the little fluid left inside my body. I don't know how much time passed, but eventually a thick layer of mud covered the stone, dried, and then cracked." Gus hung his head.

He remained in his solemn pose for several long breaths. He shook ever so slightly, and his eyes remained closed. Then, suddenly, Osric felt a calm wash over the old prairie dog. Gus hadn't moved, but the mood of the sheltered balcony seemed to shift. Serenity replaced the heavy weight that had pressed in on the two, and Gus looked up with calm acceptance in his smile.

"I've been present when you thwarted prophecy in the past. You kept the paun from killing us all, even though the vision had depicted our deaths. But I died in two prophecies that I know of, so maybe my luck will hold for the death I was shown as well. Being buried below the pillars of our training grounds after a natural death, where at least my memory can serve to nourish others, seems more appealing than my other choice. Besides, I seem to inspire inaccuracy to even the most experienced hunter, and I'm getting tired of serving as practice." Gus laughed and patted Osric's leg. "But enough about me. What news do we have from Angmar? I know we didn't stop Dredek, but I have a hard time believing there wasn't more to his plans that we don't know about."

"Well, we may never know what his plans were, but the caldereth don't seem to have any knowledge other than their native language. Even the Common they spoke on the stones seems to have been wiped from their memory over the centuries. They don't pose any danger to us now, as far as we can tell." Osric let him divert the conversation, but he intended to ask more at a later date.

"Humans were responsible for their extinction. Do they have any knowledge of the battle that led to their deaths?" Gus asked the question on the minds of nearly every Aranthian posted at Angmar.

Osric's Wand

They hadn't had anything to do with that battle, but the caldereth wouldn't know that, and if they did they may not care.

"Thankfully no," Osric replied. "But once they were revived it took a couple days for them to remember their own language. Who knows how long it will take for them to remember that we were responsible for their deaths."

"Their last days were very itinerant, long and grueling marches, day after day, having left their home in search of a miracle in a distant land. Or maybe they were looking for power and wealth. Who knows? My point is that the days leading up to their deaths were probably horrible, especially the day of the slaughter, so perhaps their minds will reject those memories out of mercy for their sanity. Maybe humans killing their race will be the last memory that comes back to them. We could have time to prove the Aranthians trustworthy before they remember." Gus's tone was almost too hopeful.

Osric laughed. "To be honest, I'm more worried about dragons attacking than I am about the caldereth. I hope we can focus our attention on that front before we have to deal with something unexpected—I haven't had the chance to devote a lot of time to the dragon problem as it is. And, for now, the irua seem to be content letting the caldereth remain isolated to a small portion of Angmar until we find them a safe place to live."

"So, they haven't developed any magical abilities yet?" Again, Gus's tone was hopeful.

"No. They show no sign of a connection to Archana—at least no connection derived of magic. But, you can never discount the emotions of a race, so maybe their connection will run deeper than ours, and they may never regain memories more than the instinctual ones." Osric tried to echo his outlook, but something kept him from committing fully to the investment.

"It's going to be difficult to find a place that is safe for them if they can't use magic. Drogma are fairly prevalent across Archana, and they can get through a lot of structures that aren't reinforced by some magical means. Maybe the caldereth could benefit from our aid in magical craft? I think our economy could afford sending several dozen to help build fences. We could check on them from time to time." Gus was thinking out loud, but he looked up at Osric expectantly.

The Weaving of Wells

"I suppose we could, but we need to find a place for them first. I've sent out scouts already. They seem to favor colder climates, so most of our attention is focused north near where the Grove of the Unicorns used to be." Osric took in a slow, deep breath and his brow creased with worry.

"Why do you look so morose? You just defeated the most experienced wizard on all of Archana, and he had mastered more gifts than even you." Gus nudged Osric's left thigh with an encouraging swat of his paw.

"It's actually defeating Dredek that is bothering me," Osric replied.

"I can't understand you sometimes. Why would you let yourself be bothered by accomplishing your goal? It seems that would be a reason for celebration." Gus leaned against a rail, looking up at Osric with concern.

"Don't you find it strange that Dredek didn't bring weapons into the Well of Strands? There was nothing more than a few crates of food waiting for the caldereth when they awoke." Osric looked back at Gus, his lips pressed in a thin line and worry creasing his brow.

"I find a lot of things he did troubling. Why would that choice bother me more than the others?" Gus answered.

"He spent decades planning everything. Every last detail was explored. But there was no way for him to know we would be able to overpower him because he was the only multi-gifted life on Archana until the unicorns created a wand that would do the same for me. I just find it troubling to think that he had no more plans after this event." Osric spoke slowly, considering his words carefully.

Gus could feel how much the thought troubled Osric, but he couldn't see the issue. "What if he didn't plan further than bringing them back? I don't see how that would make a difference. I mean, we still had to try to stop him because he has proven himself an untrustworthy sort."

"That's just it." Osric shook his head. "His entire race was killed, and he stopped at nothing to bring a couple hundred of them back, only to have no plan for after he accomplished that task?"

"And?" Gus shrugged.

"His plans stopped. Don't you see it?"

"See what?" Gus squinted his small eyes, unsure of the direction the conversation was heading in.

Osric's Wand

"He had to see it. I see it." Osric spoke with troubled eyes. "What would have happened after he raised them? He had an army that had been reduced to nearly half its original size from their attack on Angmar. If we could have coordinated a dual front attack with the irua, there is no way they could have succeeded in holding us off. He couldn't hold off our forces, and we came at him from one side. He would have known this."

"Okay, then the irua would have destroyed them, or we would have. Bridgett says they don't tolerate outsiders. It seems to me he simply overlooked one important part of the plan."

"I don't think he did." Osric sighed. "I think he planned to turn himself over to us as leverage. Hold the guilty party responsible in order to let the race survive. I can't see any other course of action that would fit the facts."

"All right, so what if that is the case. We may never know now, but so what if that was the plan?" Gus was feeling the familiar tug of his old emotions returning, but he suppressed them in favor of a sly smile.

"My worry is that if an ancient mind could plan the toppling of an ancient power and the resurrecting of a long-dead race, only to surrender when it was accomplished rather than defeat our men, then maybe we should have put our time and resources toward other endeavors." Osric hung his head. "He couldn't have foreseen my use of the other wells, but it still shouldn't have been that easy to defeat him. What if he didn't plan to keep on fighting, to keep on killing? What if I killed a man who wasn't a threat?"

"Wasn't a threat? Are you mad?" Gus's frown turned from inquisitive to stern. "Let's just get one thing straight. Even if Dredek surrendered himself to let the caldereth live, he would have been executed for his crimes. He was, by any interpretation of the word, a threat. With his crimes known, very few would have indulged him enough to offer a trial. He was a threat. Don't you ever doubt that fact."

"Maybe." Osric's grimace deepened. He looked out at the center of the Aranthian habitat, and even the sight of Pebble searching through the wooden rubble left from stumps, playfully giggling and sorting through the mess, did nothing to bolster his mood.

"Ha!" Gus's scowl faded quickly into laughter once more, and he was glad to have shed his foul nature of former years. Life was far more enjoyable without the headache caused by a creased brow. He smiled as he looked up at the tortured face of his friend. "Look at yourself! You look to be attending a feast where Kenneth is offered up as the meal. You won! Now even I recognize your genius. In fact, I've set out to find the most inexperienced Portentists as students to my trade. The strand-sight device, and the other objects we've been working on that will allow anyone to manipulate strands, can open up the trade to many creative young minds."

Gus stared out at the scene in the yard below, but he turned back to Osric suddenly with wonder and excitement in his eyes. "Can you imagine James with a wand that helps to bring out the flavor of food? I might die from happiness if he could make the food taste even better!" Osric looked at Gus, unsure of what to make of this shift in the conversation, but Gus continued. "I don't think I ever told you about Miss Carrion. Her meat pies could bring me to tears. That is the one thing that made me strive to be great in my early years of wandcraft: food!" He smiled.

Osric laughed at the change in his demeanor. "What?"

"Ah, yes. Food!" Gus nodded. "But of all the food I have ever eaten, Miss Carrion served up the best meat pie! It had the best butter crust; a thick, creamy sauce; carrots, leeks, onions, garlic, and herbs; and the most delicate dove or lamb I have ever tasted." Gus closed his eyes and swallowed, a speckle of drool in the corner of his mouth. "She made it both ways: lamb or dove, depending on what she could locate at the market. She ground the meat with pork fat, to lend it moisture and flavor." Gus tipped his head up, his eyes closing as he sighed. "Oh, I can't begin to tell you how much I loved that pie. The field outside her home may be the cleanest field in all of Archana. I would gather sticks in that area just for the hope of that smell. In my early days"—he leveled his eyes at Osric—"I even made her a spatula wand, or six, because she wore them out over the years, just to encourage her to keep making it!"

"What?" It was the second time in as many attempts that he had chosen this word, but nothing else would enter his mind in the midst of such an amusing story.

"Oh, I know I came across as a nuisance, but I was only that way to men who could hunt, or attempted it, for that matter. Miss Carrion was a woman who could inspire me to create wands of any shape or size. I would have made her a wand of silk if she would create another culinary trap for my tongue. Ah, yes." Gus sighed.

Osric laughed. There was so much of Gus's behavior that was unfamiliar yet welcome. Gus's face contorted in all of the usual ways, but for entirely different reasons.

Osric could still recognize small fluctuations in emotion, not only through the Empath gift, but through observation as well. Small hints indicated Gus was annoyed with his observations, conclusions, emotions, and the like, but it quickly dissolved each time in favor of a lighthearted playfulness. It was strange but terribly entertaining.

Gus looked out at Pebble carrying a small bag of sticks with a smile. "So, what's the next step for our Aranthians? What will my son be exposed to in the near future?"

"I wish I could say for certain." Osric frowned, his eyes directed down at Pebble and the crew working in the courtyard, but his focus was clearly on places far away. "I thought that tracking down the person who attacked the Ratification Ceremony was going to be the end of it. Then I felt that freeing the dragons might be the end of some great injustice that would set the world right. For a brief time, I let myself believe that if we stopped Dredek we could end the threat of war and everything could go back to the way it once was. You, an arrogant genius of wandcraft, and me, a quiet idiot facing no more danger than the risk of cutting off my own foot while chopping firewood."

"You're still an idiot, if that makes you feel any better. And firewood is a real threat." Gus's smile held a hint of its old smirk.

"I wish that I could say that this is over, with Dredek dead, but we both know that that would make me as naïve as I was the day they made me Contege because they wanted someone they could control in a position of power." Osric ran his hands through his sandy-colored hair, and he was almost surprised to find that it reached past his shoulders. His appearance wasn't the only thing to change significantly over the last year, and he made a mental note to get a haircut and take better care of himself. He glanced back down at Gus, noticing that most of his friend's hair had turned white, and his sharp eyes sat deeper in their sockets these days. "The dragons are a greater threat than any we have faced, and I don't have the slightest idea what we are going to do about it. It's as if this whole time they have been lying in ambush, waiting for the chaos and fear to erupt as we burn ourselves to the ground in war, providing the perfect opportunity for the dragons to sift through the ashes and bathe in the riches we leave behind. I don't know if we'll ever be able to live in the peace and quiet we once enjoyed, languishing in old age as our grandchildren become the greatest wizards to walk the surface of Archana, but I'm afraid that if we give up hope then no one will ever have that opportunity again."

"You're right. We won't get to enjoy the peace that we are striving to bring about, but perhaps we can enjoy a few days here and there before we go dragon hunting?" Gus's attention was once again on his son.

"Indeed. And based on those wise words"—Osric pulled his legs out from the rails and stood up—"I think my next step is to get myself something to eat. Would you like to join me for a morning meal?"

"No, thank you. It's such a beautiful morning, and I'm feeling like taking a walk. I've been cooped up in that wand shop since we got back from Angmar. I haven't wandered the fields outside Stanton looking for sticks in ages."

"Pebble doesn't typically use sticks." Osric smirked down at the old prairie dog.

"Oh, I know. Some habits are hard to break, and I still make my wands to sell at Pebble's shop. My wands will always be sticks—unless Miss Carrion requests something different." He winked back at Osric. "Pebble likes to gather sticks, even if he doesn't even make them into wands. Many of the best he gives to me, some he spells for games and toys, and a few he takes a fancy to and makes wands out of them himself. I guess he's picked up a lot from me over the years." Gus grinned widely. "I'm off to see if I can find better sticks than my boy today. Maybe I'll spend some time thinking over this dragon problem. I may have it solved by the next time you see me."

"Have fun, and keep an eye out for hunters. We don't want to lose you. Now that even you are willing to accept a life without the hunt, it won't be long until we see some real change in the traditions of our realm." Osric laughed.

Gus's eyes narrowed as he considered the issues of the hunt. "I think we will need to attack that on several fronts if we are to have a solution that will suit the need."

Osric's Wand

"What do you mean by that?" Osric opened the door and let Gus pass through, and they took the stairs down while they talked.

"Well, it seems to me that these are cultural issues, as well as governmental, and our ability to raise cattle should be able to provide for those who want an alternative. If we combine an anti-hunt advocacy, led by Eublin and escorted by Aranthian guards with greater farming efforts and government zones where the hunt is forbidden, and others where it is allowed, then we could have a way for everyone to get what they want out of it." Gus rattled this off as if it were simply common sense.

Osric watched him scuttle down the halls on all four legs, listing solutions as if he were reading them from a sign, and Osric was amazed. "Those may be some of the best ideas I've heard on the subject. How did you come up with them?"

"It just makes sense. Then, restrict the hunt to non-sentients in the hunt-free zones so that those living in the area can still eat, and maybe spell some tattoo ink to slightly deflect some of the force of a bolt to create another layer of safety for those who don't want to worry about hunters without scruples. Yeah, that should do it. We all get to choose then." Gus nodded once and then continued down the hall, nearing the front door of their enchanted habitat. "Yeah, even less honorable hunters wouldn't kill if their first attempt wasn't successful. Trust me, I know. Run it by Eublin and see what he thinks."

Osric stopped, placing his hand on the stone wall and leaning to one side, squinting. "By all the blazing strands, Gus! You're brilliant, and you're a jerk. We've been at it for months on that issue, and you finally join us only to solve it in the time it takes to walk from the balcony to here?"

"It's not as complicated as weaving the wells was, but I think it will do. We'll have to tweak it a bit, but the basics are all there. I'm sure Toby would want to define *non-sentient* in legal terms, and we'll need accurate maps and a way to enforce it all, but it should do what we need it to do. Lots of work ahead." Gus smiled as he stepped out the door and into the sun.

"How did you come up with that so quickly?" Osric was astonished.

"I've told you all. Once I realized I was an idiot, ideas became abundant. I had to accept the fact that I knew nothing; then I was willing to accept a multitude of options I once thought were ridiculous. I think that is how young minds work. I am trying to emulate it. If I could teach Pebble one thing, it would be to never let himself take anything for granted. He is perfect now. It isn't until you become set in your ways, like I was, that you lose sight of the exploration of things. That's when possibilities become limited and life loses its joy." Gus laughed, his face turning up with delight, and he met Osric's gaze with certainty. "If a hunter takes me today, tell Pebble what I said."

He turned away, smiling, and headed east. After exchanging greetings with a few early-morning trainees practicing dual-wielding techniques, Gus passed through the barrier and headed through Stanton.

Gus typically headed west once he left the Aranthian base. That was a habit that had stuck with him for ages. Not heading west specifically, but rather farming sticks from those fields. That had been the old Gus, and he was feeling adventurous today. He let himself explore the streets of the city as it awoke. Stanton had almost fully recovered from both the original attack on the palace and the battle with the Kallegian. He remembered the way the city had mourned and the utter devastation that the scorched and crumbling walls and the crushed or mangled remnants of the festivities had embodied.

They had come far since that day; even in the morning light they bustled about with pride and determination. None of those going about their business had forgotten what they had endured, as evidenced by their watchful eyes, always looking for any sign that would signify they needed to be at the ready. Every one of them carried out their duties with diligence, but attention to their surroundings was now commonplace. They weren't wary, but rather optimistic in expression and stance, and no pickpocket or con would dare approach the people in front of him as he walked. These days, they were too mindful of the details around them.

It was a small blessing, but to know he had been a part of the change, and to see the determination and sense of community that grew from the tragedy, filled Gus with a gaiety that almost bubbled out of him when he walked. He didn't let it, of course. He held it in; he still had a reputation to uphold, after all. The last thing he wanted was for townsfolk to be talking about how silly he was acting these days. His wands had dropped in value after Pebble took his place as the new master, but he still needed to help support the Aranthians, and his reputation aided in that endeavor.

He continued his journey as he exited the walls surrounding Stanton. He knew the battle with the Kallegian, and the early foundations of the Aranthians, had played a part in the formation of these walls. If it came to it, they wouldn't aid in defending attacks from the air. He set his mind to solutions to that problem, given the dragon issue of late. The dragons themselves were an issue that needed to be solved, but he wasn't even sure where to begin with that problem. He took a deep breath of the fresh morning air and tried to think of more pleasant things. This was a morning for enjoying the surprises that Archana could bring, and on that note he continued east as the road led away from town.

Gus skipped the less attractive—and in his mind, less interesting—areas as he went, using the traveling spell to help steer his journey. The trees were less interesting, less supple, more prone to breaking when grown in drier areas. The small bag he brought could only carry so many, after all. He needed sticks that, on their own, could last. He needed something that was flexible, sturdy, and had been moistened throughout its life. That is what makes a good stick.

He let his mind guide him effortlessly, drifting toward things that seemed interesting at the time. It felt good to just head out into the day without a goal set. He was an adventurer at heart, and his smile widened with every mile. Soon, with the use of the traveling spell, Lothaine sprang up in front of him.

Gus smiled. The traveling spell was a marvel: it would have taken him a couple days to make the round trip if it weren't for the aid of the spell. There were several areas in the local fields that should offer great wand-making material, if maps of the area were any indication.

The small town was hardly a town at all. Only a half-dozen homes were in the area, as well as a small tavern and the Lothaine Temple. Many people had traveled to this town's temple to offer thanks to Archana, but the meager activities of the small village didn't offer much to keep them there for more than a brief visit. However, several farms were situated on the southern edge of Lothaine, and that was where he was heading.

The Weaving of Wells

The farms had been established there due to the lakes and rivers located nearby; perhaps he could find something sufficient to make his search worthwhile. He regathered his bag, squinting in the bright sunlight. Gus looked to the south where the road led and continued on his way.

He turned left and followed an ill-repaired road east along the edge of town; the sound of water drifting among large trees with roping, gnarled roots drew him from the main road leading south away from Lothaine. A trickling stream was only a short distance off the right side of the road, but it turned sharply and headed south toward larger rivers on its eventual path to the Darib Sea. The distance to the other side of the stream was only an easy toss of a stone, even for Gus, but it was deep and the water moved swiftly as it rounded the bend. The left side of the road was clear of the tall-growing trees and roots, and it was unclear whether the road had been placed on the edge of the forest or whether the forest had been trimmed back to allow its passage.

Crickets were stridulating somewhere among the light cover of trees. As Gus moved along with the road, he marveled at the life around him in ways he hadn't done since he was young. A couple of young squirrels chased each other through the trees, a woodpecker hammered noisily at a tree nearby, and sprites darted in every direction. The area was alive, and Gus lost himself in the experience.

Though he took in the beauty of the surroundings and found joy in the journey, he could not ignore all the pressure of the previous months. Gus struggled to rein in the emotions that flooded his mind and to focus on the question rationally. With Dredek vanquished, their greatest threat was the attacking dragons. He didn't really understand the motivation for the attacks, and there didn't seem to be any regularity or pattern to them either. With so little to go on, he was feeling more frustrated than inspired to problem solving.

Obviously they had magic that could help—spells for offense and wards and shields for defense—but there was no way to predict where the rogue dragons might attack next. People were creatures of habit, and the dragons had been a trusted means of transportation for as long as anyone could remember, but fear was another creature altogether. Fear was causing people to spread rumors—the worst of which was that the first of the dragon attacks corresponded with Osric's releasing the elders at the Braya Volcano and that he was the mastermind behind the attacks all this time. The Aranthians didn't say these things, obviously, and they defended Osric and the majority of the dragon species whenever they heard such things being spoken, but the Aranthians spent most of their time in the protection of the spell. Rumors grew roots in outlying taverns and rural areas where there was no one to say otherwise. Gus feared that soon the people would begin to fear the Aranthians rather than trusting them to give aid and protection where it was needed most.

If there was some way to identify and track the offending dragons, then they could anticipate the location of the attacks. Gus thought about his ideas for ending the hunt, and he wondered if there might be some way to use the same solution for tracking the dragons. It would require locating them first, coming into contact with the rogues in order to mark them somehow, but he thought he could devise a spell to track them.

Gus listened to the trill of birds in the trees and the buzz of bees seeking nectar in the wild flowers, and the smile returned to his face. He was certain he could track the dragons. He was already inventorying the necessities for the spell and working out the complications of casting it, but they had the networked wells to ensure he would have the power he needed to draw on. And the others would help him find a way to locate and tag the offenders. With a rudimentary solution to the problem in mind, Gus was finally able to let the pressure fall away so that he could enjoy his foray into the forest looking for sticks.

It had been years since he had run on four legs through the forest, but he let himself slip into a younger mindset, pausing only when sounds piqued his curiosity. Now, he abandoned the traveling spell, giving himself over to the physical pleasure of bounding about, staying out of the shade, letting the sun warm his coat as he went.

He was thankful to be alone, in the mood he was in, but Gus felt that his decades spent as the greatest Wand-Maker had afforded him at least a few moments' celebration and frivolity. He paused for a moment with a ridiculous grin, looking about for any sign of observation, but there was none.

He continued, keeping one eye on the ground near the water, watching for signs that he could find the sticks that brought him out

The Weaving of Wells

this morning. Pebble wouldn't have been able to use much of anything located about, since he typically used much larger wood sources to carve a wand, but Gus was beginning to get excited.

The trees next to the stream on his right were getting larger the further he went, but the left side of the road had turned into open fields of sugarcane a while back. The distance between the road and the water grew wider, and with the growing distance and taller trees came a ground littered with even more fallen branches.

Gus stopped in the shade of a silo. It was tall and unremarkable and mostly made of stone painted white with small cracks radiating throughout. It was a very old building and had probably earned its owners fifty times the cost to build it before it became too rundown to store anything properly. And like his broken body, the attached refinery showed signs of years of too much hard work and too little upkeep.

"You and I have something in common." He stepped close and spoke to the tall structure with admiration in his voice. "We're both long past our prime, but we have done our jobs well." He ran one long claw gently over the scars on his legs and torso from botched hunts and looked back at cracks in the stone. Smoke vacated the chimney of the refinery, indicating that someone was busy working inside, so Gus decided he should be working as well. "Now, I have an idea that should put my name right back up on top of the Wand-Maker world for a while." Gus turned away and looked at the ground below the trees. "But I'll need the perfect stick for this wand." He smiled at the thought of recreating Osric's wand with the help of the network of wells they had created. With a wand like that in the hands of every Aranthian, the threat of the dragons wouldn't seem so daunting. But unlike Legati, these would be wands in the best form: sticks.

He took a few steps toward the trees, but something looked odd. The swatch of trees had grown wide, but no sounds rose from the life that surely dwelled within the cover. He looked down and was unsure if his eyes were playing tricks on him. The land below the trees looked sunken and distorted, and the trees were leaning at odd angles in every direction. He was sure they hadn't been that way just a moment ago.

Then, in a sudden rush, his Portentist gift flared to life, but danger was approaching from everywhere. The ground below his feet, all the way to the water and beyond, buckled. The area that collapsed was huge, surprising him as he shouted in alarm. Gus pictured his chambers in the Aranthian habitat and began to recite the traveling spell, but something solid smashed against the back of his head and his vision spiraled and went black.

When he opened his eyes, he could see blood mingling with the mud in the fur along his shoulder and forearm. His vision was still wavering, and the ground around him was shifting further toward the trees and water as the region was swallowed up in the sinkhole. Gus was stunned by the realization that he was witnessing the same scene that he had seen so many years before in the Seer's vision. More than anything, he was surprised that he hadn't noticed it was happening before it was too late.

Gus saw a large chunk of stone from the silo topple to the ground nearby, and he struggled to hold the image of the Aranthian quarters firmly in his mind. He fought against the fog that threatened to suck him back into the blackness of unconsciousness as he searched his memory for the words of the traveling spell. He tried to speak, to move his mouth and force the words from his throat, but he could not make a sound. He tried to push himself up from the ground, but the debris and the swiftly deepening earth that was settling around him had trapped his limbs. He struggled to draw a breath, his aged body unable to push back against the weight of the heavy stone and mud. Every breath was more shallow, and he was quickly losing his grip on consciousness As he desperately tried to breathe, to move, to speak the words to the traveling spell, a loud crack sounded behind him. Sugar dust erupted into the air when the silo split apart. He briefly registered the wash of heat that passed over him, and the last thing he saw was the bright light of the explosion when the flames of the farmer's fire met the volatile dust.

The Authors

Ashley Delay strives to live each day to the fullest with an abundance of clichés: learn something new every day, never stop dreaming, learn from mistakes, stop and smell the roses, believe the best in others, and embrace the power of positive thinking. Although writing is one of many endeavors Ashley currently pursues, it has become one of her greatest joys. She is a busy wife, mother, student, teacher, business owner, and writer who dreams of someday finding that elusive treasure called "free time." In the meantime, she will continue exploring the marvelous worlds that can only come to life in the pages of a book.

Jack D. Albrecht, Jr. always wanted to be tall, muscular, and talented with a sword. Since he was unable to convince Mother Nature to give him height or muscles, and he has no desire to lose what looks he has in a sword fight, he invents worlds where people are less shallow and swordplay is commonplace. In spite of his helpless nature, he is surrounded by an amazing array of talented women, beginning first with his mother who knew how to raise a man to respect women. She taught him to love reading by waking up early every morning to read her Bible. He can often be found doting on his daughter or cooking a gourmet meal for his wife.

Made in the USA
Coppell, TX
16 April 2022